Beneath a Hunter's Moon

OTHER FIVE STAR WESTERN TITLES BY MICHAEL ZIMMER

Johnny Montana (2010)
Wild Side of the River (2011)
The Long Hitch (2011)
City of Rocks (2012)

Beneath a Hunter's Moon

A Western Story

Michael Zimmer

FIVE STAR

A part of Gale, Cengage Learning

Detroit • New York • San Francisco • New Haven, Conn • Waterville, Maine • London

LIBRARY OF CONGRESS CATALOGING-IN-PUBLICATION DATA

Zimmer, Michael, 1955–
Beneath a hunter's moon : a western story / by Michael Zimmer. — 1st ed.
p. cm.
ISBN 978-1-4328-2613-0 (hardcover) — ISBN 1-4328-2613-1 (hardcover) 1. Métis—Fiction. 2. Frontier and pioneer life—Fiction. 3. Indians of North America—Fiction. I. Title.
PS3576.I467B46 2012
813'.54—dc23 2012013194

First Edition. First Printing: August 2012
Published in conjunction with Golden West Literary Agency
Find us on Facebook–https://www.facebook.com/FiveStarCengage
Visit our Web site–http://www.gale.cengage.com/fivestar/
Contact Five Star™ Publishing at FiveStar@cengage.com

Printed in Mexico
1 2 3 4 5 6 7 16 15 14 13 12

For Vanessa

Prologue

Feeling the Appaloosa's stride break, Pike knew his flight was coming to an end. The big gelding's gait had become increasingly jarring the last couple of miles, its breath a raw, wheezing struggle for air. Leaning forward, Pike ran his hand along the gelding's neck. It came away sticky with sweat, flecked with a pink-tinged lather that he recognized as the lung's blood. He was killing the horse, yet there was nothing he could do about it. Not with hostiles so close behind him.

There were only four of them now, but there had been more. They'd jumped him in the pearly half-light of dawn, maybe two dozen all told, appearing soundlessly from the creeping mist of the river bottom where he had been breaking camp. For a startled moment, Indians and trapper alike had stood frozen in mid-stride. Then one of the warriors slid an arrow from the quiver across his back, and the strained tableau had broken. Dropping the oilcloth-wrapped bundle he'd been toting toward a pack horse, Pike sprinted for the Appaloosa.

The leopard-spotted gelding was already saddled. Pike had only to jerk the reins free and swing aboard. He'd done so without touching the stirrups, jerking the horse around and digging in with his spurs almost before he fully had his seat. His rifle was leaning against a nearby tree, and he swayed lithely to the side as they raced past, snatching it up even as the first shrill war cry splintered the fragile peace of the small grove. A rifle cracked, the ball sailing overhead with a fluttery whine, and a flint-tipped arrow arched past his shoulder, its dark fletching disappearing into the mist.

Keeping low over the broad, flat horn of his Mexican saddle, Pike sent his horse up a shallow bank, crashing through a fringe of gooseberry bushes in an explosion of frost and crisp yellow leaves, pounding east toward the coming sun.

That had been almost three hours ago, and the Appaloosa had been running steadily ever since. Most of the dozen or so warriors who had followed him onto the open plain had dropped out within a mile, hurrying back to share in the plundering of his camp with those who had remained behind. Only these four had clung stubbornly to his tail.

Pike had hoped the Appaloosa might eventually outrun them. It had the lines for it—long-legged and trim, with a deep, broad chest that seemed made for running—but he'd underestimated the bow-legged little Assiniboine he'd traded the horse from back at Fort Union. The Appaloosa had been run too hard at some point in its past and was wind-broken; it could sprint with the best of them, but it didn't have the endurance for the long haul.

Now, as the Appaloosa's hoofs beat an increasingly ragged cadence against the hard prairie sod, Pike knew the race was drawing to a close. He would have to do something, or the Indians would be on him.

Spotting the winding path of a small stream angling in from the north, Pike reined toward it. He had no way of knowing how deep those treeless banks might be. There could be decent shelter behind them for him and his horse. Or it might not be anything more than a shallow rill, a scratch across the tawny prairie. Yet no matter how skimpy its protection, it would be more than his attackers would have.

Pike's grip tightened on the heavy, iron-mounted rifle he'd brought west with him from Tennessee. There was reassurance in its familiarity, the solid feel of its straight-grained maple stock, the cool iron of its heavy octagon barrel. With a habit ground into him from a lifetime spent on the frontier, he ran his fingers back to the jutting spur of the flintlock's cock, gliding the ball of his thumb lightly over flint and frizzen. He'd pulled the old charge last night, then cleaned the bore and reloaded with fresh powder and a newly-patched .53-caliber round ball. He'd primed it then, too, and sealed the pan with bear grease. If he hadn't jarred the frizzen too much during the Appaloosa's long flight and lost his priming, the rifle would be ready to fire. But he couldn't check it now. He couldn't risk the wind blowing away the fine ignition powder cradled in the rifle's shallow pan. He would have to trust that the seal had remained unbroken, that the priming was intact.

The Appaloosa's front legs buckled, dropping the horse out from under Pike. Instinctively he kicked free of the heavy wooden stirrups, pushed away from the falling gelding. He slammed hard into the half-frozen ground and went tumbling, sky and grass whirling together in a colorful blur. When he finally stopped rolling, he was lying face down on the ground, his chest heaving, the wind knocked out of him. Pushing dizzily to his hands and knees, he saw the Appaloosa lying several yards away, its head bent at an impossible angle, its flanks still.

Closer, he saw his rifle with a tuft of dun-colored grass sprouting from its lock. Panic swelled in his breast. If the rifle was broken, he was finished.

Still feeling off-kilter from the fall, Pike shoved to his feet, then stumbled drunkenly toward his rifle. He was aware of the pounding of hoofs behind him, and threw a desperate glance over his shoulder. The warrior in the lead, riding a chunky buckskin, had swung his mount to one side to dodge the fallen Appaloosa. A single eagle feather fluttered wildly near the head of an iron-tipped lance cradled in the warrior's right arm.

Grabbing his rifle, Pike cocked it as he brought it to his shoulder. The Indian was less than thirty yards away now, his coppery face displaying a grim acceptance of his fate as the rifle's muzzle swung to cover him—a game played, a gamble lost. Then the cock snapped forward and the flint struck the frizzen with an audible click. But there was no shower of sparks raining into the pan, no puff of priming smoke followed by the bellow and kick as the main charge caught and exploded.

With a low, raspy curse, Pike eared the cock back a second time, flipping the frizzen closed in the same motion. The pan was empty but he'd seen a lucky spark ignite the main charge without priming before. It was a slim chance, but it was the only one he had. There was no time to reprime.

The Indian had completed the outward curve of his shallow crescent to avoid the downed Appaloosa and was coming straight at him. He'd seen Pike's misfire and was already shouting victoriously. Pike pulled the trigger, cursing the sterile click of his second misfire. Lunging to his feet, he reversed the rifle like a club, locking his gaze on the spear point leveled on his chest. If he was quick, and lucky, he might, he just might. . . .

Chapter One

Big John McTavish was in no hurry. He moved slowly along the dry wash, his gaze swinging back and forth over the ground in front of his quilled moccasins. It was early yet, and still cool, but he detected a hint of warmth in the slanting rays of the morning sun, a halcyon promise in the deep blue dome of the sky. Although it had already snowed once that season, he had high hopes for the next few days, and intended to be home well before a second blustery storm swept the high plains, cloaking the land in a mantle of white.

It was peaceful along the broad streambed. To the south he could hear the trilling of red-winged blackbirds and, closer, the familiar chomp of the horses as they grazed at the ends of their picket ropes. The wind was barely a murmur, coming out of the west like the rustle of mice in the next room.

Big John was a Scotsman, tall and raw-boned like his father, with an angular face tanned to leathery hue by the sun and the wind. His dark eyes were framed by a webbing of crow's-feet, his hair, beneath his frayed Glengarry cap, was salted generously with gray, falling loosely over his collar. He wore sturdy center-seam moccasins, fringeless buckskin trousers, and a brown and white checked shirt under a red duffel coat. A black wool bandanna circled his throat, and at his waist was a wine-colored sash of woven buffalo wool, worked throughout with blue and green chevrons.

He was a trader, or had been until his recent retirement, living along the Red River of the North that separated the dense forests the Sioux called *minnesota* from the vast, treeless plains to the west. He'd dealt almost exclusively in furs and pemmican and buffalo robes, passing on in turn good Sheffield knives, sheet-iron kettles, fusils—those smooth-bored trade guns so popular among the tribes—and a sight of other merchandise, as well. His inventories had included beads and vermillion and paper-backed mirrors small enough to fit in the palm of a hand or weave into the mane of a favorite pony. There had been needles and awls and axes, linen thread and iron arrowheads and daggers the Indians sometimes fashioned into lances. Scarlet and blue trade cloth and ornamental silver trinkets in various designs that could be used to decorate an Indian's hair or clothing.

Over the years Big John had traded among the Chippewas, the Assiniboines, even the Crees, who ranged far to the west, but those days were largely behind him now. In this autumn of 1832 he lived only to live, to watch with a keen but accepting eye the changes gradually overtaking the valley of the Red. He was a hunter like the others, and mostly it was a good life and a fair living, although hard and dangerous. He had hoped to die a hunter as well, living off the great, wandering herds of bison that had once darkened the flat plain bordering the Red River, supplementing the profits of the hunt with what small grains and garden truck he could raise in the summer. But times were changing and sometimes he wondered if he hadn't lived too long, put too much faith in an economic system he'd once thought was limitless.

Coming to a flattened oval of buffalo dung, he flipped it over with his toe. A black, hard-shelled beetle scurried into the grass, but that was all. The slightly dome-shaped chip was old, and most of the nutritional value that attracted insects had been washed away long before.

Big John picked it up, adding it to the collection of dung already gathered in the sling of his coat hem. A little farther downstream, Gabriel was also scrounging for chips. On the nearly treeless prairies west of the Red River Valley, dried dung was often the only fuel available to travelers.

From the corner of his eye, Big John saw his tall roan stallion lift its head curiously, ears perked to the west. Its nostrils flared as if to catch some errant scent. Seconds later, Gabriel's horse also threw its head into the air. Stopping, Big John glanced at his partner, but the youth was concentrating on the horses, his face grave with concern.

Returning to the horses, Big John dumped his collection of chips to the ground. By now, even the small bay they were using for a pack horse had turned its attention westward, although none of the horses was able to see above the tall cutbank Big John had chosen to shelter their fire.

"Listen," Gabriel said, coming close.

Big John strained to hear but picked up only the soughing of the wind. "What is it, lad?"

"Horses."

"Wild, are they?"

Gabriel shook his head. "No, they are ridden." He looked at Big John, a trace of uneasiness shading his smooth, dusky features. He didn't need to elaborate. This was Sioux country, and they were intruders.

"Tighten the cinches on the horses," Big John instructed curtly. "We may have to make a run for it." He picked up his long, double-barreled rifle and hurried to the cutbank. He had to stretch to peer over the top.

A moment later, Gabriel leaned into the bank at his side, and Big John heard the boy's sharp intake of breath.

It seemed obvious to Big John that the man on the Appaloosa wasn't going to make it. The spotted pony's gait was choppy, and its head was bobbing erratically. The pursuing Indians were quickly gaining. Reluctantly Big John slid his double rifle over the top of the cutbank.

"They are Chippewas," Gabriel said softly, without looking around. "They are our friends."

"Aye, but there's another out there who's needin' our help," Big John replied. He cocked the rifle's right-hand hammer. "I'll not turn my back on a stranger's needs, just so our friends can help themselves to his scalp."

"Maybe he deserves to lose his scalp."

Big John's lips drew thin. "I'd do the same if it was four white men runnin' down a Chippewa, lad, and ye know it. 'Tis the odds I'm protestin', nothing more."

Gabriel didn't reply, to Big John's relief. He brought his sights loosely to bear, waiting for the Chippewas to come into range. After a moment, he added: "I'll send my first shot across their bow if I can. Maybe that'll stop 'em."

"Thank you, Big John," Gabriel replied. Big John wasn't surprised when the Appaloosa went down, but he was disappointed. He'd hoped he might be wrong about the man's chances of reaching the cutbank where he and Gabriel were holed up. He had a feeling the Chippewas wouldn't be so eager to fight if the odds against them were suddenly tripled. But it wasn't to be. The Appaloosa's front legs buckled and it went to the ground, spilling its rider.

"Ah," Big John breathed, wrapping all his regret into that single exhalation.

The stranger on the Appaloosa tumbled wildly across the short buffalo grass, and for a moment Big John feared he might have been killed in the fall. Then he rose to his hands and knees, shaking his head as if dazed.

"Hurry, man," Big John urged. "Ye've no the time for woolgatherin'."

The stranger looked up as if he'd heard Big John's muttered admonitions, then scuttled across the grass to grab his rifle. Big John felt Gabriel's desperate glance, but couldn't tear his gaze away from the drama playing itself out before him. It soon became apparent that something was wrong with the stranger's rifle. He lifted it, lowered it, then lifted it again.

"Misfire," Gabriel breathed as the stranger surged to his feet, raising the weapon above his shoulder like a club.

"So it would seem," Big John agreed, swinging his sights on the distant warrior.

The tip of the Chippewa's lance was less than half a dozen yards away from the stranger's chest when Big John squeezed the trigger. The rifle boomed, spewing a cloud of gray powder smoke across the prairie. Through it, he saw the warrior topple from the buckskin's back, saw the second Chippewa yank his horse to a plunging, head-tossing stop. Lowering his rifle, the stranger began to work frantically on his lock.

Big John sighed, feeling Gabriel's gaze, the silent accusation in his eyes. "There was no time, lad," he said with little enthusiasm.

Gabriel stared at him a moment longer, then looked away. "He is thinking about it," he said, referring to the second warrior.

"I fear ye be right," Big John agreed, cocking the left-hand barrel. Although the second warrior was farther away, he wasn't moving. Big John knew he would be within the double rifle's range if he wanted to risk a shot, but he wasn't interested in prolonging the battle, not if it could be avoided. He waited tensely as the Chippewa appeared to calculate the odds with a show of noble indifference. Finally the Indian reined away, walking his horse back to where the last two warriors had halted well out of range. Big John exhaled loudly and lowered the hammer.

"Fetch the horses, Gabriel. We'd best we be gettin' out there before they change their minds."

He clambered over the top of the cutbank, then paused to reload in plain sight. The stranger was looking his way, cradling his own long gun in a non-threatening manner. The Chippewas were also watching him, their stance more curious than aggressive. After returning the ramrod to its thimbles beneath the steel web holding the rifle's twin barrels together, Big John glanced behind him. Gabriel had already swung onto the saddle of the piebald black gelding he called Baldy, and had Big John's roan in tow. He led the stallion across the dry streambed and up through a break in the cutbank. Back on the little flat where they'd been gathering chips for a breakfast fire, the bay nickered questioningly, but didn't try to pull loose from its picket.

Big John mounted the roan gratefully, feeling more in control with a good horse under him. The buckskin the first warrior had been riding had circled around to the south and stopped some distance away. Pointing toward it with his chin, Big John said: "See if ye can catch yon pony, lad. I'm thinkin' we'll have a man here as'll be needin' it."

Nodding, Gabriel angled off toward the buckskin as Big John set a straight course for the stranger, drawing up only yards away. Meeting the man's gaze, he offered a faint smile. " 'Mornin', and a lively one ye've had, I'd say."

"Some," the stranger allowed, letting the dinged stock of his rifle butt rest on the ground between his plain, grease-blackened moccasins. He was short and gaunt and wiry-looking, with a deeply weathered face surrounding the twin pools of his faded blue eyes. A long, bushy tangle of gray hair splayed out from beneath a broad-brimmed, low-crowned hat of cheap wool felt. He wore buckskin trousers with fringe along the outside seam and an old red cotton shirt under a hooded white capote.

The stranger was studying Big John closely in return, his gaze lingering almost enviably on the roan. "That was some slick for shooting," he finally allowed, drawing his eyes away from the stallion and nodding toward the fallen Chippewa.

"Aye," Big John replied immodestly. "A hundred and fifty yards, I'm guessin', although he was movin' toward me, which made it easier." He rested the double rifle across his quilled pad saddle and nudged the roan closer, extending a hand. "Me name's McTavish, although if ye're to know me long, it'll be Big John ye call me."

"Pike," the stranger returned simply.

"Pleased, Mister Pike, and happy I am not to be buryin' ye this fine but frosty mornin'. Tell me, are there others who might be needin' our assistance, or do ye travel alone?"

"I'm alone," Pike replied shortly.

Gabriel's voice came to them across the distance, tinged with impatience. He was trying to drive the Indian pony toward Big John and Pike, but the buckskin wasn't having it. Every time Gabriel came near, it would lift its head, then trot off out of reach. And every time it did that, it would draw a little closer to the watching Chippewas.

"Easy, Gabriel," Big John said, edging a hand back to cover the twin hammers of his rifle.

The Chippewas were starting to show some interest now, as if contemplating a quick charge. Then, like a child abruptly tiring of a game, the buckskin shook its head and galloped toward the Chippewas. Howling shrilly, the bronzed trio quirted their ponies forward, circling the buckskin and driving it away while Gabriel scampered Baldy in the opposite direction.

"Damn," Big John hissed, then offered Pike an apologetic shrug. "We could have used the pony, if yon beasty was all ye owned."

"It was," Pike said grimly, turning his gaze on the fallen Appaloosa. "They got two pack horses and all my traps at first light."

"Ye're not from around here, then?"

Pike gave him a brief look. "Nope." He started for the dead horse. "I'm from the west."

"A beaver trapper?"

"Some." Pike leaned his rifle against the Appaloosa's hip, then bent to loosen the cinch on a heavy, gourd-horned Mexican saddle.

Big John looked away, watching Gabriel's cautious approach on the dead Chippewa. Pike paused, too, and in that instant Big John saw Gabriel as he knew Pike must, with an outsider's untinted clarity.

Big John had always thought of Gabriel as the boy he had been—quiet, responsible, prematurely dignified, a wise man's soul in a youth's body. Now, through Pike's eyes, he saw him as he had become—slim and capable and proud.

He was a half-breed sure, with his thick, raven-colored hair cut straight at the shoulder and his dark skin reddish-hued, after his mother's people. His eyes were black as English flint, his teeth white and even between thin lips. He wore a dark blue factory coat with brass buttons and a tail split for riding, with an embroidered floral design of dyed moose hair added to the cuffs and collar, then wisping down both lapels. Beneath the coat was a yellow calico shirt and a red sash peppered with blue and green.

Gabriel wore wool trousers the color of a mourning dove's wing and buffalo-hide moccasins that came up under tight-fitting, knee-high leggings. A blue cloth cap with a leather brim held his hair in place. His long gun was an English-made Brown Bess, at least thirty years old; he'd shortened the barrel soon after obtaining the piece, then added brass tacks along the stock and forearm and a quilled leather sling to carry it across his back.

Dismounting, Gabriel rolled the Chippewa onto his back. Looking up with a troubled expression, he said: "We know him. He is one of Tall Cloud's nephews."

Big John grunted sharply. "Are ye sure?"

"He is of the Turtle Mountain clan. I am sure of that."

A sudden regret unfurled within the lanky Scotsman. He glanced at Pike. "I've traded with old Tall Cloud and his kith many a winter. It doesn't set right to be makin' war on 'em now."

"Seems to me it was them making war," Pike said.

"Aye, and no denyin' that, I suppose. 'Twas the breath of old Clootie hisself ye must have been feelin', and no good way to die, butchered like a pup for the kettle at the hands of men ye don't know. Still, 'tis a sorry business. Especially for me and the lad."

Pike shrugged unsympathetically and turned away. He'd worked the saddle's underside stirrup free, but the cinch remained pinned beneath the Appaloosa's body. From time to time as he struggled with the horsehair cinch, Pike would lift his head to look around, but, save for their own little knot of humanity, the wide, gently rolling plains were empty. Not even the shadow of a cloud marred the landscape, and the Chippewas had vanished as if swallowed by the earth itself.

" 'Tis the huntin' of the buffalo they protest," Big John said after a while, wanting Pike to understand the Chippewas' position.

"I wasn't hunting buffalo," Pike responded without looking up. He braced a foot against the Appaloosa's hip and gave a hard yank. This time the cinch pulled free, almost dumping him on his butt.

"True," Big John acknowledged, "but even last season, I'm

thinkin', they would've rather traded with ye than tried to rob ye." Eyeing Pike closely, he added offhandedly: "If 'twas them what blackened their faces first."

Pike straightened and hooked his thumbs in his belt. "And not some outsider who bit off more than he could chew, you mean?"

"Aye, Mister Pike. I'm wonderin'."

"It was them that jumped me, McTavish."

Big John studied the gaunt trapper for several seconds, then nodded. "Fair enough, Mister Pike, and no insult meant." Looking past them, he studied the distant rim of the horizon. "There were others, ye say, besides these four?"

"A couple of dozen altogether. They jumped me at dawn while I was breaking camp. Most of 'em stayed to go through my packs, but these four hung on like burrs."

"How far back do ye suppose they'd be, them that stayed to strip ye packs."

Pike thought about it for a minute. "I was half the morning getting this far at a pretty hard run. I reckon they'd still be several hours away."

"And the others, lad?" Big John asked Gabriel. "Where are they?"

Gabriel nodded toward a little scab of bare earth about a mile to the south. "They'll wait there until we leave, then come for the body."

Big John studied the patch of dirt Gabriel had pointed out, realizing only then that it was the mouth of a coulée. Nodding thoughtfully, he turned to Pike. "Me and the lad were about to fix ourselves a bite to eat when we heard ye comin', but it might be best if we pushed on a spell. If ye've no other engagements pressin', ye'd be welcome to join us. I've a bay pony yonder that I'd be happy to make ye the loan of. 'Tis only a light pack he's carryin', and most of the *cabbri* what young Gabriel here added to the larder last night can be divided amongst us. What do ye say, Mister Pike?"

Although Pike hesitated, he really didn't have much of a choice. They were a long way from beaver country here. A long way from just about anywhere. Picking up his rifle, then hefting the saddle to his shoulder, the trapper said: "I reckon I'd be obliged to ride with you, McTavish."

Big John smiled. "Good. Fetch yeself along then and we'll be off." He reined his horse around to lead the way to the little flat where they'd picketed the bay. But with his back turned, Big John's smile faded. He knew his killing of the young Chippewa would not soon be forgotten across the northern plains. Like a stone tossed carelessly into the middle of a still pond, it would ripple outward for a long time, and no way of knowing what it might eventually disturb.

CHAPTER TWO

Gabriel put Baldy up the low east bank of the dry streambed where he and Big John had stopped for breakfast, then let him out to a lope. Although Big John and Pike were already some distance ahead, Gabriel held back. He liked to ride alone, and now he had the American to think about.

Gabriel had never cared much for the Americans he'd met. Most of them had been traders and cattle dealers up from Wisconsin or Missouri to barter with the half-bloods—the *bois brûles*—who ruled the Red River Valley of the North. In Gabriel's opinion, the Americans were a loud and swaggering lot, bold-eyed among the half-blood women, given to lying and cheating when they thought they could get away with it, and sullen resentment when they couldn't. As if they blamed the *bois brûles* for their own fumbled ruses.

So far, Gabriel hadn't detected that kind of arrogance in Pike, which only made his suspicion of the wiry trapper all the more puzzling. He felt vaguely intimidated by him, a feeling he was neither used to nor fully understood. He wasn't afraid, but he sensed a threat in Pike's presence, a need to keep his guard up.

Baldy's gait was rough and jarring, a not so subtle protest to the bouncing haunches of *cabbri* slung across the back of Gabriel's pad saddle like a pair of oblong saddlebags. He'd lashed the pronghorn antelope's shoulder across the top, behind his bedroll, while listening to the conversation between Big John and Pike.

Gabriel could tell that Big John liked Pike, which only added to his confusion. He thought Pike liked Big John, too, although that didn't surprise him. Most people liked Big John, even if they didn't always agree with him. Like about the buffalo, or trading with the Hudson's Bay Company.

Big John despised Hudson's Bay with a grudge that went back to the days of open warfare between H.B.C. and the old North West Company that Big John had worked for. After North West succumbed to Hudson's Bay by merger in 1821—about the same time the Americans had started venturing into the Red River Valley from the south and east—Big John began encouraging the *bois brûles* to trade more vigorously with their southern neighbors. It was better to take a knife in the guts from the Americans, he often said, than one in the back from Hudson's Bay.

Gabriel wasn't sure he agreed with Big John's assessment of Hudson's Bay, but then, he'd been too young to remember much about the hostilities between the Bay Company and the Nor'Westers, other than that it had been a horribly blood-soaked affair that left cultural wounds that were still unhealed.

Big John's stubborn prophecy of the buffalo's demise was a bit harder for Gabriel to stomach. Bison had once ranged throughout the Red River Valley, but time and a steady influx of settlers had driven the shaggy beasts onto the high plains farther west.

To the *bois brûles,* the buffalo's withdrawal was nothing more than a natural response to the valley's increasing population, but Big John seemed convinced it signaled the beginning of the end. Give it another twenty years, Big John insisted, and the buffalo would be gone entirely, the half-bloods forced to take up the hoe and plow.

That kind of talk generated a lot of ill feelings among the *bois brûles*, to whom the buffalo were not just a means of subsistence, but in many ways the core of who they were as a people. They heard Big John's words not as concern, but as accusation, and had anyone else made such high-handed indictments, there would have been trouble for sure, perhaps even bloodshed.

Big John was too well-respected to be challenged openly, but recently Gabriel had begun to detect something he regarded as even more disturbing, a kind of patronizing concession to Big John's beliefs, an erosion of respect for the tall Scotsman's authority, manifested in condescending smiles or furtive rolls of the eyes.

It bothered Gabriel to see it, bothered him all the more for his own occasional irritation with Big John's views. Big John had been like a father to him for as long as he could remember, had always treated him fairly and with respect, and never disciplined him without just cause. It didn't seem fair that something so trivial as a difference of opinion over a single issue could threaten all that Big John had come to stand for in the valley.

Thinking of the unrest brewing among the *bois brûles* brought sadness to Gabriel's heart. It would be good to talk to Charlo about it, and maybe talk to him about Pike, too. Old Charlo was like Big John in many ways. They had come to the *pays sauvage*—Indian country—in the same North West Company canoe brigade when they were both young men, not yet out of their teens. They'd wintered together for the first several seasons on the Jack River, at the northern tip of Lake Winnipeg, before migrating south.

Charlo had once told Gabriel that Big John had better eyes than most people, then lightly tapped his chest and the side of his head with a forefinger, explaining that Big John saw with his heart and mind as well as his eyes. Gabriel knew Charlo also disagreed with Big John about the buffalo, but that hadn't lessened the Indian's esteem for him.

Gabriel took comfort in that. It helped ease his own guilty feelings whenever he grew impatient with Big John. Gabriel knew they would stop at Charlo's cabin on the way back to their farm along the Tongue River. They would want to see what news the old Indian might have for them, and to pass along their own. With his thoughts settled, Gabriel let Baldy have his head. He had fallen quite a ways behind, and wanted to catch up. Although he wasn't overly concerned about the Chippewas slipping up behind them, he wasn't a fool, either.

They reined in atop a high ridge overlooking the Pembina River, the land dropping off sharply before them, tumbled and broken, dotted with ginger-hued boulders that seemed to reflect the sun's radiance. Groves of trees grew close in the hollows, their limbs furred yellow and scarlet and pale brown. Farther off, Gabriel could see stretches of the river itself where it wound through the steep Hair Hills that bordered the western edge of the Red River Valley. The Pembina's banks were lined with box elder and cottonwood, scattered dogwood and tremblies, that the Americans called aspen.

A gust of wind moved down the valley, causing the branches of the trees to dip and sway. Following the wind's progress downstream, Gabriel was amused by how much it looked like fall. When he and Big John had left only a week ago, it had seemed as if winter had arrived for good, with saw-toothed flurries blowing out of the northwest and five inches of wet snow on the ground. All that had changed in the time they'd been gone. The snow had melted and the wind had shifted back out of the west, drying out the land and making it all seem crisp and fresh again.

Dismounting, they loosened the cinches on their horses to let them blow. Big John put both fists against the small of his back and stretched in an exaggerated manner, groaning softly at the faint pop of his lower spine. Straightening and rolling his shoulders, he nodded toward the distant river and said to Pike: "Yonder's the Pembina. She points south here, but will turn about soon enough and flow east, into the Red."

Pike looked and nodded, and Big John went on: "There's a settlement of sorts where the Pembina leaves the Hair Hills, and a trading post at the Red. 'Tis American soil there, but no more than a good spit north to British holdin's. Rupert's Land, they call it, and a Hudson's Bay post just north of the line for tradin'."

Big John went on casually, explaining the lay of the land, the direction of rivers, the location of various trading posts and half-blood communities. Pike, Gabriel noticed, took it all in silently, his quick, sun-washed eyes following closely as Big John pointed out different landmarks.

When Big John was finished, Pike nodded toward the valley floor and murmured—"Smoke."—as if not sure he should point out something so obvious.

Spotting it for the first time, a bluish thread barely visible in the distance, Gabriel swallowed back his annoyance.

"Aye, a friend's fire," Big John explained, then glanced at Gabriel. "The eyes of a hawk this one has, eh, lad?"

Gabriel shrugged as if unimpressed. The animosity he'd felt toward Pike when they'd picked him up off the plains two days before remained as strong and as puzzling as ever. Pike hadn't done anything to earn Gabriel's distrust, but the feeling persisted, and Gabriel was powerless to ignore it.

Leaning casually against Baldy's hip, Gabriel stared back the way they'd come, seeing in his mind the rolling plains stretching westward under the deep blue curve of the sky. It was five hundred miles or more to the Rocky Mountains, and nothing in between to stop a man or even slow him down. It was his land, those plains and these hills, and on east, too, across the Red River. The best of all worlds, of Indian and white, prairie and woods. The heart of the continent, Charlo claimed, and Gabriel believed him, even though he had never been anywhere else.

Big John and Pike were unlashing their coats from their saddles. It had been comfortably warm all afternoon, but as the sun dipped below the horizon, the air began to turn cool. Gabriel could already see the wispy puffs of his breath every time he exhaled. They were still some distance from Charlo's cabin, and the trail down through the hills was a twisty one, steep enough in places that he wasn't looking forward to challenging it in the dark.

As if sharing his thoughts, Big John said: "We've a ways to travel yet, and night to hound us along. We'd best be movin' on." He glanced at the column of smoke, nearly obscured in the early twilight. "We'll spend the night at Charlo's."

"Charlo?" Pike asked.

"Beneath yon smoke ye pointed out," Big John explained. He mounted the roan, then looked at Gabriel. "Are ye comin', lad?"

"I know the way," Gabriel replied shortly, keeping his back to the two men as he tugged at the knot holding his coat across the front of his saddle. He waited until they had dropped from sight below the rim of the hill before slipping into his coat and riding after them.

They were an hour coming down off the ridge. Although the light was fading rapidly, there was still enough illumination to make out the grove of trees where Charlo's cabin sat, to discern the ebony bars of a small corral to the side. They reined up several hundred yards away, sitting three abreast, and Gabriel uneasily lifted his musket to rest it across his left arm. Big John butted his rifle to his thigh, and, noting their silent preparations, Pike saw to his own weapons, the iron-mounted rifle and a heavy-bladed butcher knife sheathed at his hip.

"Easy now," Big John cautioned. "It means nothing."

But Gabriel's heart was pounding. There was no light shining through the trees, not even the glimmer of lamplight peeking from between loose shutters, and the sky above the cabin was smokeless.

They fanned out as they crossed the meadow, keeping their horses on a tight rein. Gabriel's eyes darted, his ears straining for any sound. The breeze had died at sunset and, without it, he could hear even the faint chatter of the river beyond the trees.

Baldy pushed forward with quick, mincing steps, pulling restively at the bit by tossing his jaw forward. Gabriel kept an eye on the piebald's ears as they drew closer to the cabin, reading in the way they moved what the pony scented or heard. When Big John drew up about halfway across the meadow, Pike and Gabriel did the same. From here Gabriel could just make out the near wall of the cabin, its hewed logs a flat, dark plane.

"Look sharp there, lad," Big John whispered. "Is that a shadow in yon corral, or one of Charlo's oxen?"

Squinting in the murky light, Gabriel felt a surge of relief. "The black one," he confirmed. "The one that was snake-bit last summer and nearly died."

Big John lowered his rifle. "I believe ye be right, and we're not likely to find a war party nearby that wouldn't take time to slaughter the stock."

"The Chippewas?" Pike asked.

"Sure, it crossed my mind. The lad's, too, I'd wager. Them, or others."

But now that all seemed right again, Gabriel felt a sudden, stubborn loyalty. "No," he stated flatly. "Not Chippewas."

"Ah, Gabriel, was it not Tall Cloud's own nephew what tried to skewer Mister Pike here?"

"The Chippewas are not at war with us," Gabriel said stoutly. "They are our friends."

There was an edge to Big John's reply. "The *métis* are ye friends, Gabriel, not the Chippewas. Ye'll be learnin' that soon enough if it's war they're truly wantin'."

Gabriel's lips thinned, but he knew Big John was right. He was *bois brûle*, a half-blood—what the Canadian traders called *métis*—and if it came to war he would fight as such. But the thought of it made him half sick. A lot of Chippewa blood ran through the *bois brûles*. War would be little more than an ugly, murderous feud within an extended family.

Impulsively he kicked at Baldy's ribs, galloping recklessly into the cabin's yard. He could make out the litter of wind-blown leaves piled against the threshold of the cabin's door, and, in the corral, the snowy belly of the mostly black ox gliding toward him. But Charlo's second ox, his old, brindled riding mare, and the white buffalo runner were nowhere to be seen.

Big John and Pike rode into the yard and dismounted. Big John let the roan's reins trail on the ground, but Pike kept the bay close, using him as a shield between himself and the deeper darkness of the trees. Even in the shadows close to the cabin, Gabriel could see the disapproval on Big John's face, and knew it was from the irresponsible way he'd come in, alone and fast. But Gabriel didn't wait. Jerking the musket's big cock back to full, he headed for the cabin's door.

"Gabriel!" Big John spoke sharply.

"The white runner is gone," Gabriel said over his shoulder. "So is the mare and the ox."

"Only one ox is missin', lad, and no sign of trouble that I've seen."

Gabriel made a quick, dismissing gesture with his hand, then lifted the door's wooden latch and shoved it open. Stepping forward, Big John clamped a hand over his shoulder and yanked him back.

"Don't be outlinin' yeself that way," he grated. "Ye're no a fool, Gabriel. Don't be takin' the chances of one."

"You two'd best save your bickering for later," Pike called. He was holding the bay close to the bit, facing the deepest shadows of the woods.

Gabriel felt a flash of shame, and his anger evaporated in an instant. He didn't understand the hostility that could sweep over him without warning. At times it seemed that the whole world was changing, yet, when he looked closer, nothing seemed different.

Standing to one side, Big John lifted his voice. "Charlo! Are ye in there, man? 'Tis Big John McTavish and Gabriel."

Only the murmur of the river answered, and Big John looked at Gabriel.

"He's not here."

"I think not, but 'twas smoke we saw, there's no denyin' that."

"He's not here," Gabriel repeated, lowering his musket's cock to the half position for safety. "I can feel the cabin's emptiness." Fingering his fire steel and a piece of char and flint from the quilled moose-hide pouch at his belt, he stepped inside, then felt his way across the room to the table where a stubby tallow candle always sat in the middle in a base of its own wax. It was short work to strike a flame, and the candle's smoky light quickly nudged back the darkness, throwing his shadow boldly against wall and ceiling.

Charlo's cabin was a simple one-room affair, cluttered with a thirty-plus-year collection of treasures strewn about in chaotic disarray. The furniture was heavy and crudely built but padded with robes for comfort. Hanks of glass trade beads in a wild assortment of colors decked the cabin's walls from square iron nails, and empty rum kegs sprouted from the dirt floor like stumps. From the exposed beams overhead hung traps in a variety of sizes, from muskrat on up to beaver and wolves. Some of the traps were old and missing parts; others were new, still in their original packing grease. The yellow-toothed skulls of beavers, coyotes, and grizzly bears grinned a cold welcome from odd niches about the cabin, and against the rear wall, draped like bunting nearly from eave to eave, hung the twelve-foot-long hide of a rattlesnake Charlo had killed at Devil's Lake many years before.

"Naught but our own nerves," Big John stated with obvious relief, following Gabriel into the cabin. "I'm thinkin' 'tis that business with Tall Cloud's nephew that's got us so spooked, lad."

"Do you think the smoke we saw came from the river?"

"Aye, it's possible. Charlo's not a man to idle with his winter feed, and he's a taste for smoked fish, though I've never understood it meself. Not with good red meat to be had for the butcherin'."

As if his ebbing worry was some sort of cue, there arose a sudden and familiar sound, a mushrooming screech like a fine-toothed file being drawn across teeth. Exchanging a grin with Big John, Gabriel ducked through the door. He stopped abruptly at the sight of Pike.

The American was crouched near the corral with his rifle up but not yet shouldered, the muzzle pointed toward the still-expanding ululation that shrilled up the trail from the river. Pike had let go of the bay's bit, but still clung to its reins. He was pulling the pony after him as he waddled quickly, comically, toward a stack of firewood piled near a corner of the corral.

Gabriel clamped down on the laughter that bubbled in his throat. From the far side of the corral, the screeching broke into a series of dull, heavy thumps, then rose swiftly once more, soaring among the brittle autumn leaves. Pike thought it was human, Gabriel guessed, a tortured scream begging for death. It would be an easy mistake to make for someone unfamiliar with the ways of the valley, and all the more so by the stealthy approach he and Big John had made on the cabin. But it was funny, too, and in Gabriel's eyes it cut the American down to more tolerable dimensions.

Coming up behind Gabriel, Big John called: " 'Tis only a cart, Mister Pike!"

"He thought it was a cry from hell," Gabriel said, laughing.

There was movement behind the corral. Gabriel saw the ox first, heavy-horned and plodding, its dun hide freckled with gray. The two-wheeled cart was little more than a hulking mass behind it, flanked by a lanky figure toting a long-barreled fowler over one bony shoulder as comfortably as another man might carry a fishing pole. A pipe jutted from the corner of Charlo's mouth, as familiar as the moccasins on his feet and the stout Hudson's Bay dagger at his waist. His leathery face, deeply creviced by wind and age, was framed by a mop of snow-white hair cut square at the shoulders.

Charlo was a tall man among a notably blunt people, a stranger from the East almost forty years before. Some said he was the first freeman to settle within the Hair Hills, no small feat in those bloody, hell-hoared years. Eventually he had become something of a trader as well, although it was never anything he was serious about. Mostly he was content to hunt and trap and fish, and twice each year he would travel to the buffalo ranges with the *bois brûles.* Were it not for supplies like powder and lead and tobacco, he might have stayed forever in the Hair Hills, and never come at all to the trading posts along the Red River.

Seeing the American and the way he held his rifle, Charlo

paused at the edge of his yard. He gave Big John a questioning glance, then turned back to Pike. Speaking around his pipe, he said: "If it is my hide you seek, stranger, I am afraid you will find it is not worth much any more."

Lowering his rifle, Pike turned away in disgust. Charlo clucked his tongue and the ox came on, plodding without guidance to the far side of the cabin. The excruciating caterwaul of the cart's ungreased axle besieged them all the way.

The cart was a unique product of time and place, remarkably suited to the largely flat, treeless prairies and random marshes and woods characteristic of the Red River country. It was a relatively lightweight vehicle, all things considered. Made entirely of hardwood and rawhide, it had tall, outwardly dished wheels that made it nearly impossible to tip over even when descending riverbanks or crossing coulées. Its bed was roughly six feet long by four across, with slatted sideboards of cottonwood limbs that Big John once morosely confessed reminded him of the bars over the windows of the Montreal gaol.

As the cart shrieked past, Gabriel saw that it was carrying an oddly shaped cargo, and a second later he caught the unmistakable odor of moose.

"Here," Charlo spoke to the ox as it passed beneath a horizontal limb protruding from a sturdy cottonwood beside his cabin. Rapping the animal's springy ribs with his knuckles, he added: "Stop."

Gabriel came over, and Charlo grinned. "Upriver I found this one. God-damned lucky, eh?" He took the pipe from his mouth and knocked the dottle from it with the palm of his hand before returning it to the straps of a beaded *gage d'amour,* the heart-shaped tobacco pouch he wore around his neck. Reaching through the cart's slats, Gabriel buried his fingers in the dark, coarse shoulder hair. He pulled it out until it was stretched full-length, almost eight inches long, thick and winter prime. He said: "Isabella is wanting some moose hair for embroidery. She says she will dye it purple, for my jacket."

"Isabella is a good woman, and I have no use for the hair," Charlo said. "What you think she needs, you take." He stepped away from the cart as Big John and Pike approached, silent save for the tiny, musical ching of the American's spurs.

"So," Charlo said, smiling. "The Sioux did not get your scalps this year again, eh? That is good." He shook Big John's hand, then Pike's as introductions were made, nodding and smiling the whole time. It was a trader's greeting, Gabriel realized, with everything exaggerated for the stranger's benefit so that there would be no misunderstanding. To Big John, Charlo added: "You found more than buffalo on the plains this year."

Big John chuckled. "There's lots to be found out there, old friend, but this is a first for me."

Charlo continued to smile as he pumped Pike's hand again. "You will stay here this night, yes?"

"I'm riding with McTavish and the boy," Pike replied stiffly. "If they're of a mind to set a spell, that'll suit me."

"Good," Charlo said, dropping his hand, his smile waning. "Good. I look forward to hearing your story." He glanced at Gabriel and Big John. "We will unhitch and unsaddle and see to our stock before we talk, eh?"

"Where is the white runner?" Gabriel asked.

"He and the mare are on grass. They are near, I think."

" 'Tis thievin' the lad's thinkin' of," Big John said. "Some Turtle Mountain Chippewas tried to take Mister Pike's scalp a ways back, but got only his ponies and packs."

Charlo was silent for a moment. Finally he said: "The Chippewas tried to kill a stranger in their land, which is only natural. They will not come here." He patted Big John's shoulder. "We are friends with the Turtle Mountain band, you and I. Our ponies are safe." He looked at Gabriel. "Come, young one, help me with this meat, then get your hair for Isabella."

While Big John and Pike took the horses to the corral, Charlo and Gabriel ran an iron pole through the tendons of the moose's hind legs, just behind its hocks. With home-made block and tackle, they hoisted the carcass from the cart's bed until it hung free from the cottonwood's strong limb. Charlo led the ox forward, and Gabriel unbuckled the harness and lifted it from her back. After easing the cart's shafts to the ground, Charlo clucked softly and the ox moved away, swishing its tail vigorously. Charlo stared after her until she was swallowed by the darkness, then said, without turning around: "Did you find buffalo?"

"No. There was sign of a small herd at Rush Lake and the American says he saw a big bunch on the Mouse River, but Big John and I did not go that far."

"That far," Charlo repeated wonderingly. "And two years since I last saw a moose on the Pembina."

Gabriel shrugged, even though he knew Charlo couldn't see him. He was thinking that, all of a sudden, Charlo was sounding a lot like Big John.

Returning to the moose, Gabriel ran his hand along the gaunt flank, then down the spine. From its size he could tell it was young; from its lack of palmated antlers, he knew it was a cow. He moved his hand over the long, massive head, stopping when he came to the abrupt termination of hide, the cold gumminess of clotted blood. "You have already taken the nose," he accused.

Charlo chuckled. "For breakfast this morning," he confessed. "Had I known you would be here, I would have saved it. I remember nose is your favorite."

"Of moose," Gabriel said, "but it doesn't matter. I shot a *cabbri* on the other side of Rush Lake. We have been eating well."

"Good. Soon there will be buffalo. My belly is hungry for it."

Charlo peeled the hide back from the moose's shoulder. "Just enough for tonight," he said, slicing into the meat with his dagger. "Tomorrow I will butcher it good, and we will take it with us when we go after buffalo."

Thinking of the coming hunt brought a smile to Gabriel's face. He was looking forward to it. Sometimes he wished they could leave the Red River Valley altogether, and just follow the herds. But, of course, that would be impossible. The Sioux, the Crees, the Assiniboines, and the Arikaras controlled the buffalo ranges west of the valley, and they would never permit such flagrant invasion of their lands. It was dangerous enough going in as they did now.

Charlo draped both backstraps over the cart's tailgate, then wiped his knife's blade clean against the hide. "Enough for tonight, I think."

From the corral came the angry squeal of a horse, followed by Big John's scolding shout.

"The roan," Gabriel said, remembering what had happened the last time they'd penned Big John's red stallion with the bay horse Pike was riding. By morning the bay had been soaked with sweat, wall-eyed with terror, half a dozen palm-size patches of hide nipped off by the roan's huge, cream-colored teeth.

"Big John should tell that horse no," Charlo said, sheathing his dagger. "Then he should explain it again with a piece of firewood. A man must always get a pony's attention with something harder than its head."

"Big John will take care of the roan," Gabriel replied. "He will let the bay run loose tonight."

"I think maybe Big John would do well to watch that roan horse closely."

"Why?" Gabriel asked, puzzled.

"You watch, too, eh?" Charlo turned and smiled as if to lighten the tone of his words. "Maybe that will be enough." Picking up a slab of meat in each hand, he said: "Let's go make a good supper, young one. Moose." He smacked his lips. "God-damn, my belly rumbles for it."

Chapter Three

Pike sat cross-legged on a folded piece of buffalo robe, his back to the log wall, a cup of bitter black tea cooling on the dirt floor at his side. In the fireplace the flames had dwindled to flickering yellow tongues, wrapped in jumping shadows. He was growing drowsy in the unaccustomed warmth of the cabin. The roasted moose and a soup made of peas and barley resided comfortably in his stomach. It had been a long time since he'd eaten such grub, and the taste of fresh vegetables and recently harvested grain lingered pleasantly.

Charlo sat against the wall next to the door, paring tobacco for his pipe from the unraveled tip of a five-pound carrot. Gabriel reclined beside him, half asleep, his own white dudeen pipe, its rim stained black, held loosely in one hand. McTavish sat on an empty rum keg, his eyelids drooping. They had eaten and smoked and talked well into the night, until an easy silence had overtaken them. Pike was seriously considering seeking out his bedroll when Charlo began to speak quietly, without looking up.

"They say that already some have come from the White Horse Plain and are camped across from Pembina Post. They say they will leave for the buffalo ranges within the week, and some already speak of Paget to lead."

McTavish stirred, a frown creasing his forehead. "Within the week, ye say?"

"According to Quesnelle, whose sister has come down from

the White Horse. He says Denning will travel with them this year, that he has already left Fort Douglas."

McTavish snorted. "Aye, that sounds like Paget's doin', all right. Burdenin' the whole of a hunt with a Black Robe."

Gabriel pushed up straighter, looking at Big John. "We should have Father Denning bless our camp as well. For the good of the hunt and the safety of the *bois brûles.*"

"Aye, and let's be shakin' our *wanbangos* and tootin' our eagle bone flutes while we're at it," McTavish replied peevishly.

"It is different," Gabriel said.

" 'Tis hoodoo, lad. Christian or savage, it cuts the same."

"It doesn't matter," Charlo said mildly. "Unless you wish to hunt alone, there will be a blessing."

McTavish shook his head. "A man can no longer hunt alone, not with the Sioux lookin' to lift his scalp, damn their black-hearted souls."

Charlo looked up with cocked brow, a twisted grin. "You damn them, Big John? And you without a God?"

"Not without a God, old friend, but not blinded by a Black Robe's words, either. I'll make my own way through this life we've been given, and I'll face my own God when the time comes."

Pike's interest was piqued. He'd been wondering ever since his rescue from the Chippewas who these men were and where they had come from. He hadn't asked because he'd figured it wasn't any of his business, but curiosity finally got the better of him.

"What's this hunt you keep talking about?" he asked McTavish.

"For buffalo, Mister Pike, and the pemmican and robes we'll be harvestin' from the herds."

"And a priest?"

That brought a taut chuckle from the Scotsman. "Aye, a

priest, and what's one to do with the other, you're no doubt askin'." He turned an amused eye on Charlo.

"We have accepted the Catholic faith," Charlo explained with quiet dignity. "We have given up our heathen gods and ask only for the protection of the one true God."

McTavish sniffed in disdain and looked away. Gabriel took up the conversation. "Twice each year, in the spring and the fall, we go onto the plains to hunt buffalo. We go as a tribe, the *bois brûle,* as protection against the Sioux whose lands we must cross. We ask the priest for his blessing to guide us safely to the buffalo, and to give us strength and courage against our enemies. We also ask him to hear our confessions, so that the souls of those who do not return will be less burdened."

"The *bois brûle?*" Pike felt suddenly foolish in his ignorance.

"Of the Red River." After a moment of silence, McTavish's brows furrowed. "Ye've not heard of the *bois brûle,* Mister Pike?"

"I've heard the words, that's about all."

The Scotsman's frown deepened. "I'd figured ye for an Astor man, Mister Pike, maybe from Fort Union or Fort Clark on the Missouri River, but I cannot imagine an employee of ol' John Jacob not knowin' of the Red River Settlements."

"I don't work for Astor."

"Well, and sure, 'tis the settlements ye've come to, knowin' of 'em or not. Not the big one at Fort Douglas, at the mouth of the Assiniboine up in Rupert's Land, but the village of Saint Joseph at the edge of the Hair Hills."

Pike shook his head. Although McTavish had been partially right, he had been an American fur man for a while, but farther west, with William Vanderburg's brigade of beaver trappers in the mountainous lands of the Absarokas and Blackfeet. He'd quit the outfit cold when he learned of Arch's death, though, and had struck out across the sun-parched plains into British Territory following a trail already several months old. He'd been working his way east ever since, although jagging back and forth a lot. Sometimes he'd lose the trail for three or four days at a time, but then he'd come across some new sign to convince him that he was still on the right track, still dogging the trail of Arch's killers. Other than that, he hadn't known where he was when the Chippewas jumped him, nor had he much cared.

"The Red River Settlements was Hudson's Bay's idea," Gabriel continued solemnly. "They saw it as a way to bring farmers into the *pays sauvage,* and drive the hostiles out. It would also be a place where the old traders who did not wish to leave the north country could retire."

"Well, there's more to the story than that," Big John said after a pause. He looked at Pike, the wisp of a smile tracing his lips. " 'Twas Eighteen and Twelve when the farmers came, Scottish Highlanders like meself, though I was never one of 'em, mind ye. A trader I was, and here long before the farmers showed up, but that's another story, one I'll be savin' for another fire.

" 'Twas Lord Selkirk himself, of the Bay Company, that brought 'em here. A refuge for them that was forced from their homes in Scotland by a growin' sheep industry that needed their land, his lordship claimed, and a boon to Hudson's Bay to have the grain growers nearby, although I'd wager it was considerable less than that to the Selkirkers, as we called 'em. Fur and farmin' will never mix, we told 'em . . . us of the old North West Company . . . but it was war then between the two big fur companies, and the innocent crofters caught in between.

"There was some sorry deeds done and some good men killed, and I'll not claim the Nor'Westers were innocent in it all, although there are some who still do." He paused reflectively. " 'Twas all for naught, though," he continued finally. "The farmers are still here and maybe . . . well, maybe the country's better off for it."

After another lengthy pause, McTavish lowered his voice and went on: "It was in 'Twenty-One that the glorious North West Company lost the war and was merged with Hudson's Bay. Those of us who refused to work for the Bay Company had our contracts terminated and became freemen, meself among 'em, and proud of the title, too. A free man to sell my furs and pemmican and buffalo robes to them that wanted it most, and was willin' to pay the prices I asked. The Bay Company by tradition, but to the American traders if I prefer. American Fur is the largest of that lot, but there's always a few independents about."

"Only the robes and furs to the Americans," Gabriel reminded him.

"Sure, robes and furs and fine *métis* clothin' such as jackets and moccasins, all quilled and beaded for fancy, but the lad's right. It's our pemmican the Bay Company wants most. To feed their canoe men, their *voyageurs* and *hommes du nord* who work the far northern regions of the Athabasca, where the furs be thick and rich as gold and the rivers all flow north into the Arctic Ocean. 'Tis a far piece to that country, and the *voyageurs* couldn't make it before freeze-up without the *métis*' pemmican to feed them. 'Tis too far to hunt their own meat along the way. It would take too much time away from their paddlin'."

Pike nodded, finally comprehending the farmers' purpose along the Red River—to raise food for Hudson's Bay so that their traders wouldn't have to bother with such trifling details themselves. And the half-breed hunters—the offspring of the French, Scottish, and English traders—supplied them with pemmican, that protein-rich concoction of pulverized dried meat and melted fat, packed tightly into leather sacks and sewn shut until it was needed.

It was a good, hearty food, easy to carry, and a little bit went a long way. Pike considered it fair eating when fresh meat wasn't available, although a man had to be careful who he bought it from. Some providers took pride in their work and would add berries and herbs for flavoring; others didn't much care, and made only a casual effort to keep out excess hair, twigs, or pieces of bone.

With his pipe packed and the carrot of tobacco set aside, Charlo said to Pike: "You will hunt with us this year?"

" 'Tis not a thing we've talked of yet," McTavish interjected, glancing at Pike. "But it's one I'm hopin' he'll agree to. Tell me, Mister Pike, what do ye think of the bay horse ye've been ridin'? Is he fair, would ye say?"

"He's fair," Pike admitted.

"Aye, a six-year-old and quick as a buffalo on his feet, though smallish. Still, he'd make ye a fine mount."

"I've nothing to trade for him," Pike reminded the Scotsman.

"Well, maybe," McTavish replied vaguely. "We'll be goin' after buffalo soon. Leavin' at the end of the week, most likely. I'll be takin' three carts and Gabriel'll take one, and we'll need to fill 'em all. I could use an extra hunter, were ye so inclined."

"To run 'em?"

"Aye, that and to help some with the butcherin'. We'll be makin' pemmican in the field and carin' for the hides and robes there, too, but such is a woman's lot, and I'll not ask ye to do that. A month ye'd be, most likely, and no more than two, and I'd trade ye the bay for ye labors, plus powder and lead and what supplies ye'll need to take ye where ye wanted to go afterward. What say ye, Mister Pike? Are ye interested?"

Pike tipped his head back, staring at the light that played along the rafters. It was a fair offer for a man without a horse and only the powder and ball he carried in his shooting bag, and he figured there was a good chance the men he'd been trailing for most of the summer had been heading for the Red River country all along. If that was the case, then hunting for McTavish would provide him an alibi to nose around without suspicion. But if Arch's killers hadn't stopped at the Red, Pike knew he wouldn't waste the month or more McTavish was asking for. He'd steal the bay and whatever supplies he needed and push on, leaving the half-breeds and McTavish to deal with his betrayal however they saw fit.

"All right, McTavish," Pike said. "I'll run buffalo with you. Let's see where it takes us."

The sun hadn't yet reached the valley floor when Pike and Big John rode out the next morning, although it had been light for some time. Gabriel's trail was a dark trace across the dewy meadow, disappearing only after it started up the tall hill to the north. Gabriel himself was little more than a speck of color against the deep blue sky near the top, his piebald horse already half hidden by the brow of the hill.

"There's a trail up there the lad will follow," McTavish explained. "He'll talk to them that live along it, and let 'em know we'll be leavin' within the week. Charlo will do the same for those who live to the south."

"How many folks live up here?" Pike asked, swiveling his head to study the rugged terrain. He and McTavish were moving down the valley to the east, following a cart track that hugged the river.

"Only a few that the lad will find, but word of the hunt will spread quick enough. They're primed for it, those that will go." He lifted his reins. "What do ye say, Mister Pike? Shall we let our ponies have some rein?"

Pike nodded, urging the bay into a lope after Big John's roan. They followed the winding course of the Pembina all morning, stopping at noon where the hills ended abruptly at the edge of a broad, flat plain.

"The Red River Valley," McTavish announced, removing his coat without dismounting and tying it behind his saddle. "We'll swing wide around Saint Joseph if ye've no objection. 'Tis only a small settlement, and most of 'em will be at me cabin in another day or so anyway. We'll be most of the afternoon gettin' home as it is, but it'll be tomorrow for sure if we linger at Saint Joseph."

"It doesn't matter one way or the other to me," Pike said. "I'm following you, remember?"

They crossed the Pembina and rode south for several miles until they came to a trail leading toward a shallow notch in the ridge on their left. The climb was steeper than it looked, and they pulled up on top to let the horses blow. It was from here that Pike got his first good look at the Red River Valley. It was as big as Big John had implied, flat as the bottom of a frying pan. Even from here, the far side of the valley was hidden behind the curve of the earth.

It was the same looking north and south, too, the land just flowing outward until it seemed to fade into a metallic haze. Although level and drab, it wasn't without feature. To the north, the Pembina River cut boldly across the plain, its winding banks lined with trees ablaze in their fall colors, and here and there throughout the valley stood patches of forest, like scarlet-crowned atolls thrust from a tawny sea. Far to the south, cutting diagonally before them to the northeast, was another broad stream, banked in thick foliage. But there were no farms that Pike could see, no rippling fields of grain or feeding cattle.

"Ye were expectin' more?" McTavish asked, seeing his reaction.

"I reckon I was. You mentioned farms and settlements last night."

"Ah, they're there, Mister Pike. They're just too far away to see from here, and Saint Joseph is hidden by the point of yon hill. There are some fields there, but no real farms, and none at all along the Pembina except me own, and that's near to the other side of the valley, at the mouth of the Tongue River that ye see in front of us, angling to the northeast. The farms the lad spoke of last night lie above the border in Rupert's Land, what ye likely think of as Canada. A regular settlement, that is."

"Who lives here?"

"Hunters, mostly. Sure, they'll raise some garden truck, but farmin's not in their blood. Aye, hunters, and proud of it. Too proud, some might say."

But Pike sided with the *métis* on that. "It's a good life," he said. "I'd rather hunt than farm, any day."

They made their cautious descent to the valley floor, where McTavish lifted his horse into a lope once more. The afternoon passed without conversation, until nearly sundown when they came to the line of trees and brush that Pike had spotted from above. A cart track ran parallel to it, and they swung onto that, slowing their horses to a walk for the first time since leaving the hills.

"The Tongue," McTavish commented, nodding at the river. Jutting his chin toward a dense woods up ahead, he added: "She joins the Pembina there, then it's another hour east to where the Pembina joins the Red. Near to thirty miles between Saint Joseph and the Red River, I'd guess."

"You said your farm was here, on the Tongue?" Pike couldn't see anything ahead of them except the woods.

"Aye, beyond yon trees there, along the southeast bank."

When they came to the woods, McTavish reined his horse off the cart path and down to the Tongue. The river was deeper here than the Pembina had been in the hills, its current slow and muddy, and although no more than a dozen feet across, Pike had to lift his feet to keep from soaking his moccasins in the deep, warm waters. The land on the opposite bank reminded him of the country southwest of Missouri, where he'd spent a couple of seasons trading with the Osages for the Chouteau company. It had a muggy, Eastern feel to it, more so than even the Hair Hills.

They followed a narrow path into the heart of the woods. On either side the land looked low and marshy, marked with hummocks of coarse dead grass surrounded by stagnant ponds. Mosquitoes buzzed among the rushes, and greenheads and deerflies badgered men and horses alike.

" 'Tis worse in summer," McTavish proclaimed cheerfully. "A snaky place, too."

"Why do you live here?"

"I don't," was the Scotsman's unadorned reply.

Another half hour brought them through the dense woods. As they cleared the trees, Pike saw a cluster of buildings in the distance. There was a cabin of hewn logs with a high-peaked thatch roof, a low barn of sun-bleached cottonwood, and a small open-faced shed with a corral to one side. Maybe a dozen acres of recently harvested grain fields lay to the south of the farmhouse, sprinkled with sheaves of barley stacked haphazardly throughout.

More than a score of teepees dotted the flat plain east of the buildings, each with its own cart—or sometimes two or three carts—sitting beside it, with a sizable herd of horses and oxen spread out grazing beyond them. Children raced, screaming and shouting among the hide lodges, caught up in games of their own making, while women trudged unhurriedly from one chore to the next, toting armloads of firewood or kettles that splashed river water over their dark wool or calico skirts. Some carried infants strapped to their backs in cradleboards, others sported short clay pipes clenched firmly between their teeth like permanent fixtures attached to their lips.

The men were gathered in small groups around the buildings, talking expressively. Some sat cross-legged and slope-backed; others stood hip-shot, their arms folded in grave consideration of whatever subject they were discussing. The air above their heads was hazed with tobacco smoke, and, when they spoke, their hands flashed animatedly, as if in rhythm with the conversation.

Dogs ran everywhere. Most of them were curs, small and neutrally shaded, but Pike also noticed an uncommon number of larger canines, too, heavily-muscled brutes with tails that curled over their backs and thick, brushed coats of tan, silver, and black. Sled dogs, he realized with something of a start, displaying an air of loftiness among the lesser animals.

But it was the windmill that Pike's gaze kept returning to. It was the first he'd ever seen outside of a wood-cut illustration—a broad-based, squatty-looking structure for all its two stories, with four large, rawhide-covered blades revolving slowly in a sluggish breeze. A group of boys were playing beneath it, leaping up to catch a blade as it crept past, then hanging on until it was almost horizontal before letting go and falling back to earth.

Pike whistled, impressed. "That's some," he allowed.

"Aye, though not as practical as I'd once hoped," Big John admitted. "Farmin' did not catch on this far south. In the early years, I thought it might."

It was one of the boys at the windmill who spotted them first. He yelled in recognition, then yelled again as he sprinted toward the barn with his news. The other boys followed, shouting gleefully. The youths' caterwauling quickly brought the men to their feet. When they recognized McTavish, they burst into a cheer, and, with a full-throated whoop of his own, McTavish spurred his roan toward the waiting crowd.

Pike's fingers momentarily tightened around his rifle, then relaxed when he recognized McTavish's tactics as nothing more than a form of greeting, a bit of splash and color in an otherwise dreary world. Not much different, he reflected, from the way he'd seen lonely trappers come into rendezvous in the mountains, *ki-yiing* at the tops of their lungs, firing their rifles into the air, half froze for companionship.

McTavish slid his horse to a dirt-showering stop, leaping clear of the saddle even as the dust continued to rise around the stallion's rear legs. Several of the half-breeds were forced to skip out of the way to avoid the roan's flashing hoofs, although it didn't seem to dampen anyone's enthusiasm. Even Big John was laughing and shouting like a kid, throwing his arms around two or three of them at once, slapping others on the back or shoulder. His brogue-heavy voice rose above the clamor of the crowd.

"Baptiste! And Charles! Jules, and René, ye scoundrel! I would have thought Hudson's Bay had hung ye by now! And Joseph! By the Lord, Joseph, will ye be comin' with us again? Good, man, good! Antoine! And Etienne, and John McKay, 'tis good to see ye! Aye, laddies, 'tis a fine hunt we'll have, with most of the best of us already here, and the rest soon to follow!"

Maybe thirty men were crowded around the tall Scotsman, their voices lifting as one in a polyglot of French, English, and what Pike thought must be at least a couple of different Indian dialects. But they all turned silent when Pike rode into the yard and dismounted. They stepped back and fanned out, their gazes shifting questioningly to Big John.

"An American," McTavish announced loudly, "and a friend. Pike is his name."

Big John's proclamation released a quick prattle from the half-breeds, and several of them stepped forward.

"I am René Turcotte," said one, a short, barrel-chested man with a thin mustache and a narrow goatee. His skin was dark, his straight black hair cut square at the top of his shoulders in what Pike was beginning to realize was a common fashion among the *métis*, and his eyes were quick and bright. "You are a friend to Big John, then you are a friend to René." He took Pike's hand and shook it vigorously.

"*Oui,* and I am Baptiste LaBarge," said another, shouldering Turcotte aside to grab Pike's hand in his own. LaBarge wasn't as broad-shouldered as Turcotte, nor did he sport a goatee, but there was little difference otherwise—between any of them. A few wore short beards, others went clean-shaven or cultivated trimmed mustaches, some had hair or eyes that were lighter than the norm, although still generally dark. But mostly they were the same, made that way by the blood of their mother's people, Pike guessed. Even their dress was similar—smoked leather and brightly colored cloth, moccasins, and broad knit sashes, lots of quill- and beadwork.

When LaBarge stepped back, another took his place, and in that manner Pike eventually exchanged greetings with all of them, each introducing himself as he grasped Pike's hand, making him welcome. Several of them proclaimed their friendship for all Americans, and a few asked if he intended to open a trading post or tavern. Throughout it all, McTavish looked on, grinning broadly, until the last man had stepped away. Then he said: "Welcome to me home, Mister Pike, and ye own, as long as ye're willin' to stay."

Turcotte called to one of the boys standing nearby and a youth of ten or twelve stepped forward.

"Give the lad ye pony, Mister Pike," McTavish instructed as he handed the boy the reins to his stallion. "He'll be cared for properly, and ye tack will be brought back soon enough."

Pike handed the kid the bay's reins and the boy led both animals away. A few of his friends went along to help, but most of them stayed, their faces as eager as their fathers'.

"The buffalo, Big John, did you find them?" a half-breed asked.

"Aye, Etienne. Not personally, but Mister Pike saw 'em on

the Mouse River. They were heading south for the Dogden Butte."

"The *Maisons des Chiens?*"

"Aye."

"The heart of the Sioux hunting grounds," Turcotte added darkly, and Joseph Breland shouted: "And where else, René?"

"You are afraid of the Sioux, René?" LaBarge asked with a mock gravity that caused several of them to chuckle.

"*Non!* René Turcotte is afraid of no one!" the half-breed protested, but the others were already jumping in to join the fun, their hoots and gibes quickly overriding Turcotte's denial.

Then McTavish roared: "Lies, all! René Turcotte is afraid of no man! So says Big John McTavish, and who's to argue that?"

"Isabella!" Etienne Cyr offered in feigned innocence, bringing forth another peal of laughter. McTavish, too, was laughing, taking the ridicule onto himself, Pike noticed, and away from Turcotte, whose face had grown dark with indignation.

"Or the girl," LaBarge added, but the laughter faded when McTavish's face slowly changed. "Celine," LaBarge appended.

"Celine?" McTavish's voice was soft with confusion. "Are ye . . . are ye tellin' me the lass is here, Baptiste?"

"Ho, listen to this one!" a half-breed shouted, but no one else responded. Soon, their expressions sobered.

"I brought her," Charles Hallet explained. "She came with a Hudson's Bay dispatch canoe as far as Fort Douglas, but I brought her here."

"Then 'tis me thanks I'm owin' ye, Mister Hallet," McTavish said, although his words sounded hollow and uncertain. "And where would she be now?"

"The house," Hallet replied. "She is . . . beautiful, Big John. Like her mother."

"Aye, and what else would she be?" McTavish forced a grin that looked almost hideous from the strain, then turned toward the house with a drag in his step.

"We thought you'd sent for her, Big John!" LaBarge called after him. "We thought you knew."

Chapter Four

Celine.

How long had it been? Big John tried to remember the last time he had seen her. On the *canot du nord,* of course, the big freight canoe that had taken her away, but when? How many years ago?

Casting back into his memory, he saw a fleet of slim, birch-bark freighting canoes riding the choppy waters of the Red River offshore from Fort Douglas. A drifting mist had been falling that day. He could still remember the grumbling of the *voyageurs* as they glided slowly away from shore, damp and chilled by the inclement weather and the journey not even begun.

And alone among the nearly two score of rough, hardy canoe men, a girl of just six tender years, a frightened, tiny child crammed in among the sacks of pemmican and bales of meat and buffalo robes that were bound for Fort William and the great annual rendezvous of the North West Company. Isabella had tearfully wrapped the child in a patchy summer robe before placing her in the canoe, and the vision of her huddled there, her cramped oval face, the dark, spiritless eyes locked on his from beneath her shaggy cowl, tore at him like bloody fangs.

But his heart had been like stone then, impenetrable. He hadn't even waved good bye.

The cabin's front door unexpectedly flew open and Big John jerked to a halt. Fear welled up within him, but it was only the boy, Alec.

"Big John!" Alec cried happily. "Did you find the buffalo? Are they far?"

"On the Mouse, and waitin' for ye," Big John replied. His fingers itched to grab the boy, to lift him high until he shouted in delight. But Alec had outgrown such coltish displays of affection. Sometimes Big John wondered if he was the only one who missed them.

Alec was Gabriel's brother, and for most of his life he had been little more than a shorter version of the original, always tagging along whenever Gabriel permitted it. Yet even from the beginning, there had been disparities between the two, contrasts that had sharpened over the years, and especially of late.

There was a passion for quick laughter and high adventure in Alec, coupled with an ability to shrug off misfortune the way most people shrugged off a jacket on a hot day. Life was a celebration for him, and in that regard he was like many of the *métis* who resided in the valley, taking what came, turning his back on that which could not be changed.

There was a capacity for irreverence within Gabriel, too, although it had never been of the same free-wheeling, devil-may-care bent that guided Alec. For Gabriel there was always a tempering of impulse, a sense of responsibility that seemed to stifle pure recklessness. He was like his father in that regard, Big John mused, and wondered how well Gabriel remembered Angus Gilray. Gabriel never spoke of him, although for that matter, neither did Big John. In his mind the death of Gabriel's father had always been tied to his memory of Angelique's passing.

"Then I will go with the men to run buffalo this year?" Alec asked.

The question caught Big John off guard. Then he recalled his last remark to the boy, and nodded sadly. "Aye, ye be thirteen, lad. That's old enough, I'm thinkin'. Sure, ye can run 'em this year."

"Ai, ai, ai, ai, ai!" Alec's voice rose lustily, and he skipped back in an impromptu dance, knees pumping, arms flapping above his head. But Big John didn't smile, not even then. Sidestepping the gyrating youth, he left him to his revelry.

In his haste, Alec had left the cabin door open. Now it seemed to yawn ominously, like a gaping wound. Big John hesitated at its entrance, then took a deep breath and stepped inside. He paused to take in the room but saw nothing out of the ordinary. There was the same old table and benches, shelves cluttered with pots and pans and jars of spices. Bricks of tea were stacked one on top of the other alongside a pile of woven tobacco. In the big, arched stone fireplace a kettle of soup bubbled above a small blaze, a blackened teapot hanging from an iron arm at its side. The walls were whitewashed and the moccasin sole-polished oak floor gleamed as if freshly waxed. In the low plank ceiling, the opening to the loft gaped like an empty eye socket.

At the fireplace, Isabella rose stiffly, a short chunky woman with almond-shaped eyes and a broad, flat nose. A full-blooded Cree, she wore the simple blue wool strap dress of her people; there was a cape that went with it that covered her bare shoulders, with removable sleeves, but she kept those on the shelf above the door when she was inside or when the weather was warm.

On her chin were the traditional tattoos of a Cree woman, barely visible in the dim, early evening light—a straight line that ran from the center of her lower lip downward to a point just below her chin, then two flanking lines that flared outward as they descended toward her neck. Heavy brass earrings stretched her lobes and her fingers were encircled with thin rings of brass and copper, some spotted with glass rubies and diamonds. No hint of emotion altered the wooden cast of her face, but there was warmth in her eyes, and relief for Big John's safe return. It was a thing only a man who knew her well would notice, and he smiled to see it now. Isabella was Gabriel's and Alec's mother, and sometimes she was Big John's woman as well.

"*Bon jour,* McTavish," she said, then switched to English, which she knew he preferred. "You are well?"

"Aye, I am." His gaze circled the room.

"There is soup, and water for tea," Isabella offered.

"The lass," Big John said softly. "Where is she?"

"She went for water."

He turned and sucked in his breath to find her standing behind him, a wooden bucket hanging from one slender fist. She hadn't changed was his first stunned impression, but then he realized that she had, that she had grown and blossomed and become a woman in the years since she'd been away, and that it wasn't Celine he had momentarily seen, but Angelique. The resemblance was disconcerting, and it made him catch his lower lip between his teeth to keep from crying out.

Celine.

She stood only a few inches above five feet, slim and darkly beautiful, her eyes solemn in a dusky face. She wore a voluminous drab brown dress pulled in at the waist by a plain red factory sash that she must have picked up at one of the forts. The sash emphasized the swell of her breasts and the flare of her hips in a way the dress itself was never meant to. Square-toed black shoes peeked out from beneath the dusty, mud-splattered hem of the frock. A blue shawl had fallen back on her shoulders to reveal coal-black hair that was wavy and full, glinting with soft shades of amber in the weakening light. Framed by the V of the shawl where it crossed over her breasts was a heavy silver crucifix, suspended from a braided horsehair cord. It was her only ornamentation.

"Big John?" she queried uncertainly.

"Aye," he replied, feeling a pounding in his temples, a fuzzing at the edges of his vision.

"Father?"

"Aye," Big John breathed.

Celine.

In the bright, early-morning light her name came easily to his tongue, as natural as the flight of birds or the haunting, half-human cry of a loon. It had been different last night, though. Last night, while Isabella washed and put away the supper dishes and Alec knelt before the fire casting round balls for his fusil, Big John and Celine had sat at the table talking hesitantly. He thought she had been ready to make amends, to forgive or offer repentance, whichever he preferred, but the warmth she had reached for—his own forgiveness—had evaded her as it had him. Inexplicably he had found himself growing stiff and cold-shouldered, his words clipped with unwarranted bitterness, until their conversation had eventually faltered, then died.

Isabella had continued her chores without comment, but Alec had put away his casting tools and left the house. He hadn't returned until nearly dawn. Meanwhile, Big John had taken to his rocker, retreating into a stony silence of confusion, anger, guilt, and, above it all, shame. The ghost of that summer was twelve years gone now, yet it still tormented him. He supposed it always would. He would never know the whole truth of what had happened that day, but he knew he couldn't continue to blame Celine for it. She had been a child then, beyond fault. As much a victim as he or Angelique, if not more so.

His grip tightened on the roan's reins, his jaw rigid.

"Pembina?"

Big John looked up as Pike jogged his bay close. Pointing ahead with his chin, Pike said: "Is that Pembina?"

He glanced ahead to the bustling activity on the plain before them. Though still small in the distance, the sprawling, transient community was closer than it should have been before he noticed it. "Aye, it is," he said.

The *métis* were gathered on the north bank of the Pembina, within the angle of land between that and the Red River. From here it looked as if there were already seventy or eighty lodges set up. There would probably be another twenty or thirty before the rendezvous broke up—two hundred or more hunters, and growing every year. The prairie northwest of the camp swarmed with close to one thousand head of cart ponies and oxen, grazing under the watchful eyes of several older boys.

"A fair-size outfit," Pike observed.

"Aye, though not half as many as will go on the summer hunt in June."

"I was talking to René Turcotte last night. He says the ones who have gathered at your cabin will hunt separately from this bunch, that you'll have no more than a handful of men."

"Better a small hunt than the likes of this." Big John swept a hand toward the distant encampment. "Aye, we'll be smaller, but we'll be more than a handful, too. Maybe sixty or so hunters by the time we leave, and good men, all of 'em."

Spotting a flurry of motion at the western edge of the camp, a knot of horsemen taking shape under a rising cloud of dust, he said: "Prepare yeself, Mister Pike, for 'tis a rare sight ye're about to behold."

The horsemen came at them in a run, their tough little Indian ponies stretched low to the ground, manes flapping like pennants. Big John could see the bright reds and greens and blues of the *métis'* clothing even from here. As they drew closer, he began to pick out the feathers and bits of trade silver that danced from men and animals alike. Grouped together, they seemed to bristle with the long, blued barrels of their trade guns, but, as they came within fusil range, they began to spread out, yipping their shrill war whoops.

Big John glanced at Pike, curious to see how he would handle this feigned attack. The amused half grin that notched the trapper's face and the bright sparkle in his eyes told Big John what he wanted to know. It was good, he thought, that Pike wasn't intimidated by such displays of ferociousness. It would bode well for him in the weeks ahead.

"It appears they've heard of ye, Mister Pike, and aim to see what mettle ye're made of."

"So it would seem," Pike agreed, laughing.

"Shall we ride to meet them?"

"Wagh!" Pike cried, the sound amazingly similar to a grizzly's warning snort. Touching the bay's ribs with his spurs, he shouted: "Come on, McTavish! Let's show them some real riding!" And with that he began a wild *ki-yiing,* the equal of anyone's.

Big John let the dancing roan have its head. The stallion bolted after the bay as the Red River *métis* began to converge on the two Tongue River hunters. Lifting his rifle overhead, Big John fired his right-hand barrel into the sky over the Pembina, while the *métis* touched off a ragged volley of their own.

Still in the lead, Pike slipped down the bay's offside, hooking a heel behind the cantle of his saddle while curling an elbow around its knobby horn. Stretching forward, he pushed the barrel of his rifle under the bay's neck and fired at the prairie about twenty yards in front of the charging *métis.* Big John half expected to see the bay come undone at the rifle's thunder, but the pony kept on doggedly, more intent on keeping its lead on the rapidly gaining roan than spooking and bucking.

The *métis* roared their approval. Some of them slipped off the far side of their own horses as the party split to either side of Pike, firing into the dirt to the fore and aft of the bay. Others stood upright, their moccasined toes digging into the soft leather of their pad saddles, lifting their fusils overhead in a rigid salute.

They were among the *métis* for only a second. Time enough for Big John to fire his second barrel into the air, to note a few familiar faces. Then they were through them and the *métis* were wheeling their horses and coming back. Pike slid back into his saddle and reined alongside the roan. They both slowed to a trot.

"A fine showin', Mister Pike," Big John said, grinning broadly. "Ye ride like a half-blood, and there's damn' few who can make that claim."

Before Pike could reply, one of the *métis* caught up, shouting—"McTavish!"—in a booming baritone.

Others arrived, flanking them, adding their own greetings to the good-natured insults and laughter. These were French mixed-bloods for the most part, the children of Canadian or French-Canadian fathers. Many of them spoke limited or no English at all. It wasn't by accident that at Big John's cabin the *métis* were split about evenly between French, English, and Scottish patrimony, but that they all spoke passable English.

"Bon jour, mes amis!" Big John called. *"Vous êtes prêtes d'aller à la chasse?"*

"*Oui, nous sommes prêtes,* McTavish!" cried one.

"Quel bois brûle n'est pas toujours prêt, eh?" added another.

"Turcotte *dit que t'as amené un etranger à la chasse!*" shouted a man named Remi. *"Sacre bleu! Il est monté presqu'aussi bien qu'un bois brûle!"*

The others laughed and Big John glanced at Pike. "They be agreein' with me, Mister Pike, that ye ride like a *métis.* 'Tis a fine compliment they're payin' ye, ye understand?"

"Tell them that not even the Comanches ride as well as they do," Pike instructed. "Tell them it was an honor to see such horsemanship."

Big John nodded his approval, and, after translating Pike's

compliments, he watched the pleasure come into the eyes of the mixed-bloods. Remi stood in his stirrups, announcing in his choppy English: "You will be guests this night, Big John. In my lodge we will smoke the pipe, yes, and the feast, you and me and this American. My woman, yes, she good cooks. This you know. Now I go hunt. The finest meat I will hunt."

"Oui!" shouted a man Big John recognized but couldn't name. "We will hunt, then tonight we will celebrate with a dance!"

"*Oui,* a celebration," said another, then whirled his pony to make a dash for the Pembina. Perhaps a dozen others followed him, the air loud with shouted promises and friendly ribbings.

"They're after meat," Big John explained to Pike. "For the celebration."

"What are they celebrating?"

"Yeself, mostly, and the way ye ride, but also the compliment ye paid 'em. Not that they need much of an excuse to bring out the flute and the fiddle. 'Tis a poor hunter's life we live here, but rich in our own ways, and ready to celebrate at the drop of a hat like true *bois brûle.*"

"And you?"

"Me?" Big John laughed. "I'm *métis* in spirit, Mister Pike, if not in blood. I wouldn't trade me life here for the finest mansion in Montreal."

"A satisfied man's a rare thing," Pike said. "Tell me about the celebration."

"Sure, but I wouldn't be countin' on much to fill ye belly. Remi's a fine hunter, as he'd not hesitate to tell ye, but I'm thinkin' 'tis old pemmican ye'll be eatin' tonight if ye stay. As for meself, I'll be home in bed." He flashed a grin. "The spirit's *métis,* Mister Pike, but the body is Scottish. It demands its rest."

Pike nodded. "I reckon I'll ride back with you."

"Ye'll be welcome, and just as well. There'll be little ones who'll need any meat the hunters bring in. Ye'll offend no one if ye don't stay."

They rode in silence for the remainder of the way and the *métis* who hadn't crossed the river to hunt began veering off to the side to talk among themselves. Big John heard Paget's name mentioned several times, and knew they were discussing the upcoming elections.

As they neared the village the *métis* suddenly put their ponies into a run, racing for the lodges with neither preamble nor farewell. Watching them, listening to their fading shouts, Big John was reminded of children caught up in the unbridled happiness of being who they were, where they were. The spirit was contagious and he glanced at Pike and laughed, but the American's visage was grim as he eyed the bustling village, and he barely acknowledged Big John's gesture. Once again, Big John wondered what had brought this iron-barked little mountain man so far from his usual haunts.

They entered the village at a walk, riding past rough-housing children and skulking, half-wild dogs that growled menacingly as they passed. Among these more northern *métis,* Big John McTavish was nothing more than a retired trader in a distant land, a person they seldom saw except when they ventured south for a hunt.

The women ignored them and went about their chores, chatting in French and *michif*—that language made up of equal parts bastardized French, English, Gaelic, Chippewa, Cree, Assiniboine, and their own indigenous creations. The men lounged in whatever shade they could find, talking, gambling, swapping, telling tales that may or may not have been true. Many of them waved or called a greeting, for even a retired trader could be known and respected. But none of them rose or came forward to shake his hand. That village courtesy had already been extended by the horsemen who had ridden out to greet him and Pike along the Pembina Trail.

There were carts everywhere among the smoky-brown lodges, moving slowly but noisily beneath loads of firewood and teepee poles, spare axles, extra spokes, and wooden cassettes filled with personal belongings. Those carts not in use were lined up in a rough circle around the camp. Shortly before nightfall the livestock would be driven inside and the rest of the carts wheeled into the gaps. It was a convenience here, a handy way to bunch the horses and oxen for the night, but when they left the relative safety of the valley for the Sioux lands it would become a necessity, a rolling stockade behind which they could take shelter in case of attack.

Spotting a group of men sitting beneath a sprawling oak, Big John drew up. "There's Paget, the man I came to see, Mister Pike. Ye're welcome to sit in on the parley if ye'd like."

"No, I reckon I'll mosey around some," Pike replied. "Maybe I'll see someone I know." He reined toward a group of nearby lodges, his right hand sliding back to cover the lock of his rifle.

Big John's shoulders sagged in understanding. "Ah, then 'tis blood that brought ye among us, eh?" He watched a while longer, then reined away.

As Big John neared the knot of men gathered beneath the oak, Paget suddenly stood up and shouted: "*Bon jour,* Big John! Welcome to thee fall rendezvous."

"Ha, Paget, ye English improves! *Bon jour, mon ami.*"

"Alwees, Big John, alwees."

"*Bon jour,* McTavish!" the others called, punctuating their greetings with nods and smiles.

"Have ye spoke with René Turcotte yet?" Big John asked, drawing rein.

"*Oui,* thees morning he comes to see thee priest for thee blessing, *non?* He say you might come to see me."

"Aye, if ye've the time."

"But of course, Big John. Come, we go to my lodge."

Paget stepped clear of the circle of men and made his way toward a small, ten-hide lodge as brown as river mud. Big John dismounted to walk beside him. "The rendezvous grows, Paget."

"Every yeer a leetle more. Soon eet will be too big."

"There's some as would say it's already too big."

Paget grinned but declined to be pulled into the debate. He already knew how McTavish felt about big hunts that scared the buffalo farther onto the plains.

Making themselves comfortable beside a struggling fire, Paget added kindling, then nudged a small, fire-blackened tea kettle closer to the flames. Lifting a buckskin *gage de amour* from around his neck, he withdrew a short clay pipe from its loops, then flipped the quilled cover back to pull out a pinch of tobacco.

"We will smoke thee pipe first, eh," he said, carefully packing the bowl. When he was satisfied, he handed the pouch to Big John, then leaned forward to light his smoke with a twig from the fire.

Paget was a *métis,* which meant he was short and wiry and tough as bull-hide, quick to laugh and just as quick to anger. He was an excellent horseman, a fair shot, a trapper and hunter, and occasionally a trader among the full-bloods, most notably the Crees among whom he had relatives. He was a sometime smuggler of furs, as well, although most of them were. Hudson's Bay had held a monopoly on British pelts for more than one hundred and fifty years, but it was the Americans now, as it had once been the Nor'Westers, who offered the best prices.

Paget's woman came out of their lodge with her eyes cast toward the ground. She set a pair of dented tin mugs beside her husband's knee, then, using her apron as a pot holder, she pulled the kettle from the flames to fill both mugs. She handed the first to Big John, the second to Paget, then returned to her lodge without having spoken a word.

"Two caravans, eh?" Paget said absently, fussing with the contents of his pipe.

"Mine and yours, Paget."

"*Non,* not mine, Big John. And not yours, too. No man owns thee *bois brûles.*"

"Ye'll be leadin' this year, I'm thinkin'," Big John argued mildly.

"That ees for thee tribe to decide. I will lead only eef they ask."

They'd ask, Big John knew. He thought Paget knew it, too.

"Turcotte, he say you find *le bison* on thee Mouse *Rivière,* no?"

"Aye, so says the American," Big John said. He tapped his teeth thoughtfully with the stem of his pipe. "Tell me, Paget, if ye do lead, what route do ye think ye'd be takin'?"

"Ees not up to me," Paget replied. "I am not thee *capitaine.*"

"Aye, but I said if."

Paget grinned and shook his head. "Big John, you are so . . . what? Hurried, eh? Impatient. But ees all right. We are friends. So, you see them on thee Mouse when? Four day ago? Five day? Heading toward *les Maisons des Chiens?* Five day, that ees long time for *le bison* to travel. So me? I theenk *Lac du Diable,* then maybe we go west from there. *Oui.* Maybe that, eef I am thee *capitaine,* but thee others must agree by vote."

Big John nodded, satisfied with the answer. If Paget led, he would take his hunters southwest to Devil's Lake before turning straight west toward the buffalo ranges. It was a good thing to know.

" 'Tis the route we'd be wantin' to take ourselves, providin' we beat ye to the Ridge Trail," Big John said casually.

"*Oui,* thees I already know. But I do not theenk you will beat us this year. René says all thee hunters are not een. Ees true?"

"Aye, another day, I'm thinkin'. Maybe two."

"A last group comes today from thee White Horse Plain. Tonight then we weell hold thee election. Then we leave. Maybe tomorrow. Maybe thee next day."

Big John nodded, puffing furiously on his pipe. Charlo had been wrong about when the Pembina buffalo men would be ready to pull out. It meant they would beat the Tongue River hunters to the Ridge Trail by a day, at least, giving them access to an already well-established route that would be quicker and easier to follow. If the Tongue River caravan followed the same route, they would find the deadwood gone, the game run off.

"We'll be north of ye then, most like, but not far. Can we count on ye, Paget, in case of the Sioux?"

"But of course, Big John, and us on thee. We are brothers, *non?*"

"Oui," Big John agreed. *"Frères."*

"Eff I am elected, Big John, I weell send riders north. You weell do thee same to thee south then, yes?"

"Aye, no more than a day or two horseback between us." Both groups would send out scouts to look for buffalo as they penetrated deeper into the high plains, and to keep a wary eye peeled for the Sioux, who were familiar with the habits of the *métis* and would likely be waiting for them, looking for a chance to cause some mischief. It would be to the benefit of both parties to stay close enough to one another that their scouts, riding long loops to the north and south, would occasionally cross paths. That way, they would be close enough to help if the need arose, yet far enough away not to interfere with each other's hunt.

Big John said: "Have ye heard of the American's misfortune with the Chippewas, Paget?"

"*Oui,* I have heard. Ees bad, that, no?"

"My own thinkin', aye," he said, then added cautiously: "It could mean war. If not this year, then the next, or the followin'. 'Tis a thing they're not likely to forget."

After a moment's reflection, Paget said: "I do not theenk that weell happen. We are friends, us and thee Chippewas. I have traded weeth them many times."

"Aye, I've traded with 'em a time or two meself, Paget, and some afore ye was born, no doubt. I do not need to be told of the Chippewas, plains or woods."

Paget shrugged. "Then ees as you say, eh."

"Aye." Big John sighed in defeat. Paget was like the others, the younger ones who did not remember the early, bloody years; he refused to see what should have been clear to them all, and Big John was damned if he knew how to make them.

Paget lifted his tin mug and sipped noisily, then jerked it away. "Ah, *sacre démon,*" he swore. "Ees too hot yet, that stupeed woman." He set the cup aside with obvious disgust. "You weell eat, eh, Big John?"

"Have ye some to spare?"

"Some *cabbri,* and *rubaboo.*"

Big John winced. *Rubaboo* was a soup made of pemmican and flour. He knew it would sit heavily on his stomach for the rest of the day. But he needed to stay a while to ask after Paget's family, his summer adventures, his plans for the coming winter. Courtesy demanded as much, and, besides, it would be good to just sit and talk for a spell, to learn what was new along the Assiniboine River where Paget lived. And the half-blood would tell him everything, Big John knew. Aye, he was *métis,* and a born gossip.

Alec was waiting at Murphy's with a cart when Big John guided his roan up the slippery path from the Pembina and rode around to the front of the trading post. He stepped down and hitched the dripping horse to a rail, then loosened the cinch. The cart sat nearby with its shafts resting on the ground. Alec had unhitched the ox without removing its harness, then unsaddled and hobbled the spotted Indian pony he rode before turning both animals loose to graze. He was sitting in the shade of the front wall when Big John approached, smoking his pipe and whittling on a piece of cottonwood. Looking up with a cocky grin, he said: "I did not think you would come, Big John. I thought this year I would have to get credit on my own."

"Ye did, did ye?" Alec stood and Big John ruffled his hair, ignoring the look of annoyance that crossed the youth's face.

They waited together while Pike reined in at the rail and dismounted. To the east, Big John could see what was left of Alexander Henry's old trading post, built near the turn of the century. It had been a North West Company post then, and had still been standing when Big John first came to the valley.

After the Company abandoned it, others tore it apart for the timber. Over the past thirty or forty years there had been quite a few trading posts built along the Red River. Most of them were gone now, with only the base logs—those too rotten to carry off—remaining as artifacts of a bygone era.

Coming into the shade, Pike pushed his old, sway-brimmed hat off the back of his head, letting it hang between his shoulders by a drawstring. His forehead was as white as a catfish's belly above the line of his hatband, the hair flat and straight and parted in the middle. Big John noticed that it was considerably less gray and tangled than that which was normally exposed to the wind and sun.

"Pembina Post," Big John explained, hooking a thumb over his shoulder. " 'Tis here we'll be gettin' what powder and lead and such we'll need for the hunt . . . assumin' the man treats us fair. I'll no stand for a skinnin', not with a Hudson's Bay post only a short ride north, across the border in Rupert's Land."

They went inside to the counter. Big John leaned against it as if it were a bar in a Montreal tavern, while the trader, Murphy, haggled with a trio of *métis* over a pile of rough-looking summer furs.

It was hot inside the low-ceilinged room, and, even with the shuttered windows thrown open to admit the breeze, the air was satiated with the odors of pelts and tallow, wood smoke and tobacco. Big John idly contemplated the shelves bolted to the rear wall, filled to overflowing with blankets and hats and beads, cups and kettles and tea bricks and pigs of lead and kegs of gunpowder, fire steels and boxes of rifle flints, and bolts of calico and trade wool, corduroy, and broadcloth—half a hundred items to catch the eye of a hunter and his woman.

A rack of long guns was filled mostly with fusils, although there were a couple of better-quality trade rifles among them, and one decent-looking used Kentucky rifle with a little decorative brass. A pair of mismatched pistols lay on the shelf beneath the gun rack. Except for one of the pistols, everything sported a flintlock ignition. It seemed only Big John really trusted the newer percussion systems.

In appearance, Pembina Post wasn't all that different from the hundreds of other small trading outfits operating along the frontier—a large room divided lengthwise by a heavy plank counter, with all the trade goods on the back wall, out of reach of filching hands. A curtained door led to a storeroom; another led to the personal quarters Murphy shared with a Chippewa woman named Alice. The post was strangely uncrowded, though, considering the size of the encampment across the river. Big John would have expected the customer side of the room to have been packed with *métis,* waiting their turn to pick up some last-minute item they'd forgotten to bring along from Fort Douglas, or to buy something only the Americans carried.

The three mixed-bloods stood in stony silence while Murphy

flipped through their catch of skins, clucking his tongue at the poor quality of the pelts. His opinion was obvious, but then, he was a trader; Big John knew he would quibble with all but the finest furs. Murphy had glanced up as Big John, Pike, and Alec entered the store, but had only nodded indifferently before turning back to the bartering at hand. Now he slapped the last pelt back on the pile and made a quick sign with his hands.

"Sacre bleu!" the *métis* exploded. *"Vous nous trompez!"*

"Speak English, dammit," Murphy growled. "You know I don't savvy that parley-voo lingo." He looked at Big John. "What's he sayin', Big John?"

"He says ye be cheatin' him, Murph. He says if ye do not come up with a better deal than what ye're offerin' in sign there, he'll be takin' his butcher knife and carvin' ye a new mouth . . . under ye chin. He figures maybe it'll track a little straighter than the one ye're usin' now."

"He thinks so, huh?" Murphy glanced at the furious *métis,* then back at Big John. "You reckon he means it?"

"Aye," Big John replied gravely. "I'd say he does, and he's got friends that look willin' to help, too."

"Well, hell! All right, tell him another keg of powder, but that's it. Tell him."

"Well, sure, but do ye think it wise to offer the man powder without throwin' in the extra lead he'll need to cast bullets for it?" Big John asked mildly.

Murphy's eyes widened. "Lord A'mighty, Big John! What are you trying to do to me?"

"Give him the lead, Murph. 'Tis a fair trade."

"For summer skins! Hell, he's lucky I even allow 'em in the store." Murphy looked away, then heaved a sighed. "All right," he conceded. "I guess they're worth that." He turned to the *métis,* his hands flashing as he offered an extra six-and-a-quarter-pound keg of gunpowder and fifteen pounds of lead for the furs. The *métis* hesitated only a moment, then quickly nodded. His eyes were bright as he watched Murphy set a small wooden keg of gunpowder and three five-pound lead ingots on the counter next to the bricks of tea, cloth, and a couple of muskrat traps already there. Grabbing an armful of skins, he dumped them on the floor behind the counter to be sorted later.

Gathering their supplies, the *métis* headed for the door. The one who had done the trading paused next to Big John. "You good friend, McTavish," he said in English so broken it was hard to follow. "Friend to *bois brûle.*"

"Take ye furs to Hudson's Bay next time," Big John said sternly. "Or smuggle 'em down to Saint Peters, on the Mississippi. Hudson's Bay people will horsewhip ye if they catch ye tradin' British furs to the Americans in their own back yard."

The *métis* grinned, revealing a row of blackened teeth. "No, McTavish. Hudson's Bay no wants these furs. They summer skins."

"Well, I'll be damned," Murphy said wonderingly. "You were behind this all along, weren't you, McTavish?"

Big John laughed as the *métis* scuttled through the door. "No, Murphy, I wasn't. I don't know the man, and I wouldn't have pulled such a stunt even if I had."

"He knew you."

"Well, and sure, but ye've got to remember there's not too many Scotsmen livin' this far south. 'Tis not a surprise that he would've known me for that reason alone."

"Just the same, you might've slickered me on that deal, but you won't do it again."

"I'm not here to slicker, nor to be slickered. 'Tis credit I'm needin', for the hunt."

"Credit! You set me up with that damn' 'breed, and now you're asking for credit, as if every damn' buffalo hunter in the valley hasn't already done the same."

" 'Tis the way of the valley, Murph, and without it ye'd not have the fine robes ye get to resell to American Fur. Now, what are ye payin' for robes this year?"

"I'm paying in beaver, same as always," Murphy groused. "Three and a half dollars American equals a pound of beaver."

"I know how the system works. I'm askin' what ye're payin'."

"Three quarters of a beaver for a silk robe, a quarter for common, a tenth for poor, unless they're too bad. I won't take a robe that's nearly ripped through or poorly tanned."

"By the Lord, man, I'd as soon trade with Hudson's Bay as sell that dear," Big John thundered. " 'Tis a full beaver I'll be havin' for my silkies, and not a penny less."

"That's top dollar," Murphy protested. "American Fur wouldn't pay that, not if they had to come up here for it."

"Ye're not much of a trader if ye cannot do better than a beaver for a good silk, rare as they be. One beaver, Murph, and half for common."

"Half! Hell, I won't do it. Take your robes to Hudson's Bay, McTavish. I've already been fleeced once today."

"Ye think I won't, and take half the *métis* with me?"

Murphy's eyes narrowed. "Is that a threat?"

"Ye damned well better believe it is."

"Damn a tight-fisted Scotsman," Murphy grated. "All right, one beaver's credit for silks, providing they're tanned top-notch, and half for common, but I'll still pay no more than a tenth for a poor robe. Unless you're wanting my arm or leg, too?"

"Poor's poor, I say, and not worth the space it takes in a cart. Ye'll get none of those from us, and thank ye kindly, Murph, but no. I'm satisfied with me own arm and leg. I will be takin' some powder and lead from ye, though, and caps for me rifle. Ye carry 'em, don't ye?"

"I got caps," the trader said. From beneath the counter he withdrew a ledger, an inkwell, a couple of quill pens, and a small penknife to sharpen the quills. "Just take your time. I ain't so handy with these things."

Big John didn't need much. He was a thrifty man, and not one to throw away or lose what had taken hard work and risk to acquire. He bought powder and lead and an extra bullet mold for Alec's fusil, some tobacco and salt and tea, and a dozen good, straight-grained hickory ramrods to replace those he'd break on the hunt. For trading, he got some awls and gunflints, a gross of red-handled butcher knives, fifteen fathoms of tobacco, and one hundred paper-backed trade mirrors. He took some beads and clay pipes and fire steels, of course, but shied away from larger items, such as kettles. He still had three good, used fusils from last year's hunt. Although he didn't trade much any more, he liked to have a few items on hand. He'd bought his way out of a tight spot with various plains tribes more than once in the past.

"Is that it?" Murphy asked when Big John finally paused.

"Not just yet." He turned to Pike. " 'Tis someone here as'll be needin' some supplies of his own. He'll be huntin' for me this year, so put what he gets on my tab."

Murphy nodded to Pike. "A beaver man, huh? Don't see many of your kind up this way. Saint Louie, now, there's a place fair crawling with 'em. Forts along the river, too. I spent two years at Fort Atkinson and saw plenty of mountain men there, I'll tell you."

Big John moved away from the counter and put his shoulder against the wall, in imitation of Alec, who had watched the bartering in silence. Down the wall a ways, a *métis* man, woman, and two small children were patiently waiting their turn, and from outside there came the squeal of an approaching cart, accompanied by the murmur of several voices. A smile flitted across Big John's face. He knew Murphy would do a fair business this season, in spite of his squawking over the price of robes.

It surprised Big John a little that American Fur hadn't shown up this year, although he didn't doubt the company would get its share of robes and as much pemmican as it wanted. It was said that old man Astor was the only trader around who could buy a robe once and sell it twice, and Big John figured that was true in spirit, if not practice. Astor lived in New York City now, and probably hadn't handled a pelt or a buffalo robe in a good many years, save those he wrapped around his lady fair, but he knew how to hire the right men, the ruthless types who were as sharp in a courtroom as they were in the trading room. Sure enough, American Fur was the biggest thorn Hudson's Bay had in its side since the old North West Company went under, and maybe that was why Big John would rather soak his moccasins in the Pembina to deal with Murphy than ride a few hundred yards to the north and trade with the Bay Company on the English side of the line. Murphy called himself an independent, but Big John would have bet his fall hunt that American Fur was backing him somewhere down the line, whether Murphy knew it or not.

Pike's purchases were minimal. He bought powder and lead and flints for his rifle, a couple of twists of tobacco and two pipes, an extra fire steel, and some salt. It wasn't much, Big John reflected, although a man without a pack animal had to travel light.

"Is that it?" Murphy asked.

"No." Pike glanced at McTavish, then forged ahead. "I want some whiskey, too. The good stuff, not trade alcohol."

"I've got some high wine. It's a little better than rotgut, but not much."

"I said whiskey."

"This ain't Saint Louie, man. I got a couple bottles of Virginia bourbon, but that's dear to my heart, and runs a full beaver a bottle." Pike hesitated, running his tongue lightly over his bottom lip. Seeing that he was about to decline the expense, Big John called across the room: "Aye, and it'll be dear to our hearts, too! A bottle for Mister Pike, Murphy, and another for me. We'll be comin' home in snow, most like, and will be appreciatin' the likes of a stiff drink."

Murphy shrugged and scratched at the ledger with his quill. When he was finished, he looked up expectantly.

"That'll do," Pike said stiffly.

"McTavish?"

Big John glanced at Alec, but the boy shook his head. "Aye, Murphy, that's it. Tally the damages."

Scowling deeply, Murphy labored over the figures for some minutes, then said: "That's thirty-six beaver for everything."

Big John sighed. "I know now what the shaggies must feel, havin' their hides lifted, for 'tis a skinnin' ye've given me, sure. Ye be a bloodthirsty man, Murphy, and I do not see how ye sleep at night."

"Fair is fair, and I sleep just fine, thank you. When will you be back?"

"November, most like. Late or early, I couldn't say."

"Bring me silks, Big John. And pemmican. I'll take all the pemmican you can supply this year, and match Hudson's Bay's price for it."

"I hear ye, Murph, but we'll be bringin' in what the prairie provides, and nary a horn more." He pushed away from the wall. "Set what I've ordered on the counter there, and I'll fetch the cart."

He went outside with Alec on his heels, then stood beside the roan while the lad went to bring in the ox. A smile came unexpectedly to his face. Stroking the stallion's neck, he said under his breath: "Ye be a fool, John McTavish, feelin' like a spring buck to be off ridin' yon prairies like some wild kid. I would have thought ye'd have outgrown such foolishness."

Aye, a fool for sure, he thought, and an old one now, when he used to be just a young one. Whistling, he went to help Alec with the ox.

Chapter Five

It was past dusk by the time Pike and McTavish returned to the Tongue River encampment, the hide lodges already aglow with the soft light of the evening fires. Only a handful of people were visible, most of them women, taking care of some last-minute chore. A few men idled around the teepees, but there were no children in sight at all. The hustle of the day was behind them now, the visiting, fiddling, and dancing yet to come.

"We've grown," McTavish said, nodding toward several new lodges that had sprouted in their absence.

One of the lodges was just going up. Pike watched curiously as a *métis* woman eased her lifting pole into place, then began to work the thinly scraped buffalo hide covering over its skeleton of peeled cedar poles. He estimated there were at least thirty other teepees scattered around the plain, representing anywhere from forty to sixty warriors.

Easing his horse alongside the lumbering ox, McTavish turned the beast toward the cabin. Alec had long since deserted them, quirting his pony impatiently ahead soon after leaving Pembina Post.

Isabella appeared at the cabin door as McTavish guided the ox into the yard, her chunky silhouette slimmed down by the glow of lamplight behind her.

"Here they be," McTavish announced without dismounting. "Ye and the lass see to the sortin', will ye?"

Isabella nodded and came out to take hold of the light chain that dangled from the steer's nose ring. With her shoulder against the ox's neck, she guided it toward the door.

Turning to Pike, Big John said: "I'd best go greet them that came in today. Ye're welcome to join me, if ye'd like."

"I reckon not," Pike replied. He felt saturated by the day's events, worn out by the constant noise and chatter of an agitated village readying itself for a big move. "I think I'll put the bay up, then turn in."

"As ye wish," McTavish said, reining away.

Isabella stopped the ox with the rear of the cart even with the front door. Walking around back, she wrestled the tailgate off and set it out of the way. Then she hefted a forty-pound leather sack filled with lead ingots over her shoulder, cradled a bundle of ramrods under her other arm, along with a pinewood box of trade mirrors, and carried everything inside without once looking at Pike.

Pike smiled without malice at the Indian woman's snubbing. He knew it was just her way, the same as so many other tribes he had dealt with over the years. He was just turning away when an unfamiliar sound caused him to look back. He hauled up abruptly, unprepared for the sight of the young woman standing in the door, staring boldly up at him. She was of average height, her complexion dark without being swarthy—closer, Pike thought, to a creamy shade of chocolate than copper. Her figure was full and firm, obvious even beneath the heavy folds of a wool dress, and her face was nearly flawless. Only a hint of sadness deep within the wells of her eyes marred perfection.

Is this the daughter, Celine? Pike wondered, then decided it must be.

Although she stared at him with a quiet intensity, when he nodded a greeting, she quickly dropped her gaze and went around to the rear of the cart. Impulsively he swung down and looped his reins through the cart's tall, dished wheel. The girl was pulling on one of the robes they'd used to cushion the load, trying to pull it closer. Pike grabbed a handful of the robe, but he didn't try to move it.

"It's too heavy," he whispered, close enough to see the hair along her face stir beneath his breath.

Celine let go of the robe but didn't move away. Nor did she look up or speak. For a minute Pike didn't know what to do. Then the girl leaned forward to grab several cloth sacks from the rear of the cart and immediately started for the cabin. Pike reached out to touch her shoulder but she twisted away, running a few steps to get out of his reach. Before he could call to her, Isabella appeared at the door. She stepped aside to let Celine pass, then swung back to block the cabin's entrance with a fist planted firmly on each hip—a stocky gate of determination, firmly latched by the glare in her obsidian eyes. Then, with a loud huff, she came down to pick up another armful of goods. Returning to the cabin, she hooked her elbow behind the door and slammed it shut behind her.

Pike stood unmoving, staring at the closed door. Then he laughed under his breath and led the bay to the corral beside the open-faced shed. He pulled his saddle off and turned the pony into the enclosure to roll while he forked hay over the railing for the handful of stock McTavish kept penned there. Afterward, he lugged his rig to the windmill and dumped it under the motionless blades.

This was where he'd slept last night, staring up in fascination at the huge blades, the thinly-scraped rawhide skin made translucent by the light of a nearly full moon. Suddenly curious, he made his way around the octagon-shaped building to the door. It creaked loudly as he pushed it open, releasing a stale odor of dust and abandonment. He stepped inside, but there wasn't much to see. The single, cavernous room was empty, its grain-dusted floor trackless save for the scurrying trails of mice.

The mill itself was in the center of the building—a squared funnel, a pair of iron rollers, a deep bin to catch the flour. A shaft came down through the ceiling into a tangle of cogs and gears. Only the shaft, funnel, and bin were made of wood. Everything else was of iron, no doubt freighted into the valley at a tremendous cost. A couple of mouse-chewed leather sacks lay folded on the floor beside the bin.

A ladder to the second floor was fastened to the rear wall. Pike climbed it slowly, using the back of his arm to brush away spider webs. He felt like an intruder when he paused with just his head above the level of the second floor.

This room, too, was all but empty. He went on up to have a closer look around. A thick oak shaft ran from a side wall to the center of the room, where it met the vertical shaft from below in another snarl of cogs, gears, rusting pins, and greased joints. A small gear wheel, a joiner, had been lowered away from the two larger wheels to disengage the whole works. A second set of cogged wheels was connected to a chain that ran through the floor, obviously designed to be pulled by hand. That, he decided, was what must turn the upper section of the mill so that the blades could be positioned properly to the wind.

Pike whistled softly, impressed. The whole set-up was ingenious, especially considering that most of it had to have been constructed locally, designed right here on the Tongue, held together with hand-carved pegs and rawhide.

There were two windows up here. Pike went to the nearest one first. The back of the windmill's blades were just outside, no more than four feet away. Beyond them he could see the lodges of the half-breed camp, like cone-shaped lanterns. A large fire had been built near its center, and families were already assembling around it. Farther east he could just make out a yellow dome of firelight shimmering above the camp of the Pembina hunters.

Moving to the second window, Pike found himself looking down at the barn and the open-faced shed next to the corral, where Alec was unhitching the ox. On to the west, beyond the swampy forest cradled within the fork of the Tongue and Pembina Rivers, he saw a dark, sinuous scar crawling slowly along the St. Joseph trail. Carts, he realized, flanked by horsemen.

Two of them.

Pike's gaze narrowed, and he stepped closer to the window. He recalled his conversation with the old *métis* back at the Pembina camp. The gnarled hunter hadn't been able to speak English, and Pike couldn't understand more than a word or two of the choppy patois of French, Chippewa, and Assiniboine the half-breed seemed comfortable with, but they had been able to converse well enough in the language of the plains.

Henri Duprée? Yes, this one he knew, the old man had answered in sign. *From the White Horse Plain west of Fort Douglas. But he was gone. He would not come back. Bad, that one was, his heart black. Too much Cree blood, this Henri Duprée. He had gone away three winters ago after killing a woman in the north country. It had been during the Moon of Freezing Rivers and there was no game. Henri had been starving, but then he killed the woman and did not go hungry any longer. This is what was said. He did not know. He wasn't there. He had wintered on Red Deer Lake that season and did not return until the spring hunt. Henri went south to Fort Snelling, the American fort. But he would not come back. No. They would hang him if he came back.*

Pike's hands flashed, his pale eyes lit with excitement. *Two came from the west, from the country of the Blackfeet. Henri Duprée and François Rubiette. I followed them.*

No, the old man replied adamantly. *It would be foolish to return. They did not come here.*

Where? I followed them.

The old man thought a moment, then nodded grudgingly.

Maybe. For the hunt. But not to White Horse Plain. Not to Fort Douglas. To the Hair Hills, maybe. But they were not here. He would know Henri. Henri was foolish, but also dangerous. Very dangerous. François he did not know, but who could say? They were not here, in this camp, unless they were hiding under buffalo robes. Maybe Saint Joseph. He thought Henri had a sister there. Maybe. Who could say?

Pike had nodded in gratitude. Taking a slim, half-pound bar of lead from his shooting bag, he'd placed it on the ground between them, a gift for the old man's help, and his silence. He hadn't questioned anyone else. This was their home, Henri's, and maybe François's, too. It wouldn't do to tip them off that someone from the western country was asking about them.

Now, from the second floor of the windmill, Pike watched the approaching carts until the last of the light withdrew from the land, then made his way carefully to the small opening and climbed down. It was full dark inside the windmill, the open door in the opposite wall little more than a gray smudge, although there was a growing light spilling in through the east window from the half-breeds' central fire. He started for the door, circling wide to avoid the machinery, then came to an abrupt halt. His hand flashed to his knife and his pulse quickened. He wasn't alone in the room.

Dropping into a defensive half crouch, Pike silently pulled his knife. He turned the blade up, pressing his thumb firmly against the curled steel guard, ready to slash or stab. He sensed movement to his left and pivoted warily in that direction. A shadow detached itself from the wall and glided toward him. He caught the scent of wood smoke and clean sweat, tinged with an earthy aroma, a muskiness he identified as woman. The voice confirmed it.

"American?"

He straightened but didn't resheath the knife. "You've found me."

"Big John sends me. There is food at the lodge of Turcotte. He wishes for you to join him there."

She came closer, the scuff of her shoes on the wooden floor as gentle as the patter of slow rain. He recognized her in the faint light coming through the window—Celine. He put his hand out as she narrowed the gap between them and rested it lightly on her arm. She shivered at his touch but didn't stop, and Pike caught his breath as she came against him. Her arms circled his shoulders, then slid up around his neck. She pushed into him, arching herself into the curve of his body. Her breath was warm on his face, her lips moist and searching.

The passion of her kiss caught him off guard. The knife slipped from his fingers, thudding to the floor and bouncing away as he clamped both arms around her waist. He pulled her closer, feeling her thighs against his through the fabric of their clothes, her breasts mashed against his chest. She moaned low in her throat, a lusting sound but tinged with something else, too, and suddenly the pressure of her body against his lessened. She jerked her face away with a gasp, struggling in his arms, pummeling him with her fists until he stepped back in confusion.

Her breathing was loud in the still air, and she pressed the back of her hand to her mouth as if she'd been stung on the lip. She looked almost feral in the dim light, her black hair tousled, her eyes bright and challenging, but, when he reached for her a second time, she cried out and whirled away, fleeing through the door like a frightened doe.

Pike stood rigidly with his fists clenched at his sides, his heart pounding wildly. He felt half sick with the low-gut ache of repressed libido. Slowly he stooped and felt for his knife, mindlessly sheathing it as he hobbled to the door. He paused there, searching, but she was gone, with a hundred places to hide.

★ ★ ★ ★ ★

Dawn was a gray band of light above the eastern horizon when Gabriel came down to the open-faced shed the next morning. The dew was already whitening into frost, and in the corral the ponies' breath expanded and withdrew vaporously in the smoky light, like curtains flapping out of distant windows, then immediately being sucked back inside.

Gabriel didn't know what had awakened him. With all of the *bois brûles* camped nearby, it could have been just about anything, yet a nagging sense of foreboding had prevented him from going back to sleep. He had slipped out of bed and quietly dressed, then came down here with his sleeping robe under one arm, his musket carried in his free hand.

Settling down near a corner of the shed, he pulled the robe over his shoulders, then laid the musket across his lap. In spite of the crisp morning air, it wasn't long before his head began to bob.

Gabriel and Charlo had come in from the Hair Hills just after dusk last night, bringing with them Charlo's two carts and the butchered moose. Naturally everyone had been happy to see them, and had immediately extended invitations to sit and talk, to share in the food and the wine and the songs of the camp. And naturally, they had. It had been well after midnight when Gabriel finally turned in, and, after nearly two weeks on the trail, he'd anticipated sleeping until the frost was burned off by the morning sun.

A horse snorted and Gabriel's head jerked up. He glanced toward the sleeping camp but saw only the silhouette of teepees against the brightening sky, the occasional glimmer of a spark spiraling upward from last evening's communal fire. The lodges themselves were still dark, although that wasn't surprising. They had celebrated pretty late last night.

Gabriel's gaze was still on the camp when a shadowy form

stepped away from the far side of the shed. He caught the movement from the corner of his eye, but, when he swung his head in that direction, the ill-defined shape had already moved on.

In the corral the horses began to stir, lifting their heads toward the rear of the shed and blowing softly. Gabriel had to resist the urge to jump to his feet as a figure emerged from the shadows on the far side of the corral. He recognized the broad brim of the American's old hat first, then the rocking, bowlegged gait of the trapper himself.

Coming around the corral, Pike dropped his saddle beside the gate, then leaned his rifle against a post. No more than twenty feet separated him from where Gabriel sat under his robe, but in the dim light Pike didn't see him.

Some of the horses wandered up out of curiosity, the bay and Big John's roan near the front. Gabriel's eyes narrowed suspiciously when Pike lifted a buffalo-hair rope from the corral's gate post. The American was just stepping through the rails when Gabriel shrugged free of his robe and stood up.

Cursing, Pike untangled himself from the rails and swung around to face him. "What the hell are you doing out here, boy?"

"I was wondering which one were you going to steal," Gabriel said tautly.

Pike didn't reply right away, and, for a moment, Gabriel wondered if he might actually try to jump him. Even with the Brown Bess held ready, he felt vaguely intimidated by the American's posture, the lack of fear in his pale blue eyes. Then the moment passed and Pike let the rope hang slack at his side.

"When did you get in?"

"Last night," Gabriel replied, taking a deep breath.

Pike nodded. "I saw a couple of carts from the windmill last night, just about dusk."

"Charlo's carts."

Pike nodded a second time, glanced almost wistfully at the horses crowding the gate, then hung the buffalo-hair rope back over the post. Walking past Gabriel, he peered into the shed.

"Is this where you sleep?" he asked.

"No. I came out here only this morning."

A wry smile crossed Pike's face. "That's the way the stick floats sometimes," he said, then stepped deeper into the shed for a closer look at the bear-hide covering rigged to cottonwood bows over Gabriel's cart. It was a sunshade of sorts, although considerably more than that to Gabriel.

"Boy, that's a grizzly bear's hide!" Pike exclaimed, his head rearing back a little in surprise. "Where'd you get it?"

Feeling suddenly awkward, Gabriel said: "The *mauvaises terres.*"

"The badlands?"

"You know them?"

In his mind, Gabriel was picturing those near the Missouri River, the barren knobs and razor-back ridges, valleys that were little more than deep, broad coulées, twisting like nightmares. The bands of tinted earth—reds, blues, tans—that seemed too perfect to be real. They reminded him of the stories Big John used to tell of castles and dragons, and of a land where mountains could erupt in flames. Gabriel hadn't been able to picture such a place until the first time he'd visited the badlands.

Pike was watching him quizzically. "Is that where you shot him?" he asked.

Gabriel was aware of a new respect in Pike's voice, and couldn't help wondering at his own reluctance to bask in it. He glanced at the hide. It was three years old now, patchy with bald spots that had appeared only recently, although it had been a summer hide to begin with, and the hair had never been thick or luxurious. Worthless, old Abrams, the Hudson's Bay post factor, had gone so far as to suggest, but Gabriel knew its value. So did the rest of the *bois brûles.*

Apparently Pike also understood what it had taken for someone so young to harvest such a creature.

Impulsively Gabriel said: "Were you going to steal Big John's roan?"

Pike's expression went flat, and he started from the shed. Uncertainly Gabriel backed out of his way, though keeping the musket handy in front of him. In the east the sky was red with the coming sunrise, and he wondered suddenly why Pike had waited so long to slip away. If he had intended to steal a horse, it would have made more sense to leave last night, and that way have several hours on his pursuers before anyone noticed he was gone.

Changing the subject, Pike said: "Did you come through Saint Joseph yesterday?"

"Is that where you were going?"

"Just answer the damn' question."

Playing a hunch, Gabriel said: "Did you come here because of Henri Duprée?"

Pike stiffened, a quick, bright light flashing in his eyes. "What do you know about Duprée?" he demanded.

"I know he came back from the Qu'Appelle District a week ago, him and a man named François Rubiette. Before that, they were trading with the plains Crees in the Moose Mountains."

Pike's lip seemed to curl back in a snarl. "Is that what they said?"

"That is what I was told." He paused. "You came here because of them, didn't you?"

"Where are they now?"

"They are gone. They came to visit Duprée's sister, who is married to Nicolas Quesnelle. Michel Quesnelle is my friend."

His voice deepening into a growl, Pike repeated his question.

"They will hunt for Nicolas Quesnelle this year, as you hunt for Big John," Gabriel replied. "Quesnelle will come in today, but Duprée and Rubiette have already left for the plains. They will look for the herds, as Big John and I did, and return only when they find them."

Pike looked west toward the distant Hair Hills, and the anger seemed to drain from his face. "So this is where the bastards were headed all along," he said softly. Then, with a short bark of laughter, he went to retrieve his saddle and rifle.

"Big John trusts you!" Gabriel called after him, but Pike didn't reply. Picking up his gear, he turned toward the windmill, whistling cheerfully. Staring after him, Gabriel felt a chill trickle down his spine, like the path of melting snow.

Chapter Six

"He comes! The priest comes!"

The news sped through camp. Children ran among the skin lodges calling for their mothers. Women suspended their chores and shaded their eyes to look eastward into the morning sun. Men put aside their mending and repairs and ceased, for a moment, their animated conversations. As a group, the *métis* began to converge on the Pembina road.

Celine paused outside the barn, a wooden pail with its meager tendering of milk dangling from one slender fist. Behind her, the Jersey cow chewed contentedly on a mouthful of wild hay, unaware that this would be her last milking. She was going dry, and would stay that way until she dropped another calf sometime next spring.

Were it not for the upcoming hunt, they might have kept her wet for another month or two, but Big John wanted everyone to go onto the buffalo ranges this year. With four men hunting, there would be a lot of work, and the women would be needed.

Big John's casual attitude toward womanhood had been something of a shock to Celine after twelve years of living in the East. At the convent where she had been sent after her mother's death, she had been taught that a woman's place was at home, tending to the house and the simpler chores of the barn and garden—milking, carding wool, gathering eggs. Butchering was man's work, much too strenuous for the average female.

It was different among the *métis*, though. Here, at the very edge of the *pays sauvage,* dressing a carcass and caring for the meat and robes had always been a woman's duty. It was something she could take pride in, a reflection of her abilities as a wife and care-giver.

The male's place—after the never-ending responsibility of guarding his family against their many enemies—was to hunt, to provide those basics his woman needed to create the fine clothing and sturdy lodges, the pemmican and smoothly dressed robes that were the proof of her worth. When he had done this, when the horizons of their world were secure and he had furnished his woman and girl children with enough to keep them busy, he was free to sit with his friends and boast of his exploits, to exaggerate the speed and skill of his buffalo runners, the prowess of his sled dogs, and to keep the air above his head blue with tobacco smoke.

Such was the world of the *métis.*

The pounding of hoofs interrupted Celine's thoughts. She looked up as Gabriel galloped past on the black horse he called Baldy. As he passed close to where she stood, she saw his eyes flit toward her, then quickly shy away, as if even to acknowledge a woman was too humbling an experience for a male of his caliber. *Like the others,* she thought scornfully. Yet in her heart, she knew the truths that guided men, the desires that ultimately betrayed them. A smile tilted one corner of her mouth as she watched Gabriel race toward the half-breed village. *He was so like Peter,* she thought. *So quiet and reserved among a normally loud and colorful people . . . so proud, yet so uncertain.*

When she was sure he wouldn't look back, Celine continued on to the cabin. Pausing at the open door, she wrinkled her nose in distaste to discover Isabella moving busily about the large room. She'd half hoped the old sow had scampered off to greet the priest with the rest of the red-skinned mongrels, but, of course, she hadn't. She was hustling about the cabin as if looking forward to the Black Robe's visit.

Standing at the cabin's door, Celine wanted to laugh at the old squaw's rushed preparations. The tart odor of freshly crushed buffalo berries already permeated the cabin, as if that alone could cover the stench of a frontier hovel, and a fresh stew of moose and vegetables was bubbling over a small flame in the stone fireplace. There were new candles in the sconces, and the blue-based glass lamp on the table had been topped off with a fresh dollop of pale yellow whale's oil, its chimney scrubbed clean of soot.

Only the best for a servant of God, Celine thought acidly.

It had been no different at the convent.

Staring at the old hag's broad backside, Celine pondered the Cree woman's place in the cabin. She knew Isabella had given birth to Gabriel and Alec, although she hardly seemed like a mother to them. Once she had been the wife of Angus Gilray, a union sanctified by a Hudson's Bay contract in lieu of a Catholic ceremony—at that time the missionaries had yet to penetrate the wilderness as far as the Red River Valley—but Angus was gone now, and Isabella's relationship with Big John was a mystery to Celine.

Moving from fireplace to table, Isabella said: "Was there much milk?"

"No." Celine lifted the bucket away from her leg, swirling its contents contemplatively. "A couple of cups, no more."

"Then what there is will be for the priest to drink. Cover it with burlap and put it in the *glacière* to cool."

"There is no ice in the *glacière.*"

"It is still cool there. Go, and do not argue."

Celine went, glad to be free of the old woman's charge. Isabella hadn't mentioned additional chores after placing the milk in the underground icehouse, and Celine had no intention of returning to ask for any.

The *glacière* was on the north side of the cabin, where its entrance would always be shaded. Celine pulled the wide, right-hand door up, then let it fall open with a bang. The steps leading into the cellar had been carved out of the earth, their edges worn away until they weren't really steps at all, but a series of sloping platforms leading into darkness.

Celine paused with one foot on the top step, recalling the tiny, dank cells of the convent where she had lived, its shuttered windows and heavy doors bolted from outside. Stone walls and narrow passageways so poorly illuminated it was like walking through a cave to travel from one floor to the next. And the chill. That was what she remembered most vividly. Winter or summer, a never-ceasing bleakness that had penetrated all the way to her heart.

For a moment her confidence waned, and she swayed back from the black pit. Then, chiding herself for her fear, she quickly descended the steps. Stopping at the bottom, she instinctively crouched to make herself smaller, less vulnerable. She could feel the thin layer of mud and straw beneath her shoes, the glaciate dampness of melted ice against her cheeks. In late winter before the breakup, the people of the Tongue and Pembina regions would gather to cut ice from the rivers, squaring it into blocks with their saws and storing it on beds of straw in *glacières* throughout the valley, where it would last into July in a good year.

Like so many other functions in the valley, cutting ice was a community affair. Even for Celine, who had been gone for so many years, the coolness of the room sparked vivid images of horse-drawn carioles parked haphazardly along the banks, yapping sled dogs with their tiny, tinkling bells, and snowballs spinning through the air from the hands of laughing children.

As her eyes adjusted to the dimness of the cellar, she became aware of the heavy iron meat hooks fastened overhead, the wooden shelves along the walls grown soft with decay. There was a butter crock on the middle shelf against the rear wall. She set the bucket of milk beside it, then lifted the wooden lid from the crock to peer inside.

Although Celine loved butter, the nuns at St. Albans had deemed it a luxury too valuable to waste on the orphans in their charge. The children had churned it by the barrel, then stood by silently while it was loaded onto barges to be sold elsewhere. But Celine had her memories, a childhood before the convent when her mother had smeared butter onto thick slices of bread fresh from the fire. She would watch it melt into the brown bread, turning it a perfect shade of gold.

Impulsively she dipped a finger into the crock, then brought it to her lips, closing her eyes as the butter melted on her tongue. Such a simple act to resurrect the memories it did: her mother, small and slim like herself, but beautiful, untainted by sin. And Big John—she had called him Papa then—and Angus Gilray and Isabella. There was herself, too, and Gabriel, doe-eyed and somber even as a child, and fussy Alec, swaddled in moss-lined diapers. Summer days playing on the prairie and winter nights with Angus on the bagpipes—that great, puffing monster of cloth and horns that made such a terrifying racket as the plaid bag filled, then spilled music as sweet as Highland wine. Her mother had played the flute, she recalled, and the nights had been filled with music and laughter. . . .

The *glacière* door slammed shut with a bang that didn't quite muffle a chorus of boyish giggles from overhead. But the laughter meant nothing to Celine, the crash of the icehouse door only dimly heard above a hundred other crashes echoing in her mind, a hundred other darknesses closing in on her.

Her scream cleaved the gelid blackness, spewing butter over her chin and the backs of her hands. She spun to race blindly across the room, stumbling on the bottom step and falling hard, then crawling frantically upward on hands and knees, heedless of the mud and dirt or the suddenly frightened exclamations of the children outside. Terror clawed at her, squeezing her throat and tunneling her vision. Somewhere deep within, where the light that was the real world still flickered dimly, she knew that, if the door to the outside world was latched, she would die. Like a wild bird clutched in an over-eager hand, her heart would simply give out. She climbed with a distinct sense of her own mortality, wondering if she would even have the courage to try the door when she reached it.

Big John had constructed his *glacière* well, with three overlapping layers of oak planks for doors to prevent even the narrowest prick of sunlight from entering. In such complete darkness, Celine couldn't see anything. In her panic, it never occurred to her to put an arm out, to feel her way cautiously forward. Instead, she rapped her head solidly against the underside of the door and fell back, half stunned. The pain helped, though. It subdued the worst of her panic. Raising a hand, she let her fingers explore the rough, splintery wood until she found the centerline. Hitching herself closer, she put her shoulder to the door, got her feet under her, and slowly straightened. The door swung up and back without resistance, tottered in balance for a moment, then fell open with a sound like a clap of thunder.

Celine collapsed across the frame, burying her face in the dry grass. She kept her eyes squeezed shut as if the light she had so desperately sought just seconds before was now too brilliant to behold. She could hear the sounds from the village, the lowing of cattle and oxen in the fields. She could hear the beating of her heart, too, slowing, returning to normal, and after a while she lifted her face, blinking against the tears.

There was no one in sight. Not even the children who had slammed the door closed on her.

She rose shakily and made a half-hearted attempt to brush

herself off. From the village, the excited babble of the half-breeds changed suddenly, then grew abnormally silent, and she knew the priest had arrived. He would probably come to the cabin as soon as possible, and she panicked a little to think of him finding her this way. Beauty, Celine knew, was only a thin façade, but ugliness went all the way through. It was her ugliness she wanted to hide. Weeping softly, she hurried toward the river to wash herself.

Dismounting in front of the open-faced shed, Big John called for Alec, galloping past behind Gabriel. The youth slid his lathered pony to a stop, then spun it away from the *métis* camp where he had been headed. The pained expression on his face clearly announced his displeasure. Big John ignored the look as he handed Alec the reins to his stallion.

"Take care of my horse, lad, and put ye own pony up, too. The pinto'll be needin' all the strength he has when we get among the buffalo."

"He is a strong runner," Alec declared proudly. "He will not be slow when there are buffalo to chase."

"I believe ye, but put him up anyway, then go on up to the cabin and find yeself a clean shirt. We'll be eatin' with the priest tonight, so scrub ye face and hands while ye're at it."

"I will eat with Isidore Turcotte tonight," Alec said. "That way there will be more for the priest."

Big John grinned. "No, lad, I fear not, although I wouldn't mind doing so meself. But 'tis ye mother I'm thinkin' of. She sets a store and then some by the Black Robes, and we'll respect that."

Alec shrugged indifferently, then his expression brightened as he accepted the roan's reins. Seeing the sudden gleam in the boy's eyes, Big John's voice hardened. "Ye'll no be ridin' him, lad. I'll not have a heavy hand on my runner. Ye know that."

Alec's smile was cocky, challenging. "I can handle him, Big John. Do you think I can't? I will show you." He made a half-hearted attempt to bring the stallion alongside the pinto. He knew Big John would never permit him to mount the runner, yet he was bound by stubbornness to try.

"Put him up, Alec," Big John said firmly. "Ye own pony, too. Then get on up to the house and get yeself ready."

Starting for the cabin, Big John spotted Celine making her way toward the river. He almost called her back, then closed his mouth. He'd bungled her return badly, he knew, although he couldn't for the life of him understand why. Was it that she reminded him so much of her mother? Or did he still somehow hold her responsible for Angelique's death?

"Aye, ye be a stiff-backed old fool," he said to himself. "And ye'd best be straightenin' things out between ye and the lass, afore 'tis too late."

"McTavish!"

He turned back to the cabin. Isabella stood in the door, a rare look of impatience pinching her heavy brows. She was wearing her good dress, he noted, and had anointed her hair with just enough grease to make it shine, then painted the part on top with vermillion. The lobes of her ears were stretched from the weight of too many earrings, and her wrists were sheathed in bracelets of spun copper and brass, her fingers adorned with cheap, glass-studded rings. It made him smile to see her all decked out, and glad that he'd insisted Alec be there for the meal tonight.

Isabella was pointing to the *métis* village, where a large crowd was winding its way through the camp. The priest rode in front astride a big chestnut stallion, his long black cassock flowing into the mob around him, a broad-brimmed, low-crowned black hat shading his face.

The Church had sent Father Mark Denning this year. Big

John grunted his approval. His gaze returned to the river, but Celine had already disappeared into the thick brush along its banks. He debated going after her, but knew there wouldn't be time. The *métis* would detain the priest for a while with their greetings and questions and invitations, but Denning would be tired. He would head for the cabin as soon as he could break away, and Big John needed to be there when he arrived. Protocol demanded that much, although he would have done it anyway for Isabella.

He considered her a sensible woman in most respects, illogical only when it came to her religion. The priest was a holy man in her belief, and, as such, he deserved privileged treatment. Yet for all of Denning's religious trappings, it was Isabella's stubborn devotion to the Catholic faith that impressed Big John most. It reminded him humbly of how much she did without, the sacrifices the valley imposed upon her and all of its women. To his way of thinking, it was she who deserved special treatment, so he never balked when she made these requests for the Black Robes, no matter how much he might disagree in his heart.

"McTavish!" Isabella called sharply.

He glanced at the village. Denning must have been tired, for he was making swifter progress than usual. With a wry shake of his head, Big John headed for the cabin.

"You must hurry," Isabella said as he entered. "Soon he will be here."

" 'Tis only Denning," Big John answered casually, hiding his smile.

"Father Denning is enough." She hustled him toward a rear corner of the room, where she had curtained off his bed with Hudson's Bay trade blankets. There was a basin of water on a small table next to the headboard, a chunk of yellow soap beside it, coarsely-woven towels under the soap. She had laid out his white linen shirt—the one with the ruffled bodice—and the black silk string tie, then placed his good plaid kilt and white socks beside it. On the floor next to the bed were a pair of stiff brogans, their nap freshly brushed. He groaned at the sight of them.

"Not the shoes, woman. They'll cripple me, sure, to wear the likes of them at my age."

"The moccasins then," she snapped, quickly pulling a small cassette from beneath the bed and flipping open the lid. From the top tray she brought out a pair of moose-hide moccasins, smoked to a golden brown, decorated with quills and dyed hair. "These are good," she announced, nodding with satisfaction as she studied her handiwork.

"Aye, as fine a pair as any ye've ever made. They'll do nicely."

"You dress now, McTavish. Hurry." She stepped back and dropped the curtain. He heard her go to the fireplace to fuss with the stew. Then she went outside, leaving the door ajar, the breeze free to wander in.

Big John breathed a curse as the cool draft slipped under the blankets to bump up against the bare flesh of his calves. He knew it was no accident that she'd left the door open.

He washed quickly, then pulled on the ruffled shirt, knotted the tie awkwardly around his neck, and slipped on the knee-length kilt of heavy tartan, belting it snugly with the buckle at his back. From a rosewood and silver sheath looped to the belt he withdrew a slim, ivory-handled dirk. The blade was long and narrow and razor-sharp, with runnels along each side to vent blood. The handle was delicately carved with European hunting scenes—stags and hounds and faceless hunters carrying short-barreled Jaeger rifles.

It was an old knife, the knife his grandfather's father had carried at Culloden. Big John wore it only on special occasions. At one time, he'd envisioned passing it on to Gabriel, but it occurred to him now that such a gesture would be selfish and unfair. By rights the dirk and its heritage belonged to Celine, to be passed on to her eldest son when the time came.

Isabella returned suddenly, her voice urgent. "McTavish, hurry! He comes now!"

Big John sheathed the dirk and bent to pull on his knee-length socks, then the fancy moccasins. Isabella yanked the blankets down and shoved them, wadded, under the bed. She dumped the pan of soapy water out the back window, then leaned the pan against the wall to drain. Big John ran a comb through his long hair, then tucked the Glengarry cap through his belt. He could hear the crowd gathering out front, and Baptiste LaBarge shouting: "McTavish! Big John! Open your door to a man of God!"

Big John looked at Isabella, then impulsively made a face, bugging his eyes and sticking out his tongue, twisting his head around and up as far as it would go while his hand, clawed like a bird's yellow foot, reached slowly for the latch. Before it could land, Isabella shot forward, her eyes wide with fear. "No, McTavish," she pleaded. "You must not!"

Smiling kindly, he curled the side of his forefinger under her chin. "Now would I be doin' the likes of that to one such as yeself, woman?" he queried softly. He winked at her, then, mustering a dignified expression, he lifted the latch and pulled the door open.

A cheer greeted him. Then the crowd parted dutifully, creating an avenue between him and the priest, who sat his horse in the middle of the yard.

"Greetings, Father!" Big John called, smiling graciously. "And welcome to me home."

"Thank you, John. I accept your invitation." Dismounting, Denning held his reins out like a man who knew there would be someone there to take them. He came forward with his own large smile in place, cassock rustling. Denning's apple-like cheeks glowed red from the wind, and his eyes twinkled with good humor as they shook hands. "It's always a pleasure, John. I look forward to your hospitality every year."

"Come in out of the sun, Father. Isabella has tea and *galettes* waitin', and there's a stew of moose for later that'll make ye mouth water." Looking past the priest, he added deliberately: "And ye, René Turcotte. Would ye join us, man?"

Denning cocked an eyebrow quizzically, but Big John, facing the crowd, kept his expression carefully neutral. Turcotte also looked startled, but his wife, standing behind him, put a hand on his arm with obvious pride. Then someone gave him a shove, and Turcotte nodded solemnly and followed the priest into the cabin.

Big John went in last, closing the door firmly in the face of the watching crowd. He knew the half-bloods would drift back to their lodges soon enough, although a few might linger. The Catholics among them would expect a Mass, but that would come later, after Denning had eaten and rested and heard confessions. The blessing of the caravan would probably take place tomorrow. It had become something of a tradition for the priest to deliver the blessing on the day the caravan left, and they were all anxious to be on their way.

Father Denning went immediately to a rear corner of the cabin to hear Isabella's confession. It was one of the first things she insisted on any more, after having missed having it heard several years before because she'd been busy fixing the priest's breakfast.

After listening to the murmur of their conversation for some minutes, Big John turned irritably away. Turcotte stood just inside the door, his knitted red wool tuque pulled from his head to be twisted tightly in both hands. Feeling suddenly chagrined,

Big John growled: "Come on, man. Ye're actin' like a stranger in me home."

"*Non,* Big John, it is not that." He threw the priest a surreptitious glance, then leaned close. "Should we speak while the Father hears confession?"

"Aye, and why not?" Big John grinned wickedly. "We'll talk and drink till the good Father can join us, eh? Come, have a snort of rum with an old Scotsman. Jamaican, it is, and near smooth as silk on ye tongue."

Turcotte glanced hesitantly at the priest, but then nodded his assent. Big John knew he would. High wine was the common man's drink along the Red River, and good rum was as rare as a white buffalo.

"Perhaps a small cup," Turcotte agreed. "If you have enough."

"A drop's enough to share with a friend," Big John assured him, then chuckled. "Fortunately, 'tis more than a drop I have left in me bottle."

Turcotte grinned. "Then bring it out, Big John."

Motioning toward a bench at the table, Big John said: "Seat yeself, René."

The bottle—dark green and slope-shouldered, wrapped tightly in osier—sat on a shelf amid paper-wrapped bricks of tea and sugar cones. Big John grabbed it and a couple of tin cups from pegs beneath the shelf, then, straddling the bench across from Turcotte, he splashed a hefty portion into each cup. Recorking the bottle and lifting his cup, he said: "To the hunt."

"Yes, the hunt." Turcotte raised his cup in a salute, then quickly drained it.

"Ah," Big John breathed, smacking his lips. "Ye can have ye French wines and Virginia bourbons, René. The best of 'em will never compare to a drink from the isle of Jamaica." Then his expression saddened, and he gave the bottle a shake that produced only a gentle lapping halfway down. "Enjoy what's left, old friend, for 'tis high wine and trade whiskey after today, and naught to do about it until the next Hudson's Bay shipment comes to the valley."

Turcotte eyed the bottle worriedly. "There is more yet, though, is there not?"

"Aye, a wee bit."

René heaved a sigh of relief. "You were always the best host in the valley, Big John. A man is lucky to be a guest in your home."

In the far corner, Denning made a quick sign of the cross, then got to his feet. Coming to the table, the mask of solemnity he had worn during Isabella's confession fell away like flakes of paint. "Is that rum you're serving, John?" he asked.

"Aye, that it is. Isabella, be a lass and fetch the good Father a cup." He refilled his own and Turcotte's while Isabella brought out a shiny new one for the priest. "What's the news from Pembina?" he asked, pouring a healthy shot into Denning's cup. "Have they left for the buffalo ranges yet?"

"This morning, with Paget as captain," Denning replied. "I'm surprised you didn't see their dust, although it wasn't as pronounced as I've seen it other years."

"The snow," Turcotte said stiffly. "It settles the dust." He looked ill at ease again, in Denning's presence.

"Yes, of course," the priest replied, as if he'd already forgotten the storm that had blown through a couple of weeks before. "And now we enjoy the Little Summer of Saint Luke, eh, René?"

"Let's be hopin' 'tis a long one this year," Big John said. "I don't fancy sleepin' on damp ground any more, nor campin' without wood for a fire, and chips too sodden to catch."

"When will you leave?" Denning asked.

"Tomorrow, I'm hopin', although we won't hold the elections until tonight, so there'll be no way of knowin' what we'll decide until then."

"Is everyone in from the hills?"

"Aye, they are, and champin' at the bit to be off. I'm hopin' for an early start tomorrow."

Turcotte looked vaguely uncomfortable, and Isabella scowled.

Gently Denning reminded: "And Mass, John? And the blessing? What of those?"

"We must, Big John," Turcotte blurted.

"I daresay few would leave without them," Denning added.

Big John forced a smile. "Aye, and do ye think ye're tellin' me something I don't know?"

"McTavish!" Isabella scolded.

Denning smiled piously. "Such resentment, John. You could do so much good for the valley, working arm-in-arm with the Church."

" 'Twas born a Protestant, Father. I don't think the Church would be wantin' the likes of me . . . or me the likes of it."

"You still blame the Church, after all these years?"

"Aye, I do," Big John replied bluntly.

"Non!" Turcotte exclaimed, sitting up straight with both hands flat on the table. "It is the rum that speaks for him, Father."

"Angelique was a terrible tragedy," Denning continued gently. "For you and the Church, John. But Satan is a powerful adversary, and unfortunately evil often does triumph over good. We can only try harder."

"Ye're sayin' she burns in hell, then?" Big John asked thickly.

"You know the Church's stance on suicide," Denning replied. "I'm sorry."

"Aye, well, I suppose that'll have to do." He stood, anger making him clumsy, and thrust his cup into the air. "A toast then, to the hunt. Ye'll drink to that, won't ye, Father?"

Denning hesitated, then nodded. "Of course."

The priest stood, and Turcotte with him, and the three of

them brought the rims of their cups together, then lowered them to drink. Although Big John could feel the priest's eyes on him, he kept his own averted. He knew his hostility toward the Church didn't surprise Denning, although it had clearly shaken Turcotte. Big John's biggest regret, in fact, was René's presence. He knew that, by evening, Angelique's name would once again become common gossip among the half-bloods.

They finished the rum in short order, talking cautiously of small things until Isabella set out an early dinner of stew and hard biscuits, with milk for Big John and Denning, tea for Turcotte. Afterward, Denning and Turcotte returned to the *métis* camp, while Big John went to the open-faced shed where he kept his carts. Isabella had already sorted and packed the things they would take with them.

Gabriel was in the shed when Big John got there, checking the rawhide bindings on his own vehicle. His harness was laid out in the grass nearby, shining under a fresh coat of oil, buckles gleaming. Picking up the belly band, Big John idly flicked the small brass bell with a finger. "Ye be ahead of me, lad. Will ye be ready by morning, do ye think?"

"I will be ready in a couple of minutes," Gabriel said.

Dropping the harness, Big John went to where his own carts were parked on sapling platforms to keep them up out of the dirt. He didn't expect to find anything wrong, but he was particular about his gear, and would usually double-check everything if he had a chance.

"Denning?" Gabriel remarked.

"Aye, though better him than others, I'm thinkin'. A smidgen of sense he's got, and not afraid to saddle his own horse if he has to."

Gabriel was silent, as if gauging Denning against some of the others who had accompanied the hunt in recent years. Like Father Steele—soft, flabby Father Steele—who even the most pious *bois brûles* had ridiculed. After a time, he said: "Will there be a Mass tonight?"

"He wasn't sayin', though I'd guess tonight or in the mornin', if not both."

"Will you go?"

"Me?" Big John looked up from where he was inspecting a hub. It seemed a foolish question. Gabriel knew how he felt about the Catholic religion. He studied the youth thoughtfully for a moment, then said: "Ye can go or stay, lad. Ye know it doesn't matter to me."

Gabriel stared at him, his eyes swimming with indecision. Finally, taking a deep breath, he said: "Will she go?"

"She?" Then it hit him, and he reared back in surprise. "Celine?"

Gabriel nodded wordlessly.

"I've not asked her, but I suppose the choice is hers, the same as ye."

Speaking rapidly, as if afraid the words would bog down in his throat if he didn't get them out quickly, Gabriel said: "I would like your permission to accompany her to Mass tonight, Big John. Whenever Father Denning wishes to hold it." Meeting the older man's eyes, he swallowed loudly.

Turning toward the trees along the river where he'd last seen Celine, Big John didn't immediately reply. Conflicting emotions tugged at him. Gabriel, who had always seemed like a son, standing before him as a stranger, asking permission to escort his daughter to Mass. And his own daughter like a stranger, a creature so foreign he could barely communicate with her.

"Big John?"

He sighed, and his shoulders drooped a notch. "Aye," he said finally. "If the lass is willin', ye have me blessin'."

Gabriel nodded solemnly. "Thank you."

Not knowing how to reply, Big John abruptly stooped and

lifted the shafts of the nearest cart—the one he used most often—and pulled it into the sunlight. It was small compared to his other carts, with planed sideboards and a solid tailgate for greater protection from the elements. Its top was a sun-faded reddish-brown oilcloth stretched over the steamed cottonwood bows and fastened to the sideboards, then drawn to puckered ovals front and aft—similar to the canvas coverings he had once seen in a woodcut illustration of Conestoga wagons freighting supplies over the Allegheny Mountains.

He checked the rawhide binding on the wheels and around the box. He thought the hubs might be a little loose, but he was confident they would last. He could have Quesnelle construct new ones for him over the winter if he was still concerned about them when they got back. He always carried a couple of spare axles and spokes for the wheels, and knew that, with the cart's rawhide and wood construction, there wasn't much that couldn't be repaired on the range if the need arose. It was why the *métis* preferred such simple modes of transportation over the iron-mounted carts of Quebec or Montreal, or bulkier American-made wagons.

Big John's other two carts were simpler affairs, larger and more crudely built, with slatted sideboards and gates and no covers at all. He seldom used them except for the buffalo range, but they seemed solid enough, the rawhide tight and hard, like iron itself.

The sun was setting by the time he finished, the air dimpling the pale flesh of his legs above his stockings. Although he was tempted to slip back into the cabin to replace his kilt with a pair of buckskin trousers, he knew Isabella would be disappointed if he did. He'd explained to her years before that the kilt was a kind of badge among his people—the color and design of the plaids representing his clan in Scotland. It was his medicine, he'd explained, and her face had brightened with comprehension. Now she insisted he wear it on important occasions, and usually he didn't mind, except when it was cold.

After wheeling his carts back into the shed, he went to where Gabriel was forking hay to the horses in the corral. Folding his arms over the top rail of the corral, his gaze slowly hardened. "Have ye seen Alec lately?" he asked Gabriel.

"On the prairie to the south. He and Isidore were racing." Gabriel paused in his work. "Why?"

"And 'twas it the spotted pony he was runnin'?"

"Yes. His pinto against Isidore's sorrel."

"That sorrel doesn't belong to Isidore, Gabriel. 'Tis René's pony the lad was racin', against me own spotted horse, and me own wishes, too."

Gabriel laughed. "Alec is young. Sometimes he doesn't listen, but he will cool the pinto out before he brings it back. He is *bois brûle*, and would not put a horse up sweating."

"I had thought to use oxen for the carts this year, but maybe I'll use horses, instead. The pinto and the black and Solomon. Will ye see to their hitchin', come the mornin'?"

The smile slipped from Gabriel's face. "Alec was planning to ride the pinto this year," he reminded Big John. "There are other horses to pull the carts."

"Aye, there are, but 'tis the pinto and the black and Solomon we'll be usin', and Alec will have to walk or ride in the cart. 'Tis his own doin', Gabriel, and time enough he learns that."

"He will be mad, Big John. He will be furious."

"The lad's thirteen," Big John replied grimly. "If he cannot act as such, then maybe he still needs to be treated like a boy."

"He would not stand for that. It would destroy his pride."

" 'Tis not a thing I'm eager to do, but I'll not have him ignorin' me orders, either. Not without consequences, I won't. I told him to put the horse up earlier, and not run him against Turcotte's red horse. I told him to clean himself up for supper, too, and he didn't do it. If he wants to hunt for John McTavish, he'll have to learn to listen."

"I will tell him," Gabriel said, but Big John could see that he didn't agree with his brother's punishment. Leaning the pitchfork against a corral post, Gabriel headed for the cabin in quick, jerky strides.

Watching him walk away, Big John was struck with a feeling of sorrow. He was losing them both, he knew. At the same time, he recognized their developing independence as a natural and necessary occurrence, as inevitable as the changing seasons. It saddened him, sure, but there was a kind of pride to be taken in it, too, an acknowledgment of his own contribution toward a larger cause. They were good boys, both of them. Someday soon, they would be good men. It was all a man who loved them like a father could ask for, he thought.

With the sun just sunk below the horizon, Big John made his way to the *métis* camp. He found Father Denning kneeling on a folded piece of buffalo robe beside the cold ashes of last night's central fire, an ironwood rosary entwined through his fingers. A young girl was on her knees before him, her hands folded perfectly in front of featureless breasts. Cynically Big John wondered what sins someone so young had been able to achieve that it required the attention of God.

Footsteps padded the stiff brown grass behind him. Baptiste LaBarge appeared at his side. " 'Allo, Big John."

"Baptiste, my good friend. Have ye come to have ye confession heard?"

"*Non,* I have already had my confession heard and recited my Hail Marys and Our Fathers."

"And such will set ye straight with the Lord, then?"

"Do not mock the Church, Big John. It is very powerful, very holy."

"Aye," Big John replied seriously. "I do not mock ye religion,

Baptiste, only my own kinship with it."

LaBarge shrugged. "We will have the elections tonight. Some of us want to leave in the morning."

"And the others?"

He shrugged once more. "The day after. Yesterday. Who knows? Most want to leave tomorrow."

"Tomorrow suits me. When will ye be holdin' the elections, and where?"

"Here at the council fire, after the evening meal." He studied the fading western sky, awash in evening colors. "After full dark, I think. There will be a wedding then, also. Young Dan Keller and Saint Germain's daughter." He grinned at Big John. "They have already been living together as man and wife, but tonight the priest will make it official."

Big John's smile was large, thinking of Keller, and of Herman St. Germain's big-boned, beautiful daughter Hannah. "Aye, a fair match, that," he opined.

"She is a hard worker," LaBarge agreed. "Last spring she butchered for Charlo, and did as fine a job as any wife."

Big John nodded. He remembered it well. They had all commented on how expertly Hannah had skinned the buffalo Charlo brought down. "I'll be here, Baptiste, and Isabella, too, and I thank ye for the word."

"Is nothing, Big John. I will see you then, eh?" With a curt nod, he walked away.

The girl with Denning finished and another took her place. Three more waited in line. Big John shifted impatiently as they slowly advanced. When the last child departed, Denning rose stiffly and hobbled over.

"I believe I spent four hours on that blasted hide, John." He grimaced. "Rheumatic knees were not one of the hazards I'd envisioned of the priesthood."

" 'Twas not ye only surprise, I'm thinkin'. I'm not so old I can't remember my first sightin' of the valley, and the way my heart sank when I did."

Denning chuckled. "I remember that feeling, although it doesn't totally describe my experience. I had looked forward to hardship then. It would be proof of my love for the Lord, our Father. Even the possibility of martyrdom among the natives was appealing in its own naïve way. But in picturing my decapitated head mounted atop a pole outside some aborigine's bark-covered hut, I'd failed to consider the hordes of mosquitoes that can cover a man's face like a beard each spring."

"Aye to that," Big John replied. "I've seen 'em drive a pony near to madness with their bloody, suckin' ways. But I don't think mosquitoes'll be troublin' us much any more. The signs point to an early winter. We may be thinkin' wishful-like of 'skeeters and such before we get back to the valley."

Denning nodded gravely. He had been in the wilderness long enough to know what an early winter, with its wind-driven snows and sub-zero temperatures, would mean to hunters caught on the vast, open plains, far from wood and shelter. At forty below, a man wasn't allowed many mistakes.

"They'll be holdin' the election tonight," Big John told the priest, "though not for another hour or so. Would ye care for a spot of tea, or maybe some *galettes* to warm ye belly?"

"Perhaps some tea, thank you. I'm afraid I won't have time to eat. There are several children to be baptized yet, and a wedding tonight. Have you heard?"

"Aye, I have, and a likely pair, I'm thinkin'."

They started together for the cabin. "It's always so busy before a hunt," Denning lamented. "Always so many to see, so much to accomplish. I wish we could open a church below the border again, and damn the politics that prevent it."

"Will not the Americans allow a Catholic church within their territories?" Big John asked innocently.

A conceding smile crossed Denning's face. "Yes, the Church is partially to blame, John, I'll admit that. Trivial disputes that withhold the word of the Lord from a people who so hunger for it. Still, even a bishop is human."

Big John stared straight ahead. For some, the answers were always that simple—right was right and wrong was the other person's opinion. Still, it saddened him to recognize such Old World animosity here among the half-bloods of the *pays sauvage,* to know that the bloody seeds of war between Protestant and Catholic that burned so hotly in the British Isles had taken root here in the fertile soil of the Red River Valley. If not for the need of accord against a common enemy—the Sioux—on their twice yearly forays for buffalo, Big John shuddered to think what hostilities might have developed among the *métis.*

Watching him, Denning said kindly: "You seem so pensive, John. What troubles you?"

"Nothing troubles me, Father. Me thoughts were wanderin' a bit, 'tis all."

"To the hunt?"

Big John smiled. "Aye, to the hunt."

And in the end, he thought, it was true. The hunt. Always the hunt.

Chapter Seven

Gabriel sat at the far end of the table, braiding new reins he hoped to have finished before they left for the buffalo ranges. The slim strands of bison leather slid like silk through his fingers, the weave tight and even, for all that his attention was largely focused elsewhere, his gaze skipping randomly around the room.

Isabella was busy as always, scurrying back and forth to light candles against the deepening shadows, seeing to the men's drinks, or making last-minute changes to the packs she'd readied for the hunt the night before. Throughout it all, she apologized repeatedly to the priest for this imagined wrong or that, while Father Denning relaxed on his stool and protested that everything was fine, and that he'd hardly expected such amenities this deep in the wilderness.

Big John sat slouched in a cane-bottomed rocker close to the fireplace, silent for the most part, although his pipe, clenched in a white-knuckled fist, trembled as he observed the exchange between Isabella and the priest. Although Big John's lips remained sealed, Gabriel thought his pipe spoke volumes.

Celine tried to help Isabella in her own uncertain way, but it was obvious she was flustered by the older woman's energy, puzzled by the wide assortment of goods they would take with them on the hunt. She kept looking at the huge sheet-iron kettles leaning bottom-out against the wall, as if trying to fathom what kind of soup Isabella might concoct in them. Every once in a while Big John or Father Denning would cast her a questioning look, but no one spoke to her or tried to draw her out. It made Gabriel's heart ache to see her looking so lost and alone in her father's house.

He tried to remember what Celine's mother had been like, but Angelique was a ghost in his mind, a time-shrouded figure without perspective. He could vaguely picture a pallid face and a beautiful voice, her eyes haunted as if with fear, but of what he could never guess. He had been working on the windmill with Big John when Isabella came to them with the news of her suicide. He could still recall the shattered expression on Big John's face, the way his hatchet had slipped unnoticed from his fingers. He had seemed to cave away from the inside that day, deflating the same way a buffalo's bladder would shrivel in the sun if it wasn't cured properly.

Isabella had also looked stunned, he remembered, but there had been less astonishment in her countenance, more acceptance. Gabriel thought Angelique's death had saddened Isabella, but he didn't think it surprised her.

He remembered even less of Celine in those years. She had been a sprig even then, always standing back as if afraid of being trampled by the adults, a shy, quiet child who always seemed to prefer to play alone, rather than partake in more rambunctious adventures with the other children.

Alec, of course, had been little more than an infant, barely walking, and Angus had already left for the plains. It was possible he was even dead by then, although Gabriel supposed he would never know for sure. He'd been too young himself, the adult world far too complicated. In those days it had been easier just to drift along with the shifting currents.

Gabriel had only one truly clear image of Angus Gilray, but it was as vivid as any portrait. It was of the last time he had seen his father. A morning, it had been, with a covering of snow on the ground and the sun just peeping over the rim of the valley. Angus had been mounted on a big blood bay that seemed gigantic in memory, with a string of three or four pack horses stretched out behind it. Gabriel could still picture the bulky, buffalo-robe coat Angus had worn that day, the coyote-fur cap with its leather visor jutting out above the bright blue chips of his eyes, the reddish-blond hair that had flowed over his collar. His father's smile had been wide and unnaturally bright that morning, residing within the brush of his beard like tiny tombstones lined up side-by-side amid a tangle of russet weeds.

In the picture Gabriel harbored in his mind, Isabella stood at the blood bay's side with one hand resting on Angus's knee, forcing a smile past some uneasiness Gabriel hadn't understood. He could remember himself, too, standing with sleep-mucked eyes in the oval door of a hide teepee, wrapped in a heavy wool blanket, cold despite its weight. The image ended there, with no one moving except himself as he rubbed his eyes. He didn't know why that one scene remained so clear. He was never as sure with any of the other memories that flickered through his consciousness, never certain whether they were real or just illusions created by the words of others.

Angus had left in early spring, riding southwest to trade with some of the Missouri River tribes. When he hadn't returned by fall, Isabella had taken Gabriel and Alec to Big John's cabin for the winter. By the following spring they had pretty well given up hope of his returning, although Big John had traveled to the Mandan and Hidatsa villages at the mouth of the Knife River, then on to the Mandans at Fort Clark, to inquire about his old friend. No one had seen him, and afterward Big John had risked his life to go among the Sioux, but Angus hadn't shown up there, either.

If not for an odd set of circumstances, they probably never would have found out what had happened. It was several years later when a *bois brûle* wandering south of the Missouri met a party of Cheyenne warriors trailing a band of Crees, who had stolen some ponies from them. One of the Cheyennes was carrying an engraved powder horn that he showed to the *bois brûle* for translation. The *bois brûle* couldn't read, but he recognized the horn and traded the Cheyenne another horn and some extra powder for it. The Cheyenne claimed to have taken the horn from a Pawnee he'd killed in battle the year before.

It was several months later before the *bois brûle* returned to the Red River Valley, going out of his way to pass by Big John's cabin on the Tongue. He'd handed the powder horn to Big John almost reverently, and Big John had gotten a funny, twisted look on his face when he read the inscription scratched on its white surface. After what seemed an eternity, he'd looked at Gabriel and said: "Come here, lad."

Reluctantly he had.

"Do ye remember this?" Big John asked, holding the horn out for Gabriel to see.

He hadn't, but thought he ought to agree, anyway. Big John must have sensed his lie.

" 'Twas ye pa's horn, Gabriel," he said, his voice trembling ever so slightly. "These scratchin's here, that be writin', like what the traders put down in their ledgers, and what ye'll be learnin' yeself when ye get a little older. Ye pa put this writin' down with the tip of his knife, most like."

Understanding struck him at last, and he'd looked at the older man and asked in his little boy's voice: "What does it say, Big John?"

"Says . . . 'The Pawnee have shot me, and I'll soon be dead.' Says . . . 'May whoever finds this horn deliver it to J. McTavish, Red River Settlement, Tongue River.' " Big John had closed his eyes, his voice catching. Then he opened them and went on.

"It says 'twas the Pawnees what kilt ye pa, lad, but he wanted ye to know he was thinkin' of ye. Ye can be sure of that, or he wouldn't have scratched these words like he did. 'Twas for ye, sure, and ye ma and Alec that he did this. Ye hear me, Gabriel. 'Twas for his sons and his wife, and the love he felt for them."

Gabriel heard. Even now, he still heard.

That was the first time he'd ever seen Big John cry, for all that it was no more than a few piddling tears squeezed out of the corners of his eyes, but it wasn't the last. It was as if Angus's note had opened something inside the lanky Scotsman that he'd never been able to close since. It wasn't a common thing, but it happened from time to time, and there was never any way of foretelling what might set it off. A song, maybe, or the way a colt ran in the spring grass, or the honking of geese moving with the seasons. It wasn't the circumstances themselves, Gabriel had come to understand, but what they brought back, the memories that must have been as sharp as a winter's north wind in the old man's mind.

The rumble of Big John's voice interrupted Gabriel's ruminations, and his fingers slowed on the weave of his reins. Big John and Father Denning were discussing the elections, and Big John was angry. He was trying to convince Father Denning to lend his support to René Turcotte to captain the train, but the priest wasn't having any of it.

"I supported Paget because I thought he was the best man for the job," Father Denning was saying, "and because his leadership will directly affect my own safety on the buffalo ranges. But I won't use my influence here."

"Then why are ye here, man, if not to use ye influence?"

"Not my influence, John, the Church's."

"And does the Church not care for its wards?"

"I'm not traveling with this caravan," Denning replied pointedly. "It would be unfair to those who do if I interfered with their election in any way."

"I fear ye may be doin' them more a disservice by not interferin' just a wee bit, Father. Breland could win tonight, and such a man as captain would bring trouble to a prolonged hunt. He's too rigid in his ways. A leader needs to flex now and again, else he breaks, and pulls others down with him."

Denning shook his head. "Joseph Breland is a good man. He led the hunt last spring and you were back within the month, your carts filled and no one injured."

" 'Twas no skill involved in that," Big John replied dismissingly. " 'Twas luck alone. We ran onto buffalo less than a week out. What if we have to trek as far as the Missouri this year? 'Twill take more than luck then!"

"John," Denning admonished gently, "we are only going in circles now. I will pray for your caravan no matter who leads, but no more."

Big John leaned back in his rocker, arching a brow. "Prayers, Father? I hope 'tis ye own that the Lord hears, and not those of the Sioux, who be prayin' for fresh scalps this year."

"The Lord does not hear the drumbeats of heathens," Denning said sharply.

"McTavish," Isabella scolded.

"Aye, of course. I'm insultin' ye faith again, Father. Forgive me."

There was a knock at the door, and Big John called: "Come in, and welcome!"

The door swung open. LaBarge stood there with his hat in hand, looking humbled and uncomfortable by his intrusion.

"Excuse me, Father, but may I have a word with you?"

"Of course, Baptiste." The priest started to rise, but LaBarge quickly waved him back.

"*Non,* Father, do not get up. We, some of us, I mean, we were wondering if there would there be a Mass tonight?"

"Do you want a Mass tonight?"

"Yes, if it is proper."

Denning's smile was almost patronizing. "There is no improper time to worship, Baptiste. Yes, there will be a Mass with the wedding. Give me a few minutes."

"*Oui,* thank you, Father. We will move a cart near the fire to serve as an altar."

"Very good."

"And the election?" Big John asked.

LaBarge fidgeted nervously. "After the Mass, Big John. We thought it would be better then."

"Aye, no doubt," Big John replied dryly. He stood with Denning and set his dudeen on the mantle.

"More disapproval, John?" the priest murmured quietly, so that LaBarge wouldn't overhear. "Tell me, is it only the Church you object to, or is it me?"

"There's more to it than personal animosity, Father," Big John replied. " 'Tis a snub they're givin' the Protestants tonight, makin' them wait until after the Mass, and no reason for it."

Stiffly Denning said: "I sha'n't endorse such an argument with an answer. If you'll excuse me." He turned and smiled at LaBarge. "Shall we go?"

LaBarge nodded and ducked outside. Gabriel could see several other men waiting behind him, a couple of them holding candle lanterns to light the priest's way. Big John followed as far as the door, stopping there with his hand on the frame. Abruptly he called out: "And can I tell Joseph Breland he can count on ye support, Father?"

Denning whirled, his eyes sparking in the candlelight. "No!" he snapped emphatically. "Never!" He looked suddenly confused as the implication of what he'd said sank in. "I won't favor any man over another," he added lamely, but Gabriel thought the damage had already been done. Even if Denning refused publicly to support René Turcotte, he had clearly denounced Joseph Breland.

"Damn such treachery," Denning hissed to Big John. He turned and stalked angrily through the waiting *bois brûles,* his cassock swirling around his ankles.

Smiling crookedly, Big John closed the door.

Gabriel followed Big John out of the cabin, tipping his head back as he shrugged into his old, fringeless leather jacket with its too-short sleeves. "It turns cold again," he said, his breath puffing translucently against the black, starry sky. "But the days are still warm."

"Aye, nearer to hot at times," Big John agreed distractedly. He was staring at the *bois brûle* village, clearly uninterested in the weather.

"Will there be trouble?"

"I don't think so, though likely some hard feelin's. 'Tis best we talk it out now, though. Will ye come with me?"

"No, I will wait here a while."

"Ah, of course." His expression stiffened. "Well now, enjoy yeself at the Mass, lad, but don't forget 'tis me daughter ye're escortin'. I'll stand for no coltishness on ye part, do ye hear?"

"I hear you," Gabriel replied gravely.

Big John paused, cleared his throat, scratched thoughtfully at the back of his neck, then said: "Well, see that ye do, then."

Gabriel watched until Big John had disappeared in the direction of Charles Hallet's lodge, where a crowd of Protestants had gathered to vent their frustration at having to wait until after the Mass to hold the election. It could be a ticklish situation, Gabriel knew, but politics held little attraction for him tonight. He stepped into the shadows away from the cabin, feeling oddly dry-mouthed and jumpy, the way he had the first time he ran buffalo. His apprehension puzzled him. He'd never felt this way with any of the local girls, those he danced with at parties and festivals during the winter months, or even the bolder among them who he could sometimes coax into a midnight cariole ride, clipping along behind old Solomon, sleigh bells jingling, faces flushed with wind and wine and an intoxicating sense of daring as they'd bumped and touched beneath the heavy, curly-haired buffalo robes.

But it was only games that they'd played, he and those young ladies of the valley, with rules as old as courtship itself—flirting and teasing, promises never meant to be kept. He sensed that Celine would not be like that, neither childish nor ignorant of a man's needs. Remembering the way she had looked at him as he'd galloped past that morning, he knew her attraction to him was real. It had caught him off guard at the time, and he'd made a fool of himself by not stopping or meeting her gaze, but it would be different tonight.

The cabin door swung open and Isabella and Celine stepped out, drawing shawls over their heads. Gabriel froze when he saw his mother. It hadn't occurred to him that the two women might attend Mass together. Seeing her with Celine quickly undermined much of his determination, but, when they started for the *bois brûle* camp, he pushed quickly away from the cabin's wall.

"Celine."

The two women spun as one, and he was afraid for a moment that Celine might scream. Isabella said: "Gabriel?"

"Yes." He moved out of the deeper shadows where he had waited.

"You frightened us." Isabella sounded perturbed.

"I did not mean to." He stepped closer, his eyes on Celine. "I have come to escort you to Mass," he told her.

"Celine does not need an escort," Isabella replied curtly. "You come with us. Hurry, or we will be late."

His mother's automatic assumption that he would follow

docilely at her command embarrassed Gabriel. When the women began to turn away, he reached out to grab Celine's arm. "No," he said firmly. "She will accompany me."

Isabella scowled. "McTavish would not permit it."

"I have already spoken with Big John." Gabriel's fingers tightened unconsciously on the girl's arm.

"You have not asked me," Celine reminded him. Although she hadn't pulled away, Gabriel could sense the defiance in her words, was aware of the slight, distancing slant of her body. It hadn't occurred to him that she might refuse.

"You come with us," his mother said. "You may escort us both."

Seeing the laughter in Celine's eyes, Gabriel drew himself up. "No, I will escort Celine alone, if she will permit it."

Facing the girl, he dropped her arm and bowed stiffly. "*Mademoiselle,* will you allow me the honor of escorting you to Mass?"

The laughter in Celine's eyes dissolved, and, after a brief pause, she curtsied daintily. "*Oui, monsieur,* I would be pleased to be escorted by such a handsome gentleman."

Isabella huffed loudly at that, but the battle was over. Gabriel fixed her with an unflinching stare to remind her that he was a man grown now, and would tolerate no motherly interference in a man's business. With disapproval stamped sharply across her face, Isabella hurried away.

Taking a deep breath, Gabriel turned to Celine. "Shall we go?"

"Where?"

"To . . . to Mass."

"Why?" She pushed her shawl back to reveal the dark cascade of her hair. "I hate Mass," she informed him. "It is all pomp, don't you think?"

He shrugged, not really sure what pomp meant.

"Walk with me to the river," she said softly.

Gabriel's heart quickened as she led him toward the fringe of trees and brush that bordered the Tongue. He searched for something witty to say, some compliment that might please her, but nothing came to mind.

"You are so quiet," Celine remarked. Was she teasing him?

"I . . . the hunt . . ." He let the words trail off, not really sure where he would have gone with them, anyway.

"You have hunted buffalo before?"

"Yes, many times."

"You have your own cart?"

"Yes. I bought it from Nicolas Quesnelle last summer. He is a great builder. I took it on the hunt last fall, and on the spring hunt this year."

"You are a good hunter, no?"

"I filled my cart on the spring hunt. Ten *taureaux* from nineteen cows."

"Sacre," she breathed, as if awed by such an accomplishment—ten heavy bull-hide sacks representing over nine hundred pounds of pemmican. She put her arm through his, pressing it against the side of her breast. "You are a great hunter, then. A true *homme du nord.*"

Homme du nord. No one had ever called him that before—a man of the north. It wasn't true, of course, as he had never been above Fort Douglas, but the implication was clear. It took a special man to trap the Arctic regions, and it was no small praise to be mistaken as one who could.

Fool, a voice inside his head mocked.

"I will feel safe to know you are near when we reach the buffalo prairies." She pulled his arm more firmly against her breast. "The Sioux frighten me."

"The Sioux should not attack a *bois brûle* caravan," he assured her. "You will be safe as long as you remain close to the carts."

Coming to the trees along the river, Gabriel steered her toward a path that wound through the brush to the water's edge. It was narrow and they should have followed it single file, but Celine stiffened her hold on his arm, forcing him to suffer the scourging of thorns and branches rather than give up the feel of her body pressed against his. For a moment he wondered what it would be like to have a woman such as this, a wife to warm his bed and cook his meals, to make the best pemmican in the valley.

"Here," she said, and now it was she who guided him through the shifting patterns of darkness. In the silver-gray moonlight the ground stirred subtly in shadow, the limbs overhead swaying in the evening breeze.

It was a fishing hole she led him to, a pocket of summer-cured grass ringed by a gooseberry thicket. A narrow gap on the far side allowed access to the muddy waters of the Tongue. When the river ran deep in the spring, it was a fair spot for catfish, but after June it became too shallow, and the larger fish retreated downstream.

"I found this place on my first day here," Celine said. She released his arm and walked to the opposite side of the tiny clearing. "It is so peaceful here. I like being alone, don't you?"

"Sometimes," he acknowledged, studying her profile. In the blocky shadows he thought she looked older than her eighteen years, her features harsher. He wondered about her time in the East. He knew vaguely that Big John had sent her to Montreal, and that from there she had gone to a Catholic convent in Vermont, but that was all. Although her grandparents in Montreal had sent Big John periodic updates on her progress, to Gabriel's knowledge Celine had never written anyone in the valley, nor had Big John ever attempted to communicate with her.

Standing on the lip of the bank, slim and ramrod straight, she stared at the stars through the bare black web of overhanging branches. "My mother killed herself near this spot, did you know that?"

It was her matter-of-fact tone that rattled him more than her words. "Uh . . . I, ah. . . ."

She turned, laughing. "Didn't you know?"

Defensively he said: "Yes, I knew." Her laughter came again, taunting, and he blurted out: "Everyone in the valley knows."

She turned silent at that, then said more quietly: "Yes, I suppose they do." She came toward him, seemingly gliding over the bent, tangled grass. Her lips were slightly parted, her eyes wide and unblinking, without fear. Taking his hand in hers, she placed it firmly over her left breast.

Gabriel's breath caught in his throat, and his fingers flexed convulsively as she ran the backs of her knuckles up his arm to his shoulder. In the shadows, her eyes looked black and bottomless. He drew her closer with his free arm, while the hand on her breast grew rough with desire. Leaning into him, she breathed softly against his throat. Her hands went behind his head and she tilted his face toward hers. Her lips brushed his, light as a downy feather, and her tongue traveled along his teeth. Gabriel's arm tightened at the small of her back. Her knees buckled and she slid into the grass, pulling him with her. He moved hungrily over her, but, as he did, she suddenly twisted her face away, gasping: "*Non!* Gabriel, no!"

He grunted unintelligibly, moving his hand away from her breast to search for the hem of her skirt. Without warning she jerked her knee up between his thighs, driving it hard into his groin. Crying out hoarsely, Gabriel lurched to his side and rolled free. Overhead, the stars skittered and danced like lances of white fire.

"Animal!" Celine shouted. "Pig!"

Gabriel whimpered, his body spasming. He lay curled in a fetal position with both hands cradling his crotch. Tears streaked his cheeks, and the brassy taste of bile tainted the back of his throat. He could hear Celine pacing swiftly back and forth across the tiny clearing. The murmur of her words were too faint to catch, but the sound was furious. He rolled painfully to his knees.

"I liked you, Gabriel," she cried, stopping and whirling to face him. "I thought you were my friend."

Her words only slowly penetrated the sluggish clot of his brain, then had to be consciously arranged in order before he could make sense of them. She went on before he could even contemplate a reply.

"Big John will kill you for this."

He stared up through a tattered, blue-black veil of his own hair, hanging limply across his face. Celine seemed to tower over him, a monument of flowing dark cloth topped by the tear-blurred oval of her face.

"God and *le diable,*" he gasped. "Why did you do that?" Yet even as he spoke, his mind began to clear. Leaning weakly against a tree, he said: "Go. Tell Big John if that is what you want to do."

She looked startled by his response. "Maybe I will," she said, taking a step backward. "But maybe I won't."

"Maybe I will tell him myself," Gabriel said. "Maybe he would like to know what tricks the nuns have taught his daughter."

"Gabriel, no!" She looked stricken. "Do you hate me so?"

Numbly he shook his head. No, he thought, he didn't hate her, and the stark terror he saw on her face quickly wiped away his brief sense of triumph. The pain in his groin pulsed through his body, though, and he leaned his head against the rough bark of the tree and closed his eyes. *"Sacre démon,"* he murmured.

"Gabriel, you would not tell?"

"No," he said wearily. "I will not tell."

Whispered then: "You are my friend, Gabriel. You are the only friend I have out here."

His thoughts listed against his will, starting down a long chute into blackness.

"Peter," Celine said as if from far away. "You are like Peter, so brave and true."

Celine and Peter, a canoe sliding through the murky waters of the Pembina. He could see the Chippewa warrior Big John had shot standing tall and proud and bloodstained on the prairie. Buffalo ran in the distance. Gabriel could hear their distinctive grunts, smell the musk-tinged dust of their passage. I am dreaming, he told himself, and thought it odd that he could be so aware as he slept.

He sat up with a start. The tiny clearing was empty, the breeze calm. The moon had risen nearly straight overhead. It stared down at him like a single, elliptic eye. Teeth chattering from the cold, Gabriel started to rise, then sank back with a moan. Slumping against the tree, he took a deep, steadying breath. After a couple of minutes, he braced his hands against the rough bark and forced himself to stand.

Off in the distance he could hear the sounds of celebration from the *bois brûle* camp. The reedy sway of a fiddle and the wheezing of Nicolas Quesnelle's squeeze box added to the merriment. Mass would be long over by now, the election, too. He must have slept longer than he realized.

Gabriel's stride was slow and cautious as he made his way out of the brush. He paused at the edge of the trees, looking across the bare, lumpy ground toward the cabin and sheds. The rawhide-covered blades of the windmill were silhouetted by the dancing light of the *bois brûle* fires. Men and women moved back and forth in the orange glow. Some danced a Red River jig near the village center. Laughter rippled everywhere.

Celine was nowhere to be seen, but Alec stood on the hub of a nearby cart, staring across the camp. Following the direction of his gaze, Gabriel saw René Turcotte, looking stunned and slightly overwhelmed amid a knot of friends and well-wishers who were shouting toasts to his victory over Joseph Breland in the recent election. To one side stood Big John, a grin as taut as catgut stretched across his face.

Chapter Eight

Reining away from the caravan, Pike loped his little bay east over the flat plain of the valley. It felt good to cut himself loose from the ear-splitting shrieks of the greaseless carts, the whinnying ponies and lowing oxen, the barking, snarling dogs—more wolf than canine—and the laughter, shouts, and cajoling of the half-breeds.

To a man accustomed to solitude, the constant babble and unrelenting cheerfulness of the mixed-blood village became a weight difficult to bear. It made the air he breathed seem thick and sullied, and smothered his senses with too many sights and sounds and odors.

Clear of the noise and grit, Pike slowed the bay to a walk. It was a fair day for leaving, he thought, cool but with the promise of warmth later on. There had been frost again that morning, but the sky was clear, the breeze coming in off the Hair Hills dry and comfortable.

They'd gotten a slow start this first day on the trail, but then quickly settled into what seemed to be a familiar routine. Pike counted more than two hundred carts stretched out along the river trail that followed the left bank of the Tongue, each drawn by a single ox or wild-maned pony, driven by a man, woman, or older child who walked beside it or, on occasion, rode in the seatless bed of the cart on a folded buffalo robe, legs dangling through the front slats. The lead cart, owned by René Turcotte and driven by his wife Camille flew a *métis* flag—a white figure eight laid on its side against a scarlet background—atop an eight-foot staff lashed to the headboard.

Many of the carts were empty, in anticipation of the pemmican, dried meat, and robes yet to be harvested. Others carried personal gear and camping supplies, or firewood brought along to augment the skimpy lot the plains would provide. Maybe a third of the carts hauled lodge poles twelve to fifteen feet long, slid between the slats or canted over the tailgates and lashed in place, bobbing resiliently and rattling like old bones. Strung out single file, Pike estimated the whole affair ran close to a mile in length, with a fair-size herd of extra stock—oxen and horses—bringing up the rear.

Turcotte, his scarlet tuque settled snugly on his head like a knitted banner, rode at the head of the column. Perhaps half of the sixty-plus half-breeds who'd eventually come in for the hunt rode with him. Pike saw McTavish among them, his big roan feisty and hard to handle among the smaller, less aggressive Indian ponies. As he watched, the group began to break apart, scattering toward the hills or over the plain to the south. Only McTavish rode east, smiling as he drew near.

"Good mornin' to ye," the Scotsman boomed as he reined alongside. "Ye're still with us, I see. I need to apologize for my lack of courtesy these past few days."

"No need," Pike answered simply. "I've fared well."

"Good, good." McTavish glanced at the crawling train. " 'Tis a thing to see, is it not? 'Tis what they live for, Mister Pike. What they dream and breathe and love for. Every year I tell myself I'm too old to run buffalo with 'em, that I need to be stayin' home, proper-like for a Scotsman of breedin' and education, but I never do." He laughed, his eyes sparkling. " 'Tis a fever, running the shaggies is, and once ye've been touched by it, 'twill never let ye go, though I guess I don't need to be tellin' ye, what's hunted yon mountains a spell, the feelin's I'm speakin' of."

A smile feathered across Pike's face. "Running buff can shine, for a fact," he admitted.

McTavish fussed momentarily with the loose ends of his reins, his expression reluctant. "The lad, Gabriel. He was tellin' me the other day of Duprée, who hailed from the White Horse Plain along the Assiniboine River before he ran off, and of Rubiette, both of 'em back from the far reaches." He paused and cleared his throat, and Pike felt the muscles along his jaw tighten. The bay flicked an ear, sensing the change in his mood. "I'll not insult ye by askin' if 'tis them that brought ye here," McTavish went on. "Nor what ye intend toward them. But I will say this. Be sure that if blood's to be spilled, the man ye spill it from truly deserves it, for the mixed-bloods won't tolerate a troublemaker, and they'll hang a murderer quick if the cause isn't just."

"All right," Pike said stiffly.

"Sometimes ye have to judge a people by their standards rather than ye own, whether ye agree with them or not. I've lived among the *métis* for nigh on to thirty years now, and I don't fully understand them yet. But I accept them, Mister Pike, and to the best of my ability, I judge them in their own light.

"They're a noble race, taken as such, and not near the savage some would call them. 'Tis a thing ye may want to keep in mind in regard to Duprée and Rubiette. That's all I'm sayin'."

"I reckon I can handle my own affairs, McTavish," Pike said.

"Sure, and 'tis only right that ye do. I'll say no more on the subject, Mister Pike, and thank ye for hearin' me out this far."

The wind strengthened briefly, carrying to them a veil of dust and the strong odor of cattle and horses. Within it, Pike caught the faint stanzas of a song he remembered from the mountains, a tune popular among the French trappers, although he couldn't recall the name. Eyeing the distant line of the Hair Hills, he said: "Where are we headed, McTavish?" He nodded toward the steep, rugged slopes—a barrier to the plains beyond. "Is there another trail that'll take us through?"

"Aye. We'll be followin' the Tongue River Trail to the top, though 'tis a guess and a wonder from there. Paget's bunch left yesterday, headin' straight to Saint Joseph and the trail that leads on up past Pembina Mountain. That's the one we followed from Charlo's cabin until we swung south to avoid the settlement."

Pike nodded, putting it together in his mind. "That'll put us well south of them."

"Don't I wish it were so, but I fear not. If they spent last night at Saint Joseph, they'll be climbin' through the hills today, then turn south to follow the Ridge Trail. 'Tis what we both want, the trail. 'Tis the quickest and easiest route to the buffalo, with wood and water along the way, and plentiful game to those who get there first. We'll make fair time today with the country flat like it is, but we've got the hills ourselves to climb soon enough, and no easy road for the carts, to be sure."

"Sounds like we'll be coming out on top pretty close to one another," Pike said.

"Aye, and the caravan that gets there first will have the road to themselves, while the other will be forced onto the prairie, unless they want to follow along behind on what the lead caravan leaves them."

Pike glanced at the cart train. In the light of this new information, its plodding gait seemed unmercifully slow.

"Ye're right, of course," McTavish said, as if reading his thoughts. "But ye can't argue the point with them. They're not interested in the white man's logic so much as they are their own traditions. 'Tis the way of the land, they'd tell ye, if ye urged them to hurry. *À la façon du pays.*"

Pike didn't ask for a translation. He understood the Indian mind well enough to known that McTavish was probably right. And he suspected that, despite their declarations of conversion to a Christian religion, their carts, and even their mode of dress, their mothers' blood wouldn't be so easily displaced.

"Still, ye have to admire them for it, too. If ye think about it, there's sense to be made of their ways."

"I don't see it," Pike said.

"Ye might, was ye to quit usin' a European mind to do ye figurin' with. Tell me. What would happen if we quickened our pace?"

"We'd beat the Pembina hunters to the Ridge Trail. Isn't that what you want?"

"Well, sure, we'd beat the Pembina hunters this season. But what about the next hunt, or the one after that? Would we beat them then, or would they have learned to expect our dirty tricks by then, and maybe pull something a little dirtier? Like try to slip past us without our knowin', or not tell us when they planned to pull out at all. Maybe they wouldn't make any effort to stay in touch with us once we reached Sioux country, so that we'd be without their help, if the situation is desperate enough, and them without ours. We're rival outfits, Mister Pike, true enough, but still of one mind and one heritage. Without traditions, includin' that which sanctions collaboration, we'd . . . they'd . . . lose that thing that makes them unique. What makes them a *nation.*"

"A nation of half-breeds?"

"Exactly! A nation of people who would be without one if they hadn't created their own. Neither white nor Indian nor Canadian nor American. Not French or Scottish, Cree or Assiniboine, either. *Métis,* Mister Pike, and, aye, a mongrel nation if that's what ye want to call it, but a damn' fine one, too, and workin' pretty well, for all its peculiar ways." He studied Pike thoughtfully for a moment. "Do ye see what I'm sayin'?"

"You're talking a lot of noble crap, as far as I'm concerned. What it boils down to is that we're gonna go hungry this year because the Pembina hunters will likely beat us to the Ridge Trail, where their hunters will scare off the game we need to feed ourselves until we reach the buffalo ranges."

McTavish smiled, sadly, it seemed. "Well, 'tis true enough in its own way, I suppose, though I might argue that we'll be maintainin' our honor by maintainin' our pace, and, in that way, we'll be maintainin' the trust and co-operation between our two groups. 'Tis a fragile thing, trust is. Once it's broken, 'tis hard to repair."

Pike shrugged but didn't reply. McTavish seemed equally willing to let the matter drop. After a couple of minutes the lanky Scotsman began to whistle, the same melody the breeze had carried to them from the *métis* caravan earlier. Heard in wind-tattered snatches, Pike hadn't been able to identify it. Hearing it whole from McTavish, the name came to him quickly enough.

" *'Alouette'*."

McTavish glanced at him. "Ye know the song, do ye?"

"From the mountains. There was a Frenchman with Vanderburg's brigade. . . ." His voice trailed off in memory. They'd called him Frenchy, and Pike and Arch had trapped with him for a spell along the upper reaches of Rock Creek, which fed into the Yellowstone. Pike could hear him in his mind yet, the voice soft because it was Blackfeet country they traveled through, but rich and full all the same. It brought back a pang of sadness and loss to recall those days, and his face turned hard.

"Well, 'tis a lonely life sometimes," McTavish said after a while, averting his eyes. "Some it doesn't bother, or so I've been told. Meself, I had enough of it on the Jack River, my first winter in the *pays d'en haut.*"

"*Pays d'en haut?*"

"The North Country, Mister Pike. The land we call up there."

"I don't reckon loneliness ever bothered me much," Pike replied.

In some ways, he thought loneliness could even make a man stronger; certainly it made him more resourceful. He considered it a weakness to depend on anyone too much. Arch was the proof of that, and he was dead now because of it.

Twitching the roan's reins, McTavish began to angle away. "I'd best be gettin' back. The first day or so is always a might touchy for the harness stock. I was wonderin', though, would ye be interestin' in scoutin' some tomorrow? I'd send ye with Gabriel, if ye don't mind the lad's company."

"Fine by me. I got nothing against the boy."

"Good, and good day to ye, Mister Pike. I'll see ye at supper tonight." He rode off with a quick wave, the roan kicking up little spurts of dust that the breeze whipped away.

Reining up alongside Gabriel, Pike stared down the long, steep slope to where the *métis* camp was entrenched at the base of the Hair Hills. The loose stock had been driven out onto the plain to graze for the evening. He noticed that Turcotte had already doubled the guard on the horses and oxen. Come dusk, they'd run the whole bunch inside the cordon of carts. Tomorrow the caravan would turn straight into the Hair Hills and, barring bad luck, would be on top by sunset. The country up there was claimed by the Sioux, but they were close enough here that no one wanted to take any chances.

Pike leaned forward to ease some of the weight from his skinny buttocks, and the bay snorted and danced to one side, skittish under the added burden of a young white-tail draped behind the saddle. Pike had shot the buck that morning, after spooking it from a little strip of trees within the hills.

"They're stopping early today," he said, jutting his chin toward the camp.

"It is best that we camp here, where the grass is good and the country open," Gabriel replied. "There is no other place for so many *bois brûles* between here and the prairies."

Pike's gaze ran north along the line of brown hills. The broad coulées and narrow valleys fingering down from the hills were tinted scarlet with autumn scrub, and the sky was patchy with small, high-floating clouds. The breeze blew crisp and clean from the west. He glanced over his shoulder to the draw that wound into the hills behind them, the broken ground flanking it. Quietly Gabriel said: "I feel it, too. We are not alone."

"Sioux?"

Gabriel shook his head but didn't look around. "I don't think so." He was watching his horse, waiting for some sign that they were being stalked. Yet the stocky gelding seemed unconcerned as he stretched his neck for another bite of grass. Pulling the black's head up, Gabriel said: "They are not near."

"They're near enough," Pike replied brusquely. He swung a leg over his saddle horn and dropped to the ground, then moved back along his horse as if to check the bindings holding the deer in place. Under the broad brim of his hat his eyes strayed up the draw, then rose slowly from there to travel the hills to the south. Nothing stirred that couldn't be accounted for by the wind, but the feeling of being watched remained strong.

"Maybe Sioux," Gabriel said uncertainly.

"Or Chippewas."

"Or *bois brûle* hunters," the boy added dourly. "It would make a good story for someone to tell at the fire tonight."

A red-winged blackbird took flight from a clump of bushes about seventy-five yards away. With a curse, Pike yanked the bay around until it stood broadside to the coulée, then slid his rifle across the saddle. He thumbed the cock back to full even as he snugged the butt to his shoulder. Several yards away, Gabriel did the same. Then they stood silently, waiting tensely until laughter followed the blackbird out of the brush, and a voice called: "Do not shoot, Gabriel! You would not sleep well tonight if you killed a friend."

"Sacre," Gabriel muttered, then raised his voice. "Maybe Lizette would comfort me and help me to sleep."

More laughter tumbled from the thicket, and the voice replied: "This is true, my young friend, if it is truly sleep that you crave."

Pike swore and lowered the cock to half notch.

"It is Charles Hallet," Gabriel said. "He and Baptiste LaBarge escorted Father Denning back to Paget's caravan."

Pike saw movement among the bushes. A second later, Hallet scooted free and stood up. He laughed again as he brushed the dust and twigs from his clothing. Baptiste LaBarge appeared from behind a shoulder of the ridge one hundred yards beyond him, leading Hallet's pony behind his own. His face was split by a broad grin.

"Funny, eh?" Gabriel called.

"Could have been," LaBarge acknowledged.

Hallet climbed up the side of the draw to meet LaBarge, and the two of them rode forward together. "We must be getting old, Baptiste," Hallet noted as they drew near. "Once I would have been able to slip up on this one and tip him out of his saddle before he knew I was there."

"Older and slower," LaBarge agreed. "While the young ones grow quicker and sharper." He eyed the deer behind Pike's saddle and nodded approvingly. "A fine buck, Mister Pike. This meat will be welcomed."

Pike ignored the compliment, glowering at Hallet. "Been more than one man to go under to that kind of foolishness," he said shortly.

"Oui," LaBarge agreed. "I told him that myself, but he does not always listen to my wisdom."

"Well, sometimes I do, Baptiste, if there is not too much hot wind blowing off the prairie to confuse me," Hallet replied soberly.

"We were beginning to wonder if you two had become lost," Gabriel said.

"No, not lost," LaBarge said. "The Pembina hunters were already past Charlo's cabin before we caught up with them."

"They did not stop at Saint Joseph?"

Hallet shook his head. "I'm afraid not, Gabriel. They camped that first night at Bear Springs, instead, well inside the Hair Hills."

"Then the Ridge Trail is theirs?"

"So it would seem, but going farther onto the prairies won't be so bad. Too many people use the Ridge Trail, anyway, and the game there is about shot out. I'd prefer the prairies myself."

"It is slower, though," Gabriel said. "Timber is scarce and the coulées are not already cut down for our carts to pass."

"Ho, listen to this one!" LaBarge exclaimed. "Who is in such a hurry, eh? What is there to go home to except a long winter?"

"Better to be home in winter than a month on the prairie yet," Gabriel replied.

"That's true," Hallet conceded. "But it isn't for us to decide. We'll hold a council tonight and vote on a route."

"Oui." LaBarge looked at Pike. "A vote, eh, *mon ami des montagnes?*"

"That's not for me to say. I just hunt for McTavish."

"Then you're a hunter," Hallet replied solemnly. "You shall have a hunter's vote."

"*Oui.* It is fair," LaBarge agreed. "A hunter must have a hunter's voice."

Pike shrugged stiffly, still unable to let go of the anger he felt toward Hallet. He knew he was too edgy, but he couldn't seem to help it. It hadn't always been this way. He could remember a time when he might have tried the same trick himself, but that person was gone, and Pike didn't know if he would ever come back.

LaBarge kicked his horse forward, forcing it past Gabriel and Pike. "Good," he said, eying the camp far below. "Maybe my old woman will have meat on the fire. I am hungry." He started down the steep slope at an angle, his horse tucking its butt low to the ground for balance, but Hallet held back. "Ride with us," he offered.

"Not yet," Gabriel said. "We will go a little farther to see what else the brush hides."

Hallet nodded, glanced at Pike, then looked back at Gabriel.

"It's good that you knew I was there," he said seriously. "Maybe next time it won't be a *bois brûle.*" Reining his pony around, he started after LaBarge.

It was twilight when Pike and Gabriel returned to the *métis* camp. Pike dropped his saddle beside one of McTavish's meat carts, then leaned his rifle against the wheel. The bay, already staked out on its picket rope, tore hungrily at the short, dry grass. From the Hair Hills, coyotes yammered and yipped, garnering a response from a pack of dogs on the other side of the cordon.

Unsheathing his knife, Pike squatted next to the white-tailed buck, but, before he could make his first cut, McTavish emerged from the shadows. A look of pleasure crossed his face when he saw the deer.

"Well done, Mister Pike," he said, halting across from the carcass and lifting its hip with his toe. "Small, but winter sleek. He'll be well received by the young ones."

Pike looked up incredulously. "You intend to share this?"

"Aye, with ye leave, I do. 'Tis the only meat brought in today, and the wee ones aren't as used to empty bellies as those of us who have gone hungry before. Charlo's moose is naught but a memory now, though there's pemmican for the adults and Isabella's boilin' up a kettle of *rubaboo* for after the council."

Pike shook his head, disgruntled but silent. Standing, he sheathed his knife. "It's your deer, I reckon, but them that eats it can skin the damned thing for themselves."

"Aye to that," McTavish agreed. Swiveling at the waist, he called to the next fire. "Hannah Keller! Would ye be so kind, lass, as to see to the deer that Mister Pike brought in, and that 'tis shared equally among those that need it most?"

"*Oui,* Big John." She came immediately, a big-boned, handsome young woman, carrying a knife and whetstone. A second woman followed, older and stockier, her flesh turned nearly to leather by weather and age.

"Missus Keller, and Missus Quesnelle, have ye met Mister Pike yet, late of the Rocky Mountains?"

Hannah Keller glanced shyly at Pike, nodded quickly, then lowered her eyes. The older woman, Rosanna Quesnelle, held Pike's gaze.

"Rosanna's brother is also recently returned from yon mountains," McTavish continued innocently. "Perhaps ye knew him? Henri Duprée?"

"Never met him," Pike returned flatly.

"Ah, well, maybe ye will. Henri and another will be huntin' for Rosanna's husband this year, as ye hunt for me."

Slowly Pike pulled his gaze away from Rosanna Quesnelle and let it come to rest on McTavish. "Could be," he said softly.

"*Ce qui sera, sera,* eh?" Big John replied inscrutably. Turning to Hannah Keller, he added: "My thanks for ye help, lass. I'll expect ye to keep the liver for yeself. Will ye do that?"

"Yes, thank you, Big John." Hannah Keller's eyes came up and a smile flashed across her face. Then, drawing her knife, she knelt next to the deer. Silently Rosanna stooped to help her.

"Will ye be joinin' us at the council fire, Mister Pike?"

They were moving away from the women now, leaving behind the quick, scratching sounds of their knives. Pike picked up his rifle as they passed the cart, uneasy without it even here.

"Charles and Baptiste already told ye that Paget's bunch beat us to the Ridge Trail. We'll need to decide on a different route now."

"Seems like the captain of the train ought to make that decision," Pike said.

" 'Twould make things easier, to be sure, but such is not the way of the valley, nor of the *bois brûles.* Comes bad trouble and a need to act quickly, then René's word will be law, but not on the larger matters." He glanced at Pike. " 'Tis true democracy I'm speakin' of, Mister Pike, and there's not much we won't be votin' on. Likely ye'll be sick of it by the time we get back."

Pike shrugged indifferently. It didn't matter to him one way or the other where they went or how they got there, as long as Henri Duprée and François Rubiette were waiting at the end of the trail. "Let's go see what they want to do," he said.

The few men who had remained seated now stood. Silence gripped the council. Everyone watched René Turcotte expectantly, but Turcotte refused to be goaded. He stood before the fire, his red tuque looking as dark as kidney's blood in the flickering firelight. Doubt clouded his features. It was obvious he wasn't sure what to do, and he stole a furtive glance at McTavish, as if searching for some hint of guidance.

Joseph Breland faced him across the fire. He was a man of medium height, with thick, curly hair that seemed to fly wildly in the slightest breeze whenever it was uncapped. His eyes, green as emeralds, stood out sharply against the dusky hue of his face. Other than for his hair and eyes, Breland was typically *métis,* right down to his fiery temper. He was leaning forward now with his fists clenched—frozen, as they all were, by the sudden flare-up of animosity.

It was LaBarge who broke the strained silence. "What does it matter? René captains."

"René?" Breland scoffed openly, looking at McTavish.

"*Oui,* Joseph," LaBarge said. "It was decided."

Breland let his arms flap out, then down. He was giving in, Pike saw, but not necessarily surrendering.

Jacques Leveille said: "I have crossed the prairie many times alone, or with only a few others. As you have, Joseph."

"Such travel is the fancy of fools," Breland replied. "Two men are not enough. Not when the caravans have already started for the plains. We will find their bones on the prairie, quilled like the porcupine's back with Sioux arrows." His angry gaze swept the men surrounding Turcotte. "The Sioux know our ways. They will be watching."

"It would save time," Turcotte ventured diffidently.

"Time? Who worries about time?" Breland's eyes returned to McTavish.

Turcotte also glanced at Big John, then quickly away. Pike silently cursed the man's timidity. It had been Turcotte's proposal to send a couple of men ahead to scout for the herds, but it was McTavish who argued loudest for it now.

There was a certain logic to the idea, Pike thought, especially considering the caravan's lumbering pace. And certainly it had been done before. Duprée and Rubiette were out there somewhere now, and Big John and Gabriel had been on a scout when Pike stumbled into their breakfast camp on a dying horse. But Breland wasn't being an old woman when he argued against it, either. It was one thing for a couple of men to slip quietly onto the Sioux hunting grounds. It would be another for them to leave something as loud and colorful as the half-breeds' caravan, already penetrating Sioux lands.

Yet for all the arguments about sending out an advance party, Pike knew there was more going on here than a simple difference of opinion. If he had been blind to the politics of the camp before, he was beginning to grasp it now. There was a division here that hinged upon factors other than those of old—Catholic versus Protestant, Hudson's Bay against the North West Company, the French-speaking Pembina hunters over those of the Tongue River. This was contention closer to home, and, somehow, McTavish was in the middle of it. For a moment or two, Pike began to wonder how, to become genuinely interested. Then Nicolas Quesnelle said—"What of Henri?"—and Pike grew stiff, his fingers tightening on his rifle.

"Oui," another added. "He is already on the prairie, *non?*"

"And where would that be?" McTavish asked Nicolas.

"At *Lac du Diable,*" Quesnelle replied. "He and François Rubiette will wait for us there, after they find *le bison.*"

"I don't know your brother-in-law," Hallet said cautiously, "nor do I wish to insult him. But I don't think I want to go all the way to Devil's Lake unless I'm sure the person will be there. What if he has already decided to go on to the American forts on the Missouri River? Or offers to lead Paget to the buffalo, instead of us?"

"He would not do that. He is family."

"Almost all of us have family among the Pembina hunters," Hallet said.

"Besides, we have not decided to go to Devil's Lake," Breland reminded them.

"What does it matter?" queried a voice from the rear of the crowd. "We always go to *Lac du Diable.*"

"We do not always do what we always do," Breland countered.

"This year, some of us want to send scouts out ahead to amuse the Sioux, eh, Big John?"

"No, Joseph, to guide us around 'em, and to the herds."

"But it is always best that we go to Devil's Lake first," Noel Pouliot said, and several others murmured agreement.

"Then we will vote on Devil's Lake," Turcotte said, grasping for anything now to draw the argument away from the subject of scouts. "All in favor of going to Devil's Lake first, let it be known."

Assent rippled through the crowd. Only a few—McTavish, Hallet, Gabriel, and old Charlo among them—remained silent.

"Good," Turcotte said with obvious relief. "To Devil's Lake then." He glanced almost apologetically at McTavish. "Maybe we can consider sending men ahead from there, eh, Big John?"

McTavish shrugged, and his gaze slid to Breland. "Well, then to Clootie's swimmin' hole it'll be. We'll see if Paget's hunters have left us wood to burn or game to hunt. Does that suit ye, Joseph?"

Breland shook his head. "It does not matter whether it suits me, Big John. It has been decided fairly, by vote."

"It is best that we go to Devil's Lake first, though," Pouliot muttered, so softly Pike doubted if those to the rear of the crowd even heard him. "It is the way we have always done it." McTavish laughed under his breath and turned away. To a man, the *métis* watched him leave, watched his broad shoulders fade into the shadows.

"Sacre," Leveille whispered. "He worries too much, that one."

"Big John worries about what is important," Gabriel said. "In his heart, he is *bois brûle.*"

"Big John is a good man," Breland said to Gabriel. "But he is not *bois brûle.*"

"I don't know, Joseph, I think maybe he is," Charlo said, pushing through the crowd to face Breland across the fire. "I think maybe he was *métis* a long time before you were, eh?" He looked around at the others. "You remember the Pemmican Wars between Hudson's Bay and the North West? You remember who defended the mixed-bloods against even old MacGillivray? No? Then I will tell you. It was Big John McTavish." He turned back to Breland, but continued to speak to all of them. "Have you ever wondered why Big John never factored his own post, Joseph, when we all know he should have? It is because he always sided with us, the children of the land. The Chippewas and Assiniboines and Crees. And, yes, even the Sioux, who he has killed and who have tried to kill him. All are his friends. He has never deserted them, never deserted us. No matter what policy the company adopted, Big John's heart always remained true to the *bois brûle*."

"The North West Company is a long time gone," Breland reminded the old Indian.

Charlo's features registered disgust. "Only to the children," he said contemptuously. "Only to those who would forget the past to benefit their own future." With a slashing motion of his hand, he turned away, forcing a path through the crowd. Gabriel followed rigidly, looking neither right nor left.

Slowly the others began to break apart as well, drifting back to their fires and their suppers. Only a few remained, gathering around Joseph Breland like bees to pollen, talking in hushed tones.

Pike's brow was furrowed in thought as he left the fractured group. For the first time, it occurred to him that there might be worse storms brewing for the half-breeds than what Old Man Winter had planned for them. Maybe even worse than what the *métis* themselves were aware of.

Chapter Nine

It wasn't until they'd lined out toward Devil's Lake, still four long days to the south, that Gabriel felt as if they were really on their way. He pointed Baldy across the rolling swells of tall-grass prairie, skirting the occasional mucky slough with its fringe of cat-tails and tough-bladed switch grass. The sun was a borderless bronze globe hanging in the sky, hot across his shoulders and through the scratchy fabric of his trousers drawn tightly over his thighs. Only a light breeze stirred, and the dust churned up by the grinding wheels of the carts hung like a fog over the caravan.

Big John led today. Turcotte had dropped back to the rear of the column after leading on the first day. He would gradually work his way up through the ranks again, the same as everyone else and in spite of his position as captain of the train. A steady rotation of leaders was just one of many methods the *bois brûles* used to ensure equality within their tribe.

Isabella handled the canvas-hooped lead cart pulled by Solomon, the aging gelding both Gabriel and Alec had learned to ride on. The black mare, pulling one of the empty meat carts, followed, her lead rope fastened to an iron ring driven into the rear of the front cart's bed. Celine managed the third cart, leading Alec's pinto on a jawline bridle. Gabriel's gaze lingered on her. They hadn't spoken to one another since that night beside the Tongue, although he knew she often watched him from afar.

Gabriel wished he had someone to talk to about Celine. Big

John would be impossible, of course, and Charlo seemed an unlikely candidate. Charlo had been married to a Chippewa woman once, but that had been a long time ago. The woman had since gone back to her people in the Turtle Mountains, taking their son with her. Sometimes Charlo went to the Turtle Mountains to trap or trade, but he never mentioned the woman or the child. On the buffalo ranges, he always hired a woman to drive his carts and make his pemmican, but to Gabriel's knowledge it never went beyond that. This year he'd hired Jacques Leveille's daughter Susanne to care for his meat and robes.

Susanne Leveille was no stranger to Gabriel, either, and he twisted in the saddle to stare back down the long line of carts until he spotted her lithe form, trudging steadily alongside Charlo's dun ox. Jacques Leveille lived in St. Joseph, and Gabriel would go there whenever he could to visit and listen to Jacques's fiddle, which he played with an expert hand. But mostly, he went to talk with Susanne, or just watch her as she worked around the cabin. She was a handsome woman, not much younger than himself, with flashing black eyes, a quick smile, and tumbling laughter. He had taken her on several cariole rides last winter, and thought only the ill luck of having adults show up on some odd mission had prevented them from making love in Jacques's stable afterward.

A muscle in Gabriel's cheek twitched as he considered that. He had been a fool around women so many times he was beginning to doubt his own judgment. He thought he was probably the only person in camp his age who was still a virgin. Both Michel Quesnelle and Duncan McKay had talked girls into the bushes that summer—or at least that was their claim—and both of them were quite a few months younger than he.

Shaking his head in frustration, Gabriel turned his attention away from the caravan. He could see Big John and Pike far in advance, their rifles ready. To the east and west, the flankers were little more than tiny specks against the vastness of the horizon. Long ago, the *bois brûles* had hunted buffalo alone or in small parties or family groups, but that had made them easy prey for the Sioux. Gabriel couldn't remember who first suggested they organize their hunts into a communal enterprise, but he could recall vividly the excitement of that initial gathering. It was one of his earliest memories.

Nowadays, of course, a hunt might originate anywhere along the Red or Assiniboine Rivers and attract hundreds of participants, but Gabriel agreed with Big John about the bigger gatherings. It was better to stay small. Large enough to withstand a Sioux assault, but not so huge as to become bogged down in politics and discord. Sometimes he wondered if they weren't reaching that limit themselves.

A murmur of alarm passed along the length of the caravan, reaching Gabriel in the lead. He glanced over his shoulder, then looked west across the rolling prairie to where Antoine Toussaint, one of the flankers, was pounding toward the cart train at a gallop. His fusil was raised above his head, and, as he drew closer, his cry came faintly to the watching *bois brûles.*

"Hiah! Hiah!"

The signal that Indians approached.

Gabriel whirled Baldy toward the caravan. Isabella was already pulling Solomon off the trail, quirting him into a clumsy trot. Others were doing the same, the whole line dissolving in a dust-roiling tempest that Gabriel knew would, within minutes, form a tight, defensive circle.

Only Celine struggled alone. The pinto Alec had hoped to run buffalo with was lunging against its lead rope, the empty meat cart it pulled bouncing crazily behind it. Alec was driving Gabriel's single cart behind Celine—he'd refused to handle any of Big John's stock this year—but, when the pinto dragged Celine away from the train, he ignored her frantic cries for help and lashed Gabriel's ox after Isabella.

The pinto was trotting now, its neck bowed stiffly, chin tucked close to its chest. Its tongue protruded thickly from between its lips as it fought the rawhide bit behind its teeth. Celine was yanking on the pony's head, but she wasn't strong enough to stop it. At a gallop, Gabriel swung wide around the dust and confusion, pounding at Baldy's ribs with his heels. The pinto reared and lunged, then lunged again. Celine screamed as several feet of rawhide burned through her hands, but she refused to let go. The pony was loping gracelessly now, its gait hampered by the struggling girl hanging on and the skidding, rattling cart.

Coming in from the offside, Gabriel leaned from the saddle, reaching under the pinto's jaw to grab the lead rope close to the horse's mouth. He jerked back savagely. The pinto shook its head, snorting and slamming its shoulder into Baldy. Gabriel grunted as the cart's shaft banged into his shin, but he kept his hold on the rope. Celine was also pulling on the lead rope, and, between them, they brought the cantankerous horse to a trot, then finally to a choppy walk.

With the spotted horse under control, Celine let the rawhide fall from her hands. She turned them over slowly, sobbing as the red, broken flesh of her palms was exposed. Then she lifted her head and started deliberately for the pinto.

Gabriel knew what she had in mind. He had seen that same murderous look on Alec's face too many times in the past. Perhaps it was justified, at least to an extent. The pinto was better trained than that, and had only taken advantage of Celine's inexperience, but there wasn't time for discipline. He could see the Indians now, still half a mile away, but coming fast.

"No!" Gabriel said. He pointed toward the Indians with his chin. "We must return to the carts while there is time. There is much to be done."

Celine didn't reply. She didn't seem to have even heard him. She kept walking toward the spotted horse with her face twisted in rage, while Gabriel, still holding the lead rope, began to curve the animal away from her.

"Celine!" he called sharply over his shoulder. "Stop it! We must go back!"

The sudden drumming of hoofs caught his attention. Big John had already passed them on his way to the carts, but Pike was swerving toward them. He slowed as he approached, taking the situation in with a glance. Then he swung around the cart and caught Celine in the crook of his arm almost before she knew he was there.

Celinc squawked as Pike pulled her effortlessly across his saddle. Gabriel saw the flash of a curled fist as she tried to strike him, but her position was too awkward, the bay too jumpy, for her to do any real harm. Pike slowed only long enough to shout: "Bring in that cart, boy! I've got the girl."

Celine's fist bounced harmlessly off the American's knee, and Pike grinned. Then he whipped the bay around and rode toward the caravan at a fast lope.

Gabriel followed at a trot, the empty cart rattling loudly behind the already skittish pinto. He felt vaguely cheated out of his rescue of Celine, although he was pretty sure she wouldn't have shown him any gratitude. His only consolation was that it didn't look like Pike was going to fare any better.

Approaching the caravan, Gabriel heard Pierre Campbell calling his name, and reined in that direction. The *bois brûles* had tightened their usual cordon by running the vehicles hub to hub rather than shafts to tailgate. Then they'd tipped them back to expose the underside of the beds to the outside world. The dumped loads were left where they spilled, although, if there was time later on, they would stuff them into the gaps between the carts for additional protection. Some of the women were already lashing the wheels together so that they couldn't be roped and dragged away. Campbell tipped down one of his unbound carts and wheeled it out of the circle as Gabriel drew near.

"Leave your cart," Campbell instructed. "Just bring the horses inside."

Gabriel shook his head. "I will go with the others to face the Indians on the prairie," he said.

"Then let me have your spotted pony." Pierre glanced over his shoulder to where a large contingent of hunters was gathering on the west side of the train. "You'd better hurry, young one, or they'll leave without you."

Gabriel tossed him the rawhide lead rope, but, as he was reining away, he heard Susanne Leveille calling for him to wait. She darted through the gap where Campbell's cart had stood, but slowed as she approached Baldy. Gabriel's breath caught in his throat. She was beautiful, he thought. Firm and strong and brown-skinned, the sun setting off the auburn highlights in her hair. Coming up beside him, Susanne laid a hand on his knee, and not so long ago he would have thrilled at that, and his flesh would have quivered beneath her touch.

"Don't go," she said.

"I have to."

"Someone must stay with the carts."

"Pierre is here. So is Alec, and others."

"Only a handful. Everyone wants to ride out to meet the Sioux."

Gabriel glanced at the hunters gathering on the west side of the caravan. Most of the outriders—the flankers and point men and those who had brought up the rear—were already in, and he saw that Susanne was right. The majority of them were rallying around René and Big John. No more than a dozen remained inside the enclosure to help prepare its defenses.

"Maybe there won't be a fight," Gabriel said evasively. Since they'd started traveling in larger parties, they were often able to bluff their way past the Sioux, or purchase passage to the buffalo ranges and the rights to hunt there with trade goods. It all depended upon who they met, which individual band they had to treaty with.

"You are like all the men," Susanne scolded him, although he noticed there was no heat in her words.

He smiled. "You liked that once."

"I still do, but you do not notice any more. You have barely looked at me since we came in from Saint Joseph."

He found her candidness unsettling, and instinctively sawed at Baldy's reins to pull him away. Then he stilled the pony.

"There is no time for this," he said. Campbell had already led the pinto inside the enclosure. Now he was returning for the cart he'd wheeled out of line to allow Gabriel to enter. "You'd better get inside," he told her. "I will remind René that enough men must remain behind to protect the women and children."

Susanne's mouth leveled, and the laughter faded from her eyes. "Go then, before you miss the great battle."

He hesitated, but could think of nothing more to say. Angrily he pulled Baldy around and kicked him in the ribs, riding off without a farewell.

When Gabriel rode up, René was barking commands like a battle-scarred general to the handful of men who had already volunteered to stay behind. The rest of them would ride out to meet the approaching Indians. They would create a buffer between the Sioux and the caravan, if such were needed.

To the west, Gabriel could see Antoine Toussaint's partner, Little John McKay, riding toward them at an easy lope. Puffs of dust exploded from beneath his horse's hoofs, but he didn't look especially alarmed. Behind McKay, the Indians were slowing down and spreading out.

"Who are they?" Breland demanded of Toussaint, and Turcotte, wheeling away from the carts, added: "Sioux, Antoine? Are they Sioux?"

"Oui!" Toussaint cried, his eyes still wide with fear. "*Les Sioux,* for sure! They tried to scalp me and Little John!"

An uneasy muttering arose from the *bois brûles,* and their ponies shifted and danced under tight reins.

Then Big John's voice lifted above the turmoil. "Tried to scalp ye, Antoine? From half a league away?"

"*Oui,* Big John, they did. They come from *la coulée* and tried to scalp us."

"I don't think so, old friend." Big John nodded toward the prairie, where McKay had slowed to a trot to match the pace of the horsemen still several hundred yards behind him.

"They shoot their *fusées* at us, Big John. This I hear with my own ears!"

"At ye, Antoine, or into the air, proper-like, to show with empty guns that they mean us no harm?"

"When do the Sioux not mean us harm?" Turcotte exploded.

"When they be Chippewas, René," Big John replied calmly, tipping his head toward the prairie once more.

Someone said—"*Sacre bleu.*"—with a great expulsion of air, and several of them laughed with the release of pent-up emotion.

Smiling, Charlo said: "There is one among us who would not easily see the difference between a Sioux and a Chippewa, eh, Big John?"

A few of the *bois brûles* looked at Pike and chuckled, but Joseph Breland's features remained taut and unchanged. Forcing his horse to the center of the group, he said: "What Charlo says is true. The plains Chippewas have been our friends in the past, but maybe that is not so today. It would not be wise to relax our guard too soon."

Big John was quick to agree. "Aye, Joseph, 'tis my thinkin', too." He glanced at Turcotte. "Well, René, should we be ridin' out to meet 'em, before they get too close?"

Turcotte nodded and stood in his stirrups. He called out the names of a dozen men who he ordered to remain with the carts. "The rest of you will ride with me," he added.

No one protested. There was a time to argue, to debate and vote and debate again, but there was also a time for a man to hold his tongue and do what he was told. It was why they elected one man as captain.

Reining away from the caravan, Turcotte started for the Chippewas at a determined jog. Those hunters not detailed to remain behind followed him closely. Gabriel found himself near the front of the pack, riding between Pike and Antoine Toussaint. The American sat his horse stiffly, scowling and tense, his rifle cradled in his left arm, ready to fire. Toussaint, meanwhile, seemed distracted. Gabriel knew he was embarrassed by mistakenly identifying the Chippewas as Sioux, and was no doubt anticipating a rough time of it at the hands of the more notorious ribbers once the situation had been dealt with. He was carrying his fusil in his right hand with the cock down, the frizzen open, its pan empty.

Gabriel had unslung his own musket as soon as he joined the main party of hunters. Now, riding toward the Chippewas, he ran his hand back and forth along the sun-warmed barrel, as if he could rub away some of his own anxiety along with the trail dust from the Brown Bess. He remembered the way he'd felt that night outside Charlo's cabin, on their return from the prairies. He still didn't want to fight the Chippewas if they didn't have to.

In the past, members of the Turtle Mountain band had often accompanied the *bois brûles* on their semi-annual excursions for buffalo, adding their numbers to those of the *métis* for the mutual protection of everyone. But it would be different this year. Pike rode with them, a hunter for Big John and an accepted member of the caravan. His presence would put everyone in an awkward position with the Chippewas.

McKay had halted his horse about three hundred yards from the carts, then reined it around to face the full-bloods. The Chippewas had also stopped some distance away. As Turcotte slowed his horse alongside McKay's, about a dozen Chippewa warriors broke away from the main bunch and started forward at a walk.

The *bois brûles* spread out in a ragged line, facing the afternoon sun. Pike brought his bay in beside Gabriel. "What do you think?" he asked, squinting into the glaring sun. "Eighty? Ninety?"

"It is hard to say," Gabriel replied. Certainly there were more than their own forty-odd hunters, but he wasn't sure there were twice that many. Then a grim smile wormed its way across his face, and he nodded toward the leader of the small party approaching them, a fat-bellied old man wearing scarlet leggings and a buckskin breechcloth. "Do you recognize the pony?" he asked.

Pike grunted sharply. "Yeah, it's the buckskin the Indian McTavish shot was riding on the day they jumped me."

"That is Tall Cloud who rides it. He is an uncle of the man Big John shot, and a minor chief. They say that one time, when he was younger, Tall Cloud killed four strong Sioux braves with just his knife. At least that is the story they tell."

"He must've been skinnier in those days," Pike observed. "He doesn't look like he'd be limber enough today to dodge even one of them."

René Turcotte made a small gesture that included Big John, Little John McKay, Toussaint, Charlo, and Joseph Breland.

Those six rode forward to where Tall Cloud had halted his party halfway between the two groups. Gabriel wished he had been chosen to go along, but as it turned out, it wasn't necessary. Tall Cloud had years of experience as an orator, and his voice carried clearly across the distance.

"*Ho!* McTavish! *Ho!* Turcotte! *Ho!* McKay!" He greeted the others similarly, his hands flashing in sign to accompany his words. It was common practice among a lot of the plains tribes, an acknowledgment that not everyone understood the languages being spoken.

"My heart is sad, McTavish!" Tall Cloud bellowed, after the expected amenities had been exchanged. "Very sad. Crow Horse has brought news that makes Tall Cloud's eyes run many tears. He says that it was McTavish who killed my nephew from ambush. This is a bad thing, McTavish?"

Big John answered in kind, with voice and hand, although Gabriel couldn't make out all the words or see the signs.

"Does McTavish fight for the Long Knives now?" Tall Cloud asked, referring to the sword-carrying American soldiers.

Again, with his back to them, most of Big John's reply was lost in the wind.

"Is it not the way of the Ojibway to fight his enemy?" Tall Cloud returned philosophically, using his people's own name for the tribe others called Chippewa. "Is it not true this Long Knife invaded our lands?"

Big John's shoulders rolled in response.

"Always, the Ojibways have been friends to the white traders," Tall Cloud continued. "Did we not leave the forests of our fathers' land to hunt the beaver and muskrat for you here? Did we not venture boldly into the lands of the Sioux, who are our enemies, and take this land from them so that we might trap even more furs for your trader chiefs, and the white grandmother you call Queen? We were a people of the forests, McTavish, but we became buffalo hunters for you and Cammaron and Henry. Is that not true?"

"God dammit," Pike growled. "What's he saying?"

It was only then that Gabriel realized Pike didn't understand Chippewa, and that he had been following the conversation only through Tall Cloud's hands. But Tall Cloud had abandoned his sign about halfway through his last speech so that he could lift his old trade gun above his head and shake it vigorously to illustrate his sense of betrayal.

"He is reminding Big John of how the Chippewas came to the Red River Valley to trap for the North West Company a long time ago, before I was born," Gabriel translated. "He is making big talk about all that they have given up, but has said nothing yet of the many things they have gained."

Tall Cloud went on for quite a while, relating the numerous hardships the Chippewas had endured to come to this new land, in addition to the heartache of leaving so many of their friends and family members behind. He emphasized the cultural differences that had grown between the two bands since they'd abandoned their woodland homes, and how those differences precluded their ever returning.

Most of it, Gabriel already knew. Only part of the Chippewa nation had left their traditional forest homelands to follow old Alexander Henry to the Red River Valley. In time, they'd drifted west from the Hair Hills to establish themselves in the Turtle Mountain region, a country not unlike that from which they had come, with tall trees and rolling hills, streams abundant with fish.

It was true that in the process they had been forced to give up many of their old ways in order to embrace a lifestyle more suited to the open plains surrounding the Turtle Mountain region. They'd traded the canoe for the horse, the bark house for the buffalo-hide teepee, the flesh of the deer for the meat of the bison. But to Gabriel's mind, they had gained far more than they'd lost. He didn't know anyone among the Turtle Mountain people who had ever expressed a desire to return to the east side of the Red River, and the swampy, insect-infested forests that prevailed there. But of course, crafty old Tall Cloud wouldn't mention that. He had come for restitution, not revenge.

"My brother grieves for his lost son," Tall Cloud continued, using sign language again. "He says McTavish must pay for this terrible crime against his family, and in that way erase the shame from his own name."

"Greasy old son-of-a-bitch," Pike grated under his breath.

"It is the way of the land," Gabriel replied stoically. "Big John will pay, and if it is enough, if Tall Cloud is satisfied, then this thing between him and the Chippewas will be forgotten. It is best. Otherwise, there could be war."

"I know how it works, boy. I just don't cotton to the extra debt, is all."

"It is Big John's debt. It was he who killed Tall Cloud's nephew."

"Did it saving my hide, too. It'll be my debt, now."

Toussaint whirled his horse and galloped back to the main party. He hauled up in front of Gabriel. "Big John wants you to bring back a fusil, a horn of powder, five pounds of lead, a sixty-two-caliber bullet mold, two red blankets, ten knives, a packet of mirrors, and another of vermillion."

Gabriel jerked a thumb over his shoulder. "Tell Alec. He will get it for you."

Toussaint made a face but didn't push it. Gabriel knew he resented having to fetch what Big John told him to fetch. He had tried to pass off some of his irritation by doing the same to Gabriel, but Gabriel wouldn't be manipulated so easily—not by Antoine Toussaint.

The others had also followed the conversation between Big

John and Tall Cloud, and, although they kept their fusils handy and their eyes on the Chippewas, they began to relax, talking among themselves, laughing a little. It was good, Gabriel thought, that it hadn't come to a fight.

Toussaint soon returned with the items Big John had requested. Tall Cloud had one of the braves beside him accept the gifts. It would be enough, perhaps, but not so much that others among the Chippewas would suddenly demand proportionate compensation for past wrongs. The way of the land, Gabriel had told Pike—bribery and honor walking hand-in-hand.

Tall Cloud and Big John exchanged a few more words, quieter this time, and without sign, so that only those beside them heard. Then they parted, the Chippewas wheeling their ponies and riding off at a gallop, yipping victoriously. Big John and the others trotted back to the main party, and Gabriel saw that Big John's face was pensive as he guided his roan toward Pike.

Hauling up, he began without preamble: "Ye followed most of what was said, I'm guessin'?"

The others had already turned away, riding back to the caravan at a walk. Only Gabriel remained behind with Big John and Pike.

"Enough to know I'll be owing you for a trade gun and blankets and such," Pike said.

"Naught that cannot be earned from the hunt," Big John assured him. " 'Tis what the old bugger said afterward that's got me bothered."

"Tell it," Pike said grimly.

"It seems our friend Tall Cloud did not speak for the entire family, as a man might have expected, to hear him at the beginnin' of his windy. The lad I shot was named Wolf Slayer. His brother is One Who Limps, who I've heard of. One Who Limps has counted coup against the Sioux and Cheyennes, and stolen many a pony from 'em, to boot. He's just returned from a horse-stealin' raid against the Cheyennes, and, accordin' to Tall Cloud, he's swearin' revenge against me and the American he says led young Wolf Slayer into my trap.

"The two of us, Mister Pike, against maybe a dozen Chippewas comin' for our hides. They're makin' their medicine now, prayin' to their gods and such for the magic that'll make 'em immune to our rifles and knives. Give 'em a week, was Tall Cloud's estimate. No more than that."

Pike eyes narrowed. "Six to one odds aren't all that bad," he said.

Big John smiled without humor. "Well, it can be done, and I'll not argue otherwise, but 'tis a sorry business we've gotten ourselves into, nonetheless. 'Tis the *métis* I'm thinkin' of now. A lot of 'em have kin among the Turtle Mountain people, and most of 'em have friends there, myself included."

"You saying the half-breeds won't side with us, or is it just me they'll throw to the dogs for bait?"

Big John's shoulders were slumped. "I'm not sure I could answer that right now, Mister Pike. I doubt if many of the mixed-bloods could. 'Tis a thing we'll all need to sleep on a bit before anyone can come to a firm decision. I just thought ye ought to know the way things stand, for now, at least."

"The *bois brûles* will not turn their backs on you, Big John," Gabriel said, but that old, sick-to-his-stomach feeling had returned. He'd hoped the animosity between the Chippewas and the *bois brûles* might be pacified after today.

"Well, lad, I'm not so sure. Was the Chippewas to attack the train, we'd fight as one, and boldly so, I'd wager. But if One Who Limps comes out demandin' only me or Mister Pike, well, there could be some that would say blood's a whole lot thicker than water. Still, I see no point in worryin' the subject overmuch." He glanced at Pike. "Of course, ye could head on back to the settlements, and none here as would think less of ye for it."

"Run?" Pike snorted his rejection of that proposal. "I'd sooner give up my rifle. Besides, I have business on the ranges."

"Well, I expected no less," Big John admitted. "So 'tis enough for now that ye know what's about, and that ye watch for the Chippewas as ye do the Sioux." He lifted his reins, guiding the roan past Pike, heading for the caravan.

When they were alone, Gabriel said tentatively: "I have also heard of One Who Limps. He is said to be a dangerous man who believes, as many of the more hot-tempered ones do, that it is the guns of the *bois brûles* that drive the buffalo farther and farther west. He will not show mercy."

Pike had turned his gaze to the retreating party of Chippewas, already small in the distance. Quietly he said: "I didn't come here to fight the Chippewas, but I won't quit a country because of 'em, either." He turned his cold eyes on Gabriel. "Or anyone else, for that matter."

Chapter Ten

LaBarge returned around midmorning, reining up at the head of the caravan to speak with Etienne Cyr, who led that day. Cyr shrugged and replied, but did not stop. While the caravan creaked slowly past, LaBarge filled his pipe and struck a light to it with flint and steel.

Big John resisted thc urge to ride ahead, to see what had brought LaBarge back from his position of forward scout. Turcotte—damn his timorous soul—still lollygagged beside his cart in conversation with his wife. Once again, Big John wondered if he had made a mistake in supporting René for captain. Had his own self-interests blinded him to what was best for them all? Some men were born to lead, he knew, while others were born to follow. Only a rare few truly gave a damn for neither. Pike was one. He would lead if leading served his purpose, or be led for the same reason. But if it came to it, Pike wouldn't hesitate to cut loose and go his own way.

The *métis* had been that way themselves, before time and the slow-moving conveyances that bore the valley's name had weakened their independence. Yet they still considered themselves freemen, courageously self-reliant. It was why LaBarge halted where he did, instead of reporting immediately to Turcotte, why Etienne Cyr took it upon himself to forge ahead without even a backward glance. It required strong will and an almost Herculean patience to lead the mixed-bloods, and Big John feared Turcotte lacked those qualities. René was proving to be a follower, intimidated by the responsibilities of his position, yet too stubborn in his belief that he was the equal of any man to acknowledge it.

To a veteran of the old North West Company, the half-bloods' lack of discipline was a hard pill to swallow, and Big John had to remind himself daily that impatience was his own Achilles' heel, an enemy he had constantly to guard against.

The caravan advanced sluggishly. When finally within hailing distance of LaBarge, Big John gave in and trotted his horse forward. "Baptiste, how do ye fare, old friend?"

"Well, Big John, well."

"No trouble, then?"

"*Non.* Charles still scouts, but there is not much to see. No sign of meat, though, while the stomachs of our young ones grow emptier every day. *Sacre,* but I think we should send our hunters farther out, even if it means they have to stay away overnight."

"Ye may be right. Mention it to René and see what he has to say of the idea."

LaBarge laughed without rancor. "He will say . . . 'I do not know, Big John, what do you think I should think?' That is what René will say."

Big John caught his lower lip between his teeth, but didn't reply. It bothered him that others saw René's weaknesses as clearly as he did.

Almost as an afterthought, LaBarge added: "We found the trail of Paget's hunters. They have come inland along the Salt River, and now they have turned southwest toward *Lac du Diable.*"

"Here, man? 'Tis too soon."

"Maybe, but it is their trail, none other. Charles has gone ahead to catch up with their rear guard. We will know tonight why they abandoned the Ridge Trail so soon. Me, I think they did not find enough game there. It is the only reason that makes sense."

Hoof beats drummed the prairie behind them. Big John glanced back, expecting Turcotte, but it was Breland who slowed his black runner beside them. LaBarge quickly related his news to Joseph, who replied: "Damn such bad luck. Game is scarce enough as it is this year."

"It will be gone entirely now," LaBarge added glumly.

Others began to ride up then, Turcotte, finally, among them. LaBarge dutifully repeated what he had already told Big John and Breland. When he finished, he said: "Etienne says we will go on to the next valley and decide there what we should do."

Turcotte nodded fretfully. "Good, yes, we should do that." He glanced questioningly at Big John, but Big John refused to meet his gaze. From the corner of his eye, he caught Breland's humorless grin, but ignored that, too.

LaBarge rode back the way he had come, passing Etienne Cyr with a shout and a wave. Most of the others, including Turcotte, returned to their carts. Only a few remained clustered together, wrapped in a grim silence.

"There has been a mistake, Big John," Breland began carefully. "René does not lead, and, if the Sioux attack, he will not lead then, either."

"He did well enough with the Chippewas, and thinkin' they were Sioux, too," Big John said.

"He reacted as any *bois brûle* would, doing what we have all done a hundred times before. But it was you Tall Cloud parleyed with, not René. Tall Cloud did not even recognize René as our captain."

" 'Twas me he talked to, right enough, and yeself there to be knowin' the reasons for it, Joseph." Big John's expression hardened. "Are ye so bitter to have lost the election that ye'd cut another down so with ye words?"

"You know better than that. But our hunts grow too large to be run in the same fashion as they once were. One man to captain is not enough now. We must all have our share."

The idea was a surprise to Big John, and he studied Breland closely. "And what do ye have in mind?"

"A central captain, of course, but each man to govern the train for the day he leads. Today, Etienne Cyr should be captain. When the flag is raised on his cart at dawn, even René must heed his command. When it is lowered at nightfall, leadership reverts back to Turcotte. That way no man is chief for more than a few hours."

Big John was careful to keep his expression neutral. "And of the decisions that need to be made?"

"For the big decisions, the same as always. All men must have an equal voice. For the smaller, daily decisions, the man who captains should make those."

It was Indian logic, pure and simple. Big John had learned to recognize it shortly after coming to the *pays sauvage*, many years before, but he still had to struggle with it, to fiddle his own way of thinking into an indigenous point of view.

In practice, Breland's idea wouldn't be much different than the way the hunt was already conducted, yet it would unquestionably dilute a captain's authority, spreading leadership more evenly among them all.

Breland would find a lot of support for such a plan, Big John knew, although he personally didn't think it was a smart move. The North West Company's concept of a central government had been hammered firmly into him. Yet he knew he would never be able to convince the *métis* of that. The *bois brûles* remembered all too well the spurs of Hudson's Bay and the North West, and the control those two companies had tried to enforce in the valley. The freedom of the half-bloods had been too hard-won to give up so easily now, even to one of their own.

"We are *métis,*" Breland asserted quietly when Big John didn't immediately reply, as if that in itself was enough to clinch the proposition.

Big John forced a crooked grin. "Aye, Joseph, and when was anything more ever needed?"

A couple of hunters smiled, but Breland's face remained impassive. "We must govern ourselves, Big John," he said. "We must always listen to the wisdom of those who were first to the valley, but the time has come for the *bois brûles* to make their own decisions."

Big John knew immediately what Breland was referring to. He could hear the subtle stirring of anger in the man's voice, like water just below a boil. He wanted to deny his influence in the election, but sensed that things had gone too far for that. "And of this trip, Joseph?" he asked mildly. "And René?"

"I don't know," Breland admitted. "Not yet."

"If ye're wrong, man, 'tis the *bois brûles* who will be payin' for ye mistake."

Breland nodded soberly. "Your words ring true, Big John. We must hope that my ideas are sound. But I am *bois brûle.* I would not betray my people willingly."

So it wasn't to be a bloodless coup, after all, Big John reflected angrily. He said: "I'm not of mixed blood meself, Joseph, as ye so clearly be hintin' at, but the *métis* are my people, as ye own father, a Scotsman such as meself, was *métis.* 'Tis a kinship of the heart that I'm speakin' of, and as real as if bred there. What might have been done in the past, mistakes included, was done for the good of those we called family."

"I remember my father worked for the North West Company, Big John, and that nothing stood in the way of that."

"Then ye're rememberin' a different man than I do, Joseph. The Albert Breland I knew quit the company to stay with his woman in the *pays sauvage.*"

Breland's green eyes glinted hotly. "Then it is a different man, McTavish, because the Albert Breland I knew is the same one who beat his Stony woman regularly, until she threw herself into the Assiniboine River to end her suffering. But I suppose that would be a familiar story to you, eh? Suicide is no stranger to the house of John McTavish."

Big John's face paled, and his voice turned thick. "By the Lord, man, I did not think I'd ever hear such as that, even from you."

"Joseph talks too much," Jacques Leveille cut in sharply, glaring at Breland.

Breland lowered his gaze. "Jacques is right. I did not mean to open old wounds, as I'm sure you did not. Life in the valley is hard, and sometimes we forget that others have also suffered. Forgive me." Without waiting for a response, he reined his horse away.

Big John stared silently after him, glad he didn't have to make a reply, not sure that he could have without losing control of the rage that strummed through him.

The others remained uncertainly behind, confused by the heat of the encounter they'd just witnessed.

"And what of ye, my friends?" Big John managed after a while. "Do ye agree with Joseph?"

It was Jacques Leveille who replied. "Joseph has been to school in Montreal, and that must make a man very smart. I feel his heart is true, and that a wise man would listen to his words. But I think also that Big John McTavish's heart is true, and that his words are also wise and worthy of being listened to. So I say this . . . I know that each man speaks the truth, but I also know that the truth can be different things to different men and still be true. I don't know yet which man speaks the truth for me, but I will consider carefully what each one says, because they are both my friends, as well as friends to the *bois brûles.*"

The others nodded quick assent, although remaining somewhat subdued. Big John's spirits plummeted as he realized that, once again, Angelique's death had been thrown in his face as his ultimate failure. She was not the first woman in the valley to commit suicide—indeed, it was a fairly common occurrence in a land with such harsh winters—but she was a trader's wife, and to the Indians and mixed-bloods, that made what she did seem worse. It was as if such frailties could be forgiven a squaw or a *métis,* but Angelique had been French, her veins carrying the blood of civilized men and women, not savages.

But they didn't know, Big John told himself. *They wouldn't despise her so if they did. They couldn't know, living their uncluttered lives on the far-flung frontier, what a burden of guilt Angelique had carried to her grave.* "Damn them," he whispered. "Damn them all, and her father, old Pierre Menard, most." Big John balled a fist, but didn't have the strength to strike anything with it. With effort, he forced his fingers to unclench, his palm to lie flat along his thigh.

"*Ce qui,* Big John?" Leveille asked cautiously.

Big John looked up. They were still there, prodding at him with their eyes the same way they sometimes prodded a crippled buffalo with their lances—with a kind of morbid and unrelenting child-like curiosity. He shook his head. " 'Twas nothing, old friend. Talkin' to meself is all."

Leveille glanced at the others, and Big John knew he'd given them one more piece of gossip to be passed back and forth around the fires that night, one more quirk accepted with a consolatory shrug.

Aye, and was anything less expected from a muddled old man who was convinced the buffalo were disappearing? Lifting the roan's reins, he said: "Well, I suppose we'd best be gettin' back to our carts, wouldn't ye say, gentlemen?"

Most of the caravan had already creaked on past. The herd of spare stock was looming close, threatening to engulf them in dust and noise. As one, the half-bloods turned their ponies away without comment. Big John watched them break into a gallop, as if anxious to leave the cheerless old Scotsman behind. Saddened, he nudged the roan after them.

They nooned in the shade of cottonwoods bordering the Salt River, and turned their oxen and cart ponies loose to graze on the tall grass. The valley ran east and west like a shallow, half-mile wide trough scooped from the rolling surface of the prairie, the river meandering through it without rush, the water low but clear. Oaks and maples and box elders lined the banks, those in turn skirted by a fringe of brush and delicate, white-barked aspens, their leaves trembling like gold coins in the slightest breeze.

The sky held high and pale blue, littered with a fleet of dreary gray clouds sailing rapidly eastward. It was still hot and their faces were beaded with sweat, but there was a feeling of change in the air now, a sense of something dark and ominous brewing out beyond the horizon. The women felt it most, and had scattered through the trees to collect firewood they would carry with them in the empty carts.

The men were gathered downstream, smoking their pipes and talking. Their saddle horses grazed nearby on long rawhide or buffalo-hair picket ropes, or fettered with rawhide hobbles, hungrily cropping the rich meadow grass as if they, too, could sense changes coming in the weather.

Turcotte shifted uncomfortably, cleared his throat, squinted momentarily at the motionless *métis* sentinels etched against the sky atop the higher hills to the north and south, then finally shrugged. "Maybe we should do as Big John and Joseph suggests. Go west to Chain of Lakes. It is closer."

But Antoine Toussaint, Noel Pouliot, Little John McKay, and

others wanted to go to Devil's Lake to hunt swans, and to hell with the Pembina hunters. Old Abrams, at the Hudson's Bay post just north of the international boundary, below the mouth of the Pembina, had promised them good pay in beaver for quality swan skins this year. The Bay Company would ship the down to London for powder puffs, the quills to be turned into elegant pens favored among the wealthy.

"We thought some of us might ride ahead," Antoine Toussaint said. "Our women can bring the carts, and there are enough men here to watch over them."

Etienne Cyr chuckled crudely. "*Oui,* Antoine, I will watch your woman for you. Real close, eh?"

Some of the men laughed, and a few supplied ribald comments of their own. Charles Hallet said: "Maybe you could stay behind, Antoine, and protect my woman while I ride ahead to hunt swans for Hudson's Bay."

"No one rides ahead," Breland said abruptly. "That we all agreed to before we left the valley. Only scouts and hunters leave the caravan."

"I've seen swans at Chain of Lakes," Big John added. "Pelicans, too, although I know they won't fetch the price of a good, clean white swan skin. Still, 'tis better to be first there than trot along after the Pembina hunters like a pack of dogs."

"Big John is right," Hallet grumbled. "I'm tired of always bumping into the Pembina caravan, taking what they leave."

Leveille said: "I came to hunt buffalo, not swans. *Lac du Diable* is better than Chain of Lakes, but not if others are already there ahead of us. I also say we should go to Chain of Lakes. Maybe we will find buffalo there, as well as swans."

Big John looked at Turcotte. "What do ye say, René? Do we vote, or is there more ye want to discuss?"

"No," Turcotte said. "It is time to vote. Those who wish to go to Chain of Lakes must let it be known."

A clear majority voiced their assent. No one voted for Devil's Lake. Not even those who declined to vote for Chain of Lakes.

"Then it is settled," Turcotte said, looking relieved. "We go to Chain of Lakes."

Breland smiled broadly. "At last, *mes braves,* we turn west for the hunt."

Chapter Eleven

Chain of Lakes lay like a string of dull gray pearls dropped carelessly along the western rim of the tall-grass prairie, running north and south but with a slight westward bow. It was a land of steep, rolling hills and shaded parks, the dry, short-grass plains lying just beyond.

The caravan arrived at one of the smaller lakes late on the second day after their halt along the Salt River. After circling their carts on a slightly tilted piece of land on the eastern shore, the men unharnessed the stock and ran them out to graze while the women gathered firewood for the evening meal.

Most of the men remained with the carts after the stock had been cared for, but a few of them spread out in the hills to hunt. Pike went with them, though veering off on his own as soon as possible. He rode west, not so much looking for game as just ambling along, enjoying the solitude. There was buffalo sign everywhere—old dung and rain-washed wool snagged in the bushes, and the bark on some of the trees had been buffed slick as polished stone from about three feet above the ground to nearly six feet up, where the huge, shaggy beasts had rubbed and scratched. But none of it was fresher than last spring, and most of it was older than that.

It was nearly full dark before he started back. Pools of pitch-black shadows had collected under the trees, hiding stray limbs that slapped his face or tried to knock off his hat. A handful of stars were already sparkling in the east when he came out of the hills and saw the lights of the half-breeds' fires glinting off the corrugated surface of the lake. He was skirting the northern shore when the bay jerked to a stop with a loud, deer-like snort.

"You look so intense," a woman said from the deeper shadows of a cottonwood.

Pike's thumb had curled instinctively over the rifle's cock, easing it part way back. He relaxed it only slightly now.

"You're a long ways from camp," he said. "Does McTavish know you're out here?"

"I am a grown woman," Celine replied. "I answer to no one, not even to the great McTavish."

Pike returned the cock to the half, or safety, position. Celine stepped away from the tree, although staying well within its protective shadow, and Pike remembered that it had been dark when she approached him in the windmill, too. It made him wonder if she needed the anonymity of nightfall to bolster her courage. During the daylight hours, she always seemed shy and slightly distracted, her gaze usually on the ground.

Except for the time the Chippewas had stopped them. On that day, going after the pinto with murder in her eyes, Celine McTavish had looked anything but retiring.

"What did you shoot, Pike?" she asked, a trace of taunting in her words telling him she already knew.

"Reckon we'll be eating *rubaboo* again tonight, unless Gabriel made some meat."

"Gabriel is a boy. He could not shoot an ox unless it wandered in front of his gun."

Pike studied her vague shape thoughtfully. Her words amused him, for he had seen Gabriel and Celine together the night of the half-breeds' election, walking together toward the river. He'd assumed then that they might be lovers, and that her passion at the windmill from the previous evening had been nothing more than retaliation for some spat between them. But apparently, the rift remained. Now one seldom spoke when the other was near, and each seemed to take great pains to avoid the other. Yet he'd also observed them glancing constantly at one another when they thought no one was watching, like a couple of lovesick puppies.

"You are always so serious, yet so confident," she said. "I feel safe when you are with the caravan. Safer even than with all the *métis.* They are like children, don't you think?"

"They're your people, aren't they?"

"*Non!* My blood is pure. I am French, and my papa was of nobility."

"I thought McTavish was your father."

That stopped her for a moment, but no longer. "I meant my grandfather," she corrected. "He was of nobility."

The bay shifted restlessly. Pike was tempted to go, to leave this girl behind. But the memory of what she'd opened in him that night at the windmill was too strong. It stirred even now, like a snake deep in his belly.

"Walk with me," she said.

He hesitated, considering the possibilities. There was Gabriel, who either loved her or was falling in love with her. Then there was McTavish, Celine's father and his own friend—or at least as much a friend as anyone he'd known since Arch's death. Making a snarling sound deep in his throat, he abruptly dismounted.

They started together toward the camp, and from time to time Celine's arm would brush lightly against his. Her scent came to him, powerfully feminine.

"Who are you?" he asked.

She gave him a quizzical look.

"You're not from here. You're not a half-breed, a *métis.*"

She nodded, understanding. "Big John is my father," she began hesitantly. "I was . . . raised . . . in a convent in Vermont, outside of Saint Albans. Big John sent for me because he missed me, and because he needed a woman to manage his house. The Indian woman steals."

Pike exhaled loudly. He knew the girl was lying. He could still remember McTavish's stunned countenance when he learned of Celine's presence in the valley. He suspected she was also lying about Big John's feelings for the Cree woman. Pike had seen the expression in McTavish's eyes when he gazed at Isabella. It wasn't the look a man gave a thief.

"You don't believe me," she accused in a pouty voice.

"Does it matter?"

Stopping, she grabbed his arm and pulled him around. "Do you like me?"

"Yes."

She came closer, tipping her face toward his. Her breath caressed his throat. He wrapped his arms around her, pressed his lips to hers. She twisted her face away, gasping. "Do you love me, Pike?" she demanded breathlessly. "Would you kill for me?"

"Damn you," he said harshly, forcing her back, bending her knees until they tumbled to the ground together. His rifle fell in the grass beside them. The bay shook its head and backed off. He touched her hip, slid his hand up her ribs to her breast, then moved on to the polished bone button at her neck.

"Pike."

The button came free, another followed.

"Pike, no." She pushed at his shoulder. "Please."

Gritting his teeth in frustration, he rolled off of her, onto his back. Celine stood. He half expected her to run, but instead she loosened another button, then a fourth. Struggling briefly, she tugged the dress over her head, then dropped it on top of his rifle.

"Jesus, girl, you're driving me crazy," he said raggedly.

"Is this not worth it?" she asked, side-stepping into a shaft of moonlight.

Pike caught his breath. Her flesh had taken on a glint as coppery as any Indian's, and her body looked lean and taut. She stood before him in knee-high leggings and moccasins, a heavy silver cross gleaming dully from the shadowy vale between her breasts.

Breathing heavily, Pike scrambled to his feet. He removed his belt and dropped it beside the rifle, tossed his hat on top of that, followed it with his shirt and trousers. Naked, his body looked white and sickly compared to hers, a gaunt, caved-in wreck, hips like twin knobs, ribs a curved washboard. The hair on his chest was a sparse gray field, stiff as wire.

Celine touched it, pressed her hand against it as if it were a bed of springs, then released it. She ran her fingers down his torso until they came to a ridge of scar tissue across his short ribs. She looked at him, her eyes big. "How did this happen?"

"An Arapaho's lance," he replied huskily. "A long time ago."

Her fingers glided upward until they rested on a second scar above his collar bone. "And this?"

"Blackfoot arrow. Three, four seasons back, on the Gros Ventre."

"You are a warrior," she whispered. "As fierce as the hawk." Her fingers drifted down again to touch a small, puckered crater on his upper thigh, a purpled blemish nearly a dozen years old.

"Never really knew," he said. "It was an ambush, but I got away. An Osage, likely. It was their territory, and I traded with 'em for a spell before going to the mountains."

"Take me with you when you leave."

"To the mountains?"

She nodded, starlight skimming along the waves of her hair like silver. Her fingers moved up again, dancing lightly across his lower stomach, causing the muscles there to twitch in anticipation. Music from the *métis* camp floated across the water. "Take me away from here, Pike. Take me to Philadelphia, or Boston."

"They ain't nowhere near the mountains," he said gently.

"Please. I have to get away."

"Why?"

"Why?" She took a step back. "I do not understand your question." Then her expression softened and she put both hands under her breasts, lifting them in offering. "Do you not want me, Pike? Am I not beautiful? I would be your wife and we could ride in carriages and go to balls together. Have you ever been to a ball, where everyone wears beautiful clothing and drinks wine from crystal goblets? I have, many times. Papa took me, and there were important people there. There was music and dancing all night, and the men coveted me."

Pike's desire began to wilt. Celine's cheeks glistened with tears, yet her voice had taken on a hard and chilling edge.

"I hate it here," she said. "I hate everything about it. Everything stinks. The land is flat and ugly and the people are stupid, even though they think they are better than everyone else. I have to get out of here, Pike. Please, you must take me with you."

"When I leave here, I'll go back to the mountains. Down south, most likely, and trap out of the Spanish settlements. I doubt if you'd like that any better than here."

"Anything is better than here. Here is nowhere, close to nothing. I want to go to Philadelphia, to Boston and New York. I want to go to Paris and London. I want to see a play. Do you know what a play is?"

He had attended a play in St. Louis once, a bawdy production featuring whores in scanty costumes. He didn't remember the story, but he could still picture the bare, dough-colored thighs and flabby breasts of one of the actresses. Afterward, he'd paid $1 for a sweaty tumble with her on a lumpy, straw-tick mattress in her crib behind the stage, discovering, as he exited the blanket that served as a door, a line of four others awaiting their turn. Although the sex had been adequate, the experience had left him strangely dissatisfied. It wasn't until several weeks later that it dawned on him that he'd paid to bed a character, a good-hearted but naïve shop clerk, instead of the hardened prostitute he'd followed backstage.

"Make love to me, Pike." Celine took her hands away from her breasts and put them on top of his shoulders. "I want you. You will be the first, and the last."

He lifted his arms between her elbows to push them away, but didn't. He wanted to say no, but with her naked body so close, the warmth of her flesh almost palpable against his own bare chest, his determination wavered. Lowering his hands to the curve of her hips, he drew her roughly against him. Like fire and ice, they sank into the grass.

Jacques Leveille's fiddle drew them, set their feet to moving, their bodies to swaying. Beneath the stars, wrapped in the light of a dozen leaping, crackling fires, the *bois brûles* danced and laughed and drank high wine from kegs provided by Charlo and Nicolas Quesnelle. They celebrated the meat that had been brought in that day—seventeen fat deer, enough to feed the entire caravan—and Charles Hallet's buffalo, an old, solitary bachelor, his scarred hide too heavy to tan, his meat too tough and stringy to chew. But buffalo, nonetheless, and they reveled in its harvest as they would have a dozen tender-fleshed cows.

Deer still roasted over the flames, skewered on peeled hickory limbs slanted up from the ground, the white inner wood slick with running grease, but only a few continued to feast. Charlo brought out his fiddle to join Leveille, and Nicolas Quesnelle produced his squeeze box. Flutes and the tambourine-like *wan-*

bangos added to the cacophony, filling the cool night air with the sounds of their happiness.

In the midst of the stomping dancers, Gabriel twirled Susanne Leveille. They moved together with a lithe grace, while others stepped back and smiled their approval. Gabriel smiled too, but it was a hollow gesture, and, as they danced, his eyes searched constantly among the dancers and those who stood on the sidelines, and the emptiness inside of him grew large.

Seeing the broad grins and knowing smirks on the faces of the older ones, those already married and settled, he wondered why it was they were always trying to mold things into their own image of what was right and proper. He had only asked Susanne Leveille to dance, nothing he hadn't done dozens of times in the past, but to look at them now, a man would think it was all settled except for the asking. Gabriel resented their assumptions that he would always do what was expected of him, as they themselves, as *bois brûles,* had done. Was he no more than that? No greater than one of the cogs in Big John's windmill, identical and unimportant except for his contribution to the whole?

Gabriel's discontent grew as the evening wore on. Once he had loved to dance to the reedy scrape of fiddles and flutes, to spin and dip and laugh as if without a care in the world. But tonight the music grated on his nerves. His steps became gradually clumsier, and his grip on Susanne's fingers tightened unconsciously until at last she pulled them away with a little cry of exasperation, stepping back and stomping her foot.

"What is it, Gabriel?" she demanded.

Taken by surprise, he could only shake his head. The musicians continued to play, but several of the dancers slowed, watching them curiously. He lifted his arms and stepped toward her, but she backed away, hands clenched firmly at her sides.

"Is it her?" Susanne asked callously. "Is that who you've been pining for all evening?"

"There are others watching," Gabriel said evenly. "We should dance." He advanced, she retreated.

"Go to her, Gabriel, if that is who you wish to be with."

"Sacre," he breathed. "You are stubborn. Do not be foolish where so many can see you."

Susanne sneered at that. "I am not the foolish one. Go to her, if you can find her."

She whirled and fled, leaving Gabriel standing in the middle of the crowd, arms still lifted. Someone laughed, and Gabriel's face reddened. He lowered his hands and for a moment just stood there, until someone else said—"Go after her, young one."—as if he were an idiot without sense enough to come in out of the rain. Woodenly he followed her through the crowd, the good-natured laughter of the dancers pelting his shoulders.

He paused outside the circled carts to take a deep, calming breath. The breeze coming off the lake cooled the hot flush of his cheeks but did nothing to soothe his humiliation. Against the lighter surface of the water, he caught a glimpse of a skirted figure moving away from the camp at a run, and knew it was Susanne. He stood a moment in indecision, knowing he should go after her, that this was Sioux country, after all, and that a woman of the *bois brûle* would make a fine prize for some skulking Yankton or Santee warrior. But in that moment of hesitation, opportunity was lost.

Wearily Gabriel sank into the tall grass and put his back against the wheel of a hunter's cart. The music continued uninterrupted behind him, the stamp of the dancers' feet on the hard sod becoming a steady, insistent vibration thrumming along his spine.

Leaning back into the rough, unshaven spokes of the rawhide-bound wheel, he didn't move at all when Celine and Pike materialized out of the darkness, pausing like thieves on the rim of firelight spilling over the carts. Celine put a hand on Pike's chest and spoke too softly for Gabriel to hear. Then she hurried away, skirting the circled carts while Pike watched her hungrily. After a couple of minutes he started toward the camp, leading the bay Big John had given him by its reins. He stopped when he spotted Gabriel. Their gazes locked but neither man spoke, and after a few seconds Pike moved on, disappearing around the curve of carts toward Big John's fire.

Chapter Twelve

Indian Summer, the *métis'* Little Summer of St. Luke, was fading rapidly. Big John could smell it on the breeze that rolled in from the dry, treeless plains to the west. He could see it in the fading blue of the sky, and in the browning of the leaves still clinging stubbornly to the otherwise naked trees that grew in the glens and parks along Chain of Lakes.

He could feel it in his own body, as well, in the pop and creak of his joints whenever he knelt or stood, and in the effort it took for him to climb aboard his long-legged roan every morning. From time to time as the days progressed he would glance to the northwest, where the seasonal changes would originate in their own good time, but so far the skies there remained clear, the winds comfortable, if no longer quite as warm as they had been only a few days before.

Big John had ranged well north of the lake today, and was slowly making his way back through the rolling hills. Hunting had been good, and he had a doe draped across the roan's flanks, already gutted.

The roan stopped suddenly, arching its neck and blowing loudly. About twenty feet in front of them a rattlesnake slithered onto the trail. It paused when the roan stomped a hoof in fright, then quickly moved on. Big John waited patiently, following the snake's progress by the slight sway of the tall grass. When it was clear of the trail, he urged the roan forward. The stallion balked at first, then moved out fast, skipping wide around the spot where the snake had disappeared.

Chain of Lakes had turned out to be snaky this year. Not as bad as Devil's Lake, which some said was named after the whirring-tailed serpents, but bad enough. Two years ago a *métis* child had been bitten by a rattler at Devil's Lake and died, and a few years before that a woman had been bitten on the hand while gathering wood and lost four of her fingers. More often than not, it was one of the stock that was bitten. The oxen seemed especially susceptible, maybe one being bitten badly enough to die every couple of years. The ponies were either quicker or more attuned to the big rattlers, and able to shy away from them before being struck.

Big John stayed with the trail until it neared the lake, then put the roan up a steep incline on his left. Halting on top, he stared down at the sprawling *métis* camp, noting its strengths as well as its weaknesses. It bothered him that they were holed up in such a bowl. It made them vulnerable to long-range rifle fire and arrows that could be lobbed inside the perimeter of carts from nearby hilltops. Yet it wasn't a bad location, either. There was plenty of water and good sun-cured grass for the stock. And they desperately needed the meat the hunters were bringing in daily. Hallet's bull was the only buffalo they'd found so far, and they all knew it would be a long push from Chain of Lakes to where they'd likely find the herds. It would take a couple more days to dry the deer meat already brought in, but Big John was hoping that they would be able to pull out on the morning of the third day. He thought they would all breathe a little easier when they finally abandoned the rugged country surrounding the lakes.

Putting the roan over the crest of the hill, Big John started down the slope toward camp. He waved to Little John McKay, standing watch on a neighboring hill, but noted with annoyance that the other hills were empty, and that only a handful of men were visible at the camp. Guiding his mount through a gap in the carts, he dismounted at his own fire.

Isabella was embroidering on the jacket she had made for Gabriel. She laid it aside and came over as he started loosening the bindings on the deer. "A doe," she said, smiling approvingly. "Its meat will be tender and good to eat."

She would have been just as admiring of a tough, old mossy-horned buck, Big John knew, praising its size, or the rack that she would use for some tool or buttons, or the hide that would make fine leather. He pulled the doe from the roan's back and dropped it on the ground next to Isabella's drying rack.

Glancing around the camp, he said: "Where's Alec?"

Busying herself with the doe, Isabella shook her head.

"Is he with the herd?"

Again, she shook her head.

His eyes narrowing suspiciously, Big John said: "And where would the lad be, if he's not about or with the herd? Answer me, woman."

"He hunts."

"On foot?"

"He took the spotted pony." She looked up pleadingly. "He is thirteen, McTavish. It hurts him to be treated as a boy."

"Aye, and would ye have me treat him as a thief? Ye know the penalty for that."

"*Non,* McTavish, but I gave him permission to ride the pinto. He would not have done so otherwise."

"I cannot believe ye'd do such a thing, Isabella, knowin' me feelin's on the matter. I've no wish to punish the lad, or make him feel small in the eyes of his friends, but I cannot allow him to ignore my word. By the Lord, I won't."

Isabella lowered her eyes, then bent silently over the deer.

Big John turned a full circle. "Where's the lass?"

Once more, Isabella shook her head. "I don't know."

"She should be helpin' ye."

When Isabella didn't reply, Big John sighed. "Well, I've been needin' to speak with her for a while. I guess now's my chance." He moved alongside the roan, then paused with his hands resting on the pad saddle. "I'll send her back here when I'm finished. 'Tis time she learned the ways of skinnin' and butcherin' and such, if she's to be any help with the buffalo."

"Celine refuses to learn anything, and only mocks those who try to teach her." Isabella's knife slowed, then quickened. "She talks to herself, as her mother did."

Big John flinched, but didn't turn around. "And where would ye be gettin' such a notion as that?"

"I have walked in front of her all the way from the Tongue River, and not ridden off with my friends every morning on a fancy runner."

Her abruptness startled him. Hesitantly he said: "Ye've heard her do this?"

Isabella nodded.

"Damn me, then, for bein' a fool," his said softly.

She cast him a worried look. "Too much she reminds me of Angelique. I fear for her."

"Aye, 'tis a burden I wouldn't wish on any woman, or man, for that matter." He took a moment to collect himself, then wearily swung a leg over his saddle. He was aware of Isabella watching him, and wanted to say something to reassure her, but no words came to mind and he finally reined away in silence.

He found Celine among the trees on the north shore of the lake, and pulled up within the shelter of a towering oak to watch. At first he thought there was someone with her, perhaps reclining in the tall grass, but after a couple of minutes he realized she was alone, and the feelings that produced were like hands reaching inside him to squeeze every organ in his body. She appeared to be in argument with someone, but it was the long pauses in between, as if she were listening intently to an opposing point of view, that brought a chill to his spine.

Had it been this way with Angelique? he wondered sickly. *Had others seen her as he now saw Celine? Isabella thought so, but, if that were true, then why hadn't he noticed it himself? How was it possible for a sighted man to be so blind?*

She had been French, Angelique, the daughter of old Pierre Menard of Montreal, a partner in the North West Company who had privately financed Big John's first solo expedition into the *pays sauvage.* It was during the winter Big John had spent in Montreal, putting together his outfit, that he first met her. She was a bonny within a family of beautiful women, seventeen years old and fashionably rebellious, given to pouts and melancholy huffs and long, sad faces. But it was only with Big John that she had ever truly defied her family. After her death, he sometimes wondered if part of her attraction to him had been her father's stern admonition against involvement with a trader, a Scotsman, and an unenthusiastic Protestant, at that. On even rarer occasions, he wondered if he would have been as determined to have her if not for the same obstacles.

They had eloped in the spring, married in a civil ceremony by a local magistrate, then joined the annual brigade of freight canoes—the huge *canots des maîtres,* each shipping as much as six tons of cargo and passengers—for the first leg of their journey to the Red River.

Almost from the beginning, Big John had recognized the magnitude of their mistake. Angelique hated the *pays sauvage.* She saw no beauty in the vast forests and crystalline waters of the north country, and the mosquito-ridden sloughs and flat bleakness of the Red River Valley itself had impressed her even less. Big John's tiny cabin at the forks of the Tongue and Pembina Rivers had reminded her of the living quarters her father provided for the stablemen at their summer home, and she had been appalled by the abandonment of the mixed-bloods at their celebrations—the shouting, drinking, dancing, fighting, gambling, and romance that sometimes went on for days.

Angelique never made any effort to adapt to the valley or its life-embracing mode of work and play. She shunned every offer of friendship, never hosted a gathering, and attended as few as possible. She lived only to return to Montreal the following summer, but that dream had been shattered with the winter express. With the mail had come a letter from her father that she'd never shared. It was only over the course of years that Big John was able to extract bits and pieces of its content.

The exact wording had gone into the fireplace, with Angelique standing pale and shaken before it, but the essence had revolved around religion—her lack of a proper marriage in the eyes of the Catholic Church, and the spiritual illegitimacy of their unborn child, conceived even before they'd reached Fort William. Under such circumstances an annulment was impossible.

Apparently so was forgiveness, by either the Church or her family, although in time Big John came to realize it was the Church's repudiation that affected her most. Angelique had become convinced her soul was lost forever, and, after that, nothing else seemed to matter.

Not even their daughter.

Yet Big John had loved her, and he thought she might have loved him in her own way. And there had been some good times, at least a few. Angus Gilray had been with them then, his own small cabin and the hide lodge where he and his family normally slept standing where St. Joseph now stood, and there had been music and laughter and, for him, hope for the future in spite of his wife's discontent. A false hope, he'd ultimately come to realize. In the end, the Church had destroyed that as it had destroyed Angelique.

With a heavy heart, Big John heeled his roan into the sunlight. Celine ceased her conversation as soon as she saw him, watching his approach with suspicion. He halted while still some distance away and dismounted. "Good afternoon to ye, lass," he said, affecting a cheery tone. "Fancy meetin' ye here."

She nodded cautiously. "Hello."

Letting the stallion's reins fall, he approached with care. "Are ye alone?"

"Yes."

"Well, no harm in that as far as I'm concerned, though ye need to be mindful of the whirly-tails, for they're plentiful hereabouts. And the Sioux. 'Tis best ye not wander too much farther from the caravan than ye are right here, I'm thinkin'."

Celine greeted that with silence, her eyes unblinking as she stared at him.

Stopping a few feet away, Big John butted his rifle to the ground. "I heard ye speakin', lass," he said gently, "but I don't see anyone about." He paused expectantly, but she didn't respond. "Well, 'tis a fine day to be alone, I suppose, and no harm in talkin' to yeself, either." He cast her a sidelong glance but could tell nothing from her expression. "I . . . I came to speak with ye, Celine. 'Pears like 'tis a thing we've neglected, ye and me, what with the hunt and all, and I was wantin' to . . . just to . . ."—he made a vague gesture with his hand—"talk."

Celine said: "Can I ride your horse?"

"The roan?"

She nodded.

"Well, now, I'm not so sure about that. He's a stallion, ye see, and can be wicked with his hoofs and teeth if ye're not watchful-like around 'im. He requires an experienced hand, and I don't think ye're up to that just yet."

"Then can I ride one of the cart ponies?"

"I don't see any harm in that, and 'tis a good time for it with the weather bein' mild like it is. Aye, lass, ye can, and with me blessin', though I'd feel better if ye were to take Gabriel or one of the others with ye, in case of trouble."

"Gabriel?" She made a face.

"He's a capable lad, and handy to have around when trouble pops up."

"Gabriel doesn't like me."

"Oh, I think ye're wrong about that, I surely do."

But Celine seemed certain. "He does not. Perhaps the American could accompany me?"

"Pike?" Big John frowned. "I think I'd rather ye ride with Gabriel, if ye don't mind so awful much. I'll talk to the boy, ask him to do it."

She shrugged indifferently. "Why did you send me away?"

Embarrassed, Big John lowered his eyes. "Well, I don't rightly have an answer to that, although I wish I did, and that it was simple-like so that it made sense to the both of us." In his mind he saw her again as she had been on that misty morning when he'd sent her East—a tiny wisp of a child, eyes big and sad, not understanding. He sighed heavily, his heart breaking. "I thought I was doin' right by ye, girl, I'll swear to that. I sent ye to ye ma's people, thinkin' they'd care for ye proper-like." He looked up, meeting her gaze with effort. "I didn't think they'd send ye on to a . . . to a convent. I'd hoped they'd keep ye and raise ye to be a fine young lass like they did ye ma." He watched her closely but her face remained frighteningly unresponsive, her eyes fixed on his, yet distant and cold.

"I wrote ye. Did ye get my letters?"

She shook her head.

He nodded with resignation. He'd written only twice after learning that Pierre had refused to accept his papally illegitimate granddaughter into his home. His first dispatch had gone to the old man, offering to pay for Celine's board at the convent where

Pierre had exiled her. The second he'd sent to Celine, telling her she could come home any time she wished. When he didn't receive a reply, he had been content, perhaps even eager, to let it drop.

"Aye, well, I did," he said lamely. "Write ye, that is."

"But you still haven't told me why."

Big John looked away. "I. . . ." He shook his head.

"I hated the convent. The sisters were cruel. They beat me regularly and made me eat horrible foods. They called me a bastard child of the wilderness, and told me my mama would spend eternity in hell for her sin. They locked me in a tiny room with no light or bed or blankets, and made me work like a slave to pay my way." She paused, her face still maddeningly vacant, then added the *coup de grâce* with the finesse of an experienced swordsman. "Why did you send me there, Papa? Did you truly hate me that much?"

He took a deep, ragged breath, then let it go. "I don't know, child. I suppose I blamed ye, like a damnable fool. Blamed ye for what wasn't ye fault, for sure." He ducked his head, nearly smothering in shame, his voice hoarse with despair. "I failed ye, lass, the same way I failed ye ma. I don't know how I'll ever be makin' that up to ye, but. . . ."

Abruptly Celine started to walk away. "I wish to be alone now," she called. "I like it here, don't you? It is so peaceful. It reminds me of Vermont."

Lifting his tear-streaked face, Big John could only watch her go.

Isabella had the doe quartered by the time he returned, and was slicing thin sheets of meat from the shoulder to jerk. She'd constructed her drying stage between the two meat carts, and was smoking the wide strips of venison over a low fire to keep the flies away.

Big John unsaddled the roan, then picketed the stallion on grass outside the carts, where he could keep an eye on him. Coming back to camp, he sat down cross-legged beside a cart and plucked a blade of grass for chewing.

"Did you find her?" Isabella asked.

"Aye."

She set her knife aside and went to the hooped cart, returning a minute later with Big John's stubby, thumb- and knuckle-polished dudeen and leather tobacco pouch. "Smoke," she told him. "It will make you feel better."

Big John smiled appreciatively. "Ye're a good woman, Isabella. Angus was a lucky man."

"Angus Gilray is dead," Isabella said curtly, turning back to her work.

"Well, sure," Big John said hesitantly. "Killed by the Pawnees, or so his powder horn says."

"Angus Gilray is dead. Angelique is dead. Both are dead."

Big John eyed her uncertainly, waiting for her to go on. "Aye?" he ventured after a pause.

Without looking up, she said: "Father Denning says we live in sin."

"Denning!" Big John's lips curled in disdain. "And what would the good Father know of our life on the Tongue?"

"He knows what he hears in confession. There I must hide nothing."

Big John's face reddened. "Ye told him, then?"

Isabella nodded.

"By the Lord, woman, 'twas none of his business!"

"It was confession," she replied stubbornly.

"Then did ye tell him a man needs to . . . and a woman, too, by God."

"Father says that is no excuse."

"Aye, and what would the good Father know of such deeds,

him bein' celibate and all?"

"He represents the one true God," she retorted. "His wisdom is guided by our Heavenly Father's hand, and is not to be questioned by such as us."

"Bah! His wisdom is guided by narrow-minded men consumed with a passion for power. Denning needs to mind his own business, and ye need to curb ye confessions to true sins."

"I know what sin is, McTavish." She straightened, clutching a foot-wide section of meat in one hand, her bloody knife in the other. "Crebassa was my first husband. He was killed when his pony stumbled in the middle of a hunt. Angus Gilray was my second husband. He did not return from the prairies."

Big John waited for her to say more, but she seemed content with the point she'd made. Taking the meat to the stage, she draped it over a length of rawhide rope, then returned to the doe to start another cut.

In the silence that followed, Big John filled his pipe reflectively. What Isabella wanted came as no real surprise, he supposed. They had been nearly the same as man and wife for almost a decade now. He knew it wasn't the legal recognition she craved so much as religious sanctification. Her faith had strengthened in the years since the permanent arrival of priests to the valley, and what had been easy to ignore ten years ago wasn't as easy now.

Still, he knew, as she did, that what she wanted was impossible. His own religion—or lack of religion—would stand in the way of that. The Church would never condone Isabella's marriage to someone who so openly rejected its teachings, and his own feelings toward the Catholic faith ran too contrary to change. Yet it touched him deeply that she had voiced her desire, or came as close to it as she likely ever would.

A group of horsemen appeared from the east, riding pell-mell toward the caravan. Recognizing the pinto among them, Big

John stood and set his pipe and tobacco pouch aside.

Laughing uproariously, the boys entered the camp with their ponies at a dead run, scattering dogs and children and scolding women. They pulled their horses down in a dirt-showering slide, then leisurely began to break apart. The broad smile on Alec's face disappeared when he saw Big John.

"Hello, Big John," Alec said, drawing rein just out of reach. He looked ready to yank the pinto around and flee if he had to. "I did not have to help with the herd today, so I decided to hunt."

"So I see," Big John replied. "And did ye have any luck at it?"

Alec shook his head. "Isidore shot an eagle, but it fell in the lake and could not be retrieved."

Big John nodded carefully. He was angry enough to strike the boy, but knew he would only look like a fool if he attempted it and failed. Alec knew it, too, and a cocky smile crossed his face. "I think maybe I will hunt buffalo this year after all, Big John. The spotted pony is fast. Only Isidore's sorrel is faster."

"Faster than me own roan, do ye think?"

Alec's face sobered. He shook his head.

"Or Charlo's white one?"

Suspiciously he shook his head again.

"Or Breland's black runner?"

This time the boy made no reply at all.

"Lad, unless ye're willin' to steal every horse in camp and leave the men to ride their oxen, ye'd best be gettin' off yon pony, and be quick about it, too."

Cautiously Alec lifted his reins. "The spotted pony is mine, Big John."

"No, lad, the horse belongs to me. I traded old McBeth an ox harness and a cartload of firewood for him. Ye remember that, don't ye?"

"You said I could ride him."

"And now I'm sayin' ye can't. Get down, boy."

Alec just stared, his jaw thrusting out stubbornly.

" 'Tis best ye make this easy on yeself."

"I will buy him from you."

"He's not for sale. Now get down."

Alec looked like he wanted to cry, but, before it could go any further, Isabella called—"McTavish!"—and pointed north with her chin.

Following the direction of her nod, he saw Little John McKay riding toward the camp at a jarring gallop. Big John spun to the carts. "Get ye fusil, woman, and ye, too, Alec. Tie that spotted horse tight and be ready to fight if we have to."

Grabbing his rifle, Big John hurried to the gap in the carts where McKay was heading. His gaze skipped worriedly to the roan, the trees beyond, but he saw only children at play, and the stallion was picking leisurely at the tall grass. The handful of hunters who hadn't gone out that day were also converging on the gap. With a twinge of annoyance, Big John saw Breland among them.

McKay slowed when he reached the base of the hill where he'd been keeping guard. He was pointing to a trail that came out of some trees to the northeast. Just coming into sight was Charlo, bare-chested on his white runner. A man riding double behind him wore his shirt.

"That's Patterson he's found," Breland said, stopping beside Big John, then he laughed. "And nearly naked, too."

McKay and Charlo rode into camp together, but lanky Jim Patterson slid off the back of the white horse before they reached the carts, tugging embarrassedly at the hem of Charlo's shirt.

"Hello, Charlo!" Breland called, grinning. "What's that you've found today?"

Charlo smiled. "All kinds of prizes on the prairie this year, Joseph."

"Jim, are you considering a kilt like Big John's fancy plaid one?" Charles Hallet asked innocently.

"Nay tae that, Mister 'Allet, 'n' I'd thank 'ee nae tae bring it oop ag'in, though 'tis tae Big John I owe me thanks for such a predicament, no doubt." He turned an accusatory glare on Big John.

Big John's smile faded. "I usually know when I've caused a man any trouble, Jimmy."

"Ye've caused a barrelful this time, I'd say."

" 'Tis best ye be spillin' it, then."

"Spill it!" Patterson's brogue turned thick as porridge. " 'Tis naught left tae spill, I tell 'ee! Took it all, they did. Me 'orse 'n' gun 'n' the clothes offen me back!"

"Who, man? Who caught ye and stripped ye like fowl for the spit?"

"One Who Limps, Big John. The Chippewa that swore tae 'ave ye scalp. Ye 'n' that American."

Chapter Thirteen

Pike knew something was up as soon as he rode into camp, and reined in behind a cluster of half-breeds gathered around McTavish and a man wearing only a bright lavender shirt.

Spying him above the heads of the crowd, McTavish offered a spiritless greeting. "Ye've returned at a fittin' time, Mister Pike." He inclined his head toward the half-breed standing beside him. "It seems Mister Patterson here has bumped into a friend of ours from the prairies. One Who Limps, brother to Wolf Slayer, who I shot the mornin' ye joined us."

" 'N' others," Patterson chimed in. "Crow Horse was with 'em, sure, 'n' Otter Nose 'n' Taon 'n' Finds 'Is Lodge, plus some I did nae recognize. A baker's dozen, tae number 'em plain."

"Thirteen, then, that's wantin' our hides, Mister Pike. What do ye say to that?"

"Why, hell, I say we go see if they can take 'em," Pike replied, leaning forward over the broad horn of his Mexican saddle.

McTavish frowned. "Are ye suggestin' we take the fight to them?"

"I ain't keen on sitting around here waiting for them to make the first move."

McTavish scratched his chin thoughtfully. "Well now, I have to say I like ye idea." He smiled. "What is it Murphy says? The hair of the bear? 'Tis that, sure, ye've got, and aye to ye proposal, too. I came to hunt buffalo, not to watch me backside like a lad with a boil."

Scattered laughter greeted McTavish's remark, but it was quickly terminated by Breland's emphatic: "No!" He squared around to face the older man. "That is not your decision to make, Big John. A captain must call for a vote." His green eyes sparked dangerously. "You know that, even if René doesn't."

McTavish started to reply, but Breland cut him off with a slashing gesture of his hand.

"It is true. René hunts when he is needed here, and the caravan sits unguarded. It was not René who sent Little John to the hills to watch. It was me."

McTavish looked stunned. "Are ye sayin' the man left camp without assignin' the watch?"

Breland sneered. "Leadership frightens him like a rabbit under the shadow of a hawk. We must have another election. There is no other way."

McTavish was silent a moment, then he nodded. "Ye may be right, Joseph, but first I'll talk to René. Tonight, when he gets in."

"Tonight is too late. We must have a captain today. A true captain."

Slowly McTavish lifted his gaze to meet Breland's hard stare, and an uneasy silence fell over the crowd. The old Scotsman's face had taken on a cast Pike had never seen before, and his dark eyes blazed. Yet his voice remained mellow, barely above a whisper. "Ye'll be lettin' it drop now, Joseph, and backin' off a mite, too."

Pike eased his hand along his rifle. For perhaps a minute, Breland stood rigidly, fists balled. Then he swayed back and loudly let go of his breath. "All right, Big John. Talk to René. Lead him by the hand like a child if you have to. But never again will I follow an unfit captain onto the prairies."

A muscle twitched in McTavish's cheek. Turning to Patterson, he said: "Ye'll need a pony and gun to replace those that was stolen from ye, Jimmy. What do ye say to the spotted horse Alec rides, and a fusil from me own supplies? Would that set right with ye?"

Patterson nodded swiftly. " 'Twould be only fair."

McTavish fixed Alec with a hard look. "Fetch the man his horse, lad."

Alec opened his mouth as if to protest, but McTavish cut him off. "I'm givin' the spotted horse to Patterson, Alec. Now go fetch it."

Mutely Alec turned to obey. Although several of the half-breeds began to drift away, Pike stayed, refusing to loosen his grip on his rifle.

In a quieter tone than before, Breland said: "We will meet tonight, Big John. The *bois brûles* must decide together how this new threat is to be dealt with."

McTavish nodded curtly. "Ye're right, of course, Joseph. Ye've been right more than once of late. Call the meetin' and we'll abide by whatever decision is made." He gave Pike a lop-sided grin. "*À la façon du pays,* Mister Pike. The way of the land. Can ye set for it?"

Pike cursed softly but nodded. "I reckon so."

"Good. Now if ye'll excuse me, I'd best be findin' Mister Patterson a gun and some clothin'." He headed for his carts, and the half-breeds who lingered behind stepped quickly out of his way.

Breland followed as far as the edge of the crowd. Stopping at the bay's side, he caught Pike off guard with his next words.

"Big John McTavish is maybe the greatest man I have ever known. It is because of him, and a handful of others like him, that the *bois brûles* have become men to reckon with in the valley, the equal of any Montreal or English merchant. The young ones think we are better, and that it has always been that way, but the older ones, myself included, remember when a half-breed was little better than a dog that belonged to neither the Indian or the white world. McTavish helped change that for us. He helped us understand that we belong to ourselves."

"Is that why you're trying to knock him out of his saddle now?"

Breland shook his head. "No one will ever forget what Big John has done for us. I will see to that to my dying day. But it is time once more for the *bois brûles* to move forward as a people. To do that, we must untangle ourselves from the influences of outsiders. Even from men like Big John, because we will never truly be free as long as one white man or one Indian remains to affect our every decision. For my people, Pike, I would destroy Big John, even though it would lay waste to my own heart to do so."

Watching McTavish drag a canvas-wrapped bundle from the rear of his hooped cart, Pike suddenly grinned. "Breland," he said cheerfully, "I wouldn't be too sure about destroying Big John McTavish any time soon. Might be you ought to consider just trying to bend him a mite."

Laughing, Breland conceded: "You may be right, my friend. You may well be right."

Big John heaved into the saddle. Around the camp, others were doing the same, although many of them were lingering for a final word with their families, leaning from their skimpy pad saddles to kiss their wives and daughters good bye, or to shake hands with sons and friends. Ten men would accompany Big John and Pike in search of the Chippewas who had surprised and robbed Jim Patterson the day before. Patterson had been among the first to volunteer. He sat the spotted horse now alongside Pike, waiting for the others to join them.

Big John could tell it bothered Pike to have so many others

dealing themselves in, but the *métis* had voted overwhelmingly to face this problem as they faced all others—as a people. It didn't matter that one of them was an American. Pike rode with them. For the *métis,* that was enough.

They'd discussed other things last night as well, and although René Turcotte still captained the hunt, a solid guard of twenty men would remain with the carts at all times, and no fewer than six would watch from the hills surrounding the camp. They would continue such vigilance until they left the broken country bordering the lakes and returned to the more familiar terrain of the open plains.

Dawn's gray light was beginning to brighten when Charles Hallet finally rode over to join Big John. He looked cold, bundled up in a heavy, blue blanket coat with the hood pulled over his head and tied beneath his chin. He wore buffalo-hide mittens and leggings of the same material, although with the hair turned in rather than out. His breath was a thin cloud that tinted his dark beard with curling streamers of mist.

Others began to gather slowly around them, a quiet and grim-faced lot. As the light strengthened it revealed a land sparkling with frost. Although gauzy patches of fog draped the sides of the hills, the sky overhead was clear. Camp smells—damp-wood smoke and bubbling stews, the pungent odor of ox dung and green deer hides drying in cottonwood frames—were sharpened by the chilly dawn air.

Sitting his big roan, Big John drank it all in with a clarity honed by the prospect of a coming battle. He was careful to keep his gaze focused on the far side of the camp, and not glance in the direction of his own carts, where he knew Isabella would be fussing with the breakfast dishes while Alec and Gabriel and Celine hovered somberly nearby. Big John was afraid that if he looked, he wouldn't be able to stop the tears that wanted to squeeze past his lids and course down his weathered cheeks.

When the hunters who would ride with them were mounted and assembled, Big John heeled his roan toward the gap Breland had created by pushing one of the empty meat carts out of the way. Turcotte shuffled forward to see them off, his expression sullen. The words of Breland and some of the others from the night before still stung the goateed half-blood, yet Big John felt no sympathy for him. Turcotte said: "We will remain here two more days, Big John, then we must leave."

"Understood, though I doubt we'll be gone that long. If 'tis a fight they're truly wantin', they won't be hard to find. Look for us back any time after noon today."

Turcotte rolled his shoulders indifferently, then stepped aside. Big John urged the roan through the gap and the others filed through behind him. Breland nodded or spoke to each man as he passed, then rolled the cart back in place.

They skirted the shore of the lake until they came to a trail winding away from the basin. Here, Patterson took the lead, moving fast with the rest of them, strung out single file behind. As the sun came up, it burned away the scattered pockets of fog, but the air remained cool and the frost lingered on the northern slopes. They reached the spot where the Chippewas had accosted Patterson shortly after midmorning, the story plain to read in the tall, dry grass. After setting the lanky mixed-blood free, the Indians had ridden west. Pointing the roan's nose along the Chippewas' trail, Big John lifted him into a lope.

Noon passed and the land began to change. The grass grew shorter as they left the tall grass prairies behind. The hills leveled off and the valleys became wider, shallower. The woods thinned out along the streams to become small, scattered groves, although patches of scrub willow continued to flourish on the sandbars.

With the day's waning, the sun began to shine straight into their eyes, nearly blinding them as it neared the horizon. Big John slowed to a walk, a feeling of uneasiness coming over him as the land ahead seemed to disappear in the searing light. He'd removed his coat at the noon break, and now he could feel the dampness of sweat growing beneath his arms, a clamminess coming to the palms of his hands. When the time came, he pulled the roan to a stop, and, even though he couldn't have said why he did it, he wasn't surprised when the Chippewas appeared suddenly from behind a swell in the land about one hundred yards ahead, like board figures jerked upright by strings.

The *métis* fanned out as they had done the week before, when meeting old Tall Cloud and his band. Casually butting his double-barreled rifle to his thigh, Big John squinted into the sun. In its brilliance he was unable to count the Indians before him, but he thought Patterson's claim of thirteen would be close.

No one spoke, and for a long time the only sounds were those of their horses, blowing impatiently or stamping a hoof against the hard ground. Although Big John sensed the tension in the men around him, he could manage only a weary dread within himself.

"Well," he said finally, " 'tis come to this, has it?" He nudged the roan forward, and, even though he would have preferred to meet One Who Limps alone, he offered no protest when Pike jogged his bay alongside.

From the Chippewa contingent a wiry, bare-chested man with long, raven-hued hair rode out to meet them, a second warrior at his side. They met halfway in between and stopped with the noses of their horses almost touching.

In English, but accompanying his words with sign so that all might follow, Big John said: "Greetings, One Who Limps and

Crow Horse. I am Big John McTavish of the Tongue River, and a friend to the Chippewas for many seasons, as well as an enemy to their enemy, the Sioux. I've been told, One Who Limps, that ye're blamin' me for the death of ye brother Wolf Slayer, what tried to kill my brother, Mister Pike, here. It's been said that ye've blackened ye face against me, and have come seekin' me scalp. Can such be true?"

One Who Limps replied in Chippewa, as well as with his hands. "It is true that Big Man was once our friend," he began, using the name Big John had been given many years before by the Chippewas, when he first came among them to trade. "But this can be true no longer, for Big Man has killed my true brother, who was the son of my father. For this, Big Man must pay in blood, or there shall be war between my people and the half-breeds who have adopted Big Man as their own, even though his blood is white, and therefore corrupted."

A taut smile played across Big John's face at this insult to his place in the valley, but he didn't interrupt, and One Who Limps did not pause.

"My people would not like to rub out the half-breeds because even though their strength has been diluted by their white trader fathers, they are still of the Ojibway nation. As the coyote is a weaker brother to the wolf, so are the half-breeds lesser brothers to the Ojibway. All would agree it would be a sad thing for a stronger brother to kill his weaker sibling. This, One Who Limps would not like to see."

"Aye to that, ye cross-eyed son-of-a-bitch," Big John replied pleasantly, though careful to leave the latter part of his statement out of his sign. He could tell from the narrowing of One Who Limps's eyes, however, that the young warrior understood, just as he could tell that Crow Horse did not, and that he had only read the partial reply of Big John's hands.

" 'Tis not right for brothers to fight one another, and I'd not want to see it happen here," Big John continued with barely a pause. " 'Tis a thing between me and yeself, One Who Limps, this matter over ye brother's death, and I came to fight ye that way, man to man, if ye have the courage for it. But if ye're naught but an old woman in ye heart, toothless and smellin' of shit, then maybe there would be someone else I could fight. Ye sister, perhaps?"

This time, he said it all with his hands, and there was a quick stirring among the Chippewas, a matching restlessness within the *métis* behind him. Big John heard the dull ratcheting of several weapons being cocked in both parties, and felt an icy chill worm down his spine. The moment hung in a delicate balance, and Pike didn't help matters any when he growled: "God dammit, McTavish, this is my fight, not yours."

"Ah, Mister Pike, but it is my fight, for 'twas me what killed young Wolf Slayer."

"No," Pike said stubbornly, glaring at One Who Limps. "This is between me and him."

Big John turned to him, eyes smoldering. "Listen to me, sir, and listen well. 'Tis neither me nor yeself I was thinkin' of when I challenged One Who Limps, but them that we left behind this mornin', the womenfolk and the wee ones. They're the ones that count most, and I'll bring 'em no grief if I can help it. Nor will I start a war I can prevent, even if it costs me me own life to stop it, though I'm not so old that I don't remember a trick or two." He paused, then added in a gentler tone: "I'm hopin' to end this thing here, if I can, and I'll ask ye to respect that. I will, now."

"Son-of-a-bitch," Pike said, then shook his head in defeat. "All right, but, if you lose, I'm gonna wade into that red bastard's hide like it was the finest kind of whiskey."

"No, Mister Pike, ye won't. If One Who Limps wins, then ye'll be fetchin' me carcass back for buryin', and seein' to the women . . . Isabella and the lass. Ye'll be runnin' the shaggies for me the same as if I lived and breathed, and cartin' the pemmican and robes that Isabella makes back to Pembina Post for Murphy. That's ye debt to me for the bay ye're ridin' and what supplies ye'll take with ye to the mountains afterward. I want no killin' beyond what's to happen here in the next few minutes."

"Jesus, McTavish."

"I'm askin' ye as my friend, Mister Pike."

Haughtily One Who Limps said in English: "McTavish is an old man. There is no honor in killing someone too old to defend himself."

"Then why'd ye track me down, ye bloody damn' fool!" Big John roared, spooking One Who Limps's horse so badly it almost threw him. Some of the *métis* laughed, but Big John kept his eyes on One Who Limps, his expression grim. "Ye'll no be backin' out of this so easy, lad," he said darkly. "Ye followed for blood, and 'tis blood ye'll have. Mine, or ye own."

He threw a leg over the roan's neck and slid nimbly to the ground, then handed his rifle, shooting bag, and powder horn to Pike. He let the roan's reins fall, knowing the horse was too well trained to wander far. The *métis* edged forward, as did the Chippewas. Within seconds Big John and One Who Limps were ringed by horsemen. One Who Limps's gaze darted swiftly around the circle. Then he, too, slid from his pony's back and handed his fusil, bag, and horn to Crow Horse.

"Big Man is a fool to fight a warrior as strong as One Who Limps," One Who Limps boasted in Chippewa. "But Big Man was also a strong warrior himself at one time. One Who Limps will honor Big Man's scalp, and place it above all others on his lance."

Big John drew the slim, ivory-handled dirk from its sheath above his right hip. One Who Limps pulled a heavy-bladed Hudson's Bay dagger. They approached slowly and began to circle. A deathly silence gripped those watching. Not even the ponies made a sound.

One Who Limps made the first thrust. Big John parried it easily. They made another complete circle, then One Who Limps tried again, lunging forward to bring his dagger up in an arcing blur that sliced the air where Big John had stood only an instant before. One Who Limps recovered and spun defensively. It took him a moment to become aware of the gash in his right arm. One Who Limps stared dumbly at the wound, then lifted his eyes to regard Big John's bloodied dirk in disbelief.

They circled again. One Who Limps feigned, but Big John just smiled. One Who Limps tried another thrust. Steel clicked loudly as their blades met, and Big John skipped to the side, slicing the flesh over One Who Limps's ribs.

One Who Limps appeared puzzled as he began another cautious revolution. Unconsciously he started to move back, but was stopped by a murmur of disapproval from the Chippewas. Then the confusion vanished from his face. One Who Limps was an honored warrior, and to be cut twice without having wounded in return was a blow to his pride. Big John knew One Who Limps would rather die than suffer the humiliation of not drawing blood from his opponent.

One Who Limps came forward in a rush, yelling loudly for the first time. Big John started to the right, then went left, but this time it was One Who Limps who proved quicker. At the last moment he countered his headlong rush, dodged Big John's awkward, backhanded slash, and drove the tip of his dagger into the soft flesh beneath the Scotsman's ribs.

Big John grunted sharply and skipped back. Grinning, One Who Limps settled into a defensive crouch. In a similarly protective stance, Big John switched the direction of their circling, making little curls in the air with the tip of his dirk. He ignored the pain in his side, the warm, liquid flow that crept toward his hip. The point of One Who Limps's dagger shone red as he thrust it tauntingly in front of Big John.

Big John advanced slowly, waving the bloodied dirk in its own sinuous reel. He feigned and One Who Limps countered. Big John feigned again; once more, the Chippewa jumped clear, taking no chances. They continued their deliberate orbit, probing warily with their knives as their blood dripped into the torn, dusty grass beneath their moccasins. It was One Who Limps who made the next offensive move, a quick, forward dash that Big John side-stepped. One Who Limps spun, slashing upward with his dagger. Big John's dirk flashed. They backed away, both knives dripping fresh blood.

A cut on Big John's shoulder welled blood through the ripped fabric of his shirt, burning like fire. But it was One Who Limps who suddenly pressed his arm across his stomach and staggered backward. He stared down at the gaping wound without immediate comprehension, then, with a dawning horror, his knees buckled and the dagger dropped from his fingers. He wrapped both arms over his stomach against the push of intestines. Limbs quivering, he flopped to the ground, sitting bent forward with his legs splayed before him.

There was an angry murmuring from several of the Chippewas; the *métis* muttered a warning in return. Crow Horse slid from his pony's back and laid his weapons on the ground before going to One Who Limps's side.

Big John backed away slowly, his grip tight on the dirk. His chest was heaving and sweat sheened his face, dripping from the tip of his nose. Blood from the wound in his shoulder soaked his sleeve, but he made no effort to staunch it, nor did he acknowledge the puncture to his side. He watched stonily as Crow Horse eased One Who Limps onto his back, then gently pulled his arms away from his stomach. Crow Horse studied the wound intently for several minutes, poking tenderly at the raw, bleeding flesh, the purplish bulge of intestine. When he looked at Big John, his face was impassive, his voice without emotion.

"His intestines are not injured," Crow Horse announced in Chippewa. "I think he will live, unless you wish to kill him now."

Big John made the sign for *no,* and turned away. He saw Pike sitting his bay close by, holding the reins to his roan. Making his way to the stallion, he took the reins, then mounted awkwardly but without help. A couple of Chippewas came forward to help Crow Horse bind One Who Limps's wounds. Big John detected no animosity in their actions.

To Pike, who hadn't understood Crow Horse's words, Big John said: "The man's guts are not cut, and, with luck, he'll live, though I fear he'll be crippled. I'm not so sure I shouldn't end it here, as Crow Horse offered."

"Is that what he was saying?" Pike asked.

"Aye, finish the deed proper-like, and take the scalp if I so desired. 'Twould be within me rights."

"If you don't, he's liable to come looking for you again someday. That belly of his is gonna sag like an old woman's dugs for the rest of his life. That ain't a thing he'll soon forget."

"True enough, but a man wearies of killin', Mister Pike, and I've done my share of it over the years. I've no urge to do it again today. Let him live in peace, if he will, and meself as well."

Crow Horse stood as the others wrapped cloth around the long, horizontal cut in One Who Limps's stomach. Speaking to all, he said: "It is done, this thing between Big Man and One Who Limps. We will take One Who Limps home to his wife, and fight no more. On this, I have given my word."

Big John's relief was obvious to all. "Crow Horse speaks wisely," he said loudly. "One Who Limps was a worthy foe and a brave man. There's no dishonor to anyone this day." Taking his rifle from Pike, he calmly reined away. When they had moved out of earshot of the Chippewas, he added: " 'Twas a vale not far back. I'd like to get there, at least, before I fall off my horse."

"We can do that," Pike said.

"Well, we'll give it a try, anyway," Big John agreed weakly.

Lying on her back, Celine stared at the interlacing branches overhead. They reminded her of black cobwebs strung against the star-lit sky. The sound of an occasional falling leaf spinning into the shadows around her and the murmur of the wind in the limbs seemed to deaden the rustle of dried grass as she rocked rhythmically.

Peter, her beloved Peter, used to rock her this way. In fresh wheat straw ripe with the odor of harvest, the chattering of the other girls as they went about their chores a sweet symphony in the background, they had made long, sweaty love in narrow, freshly cleaned stalls. Afterward they would lie side-by-side. With his mop of blond hair falling into his eyes, Peter would chew on a stem of straw while gazing at her, sometimes leaning forward to play its tip lightly across her breasts. He had deep blue eyes and a reckless laugh and arms that nearly crushed the breath from her.

It was his laughter that had ultimately betrayed them. Still, Celine had always thrilled to hear it, to know that it was her and her body that brought it forth.

In her heart of hearts she knew that sex was dirty, love a filthy lie, and that being a woman was the worst sin of all. Between her legs resided Satan's chalice, a siren's call heard only by the weaker of the male breed, those most undesirable. Hogs and sheep rutted, and succumbing to temptations of the flesh with Peter had reduced her to that level, the station of animals—a mindless, godless shell of blood and bone, her soul warped and blackened as if scorched by fire.

It was Sister Bernice who had made her recognize that truth, who had so vividly spelled out the wages of her sins, then saw to her punishment, for it was she who had found Celine and Peter in near nakedness in the barn. She who had hauled Celine back to the convent without giving her time to button up or straighten out, parading her for all to see. It was Sister Bernice, as well, who had locked her in the damp, windowless room at the rear of the convent with only a bucket for her waste and a single woolen blanket, a cell in the truest sense of the word, with a solid oak door Sister Bernice had slammed shut on her in September and not opened again until March, when she was sure the younger woman wasn't with child.

She was hell bound, Sister Bernice had assured her. Without redemption. *Like your mother,* she'd uttered in a reptilian hiss. *Just like your mother.*

It was true, God had confided later, the first time He came to her. They had stood together above Sister Bernice's crumpled form, the red blood seeping through her white cowl, the stained axe-head lying across her legs.

"Hell bound, Celine," God said. "Unless you cleave unto Me."

With a final, satisfied grunt, the half-breed rolled off of her. On his back, he tilted his head around to grin broadly in her direction, releasing the foul hammer of his breath against her face. The shadows were too thick to see the yellow and black checkering of his teeth, but she remembered them well enough, those and the small, piggish eyes, a nose somewhat askew, shaded with blackheads and broken capillaries. He was at least fifty years old, with a fat Chippewa wife waiting for him back at camp and four lazy sons he was absurdly proud of.

"You liked that, eh?" the half-breed asked.

Celine didn't reply. The putrid warmth of his breath continued to bathe the side of her face, the effect slightly nauseating.

"Me, I was god damn good, no?"

The breeze off the lake was cool on her bare thighs, and for some reason that made her think of Peter, blond and slim, his flesh in those places where the sun never touched him as white as freshly kneaded dough. But when she tried to picture his face, it was the half-breed's ugliness she saw, and she cried out in revulsion and turned away.

Jumping to his feet, the *métis* exclaimed: "You come to me, right? You remember that you come to me? You no tell Aggie, eh? God damn, she cut my balls off good for this. She would."

Celine lay curled on her side, staring into the dark mat of grass.

"Sacre bleu," the *métis* groaned. He grabbed his fusil in one hand, his powder horn and shooting bag with the other. "You no tell McTavish, either. That son-bitch kill me good. Quicker than Aggie, I think." He started to slink away, then paused. *"Sacre,"* he said softly. "You was good, really good, you know? Maybe we meet again?" He waited, then added: "I could bring you something maybe. Beads, or a good butcher knife? You would like a good butcher knife?"

Celine squeezed her eyes shut, but the tears seeped through her lids anyway. A sob broke from deep in her chest, startling in the quiet solitude under the trees.

"No," the *métis* groaned desperately. "*Non, cherie,* not so loud!"

But she couldn't help it. The tears kept coming and her sobs grew fuller. Her shoulders trembled and her stomach heaved, as if attempting to purge herself of this disgrace.

She didn't know when the half-breed—this brave *métis* guardian who had forsaken his post for a coy smile and a flirtatious toss of hair—left her. After a time, her tears began to dry, her sobs to subside. Eventually she rose and straightened her dress, brushing as much grass from her hair and clothing as she could find with her fingers. Standing, she thought the breeze blowing out of the west seemed suddenly colder, and she shivered. Across the corner of the lake, the camp was growing dark, the fires dying down as the half-breeds turned in. Smiling hesitantly, Celine went in search of her own blankets.

CHAPTER FOURTEEN

"Les Sioux! Les Sioux!"

Panic gripped the hearts of the *métis* as Pouliot's warning rolled down the bare flank of the knoll behind them. Leaping to their feet, the mixed-bloods scrambled for their ponies, hobbled up and down the shallow coulée where they had camped since Big John's duel with One Who Limps.

Big John ignored the pain that shot through his side as he struggled to stand. He watched Noel Pouliot slide down the steep knoll a couple of hundred yards away. At the bottom, a shaggy brown pony was jumping in fright, almost throwing itself in its hobbles. Pouliot stripped the rawhide restraints from the pony's forelegs, then threw himself into the saddle.

Behind Big John, Pike was hauling his bay and the roan runner into camp. He tossed the lead ropes to Big John to hang onto while he began saddling the horses. "Are you up to riding?" he asked, snatching Big John's quilled pad saddle from the grass.

"I am if it saves my scalp." He kept his voice calm, but his pulse was racing.

Pouliot came pounding into camp just as Hallet, Patterson, and a couple of others swung onto their horses. Pike finished saddling the roan and turned to the bay, flinging his heavy Mexican rig over the pony's back, grabbing for the cinch in one fluid motion.

"How many?" Hallet called as Pouliot brought his horse to a

sliding halt at the edge of the camp.

"Just one," Pouliot panted as if he'd made the run himself. "A wolf, I think, riding a dun horse."

Big John paused with a handful of the roan's mane in one hand, his foot half lifted for the stirrup. A wolf was a scout sent ahead of a war party to reconnoiter the enemy's position, but he'd never known a wolf to ride a horse. It made him too easy to spot. Quite often, in fact, they would drape themselves with a wolf's hide, then haunt the ridges around an enemy's camp on hands and knees, their imitation of the wild canine so realistic that from a distance it was all but impossible to tell them from the real thing.

Hallet had also paused at mention of a horse. "A wolf, Noel?"

"*Oui,* I saw him. He came from the timber to the south and trotted . . ."—his words slowed—"toward us."

Hallet's shoulders sank with relief. "Not a wolf," he said. "Not mounted."

"But Sioux, I am sure."

"From yon timber?" Patterson queried. " 'Tis a league, a' least, from where ee was sittin'."

"I saw him," Pouliot insisted.

"Sure, and none are arguin' that," Big John interjected. "Ye saw something, old friend, for ye eyes are sharp as a hawk's. But I'm thinkin' Charles is right, too. 'Twas not a Sioux."

"An elk!" Hallet exclaimed.

" 'Tis likely," Big John agreed, aware of Pouliot's defensiveness in the sullen darting of the half-blood's eyes. "I've seen 'em that way myself, elk with racks large enough to be mistaken from a distance for a man." He glanced at the circled hunters, most of them already mounted. "Is there one among ye who cannot say the same?"

Big John wasn't surprised when no one answered. In the thin prairie air, it was an easy mistake to make.

"I could stand for some fresh meat," Pike said into the silence following Big John's query. "I'm getting tired of pemmican."

"Aye to that," Patterson emphatically agreed, bringing broad smiles to the faces of several men.

"Well, Noel," Big John said to Pouliot, " 'Twas ye what spotted the bugger. What say we be off, cautious-like just in case, and have us a look-see?"

Pouliot shrugged, although Big John could tell his humiliation had been eased considerably. *"Oui,"* the mixed-blood said. "I am hungry for fresh meat, too."

"Will you ride with us, Big John?" Hallet asked.

"I think I will, Charles. I'm not ready to discount the possibility of Sioux just yet. I'll keep to my saddle until I know for certain, though I'll not join the chase, if 'tis an elk, after all."

Hallet nodded, and Patterson shouted: "Let's be after 'im, then!" He reined his pinto around to ride toward the low ridge over which Pouliot had spied the elk, although he kept his mount to a walk in consideration of Big John's wounds.

The cut on Big John's shoulder was already scabbing over, and he would suffer no permanent damage. It was the puncture wound to his side that worried him, for all that he tried to make light of it around the others. One Who Limps's dagger had gone in several inches just under his ribs, then made a slashing exit. Big John had lost a lot of blood in the fight, and even more on the ride here, where they'd stopped. He'd burned with a high fever throughout the dark hours of that first night, and even now felt weak as a half-drowned kitten. Only the possibility that Pouliot might have actually spied a hostile could have coaxed him into the saddle at this early point in his recovery, although he knew that, if it came to a running fight, he wouldn't last long. Just the act of mounting the roan, then holding the rambunctious stallion in check, was already making him dizzy.

They had camped in a broad, shallow vale, the land sloping

up at gentle angles on either side. On top, the country returned to normal, rolling and dusty and short-grassed, mostly treeless save for sparse groves of cottonwoods that dotted the meandering, summer-dry streams.

Letting their excitement get the better of them, Patterson, Pouliot, and the others soon pulled ahead. Only Pike and Hallet remained behind with Big John. They rode to the edge of the valley, then climbed out using an old buffalo trail cut into the sod. On top, they found the others waiting for them, smiling and chattering happily.

"An elk, Big John," Patterson confirmed, pointing to a larger river a couple of miles to the south, its banks thick with timber. " 'E ran in there when ee saw us."

"A big one," Pouliot added, his embarrassment already vanished in anticipation of the chase.

Big John squinted toward the trees lining the river, but the elk had already faded into the brush.

"It's been a long time since I've enjoyed the meat of an elk," Hallet said. He glanced at Big John. "Will you be all right, staying behind?"

"Aye, I will, Charles. Go on and get ye elk, then we'll start back for the caravan."

Hallet's concern was genuine. "Can you make it that far, Big John?"

"Not straight through, no, but the day's near gone already. An early camp tonight while I lay in my robes and let the rest of ye worry about the watches and I'll be fit enough."

Hallet grinned and Pouliot yipped shrilly.

"Sure'n be damned tae the bloody Chippewa what tried tae skewer our Mister McTavish!" Patterson cried. "I say 'twill take more'n a redskin's dagger tae put Big John underground." Then he whipped his horse around and raced down the long, gradual slope toward the distant river. The others followed. Only Big

John and Pike remained behind.

"Ye'll not be joinin' the chase?" Big John asked.

"I've shot elk before. It doesn't take nine men to do it."

"Aye, but look at 'em, Mister Pike, scamperin' for the chase like pups after a goose." He shook his head, smiling. " 'Tis the Indian blood that drives 'em so, that near makes the blood boil for the hunt or the fight, or so I've always believed."

Pike shrugged noncommittally. They were riding slowly after the galloping hunters, paralleling the valley they'd just vacated, though keeping back from its rim to avoid the deeper gullies. Well ahead of them, the *métis* were funneling into a coulée that would take them back to the valley they'd just left. From there they would ride to the river where the elk had disappeared, then fan out to make a slow sweep upstream, toward the big bull.

Halting his roan, Big John studied the river and the broad reach of rolling land to the west. "It occurs to me, Mister Pike, that there be too many to slip up on yon elk quiet-like, even with the wind in their favor. I'm bettin' he'll sniff 'em out before they get close and make a run for higher ground. 'Tis a prairie elk they're chasin', and he'll feel safer in the wide open, where he can run.

"If he breaks to the south, we'll never see 'im again, or taste a bite of his meat, but, if he comes north, there's a chance he'll cut up that smaller valley yonder." He nodded toward the low height of ground that separated the valley where they'd camped and the smaller one where Big John and One Who Limps had battled.

"Be a long shot, even then," Pike said.

"Aye, me own thinkin', too, but 'tis that or naught, for the bugger did not get a rack large enough to fool a man into thinkin' he was a Sioux by careless ways. We'd have to leave the horses behind, though not so far we couldn't get to 'em in a hurry, was there need."

Pike gave Big John a dubious glance. "You sure you're up to it?"

"Well, and sure, 'tis true enough I'm a mite banged up, but I suppose I have a touch of the hunter's blood in me own veins." He flashed a grin. "Aye, Mister Pike. 'Tis meat we'll be makin' if my hunch proves correct, and nothing lost, if not."

"Hell, let's go."

They hobbled their horses below the crest of the ridge and returned to the top on foot. Just over the far side, they came to an old, grassed-over buffalo wallow, and slipped into it, thrusting their rifles before them through the tall grass.

Big John didn't know why buffalo would occasionally desert a wallow completely, but sometimes they did. The plains were dotted with such shallow depressions where the shaggy brutes had broken the sod with their short, curving horns to create bowls of mud or dust, depending on the season. In these low-lipped craters, the bison would roll and kick and paw, coating themselves with whatever was available to generate a thin shield of armor against the biting stings of insects. In the spring they would roll to loosen their scratchy, shedding winter coats.

When a wallow was abandoned, a different species of grass gradually took over—taller, greener, coarser than the short prairie growths that surrounded it. Sometimes it sprouted wildflowers in its center like a small garden. Big John had always assumed such verdant growth was made possible by the heavy deposits of manure and urine left behind, leaving these circular pieces of earth richer and more adaptable to less hardy species, more inviting to wind-blown seeds or pods carried inland on the pelts of wandering fauna. Some called these patches of green fairy rings, and claimed they were brought into existence by the tiny, dancing feet of pixies, but Big John knew the only truth to that was the ingenuity of a mother's storytelling abilities to her children.

From the edge of the wallow, the two hunters had a clear view of the valley below them, and Big John saw immediately that Pike had been right to question their chances of a clean shot. The valley was wider than he remembered it, too broad for an accurate hit at much over halfway across. If the elk did come their way, it would have to climb the east side of the valley, or they wouldn't get a chance at it at all.

"*Wagh!*" Pike exclaimed quietly, nodding toward the river. "You were right, McTavish. Here it comes."

The elk broke from the timber and trotted into the open. Big John smiled at the animal's cunning. The hunters had to be a long way off yet, but the wary old bull wasn't waiting around to let them get any closer. It stood motionlessly for several minutes, staring back into the trees. Then it started forward at a nervous trot, although continuing to look over its shoulder from time to time as it came up the valley. Big John pulled a short brass telescope from his shooting bag and put it to his eye, whistling softly as the bull's image sharpened. His gaze lingered on the mammoth, ivory-tipped rack, the muscular shoulders and broad, powerful chest. Handing the spyglass to Pike, he said: "Do they grow 'em that big in the Rocky Mountains, Mister Pike?"

The American adjusted the scope to follow the elk's serpentine path up the valley, grunting admiringly when he had it sighted.

"Nope," he admitted. "Not in the mountains. Not that big and with a rack that wide, although I've seen prairie elk nearly that size along the Yellowstone and Missouri Rivers." He lowered the scope suddenly, squinting past the elk, then brought it back to his eye. "That sure as hell ain't no elk," he said after a moment, handing the glass to Big John. "Take a look on the far side of the river, just coming out of that broad-mouthed coulée opposite from here."

Big John swept the distant escarpment with the telescope,

pausing when he came to a trio of horses halted at the mouth of the coulée a league or more away. Two of the animals carried riders. He lowered the scope, brows creased skeptically. "Some of Paget's bunch, perhaps. They're not redskins, I'm fair certain of that."

"Let's see that far-looker again," Pike said, pulling the glass away from Big John without waiting for him to hand it over. He was silent a long time while he studied the distant horsemen. He lowered the scope with a curse. "That's Duprée, and the other one's gotta be Rubiette. I'd bet my traps on it."

Big John felt a sudden heaviness in his breast. "The ones ye came to kill, are they?"

Nodding curtly, Pike slammed the telescope closed. His eyes were like ice when he turned to Big John. "I've come a long way for this, McTavish. I won't stand for anyone getting in my way."

"I'll not stand in ye way, Mister Pike, nor will I try to talk ye out of it. I'll only ask that ye remember what I said on the day we left me farm. Ye be one of us now, and proven in the eyes of the mixed-bloods, but they'll hang ye tomorrow if ye kill the wrong man, or for the wrong reason. Be sure ye cause is just, that's all I'll ask."

He took the glass from Pike. Below them, the big bull was still coming upvalley, although angling away from them now, out of reach of their rifles. The hunters were just visible within the trees along the river. He could imagine their frustration as they watched the elk draw steadily away. It was Charles Hallet who first ventured from the shelter of the trees. The others followed cautiously, and the elk broke into a running trot.

Pike pushed away from the wallow even as the *métis* hunters kicked their horses into a futile chase. Across the river, the two unknowns were gesturing animatedly, no doubt having spotted the elk and wondering what had spooked it. From their lowered vantage point, they hadn't spotted the hunters, but they would see Pike as soon as he got up. Big John kept the spyglass focused on the strangers, eager to see what their reaction would be.

Pike stood. The two horsemen remained motionless for only a moment, then made a dash for the river.

"They're heading for timber!" Pike shouted, sprinting for the bay. He jumped into the saddle and raced away. Down on the flat across the river, the two strangers were already entering the trees.

Sitting up, Big John put a hand to the wound in his side, as if he could smother the pain that throbbed there. Down below, the *métis* were sweeping up the valley after the elk, heels pounding, quirts rising and falling, though silent at this distance. The elk had already disappeared around a bend in the valley above him, and, a few minutes later, the hunters were gone as well, leaving him with only the sound of the breeze rustling the tall grasses of the fairy ring.

Pike raked the bay's ribs with his spurs, running the wiry little mustang down the slope to the side valley's escarpment, then over the edge in a steep, plunging slide. At the bottom he lined out to the south, riding hard for the distant river.

He didn't slow the pony's wild gait until he was within a couple of hundred yards of the river's wooded banks. There he pulled up to check the rifle's priming, the sharpness of its flint within the leather-padded jaws of the cock. When he was satisfied, he tapped the bay lightly with the sides of his stirrups, riding the rest of the way at a trot, his scalp taut.

The river's bed was fairly broad, though mostly sandy and dry. The main channel was no more than ten or fifteen feet across, meandering shallowly between low banks that were scarred and knocked down by old buffalo trails. There were deeper pools here and there that were crowded with flashing schools of minnows, the calm surfaces of these ponds spotted with water bugs and sodden leaves.

Pike guided the bay into the riverbed to avoid the crackle of dead leaves. Now only the occasional splashing of the bay's hoofs as it crossed the stream or the dull clip of an iron shoe striking a stone interrupted the silence around him. With his nerves strained, his senses seemed to sharpen until he was acutely aware of every sound, every movement. So attuned, in fact, that he was certain he heard the slap of flint against frizzen a split second before the boom of a fusil exploded in front of him.

The smoothbore's heavy lead slug whistled past his face, so close he instinctively jerked his cheek away. Throwing himself from the saddle, he scrambled for the shelter of a fallen log, its sun-bleached trunk as thick as a horse's chest. Crawling into the tangle of its uprooted base, Pike peered cautiously upstream. A patch of yellow cloth was visible between a couple of trees about forty yards away. A second figure stood nearly a hundred yards beyond the first, wearing a knee-length buckskin coat and a bright green tuque. Carefully Pike slid his rifle across an exposed root. He heard the more distant half-breed shout a warning, but it came too late for the man in the yellow shirt. He was already clear of the trees when Pike's ball took him low in the chest, slamming him back with his feet lifted high. Dropping out of sight, Pike quickly reloaded.

Silence drifted over the river. A gust of wind blew downstream, scattering leaves along the ground with a scratchy whisper. Far off, a hawk *kerred.* Ten minutes passed slowly, then twenty. A bee appeared out of nowhere to inspect the greased scent of Pike's moccasins, then moved on. Pike waited expectantly, sweat trickling down his face, darkening the faded red fabric of his shirt. After forty-five minutes, curiosity finally won out, and he slowly peered around the root-knotted base. The man he'd shot was slumped against a tree, his chin resting on his chest, his long, raven-colored hair falling over his forehead. Pike watched for several minutes, but the yellow shirt never stirred. Edging forward to increase his field of vision, he studied the surrounding timber carefully. He thought the man in the yellow shirt was probably dead, but he also knew that his partner could be using the corpse as bait, hoping to lure Pike into the open. At the same time, Pike knew he could lie there all day while the second man made his escape. Finally, taking a deep breath, he rose to a half crouch and stepped clear of the log, ready to drop at the first snap of a trigger. But no report split the warm air, and nothing moved that wasn't prodded by the wind. Slowly he began a cautious advance on the fallen ambusher.

It was François Rubiette, and he was still alive.

Pike paused behind a tree several yards away, his shoulder pressed lightly against the slim trunk as he watched the irregular rise and fall of the downed man's chest. Rubiette's shirt was smeared with blood, his torso twisted at an odd angle above his belt. Only his neck and shoulders were propped against the tree, the rest of him was stretched out limply in the dappled shade. His fusil lay half buried in the leaves several feet away.

François must have sensed his presence, for he tilted his head around to squint through a veil of dark hair. Coughing hollowly, he rasped: "Do not worry. Henri has left, and you have killed me."

"You're talking mighty free for a dead man," Pike said.

"Sacre," François croaked, struggling to bring Pike into focus. "Who are you?"

"A friend of a friend. Why'd you try to kill me?"

François chuckled, but the effort cost him. When he could speak again, he said: "I do not know, *mon ami.* We saw you on the ridge, then you came here. We thought you were a thief, or a

Sioux. I don't know. Maybe it was easier to kill you than to try to talk."

"I'm a friend of Arch Callahan," Pike said, watching closely for the half-breed's reaction. His words had little effect at first, but then François's face began to change, his eyes to widen.

Pike's hands shook with rage. "*Weendigo!*" he hissed.

"*Non!*" the half-breed cried weakly, forcing his head higher. "It is not true! It was Henri! I swear it! Henri!"

"I reckon it was both of you," Pike said, stepping clear of the tree.

"You are the one called Pike, *non?*"

He nodded, coming nearer. His rifle was aimed at François's chest but he didn't pull the trigger. "Tell me," he said bluntly. "Tell me, god dammit!"

The *métis* shook his head. Tears rolled down his cheeks to disappear into the curly thatch of his beard. "It was Henri," he insisted. "Kill me, but know the truth. I tried to stop him."

"You're still traveling with him, and you tried to kill me without even knowing who I was. Naw, it was you."

"*Non! Non, non . . . non.*" François's voice faded and his head lolled. "It was Henri, I swear it."

"Get up," Pike snarled. "Get up, you rotten son-of-a-bitch."

François shook his head. "I cannot," he said. "My legs will not move."

"You're lying."

"I would have run otherwise, or tried to hide. I am not lying."

Pike glanced at François's hands, but the bloody fingers were empty. Then he whirled, his throat closing, but there was no one behind him, either. Turning back to the wounded half-breed, he said: "You're telling me your partner ran out on you without even trying to help?"

"Henri was not my partner. Not after last winter . . . after what he did to Arch. We only rode together because we both had to leave the Saskatchewan district. They would have killed us had we not fled."

"Who would have killed you?"

"The Crees, the Blackfeet, the Assiniboines, the *bois brûles.* Any of them. All of them." He forced his head up to look at Pike. Spittle shone on his lips, bubbling at the corners of his mouth. "He has done it before, you know? It was why he left the White Horse Plain. He is a dangerous man, Henri, and maybe a little crazy, but he is also a coward. Like me. Maybe that is your advantage, his fear. The dreams . . . they haunt him still." He was silent a moment, then added: "They haunt me, as well."

"What happened out there?" Pike asked, the muzzle of his rifle beginning to drop.

But François only shook his head. "You must ask Henri. I did not watch."

"You were there. Dammit, you had to watch."

"*Non,* I was not there." He closed his eyes, his arms stiffening as if in pain. "*Sacre!* Kill me, Pike."

"You have a knife?"

François opened his eyes. *"Oui."*

"Use it."

Fear crossed the half-breed's face. "*Non!* I cannot!"

Pike grabbed the half-breed's shoulder and pulled him forward. François's body twisted to one side with a harsh grating sound, and he screamed until Pike shoved him back. "So it's true," Pike said, shaken.

François could only gasp for breath. In the moving his bladder had loosened, staining his trousers with the raw odor of urine. From a rawhide sheath on the half-breed's belt, Pike withdrew a dagger similar to the one One Who Limps had used against McTavish.

"Can you use your hands and arms?"

François managed a nod.

Pike dropped the dagger on François's chest, then stepped back. In a bone-dry voice, he said: "When you regain some strength, put the tip of that blade over your heart, then push it in with both hands. Make sure it goes all the way the first time. It'll be easier in the long run if you get it over quick." Numbly he turned away.

"Pike!" the half-breed cried. "Pike!"

But Pike didn't stop. He found the bay grazing about two hundred yards downstream and pulled himself into the saddle. As he reined away, François's cry came once more, muted and forlorn. Pike didn't look back.

Stars glittered like broken glass, and in the distance a wolf bayed at the chip of the bone-colored moon, floating in the southern sky. From the west a stiff, icy breeze was driving in a bank of clouds that had earlier obliterated the sunset, and was even now gnawing into the mantle of stars.

Pike sat cross-legged in the middle of a flat plain, the bay tethered nearby. His rifle lay across his lap and his dirty white capote was pulled tightly over his chest. The square-shouldered bottle of bourbon he'd purchased from Murphy sat in the grass at his side, nearly a third gone. He was staring dully into space, oblivious to the baying wolf or the chill fondling of the wind.

Weendigo. Man-eater.

Although the half-breed had denied it vigorously, Pike considered the evidence overwhelming. He'd found Arch's body himself, following the directions of a Blackfoot trapper to the *métis'* winter camp. They had left Arch in a wash, probably buried in a snowbank, but by the time Pike found him the body had not so much decayed as simply dried out. Pike hadn't realized until after he'd examined the uniformity of the cuts in

Arch's thighs and buttocks and along his upper arms how much he'd doubted the Blackfoot's story. Or perhaps how much he'd wanted to. Maybe François had told the truth when he accused Henri, but that didn't matter. He had allowed it to happen. That was enough.

"One taken care of," Pike mumbled darkly. He lifted the bottle and shook it, its fumes penetrating deep into his sinuses. "One put under and one more to go." Tipping the bottle, he drank deeply.

Chapter Fifteen

It was a bleak day, the wind coming out of the northwest laden with fine grains of dust that stung Gabriel's face and badgered his slitted eyes. His fingers, clutching Baldy's reins, felt thick and numb. Iron-gray clouds surged thickly overhead, threatening but so far dry.

In the three days since the return of Big John and the others, the caravan had wormed free of the hills surrounding Chain of Lakes and was finally penetrating the short-grass plains of the buffalo, heading almost due west. There would be other lakes and ponds along the way, of course—the grasslands here were dotted with them—but they had left the best of the timber and the easiest hunting behind. Their next fresh meat would likely be bison, and what they carried now, the deer and fowl harvested at Chain of Lakes, wouldn't last long among so many. Within a week, some of them would be eating a thin gruel of flour soup, with not so much as a handful of last year's pemmican for flavoring.

Such was a hunter's life, though, to feast one day and starve the next. With his face to the buffeting winds and his pony moving out smartly under him, Gabriel wouldn't have traded his lot for a thousand farms.

He was riding about a league ahead of the caravan today, with Michel Quesnelle at his side. He had on his new jacket, the one Isabella had been making for him from buckskin, decorated with porcupine quills and embroidered moose hair in tight, floral patterns. The familiar odor of smoked leather was strong, and he was proud of the rich, brown-gold color of the hide that allowed the vivid blues and greens and lavenders of Isabella's handiwork to stand out. It was perhaps a bit too light for the recent drop in temperature, but Isabella had finished the embroidery only last night, and he wore it as much for her as himself.

The two young hunters had ridden most of the morning without speaking, although Gabriel was aware of Michel's regular glances, as if puzzled by the prolonged silence. Quesnelle's silent scrutiny annoyed Gabriel. He wondered how much Michel had guessed about his feelings for Celine, or his uneasiness toward the American. Worse now than even the night of the dance, when Gabriel had spied her and Pike returning together from the shadows, was the *bois brûles'* return to the caravan after Big John's fight with One Who Limps. In Gabriel's mind, Celine had tarnished the name of McTavish irrevocably that day when she'd abandoned her cart to rush to Pike's side.

Gabriel's face twisted in anguish at the memory. At his side, Michel Quesnelle laughed.

"You should not think of it so much," he said. "What that woman does is not your burden."

Gabriel threw him an exasperated look. "Does everyone know?"

"Oui." Michel reined closer. "My mother says Celine speaks regularly with *le diable,* and my father wonders why you do not seek the company of Susanne Leveille."

Gabriel scowled. It occurred to him that Nicolas and Rosanna Quesnelle were two of the worst gossips in St. Joseph, and that Michel was becoming more like them all the time. He said: "Your parents do not know Celine. They should not speak of her in that manner."

"Isabella told my mother that Celine talks to herself all day now, and that she will spread her legs for any man." Michel risked a sidelong glance. "I would like to horn that one myself, Gabriel, even if she is crazy. Do you think . . . ?"

Gabriel's fist struck out blindly, slamming into the side of Michel's face. Quesnelle jerked back with a startled squawk and his horse jumped, tumbling him from the saddle. Gabriel was off Baldy in a flash, grabbing Michel by his coat and hauling him to his feet. He drew his fist back to strike again, but stopped when he saw the thin trickle of blood that ran from Michel's nose to his upper lip.

"Are you crazy, too!" Michel shouted, yanking free of Gabriel's grip. "*Sacre démon,* Gabriel, if you were not my friend, I would kill you good for that." He put his hand on his knife to emphasize his sincerity.

"Shut up," Gabriel said, turning away. Baldy had stopped where he'd jumped from the saddle, but Michel's mount, younger and less experienced, had trotted off and was already curving back toward the caravan.

"Now my horse is gone. See? Go get him, Gabriel. It is your fault."

"Get him yourself," Gabriel replied sulkily. He'd let his musket fall when he'd jumped off Baldy. He stooped to pick it up, examining it carefully.

"How can I catch him myself?" Michel demanded, his arms flapping helplessly. "I cannot run as fast as a horse."

"Then walk." Gabriel mounted Baldy and began to ride away.

"Gabriel!"

He pulled up without looking back.

"Are we not friends?"

Gabriel wondered. He knew that last year they had been friends. Perhaps even a month ago. But he wasn't sure of anything any more. "Tell them your pony threw you," he said.

"Even the best riders are sometimes thrown from their mounts."

"I won't do it! I will tell them that Gabriel Gilray struck me when I wasn't looking, and that he left his partner afoot, alone on the prairie. They will shun you, Gabriel. They will say the crazy woman has corrupted your *métis* blood."

Shrugging, Gabriel gave Baldy his heels. The wind brought tears to his eyes. He wished it would rain, or snow. Anything to force a change, even if that change made traveling more difficult. He wished they would find buffalo.

"Gabriel, you would do this?" Michel called after him in disbelief. "You would forsake your own people?"

The wind picked up, blurring his vision even more. Angrily he kicked Baldy's ribs, forcing the gelding into a lope.

Lying in his robes beneath one of McTavish's meat carts, Pike listened to the low hum of the wind through the spokes, the restless stirring of the livestock corralled inside the carts. Wide awake, he stared up at the underside of the cart's bed, his thoughts far away and troubled.

He was growing impatient with the crawling pace of the caravan, and loneliness—even amidst so many—had begun to weigh on him. He was anxious to return to the mountains and get on with his life. He wished now that he'd gone after Duprée when he'd had the chance. At the time he'd convinced himself that the odds were too much in the half-breed's favor, and that, if he would just stick it out a while longer, Henri would eventually make for the caravan and the shelter of his own family.

Now it was too late to go back. Whatever sign Duprée might have left would be old and wind-swept by now, impossible to follow. Yet as the days passed and the half-breed failed to appear, Pike's hopes began to dim.

It had been just crazy bad luck that had separated him and Arch last fall. They'd spent the winter before trapping beaver for William Vanderburg, ranging the headwaters of the Snake and Green Rivers. But Arch had been growing tired of a trapper's life. He had wanted to go back to St. Louis for a spell, to kick up his heels in a bona-fide town.

"I wanna eat meat that ain't been scorched over an open fire," he'd declared to anyone who would listen. "I wanna drink beer outta glass mugs."

Pike had been less keen on the idea. He liked his meat just fine fixed over a fire, and preferred whiskey from a jug to beer any day. But when he realized Arch was serious, he knew he'd have to make a decision, and the one he came to was that he didn't want to trap alone or break in a new partner. So he'd talked Arch into a compromise, and they'd accepted positions with James Kipp, out of Fort Piegan, on the Marias River. Arch would work at the post as a trader that winter, while Pike hunted meat for the fort's personnel.

But a twist of fate had changed their plans. Two days before they were to pull out from the main American Fur depot at Fort Union, at the confluence of the Yellowstone and Missouri Rivers, Arch had gotten into a row with an Assiniboine and taken a deep knife wound to his shoulder.

It was Kenneth McKenzie, the Fort Union factor who presided over all of American Fur's operations in the interior Northwest, including tiny Fort Piegan, who ordered Pike to go on with Kipp and his *engagés* while Arch stayed behind to recuperate.

Pike could still recall the last time he'd seen Arch alive. He'd gone to the tiny room McKenzie had assigned as a temporary hospital ward shortly after dawn to say good bye. Kipp and his French-Canadians were already pulling out in a small keelboat, but the plan was for Pike to follow along on shore with a string of pack horses. Arch had been slumbering on a pallet on the floor when Pike entered, but he'd come awake at the door's creak.

"We're pulling out," Pike said without preamble. "You need anything?"

"A gold mine would set well."

"A bucket of gold would be lost on you. You'd just go to Saint Louie and squander it all on whores and foofaraw."

"Then get on upriver and leave me alone."

Pike smiled, yet he'd felt a trace of uneasiness even then. "You gonna be all right, *amigo?*" he'd asked.

Arch nodded, mugging a grin. "Ain't gonna be my topknot parked out in the middle of Blackfeet country all winter."

Pike glanced at the Blackfoot woman Arch had hooked up with after coming into Fort Union that spring. She was still asleep, or feigning so. All he could see was the dark pool of her hair spilling out from under the blankets, the broad, round humps of hip and shoulder. Grinning, he'd said: "You'd best mind your own hair, boy, before that gal decides to lift it while you ain't looking."

Arch had laughed, even though it pained his shoulder to do so. "It ain't my topknot little Sally Mae's wantin', hoss."

"Shit," Pike had replied, feigning disgust, but Arch had only laughed harder, laughed until the pain in his shoulder made him wince. They'd been traveling together a long time.

It wasn't until Kipp sent Pike and a couple of *engagés* back to Fort Union the following spring with a raft laden with furs and buffalo robes that Pike learned of Arch's disappearance on the Canadian plains. A party of Crees from the Qu'Appelle country had come into Fort Union to trade some wolf pelts for supplies early last November, and a pair of French-Canadian half-breeds had been traveling with them. Arch, healed by then and eager to get started, had returned to Canada with them—unofficially, of course, since international law forbade the trading of furs and supplies across the border. Privately McKenzie had confided to Pike that Arch had gone north at his request to urge other members of the Cree nation to come south to Fort Union in the spring and trade with the Americans.

If not for a chance encounter with a Blackfoot who had done just that, and who had also wintered with the same band of Crees, Pike probably never would have learned of his partner's fate. It had been late spring when Pike found Arch's body, and he'd been on the trail of Duprée and Rubiette ever since.

A man stepped out of the hide lodge Isabella Gilray had put up when the weather turned cold. Pike moved a hand over his rifle, even though he'd already recognized McTavish by his lumbering, bear-like gait.

"Are ye still awake, Mister Pike?" the Scotsman called softly. He waited until Pike grunted an affirmative, then came over to squat beside a tall, dished wheel. He moved deliberately and continued to favor his side, but Pike had noticed that, after several days of Isabella's care, he was beginning to limber up again.

Taking a pipe from his mouth, McTavish held it between his hands with his elbows resting on his knees and stared across the camp. In a lowered voice, he said: "They found a dead man on the plains today, near where Mister Hallet and them lost that big bull elk."

"Jesus, are we just now coming even with that?"

"Aye, south of there, but about even, I'd say. The carts travel slow, Mister Pike, though I doubt ye need remindin' of that."

"The hell with the carts. Who found him?"

"Etienne Cyr and Antoine Toussaint. They went north today on a long scout and just got back. They didn't recognize him so they buried him there, along yon river. Gutshot, he was, with his backbone shattered. 'Twas a pony tethered nearby, gaunted up but not otherwise hurt."

"Just shot?" Pike pushed a corner of his robe back to prop himself up on one elbow. "No other wounds?"

"Just the one was all they mentioned. A huntin' accident, they figure, and not the first one to happen out here. I don't believe it meself, but his fusil was empty and that tells me he had his chance. I'll not question ye further on the matter, nor pass on what I know to the others. I just thought you'd want to know he was found."

Pike took a deep breath, then expelled it. "Yeah," he said. "I'm glad you told me."

McTavish's hands began to move with his pipe, shifting it from one to the other in an absent manner. "I feel trouble brewin'," he said quietly. "Bubblin' like tea in a kettle." He smiled uncertainly, perhaps a little sadly, then went on. "I'll be askin' ye of my daughter now, Mister Pike, and expectin' an honest answer, I will. Do ye have an eye on her as ye mate, what skins and cooks and raises the wee ones? Or . . . do ye see her as the others do, as a tart and a tramp, and weak in the mind?"

Even expecting them, McTavish's words caught Pike off guard. His fingers tightened momentarily around his rifle, then relaxed. "She's no tramp, McTavish. She's confused and scared, and I don't know why she came to me like she did that day we came back. Maybe. . . ." He let the words trail off.

"Ye've talked to her, have ye?"

"Some."

"And what would that have been about?"

There was an edge to McTavish's voice now, and Pike remembered how he'd faced down Breland, the skill in which he'd fought One Who Limps. Despite his years and the ready smile, Big John was still a dangerous man, one who wouldn't tolerate something he felt was unjust or deceiving.

"She doesn't like it here," Pike replied evasively. "She wants to go some place where the lights burn all night. She mentioned Boston."

"Boston?" McTavish sounded surprised.

"I've never been there myself, but I hear it's a fair-size city."

"Aye," McTavish replied distractedly. "I've heard such meself, but. . . . I didn't know."

Pike lay back down, pulling the robe over his shoulder. Although he kept his hand on his rifle, he didn't think he'd have to use it.

Nearby, a pony snorted and kicked, another squealed at the thud of hoofs against its ribs. Glancing toward the unsettled herd, McTavish said: "They're restless tonight."

"The wind, maybe," Pike said, although he shared their disquiet, and knew it was something more.

"Could be." McTavish stood and returned the pipe to his mouth. Pike thought for a moment he might say more, but after a pause he just walked away.

Listening closely, Pike was just able to make out the sound of the lodge door rising and falling as Big John entered the teepee. Then he was alone again, with just the mournful humming of the wind for company. He rolled onto his back, thinking of Arch and the shining times they'd had ranging the Rockies from the Pecos River country in the south to the Missouri River up north. They'd pulled in a sight of beaver over the years, and had themselves a hell of a good time doing it. It was hard to think of Arch being gone now, even though Pike had buried the remains himself.

Despite his melancholy, Pike eventually dozed off, but it was a restless slumber. The rumble of snores from McTavish's lodge seemed inordinately loud, prodding at the layers of his consciousness until it became a steady pounding, as much felt as. . . .

★ ★ ★ ★ ★

He came awake with a start, his heart racing, his breath short and gasping, and threw his robes back in such a panic that he scraped his knuckles half raw against the underside of the cart. The sudden blast of cold wind scoured away the last dregs of sleep, but the distant rumbling continued. It took him only a moment to place the sound. At that same instant a *métis* guard shouted from outside the carts: *"Le bison! Le bison!"*

Within seconds, the camp was awake.

Scrambling from his robes, Pike stood to peer into the darkness surrounding the circled caravan. Voices rose and fell around him like pieces of cork loosened on choppy waters. Isabella scurried from her lodge and dropped to her knees to feed shredded bark into last evening's fire. Around the camp, other fires flickered slowly to life.

McTavish appeared at Pike's side, shrugging into his red duffel coat. "By the Lord, Mister Pike, I believe 'tis the buffalo that's found us this year."

"To the northwest," Pike said, pointing with his chin. He felt vaguely disoriented in a darkness made complete by thick clouds, more confused than comforted by the fires sprouting up behind him. The livestock was milling restively, the oxen lowing and the cart horses blowing and whickering. Only the runners seemed unaffected; they stared into the unseeable distance with their small ears perked forward, nostrils flaring as they drank in the scent of the herd.

"Aye, and with luck they'll pass to the west of us," McTavish said after a moment. "But we'll keep the fires burnin', just in case. I'd hate to see a second herd stumble into us in the dark. 'Tis best not to take a chance when they're on the move like this."

Pike nodded. On the move, a herd of buffalo was like a slow twister, not so much destructive for destruction's sake, but just huge and unyielding, those animals caught at the front of the herd forced onward by the hundreds or thousands, or sometimes tens of thousands, behind them. Even coming on at a slow jog, like these were, they would have been hard to turn had they approached the cordon straight on.

Pike was gripping the cart's slats with both hands, heedless to the cold wind that pierced his shirt. He stared hypnotically into the ebony distance as the musky odor of the herd washed over the camp. The earth beneath the leather soles of his moccasins vibrated against his feet, and faintly he began to hear the brittle clatter of the buffaloes' short black horns, clacking together like bones in a basket. The front of the herd drew even with the carts somewhere to the west, but, from the sound and sharpening scent, Pike could tell the rear of the herd was much broader, edging steadily closer.

The women had their fires roaring now, reckless with their precious supply of wood as the danger of being overrun increased. Others came to stand with Pike, gazing over the tops of the carts at the fluctuating wall of darkness that was being edged gradually backward as the flames leaped higher. A few of the older boys were moving through the agitated livestock, crooning gentle French ballads in an attempt to soothe the animals' nerves. The guards who had been stationed on the prairie began to drift in, their faces anxious. They remained outside the carts, however, and, after a couple of minutes, others joined them. Grabbing his rifle and capote, Pike followed, though staying off to one side.

The sound of the herd seemed to overwhelm the camp, drowning out all other noises, dominating the senses. Dust and débris churned up by hoofs and carried on the wind began to pepper Pike's face. As he stared intently into the darkness, he began to discern a slight shifting of the horizon, just beyond the rim of light. It reminded him of a river's shore seen from the deck of a raft, the backward slide of the bank being buffalo now, humped and surging, and a prickle of concern skittered up both arms to terminate at his scalp. From time to time a horn made slick by rubbing in the dirt or against rocks or trees would catch the light just right and glint fleetingly, and occasionally a buffalo would stray from the herd and wander into the light, its small eyes glimmering red before it spooked away from the unfamiliar scent of the *métis* camp. Pike could sense the herd adjusting itself to this new obstruction, the nearest animals attempting to veer away as much as possible, while the herd itself bulged above them like backwater. Soon now the buffalo would have to split. Either that or overrun the camp.

A blunt horn—an old cow with horns dulled by years of digging and rubbing—wandered into the light above the camp and stopped in confusion. Pike could see others behind it, pressed reluctantly forward by those still farther back. A bull roared challengingly and shook its massive head. A cow snorted and tried to dodge away, but was thrown back into the light by the bulk of the herd. A few darted uncertainly to the east, but only a few. The line of buffalo that was the slowing bulge pressed steadily nearer.

From the entrenched carts, a child began to cry. Then someone spat—*"Enfant de grâce."*—in a taut voice. Baptiste LaBarge stepped clear of the knot of hunters and dropped to one knee. He brought his fusil up, sighted quickly, and fired. The blunt horn bellowed and jumped, then its front legs buckled and it fell, kicking.

There were several small but hopeful cheers as a number of cows crossed quickly to the east. A second fusil boomed and the bull that had challenged them grunted sharply at the slug's impact, then ran after the cows. Like a causeway suddenly breeching, other bison followed. As the herd began to split around the camp its pace picked up again. The image was still that of a river, Pike thought, but now it flowed seamlessly on either side of them, before rejoining somewhere to the south and leaving in its center a tiny island of humanity.

With the danger mostly past, several of the hunters began firing into the herd at will, choosing their targets from the strays that wandered into the wind-flaring light. With the poor light, not all of the hits were solid, and Pike knew that by morning they would find dead and dying buffalo strewn far to the south.

It took the better part of an hour for the herd to pass, the rumble of hoofs and horns shifting gradually to the south. At the fringes of the light from the still-blazing fires, Pike began to see the smaller forms of the wolves that always followed the buffalo, slinking among the dead as if puzzled by this unexpected offering. Beyond the light, the low, savage snarls of the wolves as they tore at the meat of the dead bison touched a primeval chord, and he shivered as if chilled.

The hunters noticed the wolves, too, and with scattered curses they turned their fusils on the wily canines, driving them back into the darkness. But the wolves refused to abandon the field, and soon their forlorn howls rose like ghosts from beyond the barrier of light, building steadily as more and more were drawn to the scent of blood.

The howling of the wolves frightened the livestock even more than the buffalo had, and several of the half-breeds had to hurry back inside the carts to calm the panicking oxen and horses. Others, meanwhile, rushed onto the prairie, firing at the leaping wolves or swinging at them with their empty long guns. Behind the men came the women with their knives and kettles, although they seemed less concerned with the havoc being created by the wolves than their men were. Prattling cheerfully, they moved among the fallen bison to begin their butchering. Pike understood their satisfaction. Once again, there was enough meat to fill the bellies of their children, to take away the worry of the next day's meal.

"You did not shoot."

He turned to find Celine standing just outside the carts, silhouetted by firelight.

"I was afraid that you hated me," she went on, changing the subject before he could reply. "You acted like it when you returned from fighting the Chippewas."

"I guess you caught me by surprise," he admitted. "I wasn't expecting it."

Thinking back to the way she'd come barreling out from between the carts brought back some of what he'd felt then. He'd thought at first she was angry about what had happened at the lake, and his first instinct had been to raise his rifle in defense against whatever weapon she might be carrying—a knife or a tomahawk—but her intent had been just the opposite, the feelings she'd expressed for him almost embarrassing in front of the others. Although he hadn't bought into it himself, he suspected most of the others had.

"I was happy to see you," she said. "Now you avoid me."

He had been avoiding her, in fact, unsure of his own feelings, as well as his loyalty to Big John. But seeing the round swell of her hips etched against the light, he knew he wanted her again. His desire made him bold. "We ought to find some place quiet, where we can be talk," he said, his voice growing thick.

"We can talk here."

"Not here."

She hesitated, then glanced over her shoulder. "He watches. Like a dumb, faithful dog."

Pike looked. Gabriel stood next to the carts, staring at them with undisguised distrust. "The hell with him," Pike growled.

Pulling her shawl tighter, Celine stepped close and said: "They frightened me." She tipped her head toward the fallen bison. "I did not think they would come so close to our fires."

"Buff' ain't afraid of much," Pike allowed. "Not bunched up and on the move like that. Most of the herd probably didn't even know we were here."

"You are so wise," she said a little breathlessly. She'd quartered around until he could see the firelight dancing in her eyes. Her face, honed by the flickering shadows, looked solemn. Reaching out to rest her finger lightly against his chest, she said: "So brave. A true hunter, no?"

Her fingers were like tiny coals burning through his shirt, and he shivered and blamed it on the cold. Then he shook his head and laughed. He had never met anyone like Celine before. She was young—God, he knew that—but looking into her eyes was like looking into the soul of a battle-hardened warrior.

"You laugh," she pouted.

"Not at you," he promised. "At the night." He took her arm and gave it a little tug. "Come with me. I want to show you something."

"What?"

He grinned recklessly. "Nothing you ain't already seen. Come on."

"No." She pulled away.

From the corner of his eye Pike saw Gabriel start toward them. He turned, stopping the boy with a hard look.

"He is jealous," Celine said softly, watching Gabriel with a hint of a smile on her lips.

"He's a kid," Pike said bluntly.

"Yes, I know, but I will not go with you tonight. Big John suspects, as well."

His anger flared. "What the hell did you expect . . . ?" He stopped when he recognized her ploy. "You're a hell-raising bitch, Celine, but you do grow on a man. I might just take you with me when I leave here."

Her face brightened. "To Boston?"

"Uhn-uh. Saint Louis, maybe, but then back to Taos." Taos and the southern Rockies had been calling to him for a long time now. It had always seemed to Pike that the farther north he and Arch drifted, the worse their luck had become.

"Taos?" Celine repeated doubtfully. "Where is Taos?"

"The mountains. Spanish Territory."

"The *pays sauvage?*"

He nodded. "We could get us a little 'dobe house there for the winter months, trap along the front range and into Bayou Salade, or . . . hell, on over the divide during the fall and spring. Maybe hunt buffalo in the summer. I hear they're building a fort on the Arkansas. They'll need meat, for sure."

"Non!" she cried. "I will not. I hate the wilderness. I wish only to leave it, forever."

Gabriel moved forward, drawn by the alarm in Celine's voice. Pike turned to face him, scowling. "Back away, boy. This doesn't concern you."

Near the carts, a couple of hunters had stopped what they were doing to watch.

"Celine," Gabriel said. "Are you all right?"

She nodded dully, then stepped back. When she looked at Pike, her eyes shone with hatred. "He wishes to take me away to the mountains," she accused, her voice trembling.

Gabriel glared at Pike. "Is this true?"

"Shit," Pike grunted, then his voice turned harsh. "She said it, didn't she? Are you calling her a liar, you dumb, moon-struck pup?"

"I will kill you for that," Gabriel breathed, drawing his knife.

"Do it, Gabriel," Celine whispered fiercely. "Kill him for me."

"Don't be a fool, boy," Pike said, swinging around to face him. The two hunters who had been watching from the carts started forward. Spitting a curse, Pike lifted his rifle in both hands. "I don't have a quarrel with you, son."

"You insulted Celine."

"Naw, I didn't insult her. I just asked her to go to the mountains with me." The two *métis* were close now, and Pike was aware that some of the butchers had also stopped their work and were watching.

"Gabriel," one of the *métis* said.

"Stay out of this, Etienne."

"*Non,* I cannot, mon brave," Etienne Cyr replied. "There must not be a fight."

"Yes, there will be a fight," Gabriel said. But he gripped his knife uncertainly, as if not exactly sure how to set it all into motion.

"I think you have fought enough today, eh?" Cyr said mildly. "With Michel Quesnelle this morning."

Gabriel gave Cyr a disconcerted glance. It was all the opening Pike needed. He stepped quickly forward, bringing the butt of his rifle up and around. There was a solid thunk as it struck Gabriel above his ear, and the boy dropped like a stone, without even a grunt.

Etienne Cyr and the other half-breed blinked owlishly, and there was a flurry of angry voices from the butchers.

"It's best this way," Pike said, facing Cyr with his rifle brought back up, ready to swing or fire, depending on the reaction of the half-breeds. "I'd have had to gut him if he jumped me with that knife."

"Maybe," Cyr said doubtfully. He was looking at Celine, his expression carefully blank. "Gabriel Gilray is a good man, but lately his mind has become muddled."

Celine's lips thinned, and she stalked away without speaking to anyone.

"That one," Cyr murmured, shaking his head. Then he knelt at Gabriel's side and rolled him onto his back. The boy groaned and raised a hand groggily to his head. Cyr looked at Pike. "Perhaps it was best this way," he acknowledged. "But now I think maybe you ought to go, eh?"

Pike nodded. He understood. Cyr was telling him that he was still an outsider here, no matter what Big John thought.

He headed back to the caravan, ignoring the stares of the men and women standing over their partially butchered carcasses. Tomorrow they would begin the hunt in earnest, and soon his debt to McTavish would be paid and he would be free once more. He was more than ready.

Chapter Sixteen

Gabriel loped up alongside Charlo's brindled mare, careful to approach opposite the ugly white buffalo runner the old hunter led on a short rope. He slowed Baldy to a walk but didn't speak, nor did he feel any need to. Far to the south, speckling the stark tan plain, were the remnants of the herd that had nearly overrun them last night. No more than a couple of hundred head were visible from here, but those animals were grazing slowly toward the crest of a low swell, and Gabriel knew the far side of that ridge would be thick with buffalo, a shaggy brown sea of meat and robes.

Anticipation for the hunt gorged him, so that he felt as taut as a bowstring. This was what he lived for, what they all lived for. With the chase looming, Gabriel felt keenly alive, focused and in control. Today, nothing else mattered.

The sod beneath their horses' hoofs was churned and torn, spotted with dung—a visible scar nearly a mile wide running south over the low hills. From time to time they passed the wolf-torn carcass of a buffalo, a casualty of some hunter's fusil from the night before, but they made no effort to claim the meat. Soon there would be enough for everyone. Even the wolves.

Occasionally Gabriel would glance over his shoulder, but the line of carts had vanished behind the curve of the earth. Scanning the horizon, he saw nothing but empty prairie beneath the steel-gray cap of clouds. Not even a tree or tall bush marred the landscape.

The *bois brûles* were spread out over several acres, riding singly or in small bunches of two or three or half a dozen. Many of them led their favorite buffalo runners from a slower mount in order to conserve the runners' strength for the chase. Charlo was riding his brindled mare, and Big John rode old Solomon, long-legged and humorous astride the smaller horse.

When they drew close to the herd, Turcotte curbed his pony and pulled off his red wool cap to wave the others in. White-knuckled, Gabriel tapped Baldy's ribs with the heels of his moccasins. At a gallop, he and Charlo approached the hunters congregating around René. Catching a glimpse of Pike loping in from the west, Gabriel flexed his fingers on the Brown Bess. There was a robin's egg-size lump behind his left ear where the stock of the American's rifle had struck him, accompanied by a pulsating ache that kept time to the beat of Baldy's hoofs. Sooner or later, Gabriel knew, he would have to face Pike, but he wanted to avoid a confrontation now. Although he wasn't particularly afraid of the American, intuition warned him to go slow, that there was more here than he fully understood. He had blundered enough in recent days.

They came together in a knot of horsemen, Turcotte its nucleus. Some of them hunched their shoulders to the icy wind, or thrust unmittened fingers into the sweaty warmth of their armpits. Others appeared oblivious to the blustery weather and sat their mounts with calm demeanors or high-keyed anticipation. When the last hunter had arrived, Turcotte said loudly: "We form our line here."

"*Non,* René, it is too soon," a *bois brûle* protested. "We must get closer."

But Turcotte shook his head. "No, Pierre. We will form our line here."

Turcotte had changed noticeably since that day at Chain of Lakes when Joseph Breland had publicly challenged his authority. Although still hesitant at times, he remained staunchly behind his decisions once they were made. And he was quicker to take charge of a situation now, too, willing to bull ahead on his own, without glancing at Big John for reassurance. Sometimes Gabriel wondered what Big John thought of René's newfound independence, but since his return from his fight with One Who Limps, and Celine's rush to the American's side as the hunters approached the carts, Big John had become less vocal, more inclined to withdraw than to step forward.

Broad grins and scattered, growling laughter had greeted René's proclamation. Now he lifted his fusil for silence. "I will take the right flank, and"—his gaze swept the hunters—"Charlo will ride at the left."

No one objected; a few even cheered. Turcotte waved his hand toward a spot on the prairie and the *bois brûles* quickly pulled apart, then came back together in a ragged line. Those who had led their runners quickly switched saddles, handing the reins of their slower mounts to boys too young to take part in the chase. At the western end of the column, Turcotte eased his pony half a length ahead of the others. Charlo did the same at the column's eastern terminus, then lifted an arm from his side to indicate a line between himself and Turcotte that none of the nearly sixty hunters would be allowed to cross.

Gabriel found a spot near Charlo. From his shooting bag he dug out half a dozen thumb-size lead balls that he popped into his mouth, tucking them in his cheeks until they bulged. Next he hitched his powder horn around so that it rode high on his chest, where it would be easier to reach. He'd pulled the old charge from the musket that morning, then cleaned it thoroughly with water-saturated hanks of buffalo wool twisted around the ramrod's steel worm. There was a patched round ball seated now, but, after that was fired, he would reload without patches.

Big John had left his double rifle with the carts and was toting a brace of large-bored flintlock pistols thrust into his sash. A lot of the others had also left their regular guns with their families and were carrying pony guns for the chase—standard fusils cut down until the squared stock ended just behind the long rear tang of the trigger guard, the barrel maybe twelve to fourteen inches long. They had also enlarged the touch hole—that aperture connecting the flash pan with the main charge in the barrel—in an effort to eliminate the need for priming. After firing their first patched ball, they would close the frizzen before the second charge was poured down the barrel, and enough powder would trickle through the larger touch hole into the pan so that it could then be fired. All that would remain after that was to spit a ball down the barrel, pull back the cock, lower the muzzle on a bison, and pull the trigger. It was dangerous as hell, but quick—practical only when running buffalo. None of them would dream of altering their regular hunting guns that way.

With all the charged tension flowing through the line, Baldy soon became rambunctious and hard to hold. He was bumping into the horses on either side of him, pawing at the dirt, baring his teeth, and snapping when other horses did the same. Gabriel's mouth watered around the lead balls pocketed in his cheeks. He carried his musket butted to his thigh, his right hand gripping the faded walnut forestock just below the rear thimble.

After what seemed an eternity, Turcotte leaned forward to look down the long column. He brought his hand up, then slowly swung it down in a stiff chopping motion.

"Ho!" he called, loud enough to be heard above the wind, and, as one, the *bois brûles* surged forward. Almost immediately the column became a broken, sinuous line, rolling across the

dry plain like a badlands sidewinder. In a fit of eagerness, Baldy lunged ahead of the invisible line that still stretched between Turcotte and Charlo. Hurriedly Gabriel pulled him back before Charlo could chide him for his lack of control. Others were having similar problems, though. Even Charlo's runner was half-rearing against its reins, fighting the old hunter's curb.

Advancing at a walk, the hunters managed to get within four hundred yards of the nearest buffalo before the shaggy-haired bulls—Gabriel could tell their sex by size and shape—took notice. Several of the beasts lifted their massive heads to stare near-sightedly at the approaching horsemen, unable yet to perceive any impending danger, but wary nonetheless. A few spun nervously to face them, lowering their heads and hooking up clods of dirt and dust with their horns that they tossed high over their shoulders. Others bellowed warnings or pawed the earth. But most of them just looked on until the hunters had closed to within three hundred yards. It was only then that several of the nearest bulls turned and began to walk swiftly away. Others soon followed.

"Ho!" Turcotte's command drifted down the line of horsemen. The *bois brûles* lifted their runners to a jog. The buffalo were trotting now, arching their short, tufted tails above their sloping hips, shaking their heads angrily at this unwelcome intrusion. But Turcotte wisely held back until the last bull had disappeared over the crest of the low ridge. Only then did he shout—*"Ho! Ho!"*—at the top of his lungs.

At this long-awaited signal the *bois brûles* gave their mounts their heads, the invisible line between Charlo and Turcotte disappearing under flashing hoofs. From here on, it was every man for himself.

Those with the swiftest horses—Big John on his roan, Breland on his black, Charlo riding his glass-eyed white, LaBarge astride a broad-chested chestnut, and perhaps a dozen others—quickly took the lead and began to pull rapidly ahead. The bulk of the hunters, mounted on good stock that wasn't quite the equal of the best, formed a tight pack not far behind them. It was here that Baldy ran, near the front of the second bunch, his neck stretched low, hoofs flying. Already falling behind were the dozen or so hunters whose mounts were too old or broken-down to keep up, but who hadn't been able to obtain better for the chase. They were the poorest of the *bois brûles,* those whose luck ran consistently bad. They wouldn't make much pemmican or take many robes this season because they didn't have horses fast enough to keep up with the fleet-footed bison, and for that reason they wouldn't be able to afford better mounts next year.

But these men were not Gabriel's concern today, and he dismissed them after a single, backward glance. He fixed his gaze upon the low ridge before him, and, when he finally streaked over the top and saw the prairie for ten miles ahead darkened by buffalo, he wanted to whoop for the sheer exhilaration of it.

The buffalo were already on the move, a mottled undulation fanning outward from where the straggling bulls had entered the main herd. Within seconds, the whole prairie was rolling and pitching. Gabriel raced Baldy headlong down the slope into a wall of dust. He kept his mouth clamped shut and squinted his eyes to slits. At the bottom of the ridge the hunters began to pull apart. Those mounted on the best horses were already threading their way through the slower bulls at the rear of the herd, huge lumbering beasts whose meat would be tough and stringy and next to impossible to chew. In a mixed herd such as this, the older, heavier bulls always had to be breached first, in order to catch up with the swifter cows whose meat made the finest pemmican, their hides the best robes.

The dust was suffocating. Clods of hoof-shaped sod smacked Gabriel's chest and shoulders like stones, and he knew that, by evening, his flesh would be dappled with bruises, every crevice packed with grit. A huge bull emerged from the roiling, earthy haze on his left, its short, curved horns blunted by a lifetime of scooping up dirt and fighting boulders. Gabriel could hear the popping of its aged, weight-strained joints even above the roar of the stampede. The bull snorted as Gabriel drew abreast, then suddenly angled closer to hook at Baldy with a stubby horn. But Baldy was an old hand at running buffalo, and dodged nimbly out of the way without even breaking stride. Other bulls appeared, monarchical beasts with angry, red-rimmed eyes and pulsing nostrils. Giving Baldy his head, Gabriel allowed the piebald gelding to find his own path through this bobbing rear wall of giants. Muted by the din of the rushing herd, he heard the first scattered reports of gunfire from those who had already reached the cows.

Gabriel rode alone. The anticipation that had earlier stretched his nerves almost to their limits had since given way to a peculiar kind of serenity. He had become part of the whole, mystically joined with his pony and the flowing stream of bison that carried him forward.

Slowly Baldy began to pull ahead of the older bulls. He had also settled into the chase, his gait smooth and rocking. A young spike—a bull—appeared in front of them and Gabriel tipped his musket toward it. Obediently Baldy veered in that direction. It wasn't a cow, but it was young and its meat would be nearly as good. And Gabriel knew Baldy wouldn't be able to match the rapid pace of the herd for long. Only the swiftest runners, those with the best wind, could rival a buffalo over any distance. Only the bulk of a large herd slowed it enough for the others to dash in for a few minutes' shooting—seldom more than half an hour—before the average horse began to lose ground.

The spike grunted as they drew alongside but made no effort either to pull away or to charge. Slanting the musket's barrel toward the young bull's rib cage, just behind its pumping shoulder, Gabriel squeezed the trigger. The Brown Bess slammed back against his shoulder, belching a cloud of gray powder smoke that blossomed against the buffalo's heavy wool. The spike bellowed and swerved sharply away, ramming a larger bull and bouncing back, tumbling off its feet.

Gabriel raced on. He spotted a cow just ahead, and Baldy tacked toward her without guidance. Gabriel let the musket's scarred butt slide down the inside of his calf until it was cradled in the notch of his foot and the stirrup strap. Thumbing the wooden plug from his powder horn, he poured a charge into the antler-tip powder measure he kept fastened to the horn's strap. After pouring the powder down the barrel, he let the charger drop and dangle, then lifted the muzzle to his mouth, cushioning it with his lips while he spat a lead ball into the bore. Then, leaning almost casually from the saddle, he rapped the musket's butt once against the hard ground to seat the ball, allowing the momentum of the blow to vault the weapon back up the curve of his hand. Sloping the musket across his left arm, he hitched the large powder horn around to fill the pan, then quickly flipped the frizzen down before the wind could blow away the priming.

Reloading had taken less than a minute, and by then Baldy had come alongside the cow. Gabriel cocked the musket and leaned forward, firing swiftly. The cow grunted and shook her head, lunging aggressively at them, but Baldy had already taken them out of reach and was racing after the next animal even as the cow stumbled and fell.

From the back of the roan, Big John watched the herd disappear over the brink of the horizon, leaving behind only the scent of dust and buffalo and a litter of dead animals.

He had quit the hunt early, fighting the stallion and a reeling dizziness that pulsed at the edges of his vision. He could feel the slow seepage of blood through the bandages Isabella had wrapped around his side, and called himself a fool for allowing his craving for the chase to override common sense. Isabella had warned him that he was still too weak to run buffalo, but he hadn't listened. At this late date in his life, he supposed he probably never would.

He rode leisurely to a shallow coulée where a single sapling, no more than a couple of years old, was nearly twisted off at its base—a victim of the stampede, although he figured the willow's chance for survival on the buffalo plains would have been slim, regardless. Only the tough, deep-rooted buffalo grass lasted long out here; prairie fires and rubbing bison soon destroyed the rest.

Alone, Big John permitted himself the luxury of a small groan as he dismounted next to the sapling, then sank down cross-legged beside it. Taking out his pipe, he absently filled it while surveying the plain around him. Already a few wolves were venturing cautiously toward the dead buffalo. Even from his position on the ground, Big John could count at least thirty carcasses scattered from north to south. Adding up the totals in his mind tarnished his satisfaction with the hunt. It wasn't the by-products of a successful run—the meat and hides that were the mixed-bloods' livelihood—that saddened him so much as the waste he knew would come with it. For every pound of buffalo the *métis* utilized, at least twenty would rot or feed the scavengers. And even then, he knew half of them would return home with only partially filled carts.

A rider appeared from between a couple of low hills to the west and cantered easily toward him. Big John stood and put a hand on one of the pistols in his sash until he recognized Charles Hallet.

Hallet nodded as he rode up, but his expression lacked the characteristic grin of a man completing a profitable hunt. Stepping down smoothly from his pad saddle, he said: "Hello, Big John. How went the chase?"

"Well enough," Big John replied. He hesitated, then fingered a wire pick from his tobacco pouch and began unloading his pipe.

"What troubles ye, Charles?"

Hallet's gaze was wandering. "I'm looking for Etienne Cyr. Have you seen him?"

"He's missin'?"

"Baptiste found his horse half a league or so back. It's lame and skinned up, but not hurt otherwise. He was trying to backtrack, but I said I'd come on ahead. Baptiste'll be a bloody long time sorting out that trail, if he even has the eye for it. I figured Cyr would be closer to the rear of the herd, his pony being slower than most."

"I've not seen him, but I'll help ye look."

"He wouldn't be the first to get thrown from his horse, but I'd hate to think of him being caught under the hoofs of a herd this size."

"Have ye talked to any of the others?"

"No. Everyone else is still with the chase. I only stopped because I saw Baptiste with an extra horse."

Big John put away his tobacco and pipe, then mounted the roan. "I'll swing east, then work me way back. If ye do the same to the west, we ought to find something."

Hallet nodded glumly. "Look sharp, Big John," he said as he moved back alongside his runner. "My heart feels bad about this."

"Here," the moon-faced bitch grunted.

Celine stopped and turned.

"You skin this one with me," Isabella said. "Watch, then you will learn."

Celine stared at the mound of curly brown hair lumped on the prairie in front of the meat cart. Only slowly did she recognize it as a dead animal, a buffalo. Around her she became aware of the other women stooping above similar mounds.

"Is this Big John's buffalo?" she asked.

Isabella nodded.

"How do you know?"

Isabella pointed to a piece of green cloth trampled into the ground several yards away. "McTavish marks his kills in this manner," she replied impassively, then tied the cart pony's lead rope to the dead buffalo's horn and walked around to the rear of the vehicle to gather her tools. When she returned, she handed Celine a pair of knives and a worn whetstone. As Isabella stripped off her heavy capote, Celine idly contemplated plunging one of the sharp blades into the woman's soft abdomen. She didn't, but there was a pointed sense of gratification in visualizing the quick spurt of warm blood over her hand, the look of shock on the old squaw's round face.

"Now you will learn to butcher," Isabella said.

Celine glanced at the fallen buffalo. It lay on its chest with both front legs broken and tucked back along the body. Grabbing the nearest limb close to the hoof, Isabella hauled it roughly around, then cocked the knee at an angle to the body to hold it in place. She made an impatient gesture with her hand, and Celine went around to the opposite side and did the same with the other front leg. Then Isabella drove one of her butcher knives into the back of the buffalo's neck.

Steam rose from the laceration as the warmth of the buffalo's meat was exposed to the cool air. With both hands and an aggressive sawing motion, Isabella drew the blade back over the hump and along the spine. At the base of the tail she repositioned the knife to cut down the back of one leg as far as the hock. Then she moved to the front of the shoulder and did the same there, ending her cut just above the knee. "Now," she said, puffing a little as she grasped a double handful of curly hair at the juncture of the shoulder and spinal cuts, "we pull. See?"

She gave a hefty tug, and an inch or so of hide flaked back to reveal the marbled flesh underneath. A warm, cloying odor was released into the air. Celine breathed deeply, finding the scent strangely intoxicating. She leaned forward to peer into the triangular cavity while Isabella worked her fingers under the leathery rind. Bracing her foot against the buffalo's shoulder, Isabella strained backward, expertly separating hide from body. From time to time she was forced to sever a particularly stubborn piece of membrane with the knife she kept clenched in her right hand, but, to Celine's surprise, the hide came off fairly easily. Within minutes Isabella had one whole side skinned to the ground.

Stepping clear, the old woman straightened slowly, pressing both hands against the small of her back. Glancing at Celine, she said: "Now you do the rest."

"The rest?"

Isabella's lips thinned with impatience.

Celine circled around to the offside. Tentatively she extended a hand over the abrupt termination of hide at the top of the hump. She appreciated the warmth of the meat on her slender fingers. Her hand, stretched horizontally from her shoulder, came just even with the highest part of the buffalo, causing her to marvel at the animal's size. Once she had wondered why the half-breeds didn't train bison to pull their carts, picturing them from memory as little more than mop-headed oxen, but she could see now that any such attempt would be doomed from the start. She could as easily imagine emptying the Great Lakes with buckets.

"Cut," Isabella said gruffly.

Celine placed the tip of her knife against the hide above the neck and pushed down, but nothing happened.

"Hard!" Isabella snapped. She made a quick, downward motion with her hands to illustrate what she meant.

That was all it took. Celine's rage exploded, and with a shrill cry she lifted the knife high in both hands, then plunged it down with all her might. The blade sliced cleanly through the matted hair and hide, going an inch or more into the meat. She screamed and jerked the knife savagely toward her, but her grip slipped and she lurched backward. She remained where she stopped, feet splayed, fists clenched, glaring at Isabella, who held her own knife up defensively.

For half a minute the two women stood frozen, gazes locked. Then Isabella came around the carcass without taking her eyes off of Celine. Returning her own knife to its sheath, she grasped the wooden scales of Celine's knife and worked it back and forth until she'd freed it from the bison's hump. In a calm voice that belied the emotion clearly visible on her face—the tattoos on her chin were wiggling like tiny snakes as her lips trembled—Isabella said: "Jab only to start your cut, as I did. Then you slice. See?" She indicated the top of the hump where she had already peeled the hide away on the opposite side. "Now I will do this side, too, but you must watch and learn. A woman must know how to skin a buffalo. It is her life." She began to slice awkwardly down the side of the neck, though keeping her eyes on the younger woman.

"Are you afraid of me?" Celine asked suddenly.

Isabella stopped and turned, holding the butcher knife in her right hand with the cutting edge turned almost casually up. She shook her head.

"I think you are," Celine said, surprised. She moved closer, and Isabella instantly stepped to one side, away from the buffalo. Celine laughed and said: "Yes, you are." Then her expression changed and she pointed to the carcass. "Show me," she demanded. "Show me how a woman of the *pays sauvage* butchers a buffalo."

Isabella took a deep breath, then turned back to the fallen animal. "Good, yes. I will show you. Like this, see? Slice."

Sweat was glistening from Isabella's forehead by the time she finished butchering the first buffalo. As Celine watched, she skinned the hide down both sides, then laid it out flesh side up like a pink and white tablecloth. On it, she placed only the choicest cuts—the *petite bosse,* that small hump above the cow's neck, the *dépouilles,* from each side of the spine and above the upper ribs, the *grosse bosse,* or large hump above the shoulders, the *plats-côtés,* the *croupe,* and the *brochet.*

She took the liver and the finest fats—both hard and soft—for her pemmican, and the best strips of sinew that she would dry and use as thread. Only at the last did she take that most select of all meats, the tongue. Wrapping it all in the two halves of the hide, she carried both to the cart and pushed them toward the front of the bed. Stepping back, she eyed Celine curiously. "See, it is a simple thing, but you must learn it well if you are to attract a husband."

"Are there not other ways to attract a man?" Celine asked.

It was clear from the immediate shift in Isabella's demeanor that she understood the innuendo, but she didn't acknowledge it. Celine looked to the south where a small party of horsemen was returning. She recognized Big John first, then Charles Hallet, and finally Baptiste LaBarge, leading a fourth mount that was riderless. But she didn't see Gabriel's Baldy among them, and a prickle of alarm coursed down her spine. Whirling toward the old woman, she said: "Does Gabriel mark his kills with pieces of cloth, like Big John?"

Isabella looked momentarily perplexed, but shook her head. "*Non,* he does not."

"Then how does he know?"

"How does he know what?"

"Which buffalo is his."

Isabella just stared for a moment. "Why would he not know which buffalo is his?" she asked finally.

Impatiently Celine flung her arm toward the far-off southern horizon, where so many black lumps of dead buffalo awaited butchering. "They all look alike!"

Isabella's confusion vanished, as did the lingering tendrils of her earlier fear. Deep down, Celine knew she had erred, had lost her leading edge. Laughing softly as she ran the blade of her knife between pinched fingers to clean it, Isabella called to Lizette Hallet, who was dragging a hide toward her own cart a short distance away. She spoke in Cree so that Celine wouldn't understand, but she knew Isabella was ridiculing her by the tone of her voice, and by Lizette's low, answering snicker. Turning back, Isabella said: "Would you not know your own handwriting on a piece of paper, fancy girl, even if a hundred others wrote the same message all around it? A *métis* knows because he is *métis*. A woman knows because she is his woman. A wife, a mother, a daughter, it does not matter. She knows."

"But how will I know?" Celine pressed. "How will I know which buffalo to skin?"

Isabella's voice grew stern. "You will butcher the buffalo I tell you to butcher. None others."

Under her breath, Celine said: "But I must butcher for Gabriel if I am to be his woman." She frowned uncertainly. Was that what she wanted, to be Gabriel's woman? Or was it Pike's? The two images blurred in her mind—young and old, gray and dark.

Isabella had put away her knives and whetstone and was slipping into her capote. Brusquely she said: "You will butcher for your father. Gabriel can dress his own meat." She loosened the cart pony's lead rope, then started south across the barren plain.

They passed a dozen buffalo in the next mile without stopping to examine any of them. Then without warning, Isabella altered her course to approach a smaller bison with short, spikelike horns. After studying the animal for a moment, she glanced at Celine with a wry smile. "You want to butcher Gabriel's buffalo? Then good, I will let you. This is Gabriel's."

Celine walked over to inspect the carcass. A few gnats were still spiraling around the twisted head, and the black nose was clotted with ropy, bloodied snot. Its eyes were open but lifeless, filmed with dust. Hesitantly she toed a small, neatly rounded black hoof. It shifted slightly, then rolled back into its original position.

"You butcher this one like I showed you," Isabella told her. "Then wrap the meat tight in the hide and catch up. We will pick this up on our way back."

"You want me to butcher this one by myself?"

Isabella didn't reply. She brought out a couple of knives and a whetstone and dumped them on the ground beside the buffalo. Then, giving the cart pony's lead rope a series of short, quick tugs, she went on in that slow, waddling gait Celine had come to despise.

It surprised Celine to see how quickly the cart seemed to shrivel as it rattled on along the trampled path of the buffalo. Soon even the shrieks of its axle were silenced by the wide-open spaces. The strengthening wind whipped her dark tresses and her body swayed like a stem of long grass. In the middle of the broad plain she felt suddenly small herself, as if she were shrinking right along with the cart.

She spun a slow circle. In the east, far away, Monique Pouliot was toting a dark bundle toward a minuscule cart. To the northwest, a cluster of women surrounded the men who had returned early from the hunt, although they were too far away to recognize, and much too far to hear her screams, should her life come into jeopardy. Taking a deep breath, she lifted her eyes to the solid mantle of clouds and her heart thrilled. She was alone, completely alone. The freedom of it made her laugh and cry at the same time.

She should have watched more closely. Almost as soon as she picked up one of the knives, Celine realized she didn't know what to do. Her immediate problem seemed to be that Gabriel's young spike had fallen on its side, rather than its chest, as Big John's buffalo had been considerate enough to do. So the wisdom of running her first cut down the spine seemed questionable, especially if she wanted to remove anything from underneath the animal. Although she considered slitting the belly as she'd seen Isabella and others do when skinning deer, she was too daunted by the thought of spilling the intestines. Besides, skinning buffalo with a center cut down the spine seemed to be the accepted way of doing things in the *pays sauvage*. Isabella had done it that way, as had Lizette Hallet. Isabella claimed that a buffalo's hide was larger and thicker than that of a deer or even a moose, and that it was easier to tan if halved first, then sewn back together later. Her own sleeping robe had been cured that way.

Walking around the bull's shoulder, Celine put both hands under the hump and shoved upward, but the massive body didn't even budge. With a small cry of frustration, she kicked the woolly shoulder as hard as she could.

She went around to the belly side. *This is Gabriel's doing,* she thought peevishly. She wasn't his woman, so why did she have to skin his buffalo?

Squatting with her forearms resting on her knees, she stared uncertainly at the buffalo's belly until she suddenly became aware of the jutting sheath of its maleness. She became instantly fascinated. Pushing at the rear leg, she exposed the pouch that held the testes, lying flaccid against the inside of the bull's upper thigh. Stooping closer, she probed the scrotum with her knife, her eyes widening as the tip of the blade easily pierced the finely-haired sac.

There was a plop in the grass beside Celine's knee. Another struck the ground behind her, the sound like a fishing cork hitting the calm surface of a lake. Two more fell on the far side of the buffalo, and thunder rumbled overhead. Within seconds, rain began to splatter the ground around her. She looked up and saw that the clouds had lowered ominously, a dark craggy plate racing past dizzily. Even as she looked, a drop struck her cheek like a miniature slap. With her head tilted back, she opened her mouth wide to catch the icy liquid.

A pony's hoof stamped the ground nearby. Turning, she discovered Lizette Hallet standing behind her, staring. Hallet's expression frightened Celine, and she jumped to her feet, convinced that Indians had somehow crept up on her while she worked. But the plain was empty, and, when she looked again, she realized it was she the Hallet bitch was looking at. Glancing down the length of her body, Celine gasped at the smeared blood and chunks of pale fat that fouled her clothing. Her hands were slick and red, the sleeves of her cloth dress soddened.

"Oh, God," she whimpered, staring at her crimson arms. Then she closed her eyes to shut out the sight. "Oh, God, save me. Please."

Chapter Seventeen

Weary in bone and muscle, his eyes gritty for want of sleep, Big John leaned back against his rolled-up sleeping robe. His legs were stretched to one side of the dying fire, crossed at the ankles. His dudeen sat beside him on a hummock of grass, flint and steel and a half used bit of char lying next to it. Staring reflectively at the hard-packed mud just inside the lodge door, where the grass was already matted flat and nearly worn away, he was only dimly aware of the rain that pattered gently against the thin, bowed hides of the teepee.

Etienne Cyr was still missing. LaBarge had recovered his torn, leather-visored cap and a hoof-scarred fusil from the prairie less than a mile from where he'd come upon Cyr's lame horse, but the little bowlegged hunter hadn't been found. His wife Marie had taken the news stoically, gathering her four young daughters around her and retreating to their lodge. Friends, mostly women, had gone to call, although, according to Isabella, they'd been sparing in their sympathy. No one was willing to admit defeat just yet, or to initiate anything that might be misconstrued as mourning. And everyone had stories to bring, like pies to a picnic—narratives of their own men stranded overnight and surrounded by Sioux or blizzard or flood, then showing up the next day, fit as a fiddle.

There was a stirring against the inner wall of the lodge. Big John's gaze was drawn to the bundle of robes where Alec slept. It occurred to him that he was on the brink of losing that one.

Alec's mood had darkened steadily since Chain of Lakes and the loss of the spotted pony. He had become sullen and insolent, his manner around the stock, Big John's in particular, almost brutal. With an oddly detached curiosity, Big John wondered how the final break would come, never doubting that it would. Drink, perhaps—it was the bane of many of them—or a full-blood's lot, abandoning the *métis* altogether to live among his mother's people.

It pained Big John to think of him that way, turning his back on civilization. Yet it wasn't an unheard-of event among the mixed-bloods, and he could see the appeal of it to a lad of Alec's temperament. A Cree, he would become, if he joined Isabella's tribe.

Envisioning the possibilities left Big John feeling empty and at a loss, for he didn't know how to deal with Alec's willfulness, or if it could even be dealt with at all. Defensively his mind shied away from that problem only to land smack in the middle of another, as it had a dozen times already that evening—Celine.

When Lizette Hallet brought her to him that afternoon, he'd thought at first she'd been gored by a wounded buffalo, some animal lying unconscious until the sting of a butcher's knife broke its paralysis. But as she came closer, he'd recognized the stumbling gait, the loose, vacant expression. She'd looked so much like her mother during those final weeks before her death that Big John had trembled.

Celine lay against the far wall now, buried in buffalo robes, although Big John knew she wasn't asleep. He wondered where her thoughts were, and where they had been. Could they be brought back? He had tried to help her mother and failed. Was that what thwarted him now? Had fear of a second failure so warped his nerve that he could only stand back and watch?

The pattern of the rain changed abruptly, popping louder

and sharper against the sagging lodge covers.

I'm losing them all, he thought with a sudden, sickening clarity. *Celine and Alec, even Gabriel in his own way, like cottonwood spores in a dry summer twister. Only Isabella remains constant.*

As if awakened by his thoughts, Isabella shifted under her robes. Her voice came softly from the rear of the lodge. "It sleets."

"Aye, it does," he replied quietly. " 'Twill be ice over everything by mornin' if it keeps this up."

"You should sleep, McTavish."

He nodded agreeably but made no effort to comply. After a couple of minutes, Isabella settled back in her robes. His thoughts drifted to Pike, bedded down beneath one of the meat carts. Although he told himself Pike couldn't be held accountable for any of the events that had occurred since the beginning of the hunt, he couldn't suppress a niggling sense of unease. He would watch Pike, he decided. The American's strange influence over Celine and his altercation with Gabriel the night the buffalo nearly overran the camp warranted that much. For the first time, he began to grasp some of the apprehension he knew Gabriel had always felt toward the wiry mountaineer.

The last tongue of flame retreated into the coals, plunging the lodge into darkness. Big John lifted his face to the cool draft that, at the same moment, slipped down through the lodge's shuttered smoke hole, stirring the smudgy air the storm had trapped above his head. But if there were any answers in the darkness up there, he couldn't see them.

The storm was gone by morning. The sun rose into a fragile-looking blue sky, strewn in the east with a few small, tardy gray clouds. The land beneath glistened in a husk of ice, all things coated equally—the ground, the carts, the piles of meat, even the horns on the oxen. The hide lodges sagged under the added weight, although the ice was already starting to melt away from the blackened leather at the smoke flaps as the *métis* began their breakfast fires.

With a crisp rattle, Big John flipped the stiff *cabbri* hide back, then paused in the doorway. The slant of the teepee allowed him to stand upright with the lower portion of the entrance tight against his shins, the upper part pressing into the small of his back. He stood quietly looking around, humbled by Nature's display.

There wasn't much activity about except for the little ones, already scampering forth to play, skating over the ice in their heavy, greased winter mocs, laughing and falling and laughing again. Even the dogs stayed close to the lodges, and the stock looked pathetic in the brittle light, miserable and cold, their wet hides steaming. Little balls of dirty ice clung to the long hairs of the animals' bellies, and every now and then, when bumped against another horn or the side of a cart, the ice covering the oxens' horns would shatter and fall with a sound like breaking glass.

On his picket rope behind the lodge, the roan nickered pitifully. In concern, Big John stepped carefully onto the treacherous ground, yet managed only a couple of steps before he was forced to stop with his arms spread wide for balance.

"Easy there, McTavish!" Pike called with a grin. He was sitting cross-legged beneath a cart, his buffalo robe drawn around his waist. His hat was on the ground beside him. He'd pulled the hood of his capote up and tied it snugly closed under his chin to keep his ears warm.

"Ah, Mister Pike, I see ye fared the night well enough."

"Fair to middling." He chuckled. "This is a hell of a note, McTavish, the hardest damn' frost I've seen in a 'coon's age."

Big John laughed, blowing a puffy cloud of breath into the air. "Tell me, Mister Pike, can ye see me runner from where ye sit? He called, but I fear I may not be able to reach him just yet."

"He's fine. So is the bay and the piebald. Just spoiled and uncomfortable, although I don't blame 'em much."

"Well, I wouldn't argue with that. If ye feel up to the adventure, ye're welcome to come to the lodge for a bite of breakfast. We'll be eatin' good after yesterday's harvest."

"I'd be obliged if you'll give me a minute to belly over that way."

"Aye, a minute at least." He grinned, but then the grin faded and for a while they stared silently across the icy gap separating them, each measuring the other in a new, veiled light. A scream from the center of camp severed the moment.

Jerking awkwardly around, Big John spotted a small child on its back, legs cocked skyward. The other children had stopped their play at the panicky cry, and were staring, wide-eyed and frightened. At the same time, a huge sled dog rushed, snarling, from beneath a cart, drawn by the helplessness of the scream, the diminutive size of its prey. Big John's heart slammed into his throat. He felt frozen in place, unable even to call out a warning. Then in the next instant a lodge door flashed open and a *métis* woman leaped out. She slipped immediately on the ice and fell heavily but didn't let that stop her. She crabbed forward on her hands and feet, and Big John breathed a sigh of relief when she reached the child's side. The dog halted about thirty feet away, wagging its tail congenially.

The child's wailing dropped off to whimpering sobs as the woman lifted the youngster in her arms. He recognized Monique Pouliot and knew the child was hers. Even from here, he could see the odd bent of the youth's arm.

Isabella poked her head out of the lodge's entrance.

"Ye'd best be riggin' up some sort of splint," Big John said.

Isabella ducked from sight. Pike sat where he had before, but his rifle was drawn across his lap, ready to fire had the dog gotten much closer.

Big John nodded gratefully to know someone would have done something. Taking his time, he started across the field of ice. Noel Pouliot came out of his lodge, shrugging into a bulky buffalo-robe coat. He slipped as soon as he stepped away from the lodge door, striking the bed of ice with a loud *whoof*. His face paled and blood spurted over his mustache from his nose, but, like Monique, he stayed down and started crawling toward his wife and child.

Big John kept on doggedly, sliding one foot after the other without lifting either. Several children were already gathered around Monique, but none of them were helping. With the child on her lap and clutched in one arm, she began scooting backward on her buttocks toward the lodge. She stopped when Noel reached her side. That was where Big John reached them, helpless on the ground with the child between them.

Noel looked up when Big John's shadow fell over them. "It is broken, Big John," he said, leaning back to reveal a seven-year-old with gentle brown eyes. The sleeve of the girl's leather coat had been pulled up to reveal a protruding knob of flesh just above her left wrist.

Noel's eyes fixed steadily on Big John, and Big John nodded without making him ask. "Aye, old friend, I'll set it as best I can, if ye wish."

"I will give you a fine robe for your help," Noel promised.

"A silk," Monique added, and Noel quickly nodded.

"Ye can pay if such pleases ye, but I'll not be askin' for it, and naught would be enough." He squatted cautiously beside the trio, smiling at the small face that watched his so solemnly. "Aye, and have ye a name, child? Something I can call ye, face up?"

"Her name is Emmaline," Monique said, smiling reassuringly

when Emmaline turned to her.

"Emmaline, eh? Well, 'tis a fine name, and pretty as a spring flower. What happened to ye, lass? Did ye fall while playin' on the ice?"

The child nodded gravely, and Big John, who had suffered a broken bone or two in his own life, knew the real pain hadn't yet set in. It would, though, with a feverish heat and a terrible swelling. Glancing at Noel, he said: "Best we be gettin' to it."

Noel nodded, and, between them and others who had come to their aid, they dragged Monique back to her lodge like a lumpy sleigh, Emmaline cradled firmly in her arms. At the door, Noel took the child from his wife and stepped inside. Monique quickly followed.

"We will be here if our help is needed," Lizette Hallet assured the Pouliots, and Big John nodded and ducked inside, pulling the flap closed against the frigid air.

Monique instructed one of the older children to build up the fire while she and Noel stripped off Emmaline's outer garments. Big John knelt at the girl's side and gently lifted her arm. It seemed so soft and delicate, dwarfed by his own huge, leathery paw. He had set broken bones before, but never one so small.

Holding the arm gently in one hand, he lightly stroked her fingers with the other. Looking at Noel, he said: "Ye'll not be ridin' with them now, I suppose. Breland and them that go out to look again for Etienne?"

Noel shook his head. "*Non*, not now. I will stay and help with the fires and the meat."

" 'Tis just as well. Nine will serve as tolerable as ten, and ye help will be needed here." He smiled disarmingly at Noel's puzzled expression and his grip tightened ever so slightly around Emmaline's hand. Without looking down, he gave it a firm, steady pull. There was a quick grating sound as the broken bones snapped back in place, but that was all. Emmaline, who had been listening almost drowsily to Big John's voice, gave a start, then gawked at her straightened arm.

Big John smiled at her and winked. "Isabella Gilray will be here soon to splint that arm for ye, but I'm thinkin' the worst will be over for a while. Was it so bad?"

Emmaline shook her head.

Smiling, Noel gave Emmaline's shoulder a quick squeeze, then went to their packs at the rear of the lodge. From a painted rawhide parfleche he retrieved a bottle of high wine. "For you, Big John. To keep you warm until I find that silk."

"Aye, Noel, and I'll be takin' it, too, but only if ye help me with the drinkin' later."

Noel laughed. "You are a good friend. Yes. Tonight your family will come to my lodge, and we will eat fresh buffalo and drink until we fall down."

"Until tonight, then." Big John nodded his good bye to Monique and left the lodge just as Isabella appeared with a splint carved from a willow limb. She smiled warmly as she passed, and Big John returned the expression, knowing that, if he wasn't too drunk tonight, she would come to his robes for an hour or so and they would make love. The prospect pleased him, and the smile clung to his face as he made his way back to his own lodge.

It was afternoon before the ice melted off enough for the adults to get safely around. When it did, the women began unloading the saplings they had brought with them from the Salt River, and with strips of rawhide and excited chatter they erected their drying stages. Over these they draped the thin sheets of buffalo meat harvested the day before, most of them averaging eight to ten inches across and as much as two feet long. Under the stages they built small fires to accelerate the drying process, although had the temperature been warmer or the meat not so soaked in yesterday's rain, they would have let it dry naturally in the sun and wind.

While the women cared for the meat, the older boys drove the oxen and cart ponies to a long, rain-freshened slough a couple of miles away to drink, then turned them loose to graze. The caravan itself was camped just west of the low ridge where the run had started the day before, in the middle of a flat, treeless plain. Although there was no wood and only the tainted water of the distant slough for their stock—the *métis* had set their kettles and pots out overnight to catch as much rain water as they could—no one was willing to leave until news of Etienne Cyr was received.

In an election the night before, Joseph Breland had been chosen to lead the search. He would take eight men with him, now that Pouliot was staying behind, and scour the plains from the ridge southward. They would pack enough food with them to last several days, remembering the time Charlo's buffalo runner had stumbled in the middle of a chase. Charlo had kicked free of the saddle just as the pony fell, and managed to grab a handful of curly hair behind a cow's surging hump before he was trampled. He'd run alongside the galloping bison until he was able to swing astride, but it was late in the day before the spooked herd slowed and scattered enough that the old hunter felt safe in dropping to the ground and making his escape. The trouble was, by that time, the stampede had carried him nearly forty miles from where the caravan was camped.

Charlo's misadventure was what they were all hoping had happened to Cyr. By this time, it seemed like the only real hope they had left.

Breland was lashing his sleeping robe behind his pad saddle when Big John walked up. "You have come to wish me luck, Big John?" the lanky mixed-blood asked, his blue eyes crinkling in a rare smile.

"Ye'll be makin' ye own luck, Joseph, and doin' a fine job of it, too. No, the truth is I came to ask ye how far ye planned to go."

Breland gave him a measured look. "That would depend, Big John. You know that."

Big John waited patiently, without reply.

"All right," Breland said quietly. "I do not think Etienne lives, although I would give my runner and all that I own if that were false. If we find him, we will return immediately, either to celebrate his survival or to bury him where his family can say good bye. If we do not find him, I have a desire to know how far the buffalo ran yesterday, and in which direction they are traveling. It could save us many days' effort to have that information when the caravan is ready to pull out."

Big John nodded. It seemed like a wise decision. He stepped back, and Breland mounted. "Be safe, Joseph, and watch yeself."

"We will be back in no more than four days, one way or the other," he said, reining his horse around.

After the search party left, Big John returned to his lodge. He passed Alec and Isidore Turcotte on the way. The two young men were sitting on a cart shaft, smoking their pipes and watching some of the girls and younger women scrape hides. Neither spoke as he passed, and Alec turned his face away in a deliberate snub.

Big John found Isabella working on the meat he'd harvested yesterday. She had already set the best pieces—the tenderloin, the two humps, the tongues, and the belly meat—aside to be eaten fresh. The rest she would dry, then flay into tiny splinters to which she would add tart buffalo berries and plums, picked and crushed and dried last summer. Later she would shovel the flayed meat and berries into a kettle of melted fat, mixing the whole to a uniform consistency. The liquid pemmican would then be poured into a bull-hide *taureau* and sewn shut. As the green hide dried it would shrink considerably, compacting the pemmican into a hard mass. A single *taureau* weighed about ninety pounds, fifty of meat to forty of fat, but, because Isabella used only the choicest cuts, it would require the yield of nearly two young cows to fill one sack. Big John had only killed two on his first run, enough for a single bag. It would take another four or five *taureaux*, along with the hides and baled meat, to complete the load of a single cart.

Isabella's pemmican was some of the best in the valley, and she was always able to command a high price for it. Normally the post factor at Fort Douglas kept her pemmican for his own consumption, and sent a lesser quality on to feed the *voyageurs* as they made their way into the deeper recesses of the Bay Company's empire. There was no secret to Isabella's success with pemmican. Berries and fruit when the season provided it, and the use of both hard and soft fats, gave it a better flavor.

Sitting in the sun nearby, Big John quietly smoked his pipe while the women busied themselves with the meat and hides. Celine toiled docilely alongside Isabella, withdrawn but efficient. She wore a Cree dress of blue wool today, decorated with silk ribbons sewn across the bodice. Last night Isabella had washed the girl's old, blood-spattered outfit as best she could in the slough, then hung it from the lodge liner to dry, despite Big John's suggestion that she burn it. He knew he would never be able to look at that dress again without envisioning Celine as she had been when Lizette brought her to him.

The feeling of melancholy that had begun to engulf him last night deepened. Etienne Cyr's absence loomed over the camp, and the twin enigmas that were Celine and Alec were like splinters in his shirt, pricking his flesh every time he moved. But he knew there was more to his depression than that. The truth was, his knees hurt and his back ached, and looking at the pipe in his hand generated only a blurred, cream-colored smear.

I'm growing old, he reflected in something like surprise. *Old and losing my children, and my life is changing forever.*

He wasn't ready for that. Not yet.

He was also just beginning to realize that he was losing his position of leadership within the *métis* community, although that didn't bother him as much as he once would have imagined. His constant warnings about the decline of the buffalo, and overhunting in general, plus his unyielding stance toward Hudson's Bay, weren't helping his cause any. But what really hurt was that he seemed to be losing the respect of some of the *métis.* Not all of them, for sure, but a few.

Respect was a thing Big John had always taken for granted, and he was discovering that its loss, no matter how minute at the moment, struck a chord of uncertainty within him, a fear for the future. What would tomorrow hold, he pondered, when all he had ever cared about appeared to be slipping irretrievably away?

Gabriel sat cross-legged on his bedroll inside the lodge, lazily tending to the fire where he was was melting a pig of lead in a small iron pot to run some balls for his musket. He barely looked up when Alec ducked through the entrance and flopped down against the wall across from him.

"I am leaving as soon as we return to the valley," Alec stated boldly.

Carefully Gabriel spooned the multi-hued dross from the top of the bright silver liquid, giving himself a moment to think. A year ago, he might have guffawed at his brother's declaration. Today he took the threat seriously. "Where?" he asked without looking up.

"To the North country. I will work for Hudson's Bay."

"A thousand men would work for Hudson's Bay if the jobs

were available. What makes you think they would hire you?"

"Because I am young and a hard worker, and because I know how to read and write and figure."

"Not so good, the figuring, though?"

"It does not matter. I will not stay with McTavish another year."

Gabriel nodded, but kept his eyes on the low flames. He knew Big John had made a mistake in taking the pinto from Alec, humiliating him in front of his peers.

"Or maybe I will become a *voyageur,*" Alec said. "I will go to Montreal and horn the girls plenty."

Gabriel laughed. "What do you know of horning girls?"

Alec's smile faded. "I know you should be horning Susanne Leveille, instead of rutting after the dim one. It does not seem right, anyway. She is Big John's daughter."

"I am not Big John's son. Neither are you."

"Maybe, but it still does not seem right. Even Isidore says so, and he is stupid."

"Then why do you listen to what Isidore says?"

"It is also what Charlo says," Alec replied somberly. "Charlo, Gabriel."

Gabriel leaned forward to nudge the melting pot closer to the flame. Staring at the softening lead, he said: "Charlo does not know everything."

"Once you thought he did."

And not that long ago, either, Gabriel acknowledged to himself. But things had changed recently, and he was no longer sure what he believed. He supposed his feelings toward Celine were foolish, especially in light of the way she acted around Pike, but down deep he thought she was only frightened, and that sooner or later she would realize that she was wrong about Pike, and about him, too.

"Do you believe she bathed in the blood," Alec asked, "and

wallowed in the intestines?"

"No," Gabriel replied, looking up in disgust. "That is the foolish cackling of gossips. I remember the first time you butchered a deer. You made a fine mess of it."

"I knew enough not to stick my hands in blood up to my elbows," Alec countered. "Besides, Lizette Hallet saw her."

"Lizette Hallet hates Celine. They all do, but not because she is dim. They hate her because she is different, because she doesn't know how to butcher a buffalo or make pemmican or tan a robe. And because once her life was easier than theirs."

Alec shrugged, and Gabriel knew he had already dismissed the subject of Celine McTavish. "As soon as we return, I will go to Fort Douglas and find work. Then next spring I will harvest my own buffalo. Maybe I will go to the Saskatchewan District and hunt there."

"Or maybe you will be back on the Tongue, asking Big John if he will feed you," Gabriel replied.

Laughing, Alec said: "I just wanted you to know that you can come with me, if you want."

"I don't need you to tell me where I can go. I do as I choose."

Alec shrugged and pushed to his feet, exiting the lodge but leaving the antelope hide back, the cold air pouring in. Gabriel watched until he turned from sight behind Quesnelle's teepee, then pulled the pot off the fire and brought out his ladle.

Chapter Eighteen

Pike's nose ran and his eyes watered. Cursing the icy blasts of wind that sliced down over the plain from the northwest, he scanned the flat thread of the horizon. His lips curled back in distaste. It was an empty land they traveled through, made all the more desolate by the season, that time between fall and winter when everything, even a man's spirit, seems gray and lifeless.

To the south, the cart train was creeping across a broad, shallow basin, the shrieks of its many wheels mercifully silenced by distance and a stiff, quartering wind. The caravan was formed into three stubby columns today, as it had been ever since they'd departed the broken country around Chain of Lakes. The spare stock brought up the rear like a huge oval rug being pulled behind the carts.

The caravan was angling west by southwest toward a place called Turtle Lake, where McTavish claimed there would be a smattering of trees to give the country perspective, and plenty of clean water if the buffalo hadn't gotten there first to foul it. It was four days now since the hunt, and neither Etienne Cyr nor Joseph Breland and his eight had returned.

With his head turned to watch the caravan, Pike thought he caught a glimpse of movement from the corner of his eye, to his rear. He twisted in the saddle to stare back the way they'd come, but nothing stirred on the barren plain. Yet the impression remained, and he stopped the bay and swung it around to face east. Nearly a quarter of a mile in front of him, Jacques Leveille saw him pause and reined up his own horse. After a couple of minutes, the goateed half-breed loped back to join him.

"You see something?" Leveille queried, pulling up.

"Maybe," Pike replied, rubbing the stiff wool of his sleeve under his dripping nose. Leveille looked doubtful but kept his opinions to himself. After another few minutes, Pike shrugged. "Maybe not," he allowed.

"What was it?" Leveille asked.

"I thought I saw something move."

Leveille continued to stare along their back trail. Pike thought he looked more worried now. Pike felt the same way, an uneasiness he couldn't put his finger on was toying with his scalp.

"Sioux?" Leveille asked.

"I don't see anything now."

"To tell you the truth, *mon ami,* that kind of worries me."

Pike knuckled his wind-blurred eyes and squinted toward the horizon, but the prairie remained empty beneath its vast canopy of blue, and he felt suddenly foolish. With a stiff grunt, he said: "Hell, it wasn't anything. Just the wind in the grass, most like."

"Sacre bleu," Leveille responded dryly. "It was no trick, *Monsieur* Pike."

Pike looked again, and his mouth went dry. Leveille watched a moment longer, as if mesmerized, then with a terrified squawk he jerked his horse around and quirted for the caravan, shouting: *"Aux armes! Aux armes! Voila les Sioux! Les Sioux! Voila les Sioux! Aux armes!"*

Pike held the bay back a while longer, staring at a horizon that seemed to spit up feathered horsemen by the dozens. Then he swore, softly and in awe, and raced after Leveille.

Curling himself over the broad, mesquite horn of his Mexican saddle, Pike raked the bay's ribs with his spurs. He kept glancing over his left shoulder as the bay stretched out toward the distant caravan. He estimated at least two hundred warriors were charging down on the cart train. He could see the brittle glint of sunlight flashing off steel lance heads, the blue sheen of fusil barrels, the occasional sparkle of a polished sword. The Sioux were coming on with everything they had, howling their war cries.

Turcotte was already running the carts into a circle, tailgates butting the earth, wheels lashed together with rawhide and rope, shafts projecting skyward like the spears of an ancient army. The herdsmen were driving the extra stock into the corral of carts even before the circle was completed. It took only minutes for the *métis* to enclose themselves and their animals. After that, it was only a matter of stuffing dried buffalo meat, wooden cassettes, and bundled hides into the larger gaps, then finding a hole to shoot through. They would be ready by the time the Sioux came within range, but it wasn't the mixed-bloods sheltered behind the carts that the Indians were after now.

Eyeing the forward line of warriors, those on the fastest ponies, Pike tried to gauge the bay's speed against theirs. With a sinking sensation, he knew the bay would never make it. The little gelding was giving everything he had, but he was too small, his legs too short, and, although the caravan was less than five hundred yards away, the Sioux were one hundred yards less than that on his left, coming at the train from its rear.

Most of the *métis* guardsmen were already in. Only the flankers—Leveille and Pike on the north, a couple of others to the south—were still out. The bulk of the Sioux war party was trailing perhaps thirty warriors who rode the swiftest mounts, and Pike figured it would be one of these who would raise his hair if anyone did.

A few ineffectual rounds were already being fired from the caravan, although they were mostly for effect. The Sioux were intimately acquainted with the *métis'* marksmanship within the limited range of their smoothbored trade guns, and were even now veering wide to avoid drawing too close.

The advance group of thirty had split to skirt the train on the north and south. That left slightly more than a dozen yipping warriors pressing forward to cut off Pike's escape. Leveille had already passed through that protective ring of the half-breeds' fusils, but Pike had held back too long when the Sioux first appeared. He judged now that at least three of the dozen or so warriors riding down on him would intercept him before he passed within range of the *métis'* weapons.

As the gap closed, Pike began to pick out details. The lead warrior was a tall, broad-chested man with a lance in one hand, a painted, buffalo-hide war shield in the other; a bow and quiver of arrows were slanted across his back. He rode a long-legged black horse that was dotted with silver-dollar-size vermillion spots across its chest and down both front legs as far as its knees.

The other two Indians carried flintlocks, although both of them also bore bows and quivers. The outside brave rode a sorrel nearly the match of McTavish's big roan, the other a gray that was also covered in designs of vermillion and yellow. These three were about forty yards ahead of their nearest followers, and, when Pike was sure he wouldn't be able to outrun them, he swerved the bay toward them in a sally that caught all three warriors off guard.

Even though he knew a shot would be chancy, Pike figured it was worth the risk. He threw the rifle to his shoulder, and, when the lead warrior's black horse bobbed into view at the end of the barrel, he pulled the trigger.

There wasn't time to reload. The black horse squealed as it went down, throwing its rider over its head. Using the crippled animal as a shield—keeping the bay behind it for no more than a few seconds, yet time enough to break the stride of the other two horses and buy himself a few precious yards—Pike reined toward the caravan.

But a few seconds wasn't enough. The brave on the sorrel closed next. Leveling his fusil from less than a dozen yards away, he triggered a shot that was impossible to dodge. Pike felt the tug and burn of the ball as it seared his ribs, and stifled a cry. He didn't try to examine it. What was done was done. He would have to fight with everything he had, and worry about the damage later.

As the sorrel pounded closer, Pike abruptly reined the bay into it, slamming the butt of his rifle against the side of the animal's head. At that same instant, the warrior leaned forward to bring his empty fusil down like a club. The round blue barrel slammed into Pike's thigh, skidding along his leg in an explosion of pain that blossomed in his left knee. The Indian swung again but Pike deflected the blow with his rifle this time. Then the sorrel's front legs buckled and it dropped unexpectedly from the bay's side.

Before Pike could glance back to see what had happened, the rider on the gray touched off his charge. There was another quick burst of pain, this time in his hip, and he grunted loudly and nearly tumbled from the saddle until he grabbed the horn and pulled himself upright. But the bay never broke stride, and, before the warrior on the gray could bring his mount any closer, they had passed through that indistinct ring of relative safety within the range of the half-breeds' weapons.

A ragged volley was loosened from the wall of carts. Pike heard the thumping whine of lead passing on his left like a swarm of bees. The warrior on the gray must have heard it, too, because he suddenly pulled away, angling back out of range. For the first time since his race for the carts began, Pike started to think he might have a chance. The caravan was less than eighty yards away and the Sioux were pulling back. Leveille was already swinging down, securing his pony to an axle. Soon his fusil would add to the covering fire.

So convinced was Pike that he was going to reach the carts that, for a second, he couldn't comprehend the stubby war arrow that thunked solidly into the bay's dusty hide just behind its shoulder. The horse stumbled and almost went down. Sawing back on the reins, Pike managed to bring the gelding to its feet. But the wound was severe, and after a few more faltering strides, the bay started to fall. This time, Pike couldn't keep the horse up. As the bay began its long slope onto the ground, Pike tried to kick free of the heavy wooden stirrups, but his left leg refused to work properly, and he was still trying to push away when the ground came up like a sledge-hammer.

Bloodied and dazed, Pike eased onto one elbow. He heard a distant crack, like the pop of a teamster's bullwhip, then several more in quick succession. A lead ball smacked into the earth a couple of feet in front of him, and suddenly the world snapped back into focus. Pushing to his hands and his good knee, he scrambled toward his downed horse. His rifle lay nearby and he grabbed it on the way, then dived into the curl of the dead pony's legs. Twisting around to a sitting position, he quickly reloaded.

Most of the Sioux had seemed willing to give up on him while he'd been mounted, but, with the bay's fall, they were returning. Although Pike was too close to the deadly guns of the half-breeds for the Indians to try to overrun him with one fatal charge, they continued to harass him by urging their horses in close enough to loosen an arrow or two or touch off a fusil before curving back out of range. The ground surrounding the bay was soon stubbled with a crop of arrows, the sod ripped and torn by gunfire.

Grimly Pike slid his flintlock across the bay's shoulder. A

Sioux on a short-coupled dun was galloping toward him, coming close enough to let fly an arrow that thudded into the frame of his saddle. Lining his sights on the brave's torso, Pike squeezed the trigger. When the smoke cleared, he saw the Sioux sprawled limply in the short grass. Yet it seemed a shallow triumph; no sooner did he fire than a dozen others raced in to finish him off before he could reload. Only a ragged volley from the caravan stopped them.

In the east, Pike noticed a growing number of warriors dropping out of the battle. With the advantage of surprise lost, their chances of routing the half-breeds would be slim, at best. Still, Pike knew the fight was far from won. Even from his crouched position behind the bay, several hundred yards away, he could see the animated gestures of a number of warriors pressing for another charge.

"Sons-of-bitches," he muttered, snapping the frizzen closed over a freshly primed pan.

There was a shout from the caravan. Pike glanced over his shoulder to see Jacques Leveille's horse pounding toward him, hoofs flashing above the tawny plain. Pike's fingers tightened around the stock of his rifle, and he closed his eyes in a moment of overwhelming gratitude. Here was an unexpected second chance—if they could pull it off.

Already a few warriors were racing in from the opposite direction, and it occurred to Pike that this was an unanticipated opportunity for the Sioux, as well—two fine scalps and maybe a good *métis* buffalo runner, to boot.

Clouds of powder smoke began to mushroom along the line of carts as the Sioux drew close. Pike pushed to his feet, sucking in his breath as a fresh burst of pain surged along his left leg from groin to knee. Stubbornly he plunged toward the carts in an awkward, lurching run, while the drumming of hoofs grew louder from behind. At the last minute he spun and threw the rifle to his shoulder, snapping off a shot that spilled a warrior from his horse. Then he turned to the carts and Leveille's horse was there, but it wasn't Leveille riding it.

"Get on!" Gabriel shouted, pulling the horse down to pivot it tightly around Pike. Pike grabbed the half-breed's waist, then let the momentum of the wheeling pony help yank him up. With his injured leg gone nearly to rubber, he almost didn't make it, but then he latched onto Gabriel's sash with his other hand and jack-knifed up behind the saddle.

The Sioux were on them then. Gabriel fired his musket point-blank into a brave's chest. Pike slammed his rifle across the face of another. A ball from the caravan tumbled a third from his mount. Gabriel lashed the runner with his quirt. Pike beat at its croup with his rifle. The Indians didn't attempt to follow, but they were laying down a withering fire. An arrow sliced the air next to Pike's cheek, tugging at his long, wind-tangled hair. Another struck the steel buttplate of his rifle and almost tore it from his grasp. Finally, miraculously, they passed out of bow range. Clouds of gunsmoke nearly obscured the wall of carts as the half-breeds quickened their rate of fire, and the Sioux were forced to withdraw.

Gabriel didn't pull up until they were almost at the carts. For a second Pike thought he was going to crash the horse into them. Then Gabriel hauled back on the reins and the horse went into a slide that rattled the wooden beds with chunks of sod. Pike jumped clear, and this time his leg did give out, dumping him on his face. Gabriel swung to the ground and quickly hitched the reins to an axle, but the horse was half crazy with fear and immediately jerked back and broke free. Although Gabriel grabbed for what was left of the reins, he was too slow, and the horse took off down the length of the caravan with its nose high in the air, disappearing around the bend.

Pike rolled onto his back and tried to reload, but suddenly

nothing seemed to work right. He could see and hear clearly, yet every time he made an effort to pry the stopper from the powder horn's throat, the ball of his thumb would skid clumsily away. He started to swear, but the words came out garbled, and finally he just lay back.

Kneeling at his side, Gabriel asked: "Are you hurt badly?"

Pike shook his head. With his face turned away, he was staring past the littered plain to where the Sioux were abandoning their attack. Even as he watched, several of them began to drift toward the larger group, those Indians who had dropped out of the fight earlier.

"Gonna be hell to pay here in a few minutes," he croaked.

"I know," Gabriel said, tugging at the sash holding Pike's capote closed.

Pike struggled to bring the younger man's face into focus. "Looks like I owe you a heap now, too. I'm gonna be running buffalo out here for the rest of my damn' life."

Gabriel didn't answer. He pulled the coat back, scowling at the wound in Pike's side. "It is not bad, but it is not good. A crease, but deep." He met Pike's gaze impassively. "Another inch and you would have died, very slowly and very painfully."

"Another inch the other way and it would've only scratched me," Pike pointed out. Around him, half-breeds were dropping over the carts, scurrying onto the plain with their fusils in one hand, shovels, axes, and hide scrapers in the other. "What the hell?" he mumbled.

"They will dig trenches if there is time," Gabriel explained. "Already an ox has died from a fusil ball that found its way through the carts. We must keep the Sioux as far away from the train as possible. Roll onto your stomach. I want to look at your back."

"Don't be frettin' over my hide. Go help 'em with the digging. I'll slap a patch over this when things slow down a mite."

"You talk too much," Gabriel said. "Roll over while there is time. The Sioux will not wait forever."

Pike twisted onto his stomach, gritting his teeth against the harsh burn of his wounds. He had been pushing on adrenaline ever since spotting the Sioux, but that energy was beginning to ebb.

A woman's voice came from inside the carts, and Gabriel replied: "There is a musket ball in his hip, but it is not too deep. There are splinters of wood and rawhide around it, though. I think the ball must have passed through the back of his saddle first. It is his side that needs the most attention. Bring sinew and a needle."

"God-dammit, get on out there," Pike said huskily. "I'll be along as soon as I catch my breath."

"I do not think so," Gabriel replied. "Isabella will see to your wounds. When she comes, I must leave."

McTavish's chunky squaw soon hove into view, carrying a buffalo bladder filled with water, a small rawhide parfleche painted in muted colors, and a length of amber sinew. Placing her medical kit on the grass next to Pike, she lowered herself to her knees at his side. Gabriel touched her shoulder lightly, then left without speaking. Isabella's eyes rested on Pike's face a moment, then she went to work, freeing the long tails of his shirt first to examine the wound in his side. After a couple of minutes of poking, she sat back on her calves.

"The ball touched a rib but did not break it. Your medicine was good this day, otherwise you would be dead."

"More likely it's because a Sioux can't shoot a long gun worth a damn," Pike said.

Isabella peeled a length of thread-size sinew from the narrow strip and rolled it into a marble-size ball that she placed in her mouth, leaving about a quarter of an inch of one end protruding from between her lips. While the sinew softened in saliva, she untied the whang from around the mouth of the bladder and spilled a little water onto a cotton rag.

Pike flinched when the cold cloth touched his bruised flesh, then hardened himself to it. Isabella swiftly cleaned the wound, then set the rag and bladder aside. From the parfleche, she brought out a brass needle case and a pair of tiny, gold-inlaid scissors that looked too delicate to cut much more than the thinnest of papers. Setting those aside, she took the moistened sinew from her mouth and threaded it through the eye of a stout harness needle.

"This will hurt bad," she told him matter-of-factly, snipping off the stiff, quarter-inch section she'd used to guide the sinew through the needle.

But Pike already knew that, and was focusing his attention on the half-breeds as they chipped frantically at the hard soil. The Sioux were stirring again; a bunch of them that he took to be leading warriors and war chiefs were edging around to the northeast. They seemed to be arguing, gesticulating wildly to make their points. After several minutes of this, half a dozen or so Sioux extracted themselves from the larger party to cautiously approach the caravan. They stopped just out of range, and from there a single horseman advanced another thirty yards, his warbonnet flapping gently in the wind. Raising an eight-foot lance furred with the scalp locks of his enemies, he began to speak loudly in Sioux.

"What's he saying?" Pike demanded of Isabella, then grunted and slammed the side of his face against the ground as she ran her needle through the edge of his wound on both sides and tugged it closed. "*Jesus Christ,*" he hissed.

"The pain cannot be avoided," she said with what might have been a trace of compassion, "but it will soon pass."

"The hell with the pain," Pike grated, panting. "What's that redskin saying?"

"He says he is Black Fish, and that he is war chief of his village. He says that they are Yankton Sioux, and that this is their land. He says the *bois brûles* are trespassers and thieves who steal the Yankton's buffalo and wood and water and grass, and that the *bois brûles* have killed brave Yankton warriors this day, and that for this, they . . . we . . . must pay. He says twenty guns and enough powder and shot for one hundred rounds for each gun, and one hundred knives and belt axes, and ten good buffalo runners. He says that if the *bois brûles* do this, we can go on, but that if we do not, then the Yankton will surely wipe us out and sell the women to the Pawnees." She took another pass with her needle and pulled the flesh tight. "You will scar," she remarked absently, eyeing her work. "Perhaps if I took smaller stitches. . . ."

Turcotte was speaking now. Pike tried to hitch himself around to watch, but Isabella pushed him down. "Do not squirm so much. You do not have to see in order to hear. I will tell you what is said."

"Where's my rifle?" Pike asked suddenly. He forced himself up on one elbow, batting her hands aside. "Where's my goddamned rifle, woman?"

"There!" Isabella snapped, pointing behind him. He twisted around to see it leaning against one of the carts. He didn't remember putting it there, and wondered if Gabriel had.

"Is it loaded?"

"I do not know. Hold still. I must finish this if you are to fight later."

Pike swiveled back to listen to Turcotte. "Now what's he saying?"

"You must be still!" Isabella scolded. "I cannot work this way."

Pike swore and tipped his face into his arms as another wave of dizziness pulsed through him. "What's he saying?"

Isabella slowed her sewing almost imperceptibly, then went back to work. "He says no," she replied without fanfare.

Pike smiled into the grass. "*Bueno,* that's good." He chuckled. "That shines for a fact." He tried to relax, taking deep breaths. "You about finished?" he asked.

"I am maybe half done. I could have been finished if you did not wiggle so much. Sewing on you is like trying to skin a live snake."

Pike didn't answer. He could hear Black Fish continuing to harangue Turcotte and the others, but he didn't have to understand the language to know what was being said, or what would happen next. Turcotte had refused the Yankton's first demand. Perhaps he would give in later, through negotiation, to a lower price. Or maybe he wouldn't. Either way, it would take some time to sort out, maybe as long as an hour. And it was good that Turcotte hadn't given in too readily. It might have gone harder on them in the long run if he had. Dealing with hostiles was something of an art, Pike knew, a fine balance of bluff and deference; too much of either could convey the wrong message. In the meantime, he could relax a few minutes, let some of his strength return. He was hoping the light-headedness would pass, too. He wasn't going to be much good if he passed out in the middle of an attack.

After suturing the crease in his side, Isabella bound the wound with a length of cotton cloth, then leaned back and said: "Now I must look at your butt."

Pike almost refused, but then he laughed and said—"What the hell."—and thumbed his trousers down far enough to expose the mangled flesh on his hip. Isabella leaned close to peer at the damage, softly clucking her tongue.

"I think Gabriel was right," she said after a while. "The ball is still in your hip, but it is not deep. It must come out, though, or it will maybe poison your blood and kill you anyway."

"Then get it out," Pike said gruffly.

Her touch was gentle as she probed the bruised flesh, but still he had to grit his teeth to keep from crying out. "There are splinters of wood and rawhide that must also be removed," she said, peering intently into the bloodied wound. "The rawhide may not be too painful, as it already turns soft in your blood, but the wooden splinters are small, and the skin here is much torn. It will not be easy."

"If they gotta come out, do it."

"They must come out," she agreed, then tapped his shooting bag. "Do you have a bullet mold?"

She opened the flap without waiting for a reply, rummaging through the leather bag until she found his mold. She studied the steel, pliers-like contraption for a moment, opening and closing the jaws speculatively, then nodded her satisfaction.

"This will work," she said, running a finger along the slight, inward curve of the two hafts. "I will use the handles to remove the ball. That will cause less pain than cutting it out with a knife." She gave him a sober look. "Maybe that way you will not scream so loud."

"It ain't deep enough to scream over," Pike returned as nonchalantly as his ragged breathing would allow.

Isabella washed away as much of the blood as she could, then began to probe for the spent ball. Pike's face twisted in a grimace, and, although he was determined not to cry out, he couldn't prevent a thin, sputtering whistle from escaping between his teeth. Isabella continued to cluck her tongue against the roof of her mouth as she labored over his buttocks, but soon she sat back with a small exclamation of delight, thrusting the misshapened ball in front of Pike's face.

"See, it was so near the surface it almost fell out. It is a good thing it did not go any deeper, though. It could have crippled you." She fingered the handles apart to allow the bloody chunk of lead to drop into the grass in front of his nose.

Pike concentrated on slow, deep breaths as Isabella began the tedious process of digging for splinters with the tip of her knife. Sweat poured off his face and stung his eyes, and his throat felt as dry as the inside of an abobe brick. He tried to focus on the half dozen or so *métis* within his vision. They'd already scooped out shallow craters about fifty yards from the carts, and were packing the dirt down in front them. It would be scanty shelter, at best, he figured—they would have to sprawl belly-flat to fire, and reload from the same position—but it was something, and more than the Sioux would have.

Turcotte and Black Fish were still palavering, but their voices seemed muted, more fuzzy than distant. Pike blinked suddenly and shook his head, fighting back a slowly descending curtain of blackness.

"You must not pass out," Isabella reprimanded him sharply, jabbing his shoulder with her finger. "Do you hear me, American?"

Pike lifted his head to look around. On the prairie, the *métis* had stopped digging and were standing next to their pits, their fusils at the ready.

"The Sioux have rejected René's offer of ten Northwest guns and fifty rounds of ammunition," Isabella said. "Now I think maybe we will fight again." She gave the waist of his trousers an upward tug. "Come. I have removed the largest splinters. The rest will have to wait until later."

Pike struggled to his feet, staggering a little. Isabella shoved his rifle into his hands, then linked her arm through his and led him to a gap between two of the carts.

"We must hurry now," she urged. "There is not much time left."

He had to get down on his hands and knees to crawl through. As soon as Isabella had wiggled in after him, she and another woman began shoving slabs of dried meat and bundles of untanned hides back into the gap. Pike had to wait until another wave of dizziness passed, then he began methodically to reload. By the time he heard Turcotte's warning shout, he was ready.

Chapter Nineteen

The Brown Bess rocked Gabriel's shoulder. Through the smoke he saw a warrior lurch atop his pony, then pull it around and race out of range. Rolling onto his back, he slanted the musket across his chest and quickly reloaded. As he did, a fusil's ball channeled a path through the sod several feet to his right. Seconds later, an arrow thudded into the mound of dirt in front of his pit.

The Sioux were circling the entrenched *métis* at a gallop, darting in occasionally to fire an arrow or gun, then immediately withdrawing. A few abandoned their mounts to run in on foot, seeking shelter behind the bodies of the dead horses that littered the field. These Yanktons were keeping up a steady sniping, but the war party had so far avoided a direct charge. That was more or less what the *bois brûles* had expected. The Sioux wanted glory and honor. They wanted ponies, scalps, and plunder. What they didn't want was the heavy loss of life a pointblank assault would incur. The *bois brûles* wouldn't have risked pits on the open prairie if they thought the Yanktons would attempt to ride over them *en masse*.

A lot of the Sioux, Black Fish among them, had refused to take part in the battle altogether. They sat their ponies well out of range, watching as their more obstinate comrades threw themselves futilely against the line of *métis* marksmen. As time passed, the confidence of the *bois brûles* began to grow. Between shots they would call out derogatory comments or flash obscene gestures. In the rifle pit to Gabriel's right, Nicolas Quesnelle leaped impulsively to his feet. Raising his smoothbore above his head, he shook it toward the Yanktons as he broke into an impromptu jig.

"Coyotes!" he shouted at the top of his lungs. "Old women who pee in their robes!"

He was still gleefully prancing from one foot to the other when a bullet slammed into his chest, knocking him flat on his back.

There was a scream from the caravan, followed by a distant, horrified: "Papa!"

Keeping low, Gabriel scrambled across the intervening distance, dropping to his knees beside the stocky half-blood. "Nicolas, are you all right?"

Quesnelle was struggling to sit up. He looked pale and a bit muddled, and there was blood on his chin from where he had bitten his lip, but Gabriel didn't see any evidence of a wound.

"Sacre bleu," Quesnelle mumbled, rubbing his chest. Then, from his lap, he picked up a lead ball, slightly flattened on one side. He pulled the deep-cut neck of his shirt out to peer down his chest. "A spent ball," he said, chuckling with relief. "I got a bruise, Gabriel, but that is all."

Gabriel waved to the caravan to let those inside know that Quesnelle was all right. Patting the *bois brûle* on the shoulder, he said: "You must keep your head down, Nicolas. Next time, the ball may not be fired from so far away."

But Quesnelle was concentrating on his breathing, which seemed to be coming with more difficulty now that he was sitting up. Hanging onto Gabriel's arm, he puffed: "I cannot . . . breathe so good . . . my friend."

Gabriel brushed the lapels of Quesnelle's capote aside, then pulled his shirt up until he could see the fist-sized bruise and lump of swollen flesh where the ball had struck him. He said:

"There is a broken rib, perhaps."

Quesnelle swayed suddenly and his eyes rolled back until only the whites were visible. With a gasp, he flopped onto his back. For one terrifying moment, Gabriel thought he was dead. Then he saw the slow rise and fall of the *bois brûle*'s chest and knew he had only passed out. But there was nothing he could do here.

As if Quesnelle's falling were a signal, a bone-chilling howl arose from among the Yanktons, and a band of forty or more charged across the plain toward Gabriel's and Quesnelle's position.

"Sacre démon," Gabriel said hollowly. Then he dived into the tiny crater next to Quesnelle and slid the Brown Bess across the little mound of dirt in front of him. While the Sioux were still at the far end of his musket's range, he pulled Quesnelle's trade gun up beside him and checked its priming. To his left, one position over from the pit he had occupied earlier, Big John's double rifle cracked once, then a second time. With each sharp report, a Yankton pony went down, effectively taking out of the action the tiny figure crouched atop it.

As the Sioux came within the shorter range of the *bois brûles'* fusils, the half-bloods added their own ragged fire to the struggle. Gabriel saw a warrior knocked from his pony. Another jerked and dropped his bow, then reined away, shaking his hand as if it had been stung. Snugging the Bess to his shoulder, he picked out a target and squeezed the trigger, tumbling a brave from the back of a leggy buckskin. Then, as the brave he'd knocked from the saddle jumped to his feet and raced away, Gabriel dropped the musket and shouldered Quesnelle's fusil. But by the time he brought the tiny, turtle-shaped brass front sight in line with the brave's shoulders, the Indian was out of range. Before he could locate a new mark, the *métis'* fire abruptly intensified, and the Sioux charge crumbled. Whipping their ponies around, the Indians galloped back the way they had come, retrieving as many of their wounded along the way as they could.

The beaten warriors congregated around those who had sat out the fight. After a couple of minutes of heated conversation, Black Fish raised his lance and the Sioux quieted. Wheeling his horse, the chief rode toward the horizon where the Sioux had first appeared. Most of his followers went with him. Perhaps two dozen held back, but then, one by one or in pairs, they began riding after the larger party. Within twenty minutes the field was empty save for a clutter of dead horses and the bodies of three fallen warriors the Sioux had been unable to recover.

Rising slowly to his knees, Gabriel stared uncertainly after the retreating Sioux. At his side, Nicolas Quesnelle lifted his head and rasped—"God damn."—in disbelief.

Night seemed to fall without warning. At dusk, the *bois brûles* who had manned the pits during the day returned to the shelter of their carts where they wouldn't be as exposed to arrows arched in from the darkened plains, or skulking warriors creeping up on their bellies. Almost everyone remained tautly on guard. Even though an attack after dark was unlikely, they had fought Indians long enough to know that anything was possible. And no one believed the Yanktons had pulled out for good.

The livestock was as restless as the night the buffalo had nearly overrun them. The oxen were spooked by the smell of blood—three of their own numbers had been crippled by arrows, and Patterson's roan steer had been killed by a roundball—and the horses were agitated by the gunfire and the chaos of the humans. Added to that now were the heart-rending wails of several women, mourning the death of Little John McKay.

Although a number of men had received minor wounds, Little John was the caravan's only casualty. He had been one of the flankers to the south when the Sioux attacked, and the iron-tipped shaft of an arrow had pierced his back just below his shoulder blade on the ride in, puncturing a lung. Little John had clung stubbornly to life throughout the afternoon, with his wife Eva and all but his eldest son Duncan at his side. He'd died just before sunset, drowning in his own blood.

Duncan McKay was Gabriel's age, and he and Gabriel and Michel Quesnelle had been good friends before the events of the past few weeks had come between them. It was Michel who'd helped Duncan rescue Little John from the prairie before the Sioux could reach him. In spite of Duncan's desire to remain with his father, he had dutifully returned to his post beside Michel. They had fought on the east side of the caravan that afternoon, and neither of them was aware until day's end that Michel's father had also been shot.

It was after dark when Michel came looking for Gabriel who was sitting in the deepest shadows of an upturned cart. Gabriel saw him approaching but didn't call out. It was the glow of Gabriel's pipe that ultimately betrayed his position.

Michel squatted several feet away, as if wary of coming closer. "I was told of what you did for my father," he said. "I was told also that you stayed at his side, even when the Sioux charged."

"It was nothing your father would not have done for me, or any other *bois brûle*."

"That is true, but I was not sure you would have done the same. My thoughts are confused when I think of you, Gabriel. After leaving me on the prairie without a horse, I have begun to wonder if you are even *bois brûle* any more."

"For what you said that day I should have killed you," Gabriel replied flatly.

Michel was quiet a moment, then he stood. "I do not understand you, Gabriel Gilray, but I think maybe you saved my father's life today, and for that I wish to repay you. A knife from Hudson's Bay. I will bring it in the morning."

"I do not need another knife from Hudson's Bay," Gabriel said. "Bring the American a horse if you wish to repay me. He needs a pony if he is ever to return to his cursed mountains. Is your father's life worth a pony, Michel?"

Michel stiffened. "Yes, my father is worth a thousand ponies. I will see that the American gets one."

Gabriel felt a moment's shame for his anger, but bull-headedly refused to back away from his demand. "Good," he said. "I will be a satisfied man when Pike is gone."

"Will you?" Michel asked, then walked away without waiting for an answer.

Gabriel stared after him until he was swallowed by shadows, then he tipped his head back against the cart's rough bed and closed his eyes. He felt torn between sorrow and anger and a child's helpless frustration, yet he thought Michel had a point when he'd questioned whether Pike's leaving would be enough.

"Gabriel?"

He opened his eyes. Celine stood before him, the pale light of the rising moon casting her in an odd glow that sent a shiver down his spine. He set his pipe aside and got to his feet, bumping his shoulder on the rim of the cart's wheel as he did. "Celine?"

She came to him and put her hands on his chest, leaning forward until her forehead rested under his chin. "I've been so worried," she said, barely above a whisper. "So many were injured, and poor John McKay. Oh, Gabriel, what must his family feel? How can they bear the loss?" Cautiously he put his hands around her waist. Tipping her head back, she said: "You do not hate me, do you? After today, I don't think I could stand it if you did. Please, Gabriel, you must tell me you don't hate me."

Mutely he shook his head.

"I have been so foolish," she murmured. "I have done such terrible things that I thought surely you must."

"I . . . ," he began.

"Hush." She leaned close again, putting her arms around him. "It does not matter. I've been so frightened, Gabriel. You don't know how many times I've wished to come to you, how much I yearned to be alone with you. The American terrifies me. I fear each night that he will kidnap me, drag me away to some dreadful hovel in the mountains. That is his desire, you know? He has told me so, and that night . . . the night the buffalo came. . . . I thought surely he would do it then. *Oui,* I think he might have, if you had not been there to stop him."

"He will never take you away," Gabriel said tautly. "Not as long as I am alive." His arms tightened around her, and—*sacre bleu*—she was pushing against him, rubbing her thighs across his, mashing her breasts to his chest. Her fingers dug at his spine, pulling him closer. He wanted to laugh because he knew she was just playing with him, but it didn't matter. Crazily he said: "I will kill him first."

"Will you, Gabriel? Will you promise me that you will you kill Pike before you let him take me away?"

Gabriel nodded, his voice trembling. "I promise."

Pike sat with his back to a pile of untanned hides, the bottle of bourbon he'd purchased at Pembina sitting beside him, open. Pain gnawed at his side and hip like half-starved wolves, and his knee was swollen and hot to the touch. He was gimped-up for fair, he thought, and knew it would be a long, sleepless night if he couldn't drink enough to deaden the pain.

The half-breeds hadn't built any fires because of the possibility of Sioux snipers, but even without them, a man could get around. The stars were bright and the moon had come up fat as a tick, though still somewhat lop-sided. There were a few people wandering about, but not many. Save for the posted guards, most of the half-breeds had returned to their own carts, staying close to their families. Pike figured the keening of McKay's widow, daughters, and sisters had a lot to do with that. His death was a stiff reminder to them all of the fragility of human life.

Pike heard the low rumble of Big John McTavish's voice from down the line. A few minutes later, the raw-boned Scotsman came into view against the star mist, shoulders sloped in weariness.

"Mister Pike? Is that yeself I see there?"

"It is," Pike replied, somewhat surprised by the thickness of his tongue. From the pain, he'd assumed the liquor hadn't taken any effect yet. "Sit down, old man."

McTavish made himself comfortable at Pike's side. " 'Tis that bourbon I'm smellin'?" he asked, sniffing the air.

Pike held the bottle toward him, sloshing it a little. "What's left of it. Help yourself."

McTavish accepted, tipping it to his lips and drinking deeply. When he finished, he handed it back, then settled against the cart's bed as if he planned to stay a while.

"Isabella says ye took a bad one across ye ribs."

"I've been banged up worse than this."

"And ye hip?"

"I'll be ready to. . . ." He let the words trail off when he remembered that he'd lost the bay.

"I've talked to Hallet. He says he has a spare pony he'd make ye the loan of for the rest of the hunt. 'Twill be a small fee, ye understand, but likely no more than a robe or two, or some meat. Another good hunt and ye'll have it all paid off, and like as not enough to buy ye another. Charles wasn't wantin' to part with this one, but ye'll have ye pick of horses back at the settlement. Especially with winter comin' on."

Pike's lips thinned. *Just one more god damned debt,* he thought sourly, and not a thing he could do about it, either—short of theft. He took a swig out of the bottle and handed it to McTavish.

McTavish drank and belched, then said: "I shouldn't be drinkin' with me belly empty like it is and the Sioux likely to come visitin' again with the mornin's first light."

"Have some jerky," Pike said, fumbling in his saddlebags for a strip of dried meat he'd stolen off a stage days earlier.

McTavish shook his head. "I don't think I could stomach the likes of that," he admitted. "I could never understand an American's passion for something that tastes like bark, and fair looks like it, too."

Pike laughed. "That's bold talk from a man who's ate moose nose. Jerky's all I've got, and a heap better than crickets, which I've ate when starving times were upon me. Best wrestle some down, *amigo,* if you aim to drink much tonight."

Sighing, McTavish returned the bottle. " 'Tis with regret that I do this, Mister Pike, though maybe we'll share us a mug of something better back to the settlements. But for now, I'd best keep me head clear and tight, and not spinnin' around like a child's whirligig."

Pike laughed at the image, discovering, as the bourbon's warmth began to spread throughout his body, that a lot of things were looking funnier.

The liquor seemed to be having the opposite effect on McTavish, though. With just a few swallows, he had begun to turn morose. Lifting his face to the sound of Eva McKay's grief, he snorted. "Listen to her, Mister Pike. A Catholic, she calls herself, but are those the tears of a papist? No, 'tis an Assiniboine's cry, that, and an Assiniboine's heart what's breakin' tonight."

"Her husband's death wasn't your fault."

"No, it wasn't, but 'tis faith I'm speakin' of now. I asked the good Father Denning once just why it was he could believe so strongly in the words of men he didn't know or ever would, and he said to me . . . 'I read the Bible, Mister McTavish, and I believe.' 'Twas all the man said, too, and if smugness were a sin, he would've damned himself for all eternity right then and there. 'I read the Bible, and I believe.' As if any Protestant cannot say the same, and with the same heart-deep conviction. And do ye think, Mister Pike, do ye truly think any of 'em believe any stronger in their God than the redskin does in Man Above or the Great Spirit or Manitou, or a hundred other names for a hundred other gods?

"I'm not knockin' another's religion, mind ye, but I'm sayin' don't try to convert others to what ye don't rightly understand yeself, and cannot understand, bein' only human, with a human's weaknesses and blindnesses inherited into ye. Don't be so damn' righteous as to believe only ye own religion can be the one true religion when all ye have to go on is what some man ye've never met has writ himself, and maybe no more knowin' of the subject than ye or me. That's all I'm sayin'. If ye want to believe it, then do, and with me blessin' if such would make ye happy, or without if ye don't need it. But don't say me own beliefs are wrong. By the Lord, man, don't tell me that."

He paused, then waved his hand in a manner that included the whole camp. "Aye, Mister Pike, Catholics all, and Protestants, too, but come the Northern Lights all a-glowin' and dancin' and lightin' up the darkest sky until the hounds see fit to bay, and ye can hear 'em up and down the valley shootin' off their fusils to keep 'em at bay, for 'tis evil spirits the Northern Lights are, and taught that by their mas and pas from a thousand years past. Maybe taught that before Christ died on a cross, then raised up afterward, or maybe not, because who's to know for certain when the story's been taken from a book that's been translated a hundred times over the centuries? Who's ever to know when ye haven't seen it yeself, or at least talked to men who have, and them ones ye can trust proper-like, and not some salesman out toutin' his own brand of faith like it was a new carriage with shiny wheels?"

Pike kept quiet, waiting it out. After a time, McTavish hiccuped and said: "Well, sure, look who's preachin' now, eh? I suppose 'tis a thing that grates, though, and I won't deny that, but still. . . ." He fell silent, ducking his head.

Gently Pike said: "I figure the Sioux'll come back at first light. Best be getting some sleep. Tomorrow could be a long day."

McTavish stirred as if to rise, but didn't. In a low voice, he said: "They were better off before we came, Mister Pike. The Assiniboines and Crees and them. Any man with a half-blind eye can see that. But we came anyway, traders and missionaries and such, and offered 'em our geegaws and bright cloth, and, maybe worst of all, our Christian gods. And when none of that caught their fancy, we turned 'em into drunkards and whores, no better than ourselves right here."

"That seems a mite harsh," Pike said mildly.

"Is it? I say a man can only be proud of what he's accomplished among the savages if he doesn't look too closely at what they were before we came." He heaved a shuddering sigh, then shook his head. "Well, 'tis enough blubberin' for one night, wouldn't ye say?" He stood and pulled the collar of his duffel coat tighter around his neck. "Good night to ye, Mister Pike," he said sadly, then shuffled away like a stoved-up old man, a gait Pike had never seen him use before. He watched until the darkness took him, then gently corked the bottle and put it away.

Pike came up with a start, reaching immediately for his rifle. He relaxed only when he saw the half-breed who had shaken him awake sitting back on his heels with a grin. "You should have told me you wanted to get drunk last night, American. I would have helped good, eh?"

"What the hell do you want?" Pike growled, rubbing the scum feel from his lips with the back of his hand. His tongue felt like a half-dead fish, flopping loosely in his mouth. Its taste was worse.

"Look to the east, *mon* friend. See? The sun, she awakens. Soon they will come, them devil Sioux." He hefted a shortened trade gun to draw attention to it; his grin broadened. "We'll give 'em hell again, eh?"

Pike grunted noncommittally and pushed his robe back, but, when he tried to sit up, the pain in his hip and knee and side was like multiple hammers clubbing him back. He clenched his teeth to keep from crying out, but couldn't stop from writhing as the muscles over his ribs mutinied. He'd drawn himself into a fetal position in his sleep and lay curled that way now, his side muscles twitching warningly.

The half-breed chuckled with compassion. "The wounds, they do not wake up so fast as the body, eh? Go slowly, *mon ami.* We must be limber to fight the Sioux, no?"

"Don't worry," Pike managed, although he kept his face turned to the curly hair of his robe. "When the fighting starts, I'll be there."

"*Oui,* this I already know. I saw you fight yesterday. You come when you are ready, American, and if you want some breakfast, ask for Pierre. He will feed you good, eh?" The half-breed gave his shoulder a quick, friendly pat, then moved on down the line.

When he was alone, Pike cautiously unfolded his legs, then worked on straightening his torso. He could feel Isabella's stitches stretching reluctantly, the old blood cracking and flaking away, a trickle of fresh taking its place. He used his rifle to help him stand, then hobbled painfully over to where he'd fought the day before.

Charlo was already there, his pipe clamped between his teeth, a column of blue smoke curling past his squinting left eye. He nodded as Pike came up. "All quiet so far."

Leaning against a cart, Pike peered out at the prairie. The view beyond thirty yards or so was indistinct, a lead-colored barrier behind which might have lurked death and destruction, or nothing more gruesome than another chilly, sunny day.

"Be light enough in another twenty minutes," Charlo predicted. "We will know then, damn' sure."

Pike cradled his rifle to check the priming, blowing out the old and sprinkling in a fresh charge. He'd cleaned the bore haphazardly last night, and wished there was time to do a better job now, with light to see by. He'd been remiss in not waking up sooner to care for his weapons, but figured he could blame the bourbon for that.

"You did good yesterday, American," Charlo said. "A *bois brûle* could not have done better. The way you fought while trapped on the prairie is the talk on everyone's tongue this morning." He handed Pike a chunk of pemmican. "Eat. It will help you mend."

Pike eyed the fat-laced ball of meat suspiciously, then shrugged and pinched off a bite. He wadded it in his cheek like a chaw of tobacco to allow the fat to melt at its own pace, then set the rest of the ball on a cart hub where it would be handy. The light changed slowly. What had been obscure only seconds before now began to take shape, though it revealed nothing new.

"If they come, it will be soon," Charlo said tersely. He stood ready, legs braced, shoulders rigid. His long-barreled fowler was poked between the spokes of a wheel and the cart bed, the big cock eared all the way back. The hazy light receded slowly to reveal an empty horizon. Not even the dead warriors who had been left behind yesterday remained.

An uncertain silence gripped the camp. They could see clearly for nearly a mile in every direction, yet nothing seemed to threaten them. After nearly half an hour, Charlo began to relax. He stepped back and glanced around curiously. Others were doing the same.

"This is not like the Sioux," he said to no one in particular.

"Maybe we hurt 'em too much yesterday," Pike ventured.

Then the call they waited for came. *"Voila les Sioux! Voila les Sioux!"*

The cry was raised from the opposite side of the camp. Pike looked in that direction but couldn't see beyond the wall of carts.

"Sacre diable," Charlo muttered passionately. "You cannot trust a Sioux." He spat for emphasis, but held his station.

"How many?" someone called.

"Only a few," was the answer.

"They come slowly," added another.

Charlo looked at Pike. "What do you think, American? Does that sound like them god damned Sioux to you?"

Pike shook his head. "Not even to parley."

Far to the south, a fusil was discharged. A hopeful murmur began to spread among the half-breeds. It was Marie Breland who made it official. "It is Joseph! Joseph has returned!"

Charlo chuckled. "I think she must be right, eh?"

He and Pike walked across the camp to the southern rim of carts to watch the small party of horsemen loping in. Joseph Breland did indeed ride in the van, but, as they drew near, Pike noticed that there were ten riders, rather than nine, with an extra pack horse bringing up the rear. With a gasp of anticipation, Marie Cyr pushed through the crowd, but her hope was short-lived. It wasn't Etienne Cyr who returned with Breland, but a stranger.

Pike's grip tightened on his rifle. Although he'd never seen the man up close, he recognized him from the description McKenzie had given him, that and the knee-length leather coat and the bright green tuque he'd seen the day he shot Rubiette.

It was Henri Duprée.

Chapter Twenty

"*Beaucoup* buffalo to the southwest," Joseph Breland said tiredly. He was drinking tea from a china cup with a blue willow pattern, his big, sun-darkened hand dwarfing the fragile vessel. With breakfast behind them and the land still empty of Sioux, the *métis* had gathered in council to listen to Breland and the others speak, and to decide what their next move should be.

"In places the land is made dark by their numbers," added another.

" 'Twas Paget's bunch wha' spooked 'em our way," Jim Patterson chimed in.

"Paget?" Big John seemed to perk up. "Ye found the Pembina hunters, did ye?"

"On the Sheyenne," Breland confirmed. "We almost stampeded the buffalo into them last week, but they were able to turn the herd away before any harm was done. Then they ran the same bunch. It was some of these that splintered off to the west and a little north, toward us again. Maybe three days from here, with the carts."

"Hah!" Turcotte cried, grinning broadly. "So we beat the Pembina hunters to the buffalo, after all."

Several of the men cheered. Gabriel knew it had galled everyone to have to turn away from Devil's Lake because of the Pembina caravan.

"And of Etienne?" Big John inquired, bringing up what had only been lightly touched upon before.

"No trace, as I have already said," Breland replied. Then his voice took on a more thoughtful note. "None at all." He seemed baffled by that.

"And ye, Henri?" Big John turned his gaze on Nicolas Quesnelle's brother-in-law, his expression flat. "Do ye bring us news from the plains that we can use?"

With the council's attention fixed suddenly upon him, Duprée shifted uncomfortably. He was a short, pot-bellied man of forty or forty-five, with a dark beard and shaggy brows, his long hair unkempt beneath a wolf-skin cap. He seemed to weigh his answer carefully before voicing it. "*Non.* I see no one until Breland."

"And ye partner? What of him?"

Duprée glared at Big John. "François returned to the Qu'Appelle."

Antoine Toussaint scowled. "Big John, the man we found. . . ."

"Aye, Antoine, 'tis me own thinkin'." To Duprée, he added: " 'Twas a man found a few days back, taller than yeself but just as dirty, wearin' a yellow shirt. He'd been shot."

Duprée's eyes darted like a trapped animal's, but he shook his head. "I do not know."

"Ye don't know if ye partner owned a yellow shirt?"

Again, Duprée shook his head.

Big John laughed softly, with disdain. "Well, sure, who'd expect a man to know the color of his partner's shirt?"

Eyes narrowing dangerously, Duprée repeated his earlier declaration that François Rubiette had returned to the country along the Qu'Appelle River, to the northwest. Inexplicably Gabriel's attention was drawn away from the core of speakers at the center of the council to Pike, who stood alone outside the circled hunters, hunched painfully with his wounds. Pike was watching Duprée with a rattlesnake's obsidian stare, and Gabriel realized suddenly that Duprée was aware of it, too, and that he was more nervous because of that than from Big John's interrogation.

"The Pembina caravan?" Charlo said to Breland, changing the subject. "Have they had trouble with the Sioux this year?"

Breland shook his head. "*Non,* Charlo. From *Lac du Diable* they sent a delegation to Renville's post to treaty with the Sioux, and have paid in blankets and ammunition for the right to hunt unmolested along the Sheyenne."

An uneasy murmur greeted Breland's announcement. Turcotte said: "What will they do if they do not fill their carts along the Sheyenne?"

Breland's smile was as thin as stretched gut. "They will go where there are buffalo, René, for they are *bois brûles,* and could do no less. But for now they hunt in peace, which is good for them but maybe not so good for us. Paget said that a lot of the Yanktons did not wish to see such a treaty made. But, it is done, and, for the time being, it is being honored by our red brothers."

Musing aloud, Big John said: " 'Twas a wise move on their part, though, and one we should have pushed for ourselves."

"The Sioux dae nae own the buffalo, Big John," Patterson said with an edge to his words.

"I was thinkin' of Little John, Jim, and his wife and the small ones. A treaty might have saved the man his life."

"The Yanktons did not want a treaty," Gabriel reminded him. "They did not come to parley. They attacked from ambush and killed Little John and wounded four others without warning. I think they will attack again, sooner or later."

"Gabriel's right," Hallet said. "It was the Sioux who tried to slip up behind us like snakes in the grass. Now a man is dead, and the blame is theirs, not ours. I say Paget's a fool if he thinks they won't attack because of a treaty only a few of Joseph Renville's relatives signed."

"Paget is no fool," Breland said. "He watches like a hawk and will not be taken by surprise."

"What does that matter?" Gabriel asked. "If there are buffalo to the southwest, then that is the direction we must go in, not toward Turtle Lake."

"What of the Sioux?" asked Toussaint.

"Let the devil take the Sioux," Hallet replied darkly.

"*Non,* Charles," Turcotte said grimly. "*Le diable* would not want Black Fish or his warriors cluttering his fire."

There was a general burst of laughter at that. When it died, Turcotte continued. "We must go forward, as young Gabriel says, for we cannot squat here forever like old men with stoppered bowels waiting for our enemies to return. But we must also be cautious, for now the Yanktons have shown us that their hearts are bad this year." He glanced around the circle of men. "And now, also, we must send scouts ahead, so that we know where the buffalo that Joseph spoke of have gone. Also, we must know if the Pembina hunters are following them, scattering them even more. The caravan should continue southwest, but someone must ride ahead to find the buffalo. It can be delayed no longer."

Turcotte had been arguing for sending scouts ahead ever since their first camp at the base of the Hair Hills, but this time, no one objected. In the silence that followed, Big John said: "I'll go, René."

"No." Breland leaned forward, his eyes on Big John. "To scout is a younger man's duty."

"Enough younger men have died, Joseph," Big John replied. "I'll go, alone."

"Big John cannot go alone," Charlo interjected. "Yet he speaks the truth when he says enough younger men have died. We have too many widows and fatherless children as it is. I will go with him."

Before anyone could second it, Gabriel stood and let the butt of his musket strike the earth between his feet. "No, I will go with Big John." He said it boldly, and, when no one spoke against him, he nodded, relieved that he hadn't been challenged.

Turcotte said: "It is settled then."

"But what of water?" a *bois brûle* named Grahm asked. "At Turtle Lake there is plenty for our oxen."

Others took up similar issues, but Gabriel didn't wait to hear them out. He had no patience for details today. And he was looking forward to riding with Big John again. He wanted to reëxperience the solitude of the plains with someone capable of appreciating its silence. The possibility of running into more Sioux didn't worry him. The Sioux were always a threat when a man traveled across their lands, but when had that ever stopped a *bois brûle?*

He roped Baldy out of the restless herd still penned inside the cordon and led him to his cart. Alec was already there, standing where he could watch the plain for Indians, yet also keep an eye on the council. He grinned when Gabriel came up.

"Let me go, big brother."

"Shoo, you and Big John? You would kill one another within an hour." Gabriel saddled Baldy, then got his bedroll from behind the cart. He packed some pemmican and tea and a little tin kettle inside his sleeping robe, then lashed it behind the seat. Inside his heavy coat he wrapped mittens and extra moccasins, then tied that across the front of his saddle. When he was ready, he went to sit with Alec so that he could listen to the men from a distance, yet also allow his thoughts to wander.

"Now it comes," Alec said with obvious relish, nodding toward a group of women who had been standing at the edge of the council. Charlo was already speaking to Marie Cyr.

"We have come to hunt buffalo, Marie," the old, white-haired hunter was saying. "We cannot remain here and wait for the

Sioux to return."

"We've searched for Etienne," Hallet added. "He couldn't be found. We must go on."

In Assiniboine, Marie Cyr said accusingly: "Would you leave behind one of your friends, Charles Hallet? Or is it only those who are not close to you that you would abandon?"

Hallet's face darkened, and a grumbling passed through the council. Several of the men turned to glare at their wives for allowing this breach of etiquette. Others refused to look up at all.

"We have searched," Breland insisted. "Perhaps he was found by others."

"What others, Joseph? Did you see him or hear of him at Paget's camp? Or is it the Sioux you speak of when you say *others?*"

In English, Big John said: "What would ye have us do, Marie? Say it, and I'll do it meself, for Etienne was me friend, and as fine a man as any who's ever run the humped ones. But"—he spread his hands in a helpless gesture—"what more can we do? Tell me."

Staying in Assiniboine, Marie said shrilly: "What am I to do, Tall Man? What am I to do without a husband, or a father for my children?"

Big John's words were audible to them all. "Ye'll be doin' what every other widow has done before ye. Ye'll find yeself another to hunt and farm for ye, whose hides ye can tan and whose pemmican ye can mix. Ye're a fine worker, Marie, and ye'll be comin' with us in the spring, proud as a swan with a new husband. Ye will now. I'd bet prime beaver on that."

But Marie just stared until Big John's face turned red and his eyes slowly lowered. Then she turned away, her movements as measured as those of an ancient grandmother, and went back to her carts. The wives of Quesnelle, LaBarge, Leveille, and several others walked with her, their heads bowed under their shawls.

Alec shook his head in disgust. "She should know better," he said. "It is not right for a woman to speak that way to men."

"She has a right," Gabriel replied quietly. He watched as she sat down in front of her small lodge, her children gathering silently around her like chicks to a hen. Only she, among them all, kept her head up, although she didn't speak or even seem to notice the other women standing nearby. Yet in spite of the rigid way she held herself, her grief was obvious, and Gabriel wondered how anyone could say she didn't have a right to speak her mind. He stood and gathered Baldy's reins above the piebald's neck.

"Where are you going?" Alec demanded.

"To wait for Big John." Stepping into the saddle, Gabriel rode over to where a cart had been wheeled out of the way for Breland's return. Alec's friend, Isidore Turcotte, stood guard there, his fusil clutched across his chest. Gabriel pulled up and cocked a leg above the coat tied across the front of his saddle. He was aware of Isidore watching him, but neither glanced at the youth nor spoke. He was still there an hour later when Big John finally rode up, his roan packed for the long journey ahead.

It was late that same afternoon when Gabriel and Big John came to the site of an old prairie fire, something from before the rains. It lay before them like a giant brand on the earth, the blackened grass beaten down by wind and weather, discoloring the soil. Letting his gaze run along the distant line of the southern horizon, Gabriel saw nothing that wasn't black.

"Well, 'tis a surprise, to be sure," Big John said after several moments' reflection. "But, I see no choice other than to cross it. If the buffalo are headin' west, like Joseph says, it would take too long for us to backtrack around the burn with our carts."

"If it is a big burn, we could travel for days without grass to feed the stock. The water may be bad as well."

" 'Tis a possibility, though I'd be more worried about grass than water, what with all the rain we've had of late."

Gabriel shrugged and looked away, knowing Big John had already made up his mind, and that they would push on across the burn in search of buffalo somewhere on the other side. Abruptly he heeled Baldy into the blackened grass.

"Where are ye goin', lad?" Big John called. "I've not heard ye opinion yet."

Gabriel hauled up and looked back. "The decision is already made, Big John. Now we must go on to see where the burn ends and the good grass begins again, before the carts follow too deeply in."

But Big John seemed wary. "Are ye thinkin' we should turn away, Gabriel? 'Tis Breland's route ye'd rather follow, where there's grass, sure, and water along the Sheyenne?"

Gabriel's lips narrowed in resentment. "And Paget's hunters already ahead of us?"

A smile touched Big John's face. " 'Tis what I was thinkin', as well, for such is what we'd surely be doin' was we to backtrack. Ye made a wise decision, lad."

His anger flaring, Gabriel pulled Baldy around and rode back to Big John's side. "But it wasn't my decision, Big John. It was yours. You had already made up your mind that we would cross the burn. Don't try to make it sound like it was my idea."

Big John sighed. "Well, there's truth to ye words, Gabriel, and I won't deny it. Still, it did me heart good to have ye tell me why ye agreed that we should go on, to consider all the facts and. . . ."

Gabriel's voice rose sharply, cutting him off. "Like a good little half-breed? Is that what you mean?"

Big John's eyes widened. "I said no such thing, lad!"

"Didn't you?" Gabriel drove his heels into Baldy's ribs, forcing his smaller horse into Big John's roan. The roan bared its teeth and laid back its ears, but Gabriel used his quirt to slash the horse across its nose before it could bite.

"Here now!" Big John roared, pulling the stallion's head around. Shock replaced the anger on his face when Gabriel raised his quirt once more. Instinctively Big John lifted an arm in self-defense. They froze that way. Then the rage in him quickly abated, and he lowered his quirt.

"By the Lord, Gabriel," Big John breathed. "Has it come to this, that ye'd try to lash me like I was naught but a thief?"

Shamefully Gabriel said: "I did not mean that."

"Well now, I'm thinkin' ye did, or ye wouldn't have come near to doin' it." Big John's voice softened. "What I'd like to know, son, is why?"

Gabriel looked away. Far to the southwest, little more than a knob on the horizon, lay the heights of Dogden Butte. It was an old and familiar landmark to the *bois brûles,* a sight he'd seen many times and from many different angles. Yet he had never been there, had never scaled its heights to view the eagles' nests some said dotted its sheer southern slope, or rolled stones down its side. For all he knew, there weren't even any stones on top of the Dogden, or eagles, either.

"Times," Big John began hesitantly when Gabriel didn't reply. "Well, they're not the same as they used to be, are they? I suspect maybe ye were right that night in Charlo's cabin when ye said the mixed-bloods have taken root, and that the valley belongs to them now. Likely it has for a long time, and I've been too blind or stubborn to see it." He smiled sadly. "And I suppose ye're right to think I'm naught but a patronizin' old fraud, always thinkin' I know what's best for ye and the others, and none who would speak against me simply because I was John McTavish.

"Well, that's changin', too. It's changin' with ye, though I'm not sure ye see it yet. But I'll tell ye this, lad, and I tell it true.

Ye've made me proud near to burstin' for the way ye've grown, and I'm thinkin' it would have done as much for ye pa, was he still with us."

Gabriel knew Big John meant for his words to give comfort and reassurance, but they kindled a fear inside him that had been smoldering for a long time. Big John was speaking like a man who thought his time was finished, and the implications chilled Gabriel's soul.

"Ye'll be captainin' a train yeself, soon enough," Big John went on. "Takin' ye a wife, too, someone to care for ye and keep ye clothed and fed and on the straight and narrow, and who'll raise ye bairns up proper-like. 'Twill be a different valley then, and not so far off any more, either. One ye children will consider as normal as blood pudding, but I can't help but wonder what ye'll think of it. If it'll seem as strange to ye then as this one does to me now."

"The valley will not change," Gabriel replied.

"The land will not change, 'tis true, save for the scarrin' put on it by the farmers and the town builders and such. 'Tis the people I'm thinkin' of, Gabriel. 'Tis them that will change."

"The *bois brûles* will not change, either."

"Lad, the *bois brûles* are changin' constantly, and they'll keep on doin' so. Listen to Joseph Breland when he speaks. And, aye, to Paget, as well. 'Tis change they're preachin' even now, and more to come. Evolution, Gabriel, as natural a progression as young into old or night into day." He laughed at the confused look on the younger man's face. "No, I'm no losin' me mind. Not about that or the buffalo. I'll be wrong on some of the details, but 'tis comin' still. Ye can count on that." Looking out across the burn, Big John's voice deepened. "Did ye notice, lad, what a beautiful day it's turned out to be?"

Gabriel shook his head in frustration, yet he couldn't stop a small smile from coming to his face. "It is cold and windy, and there will be no grass for the horses tonight, or water for us. And the Sioux are still out there, not very far away. You know they are, and that they are watching closely, waiting for the smallest mistake so that they can attack again."

"Sure, 'tis likely, but all the more reason to be enjoyin' today, wouldn't ye say?"

Gabriel reined his horse around. "It is time we went on, Big John. The sun will set before long."

"Aye, well, there's one more thing I wanted to discuss with ye." He let the roan have its head, and they started across the burn at a walk, stirrup-to-stirrup. " 'Tis why I was glad ye came with me today, and why I didn't argue against it."

"What is it?"

"The girl, laddie. Celine."

Gabriel stiffened. "What of her?"

"Ye've heard what the others are sayin' about her behind me back, and ye've seen some of it yeself . . . the butcherin' of the young bull ye shot, and the way she wanders around camp without. . . ." He paused and breathed deeply, as if to gather his emotions. "What I want to say is, she's not the lass for ye, Gabriel. It pains me to say such of me own kin, but 'tis the truth, and ye need to hear it, and to heed me on this one."

"How can you say that about your own daughter?"

"Because I see too much of her mother in her. Mutterin' to herself and the look in her eyes as if she's . . . not here, in the present. Ye were too young to remember Celine's ma, but . . . well, I don't want ye goin' through what I did when . . . when she. . . ."

"Killed herself?"

Big John released a large sigh. "Aye, when she hung herself. 'Tis that I'm speakin' of, and the hurt that came with it, the guilt of always thinkin' I must've done something wrong but never knowin' what it was." His expression had turned as grim as cold death, but he pushed on doggedly. "Ye be Angus Gilray's son, but I've raised ye as me own, and 'tis how I see ye now. So I'm tellin' ye, lad, with a father's love, to stay away from her."

Staring straight ahead, Gabriel said: "I think you are mixed up, Big John. I do not think it is me you should be giving a father's love to." He was going to say more until he saw the look of anguish that came over the older man's face, realizing then that he'd said too much.

"Aye," Big John agreed, his voice shaky. "Ye're right, of course. I'm not one to be speakin' of a father's love."

"I did not mean it that way."

"No, don't deny ye own instincts. Ye see more than most, and what ye said was the truth, plain as life itself. 'Tis something I should be facin' squarer than I do, most days."

A single tear slipped free from the corner of Big John's eye and began a winding journey down his cheek. He swiped at it clumsily with the back of a mittened hand, then quickly turned his face away. After a moment, shoulders heaving silently, he kicked the roan into a lope.

Gabriel tightened his legs around Baldy's ribs to catch up, then let them relax. He thought that maybe it would be a good idea if they both rode alone for a while.

They made their slow way across the burn without conversation. Gray-black grass rolled away in every direction, and fine clouds of wind-blown ash swirled around them like dark-skinned dancers. There was eeriness to the landscape that prickled the flesh across the back of Gabriel's neck.

The temperature began to drop noticeably as the sun started its slide into the horizon. Freeing his heavy coat from the front of his saddle, Gabriel slipped into it without removing his fringed buckskin jacket. He snugged his cap down over his forehead and pulled mittens on over his gloves. He wished he'd thought to bring along some wool socks to put on under his moccasins, even though he knew Alec would have made fun of him for it. It wasn't much of a man, in Alec's opinion, who had to wear socks when the temperature was above freezing, no matter how sharp the wind might blow.

As the sun slipped from view, the western sky lost its pale, robin's egg tint and began to segue into deeper shades of blue and violet. Flat-bellied clouds floating above the horizon were trimmed suddenly in rust and gold. Arriving at the lip of a shallow coulée just as the last of the light bled off the land, the two Tongue River scouts dismounted to stretch their limbs and chew on some pemmican. But when the moon came up a couple of hours later, they were back in their saddles, pushing on into the night.

They continued their silence, comfortable together in the depthless quiet of the burn. Although the moon was nearly full, its light seemed anemic and peculiar, as if its strength was being absorbed by the charred, blackened grass, and there was an acidic taste on the wind that irritated Gabriel's throat and sinuses. From time to time he sniffed the breeze for water or grass, but scented nothing, and by dawn they were still surrounded by a Stygian plain. It wasn't until a couple of hours after sunup that he spotted the southern edge of the burn several miles ahead. In the lead, he reined up to wait for Big John, laughing when he saw the gray-black hue of the older man's face, knowing his own must look just as ridiculous.

They found a rush-lined slough less than a mile out of the burn and rode their horses into it to let them drink. Gabriel dug the kettle from his sleeping robe and leaned down to dip up a pailful. He drank greedily, then offered the kettle to Big John, who drained it, refilled it, drank some more, then passed it back.

After slaking their thirst, the two men rode to the crest of the next hill, where they stopped to stare south and west over the rolling plains. As exhausted as Gabriel felt, he couldn't deny a deeper satisfaction that numbed the edges of his weariness. As far as he could see, the land was brown with buffalo. Not in one huge, compacted herd, but scattered into a thousand herds of anywhere from twenty to two hundred head, with smaller bunches in between. *Cabbri* moved delicately among the massive beasts, and cowbirds flitted from hump to hump. Wolves and coyotes prowled cautiously among the bison, ever on the look-out for weakened, crippled, or unwary animals. Gabriel and Big John gazed silently at the buffalo for several minutes, then turned and made their way back to the slough.

"We'll rest here for a spell and let the ponies fill their bellies," Big John said, his voice roughened from the ash he'd ingested last night. "Noon'll be soon enough to head back."

Gabriel nodded, but, as he worked at Baldy's cinch with stiffened fingers, he realized he was disappointed that they were returning so soon. Despite their blow-up the day before, he'd enjoyed this otherwise quiet sojourn with Big John. Often in the past when the two of them had turned back from similar rides, Gabriel had found himself feeling as he did now—a reluctance to end the adventure, a desire to keep going, to see what lay beyond the horizon. It wasn't all that long ago, as a boy, that he'd fantasized about all of them traveling with the buffalo forever, patterning their lives around the migratory habits of the shaggy bison in much the same fashion as the plains tribes did.

He dumped his saddle in the grass, then picketed Baldy close to the rushes along the slough. When he returned, Big John was sitting on top of his sleeping robe with his double-barreled rifle across his lap. He looked tired but not particularly sleepy. Unfurling his own robe, Gabriel flopped down cross-legged. "We must keep watch."

"Aye."

"Two hours for each?"

"I thought perhaps three."

Gabriel nodded solemnly, as if considering three, but in truth he was staring listlessly at the rushes behind Baldy, entranced by their slight swaying in the wind, his thoughts already skittering wildly in exhaustion.

Noticing the droop of his eyelids, Big John said: "Ye be dead on ye feet, lad. Go ahead and lay back. I was thinkin' of havin' a pipe, anyway."

"You will wake me?"

"Aye, when the time comes."

Gabriel rolled into his buffalo robe without removing his moccasins or coat. Twisting around on his side, he curled his left arm under his cheek as a pillow and closed his eyes. But he couldn't sleep. As tired as he was, his thoughts continued to race and dart, his limbs to twitch from weariness. Finally, after twenty minutes or so, he sat up to find Big John dead to the world.

Gabriel stared in disbelief, hardly able to credit the slow rise and fall of the older man's chest, the slack expression on his face. Big John was still sitting upright, half propped against his saddle and some of the robe that he'd wrapped around his waist. His stubbled chin rested on his chest.

The sight so astonished Gabriel that, for a moment, he didn't know what to do. To sleep while on guard in a hostile land was almost incomprehensible, a crime among the *bois brûles* punishable by flogging. Yet Gabriel knew he could never again judge Big John by those old, inflexible standards. He wasn't sure what had changed within himself in the past twenty-four hours, but, toward Big John at least, he felt a sense of peace he'd never known before.

Quietly he lay back down. He could still see Baldy cropping

hungrily at the short prairie grass, and knew that by watching the piebald's ears he would be forewarned if anyone approached. And it was best that Big John not know he had been caught napping. He had been through enough recently. He didn't need this added embarrassment.

Chapter Twenty-One

Pulling out early, the cart train crept southward, following the general route McTavish and the boy had taken the day before. They made no effort to hide the dark swath of their trail across the frosty grass. It was too late for that, and would have been impossible anyway. Instead, Turcotte sent out twice the usual number of flankers, scattering them in every direction with instructions to range out as far as they felt necessary. But as the hours passed without any further sign of Black Fish or his warriors, the mood of the half-breeds became one of confusion. They had fought the Sioux too many years to believe they could get off this easily.

As one—man, woman, child—they eyed every distant ridge with suspicion, passed every coulée with dread. It was as if they expected the Sioux to sprout magically from the plain to fall upon them like the plagues of old. And yet in spite of the fear Pike saw on every face, no one suggested retreat. If there was fright, he began to realize, there was also an uncompromising stubbornness in their lives, a simplicity of purpose that somehow equaled courage. They were buffalo hunters, by damn, nothing would stand in the way of that. Not even the Sioux.

With this understanding of the *métis* mentality, Pike finally began to grasp some of the mixed emotions McTavish felt for the half-breeds, the pride that ofttimes vied with exasperation.

They'd buried Little John McKay inside the circle of carts yesterday, with Catholic prayers in lieu of a priest and a proper ceremony, the beating of a *wanbango* and spirit songs chanted in Assiniboine for those gods not covered by the Roman faith. Afterward, Turcotte had ordered the livestock driven over the grave until no trace of it remained—a precaution against the Sioux who might have come back to open the grave and scalp and mutilate the corpse, or wolves and coyotes that would have dug up the body for food. There would be no cairn to return to, no landmark by which they would ever again find its location. Save for what remained in the hearts of family and friends, Little John McKay was gone forever.

Three of the wounded men rode in carts when the train pulled out, cushioned on robes against the harsh jolting of unsprung axles. Pike, his knee still too swollen to accommodate comfortably the curve of a horse's barrel, started the day in one of McTavish's meat carts, but by noon he had endured all he could of the vehicle's slow, tooth-rattling pace and caterwauling shrieks. Dropping painfully to the ground, he saddled the seal brown gelding Michel Quesnelle had brought him that morning, then heaved himself astride the leggy animal. Leaning awkwardly to one side to allow his injured leg to dangle free, he'd kept pace with the carts.

Quesnelle had come to the McTavish camp in the murky light just before dawn while Pike, Alec, and Isabella were finishing their breakfast. He'd tied the seal brown to a cart wheel, then came over to stand in front of Pike.

"The pony is yours," he'd announced without preamble. "It is a fine runner and is not afraid of buffalo. It will serve you well."

Pike didn't reply or even acknowledge the boy until after he'd left. Then he'd grunted softly, in wonder, and resumed his eating. He didn't know what had prompted the youth's generosity, nor did he care. It was enough that he had a horse again—seemingly free of any debt that might bind him tighter to the hunt—and that soon his time among the half-breeds would be over. Only McTavish held him back now. Not so much for the debt he still owed him, but because of his new-found respect for the iron-willed old Scotsman. Pike had already made his decision. He would wait for his wounds to heal, then run buffalo at least once more, adding as much meat and as many hides as he could to McTavish's larder. After that, he would consider his obligation paid, kill Duprée, then flee to the mountains. Quesnelle's gift would only make his leaving that much easier.

The frost was a long time burning off that morning. The days were continuing cold, with the scent of distant moisture. Soon now, Pike knew, the weather would change for good.

The caravan arrived at the northern edge of a huge burn late in the afternoon, the lead oxen halting as if they'd come to a solid wall of stone. Riding ahead, the men gathered around Antoine Toussaint, who had piloted that day, and the two forward point riders who had waited there for the train to catch up.

Toussaint was watching Turcotte questioningly. The latter stared across the blackened plain in the direction of the horse tracks leading into it.

"Big John and Gabriel," Toussaint said needlessly, pointing out the trail with his chin.

"We cannot wait," Breland said, as if to head off any discussion on the matter. "Already the season grows short."

"But we must wait," Noel Pouliot quickly countered. He, too, was watching Turcotte. When he saw the indecision on the captain's face, he added: "What if there is no grass, René? What if the burn stretches all the way to the Missouri River?"

"There was grass to the east when I returned from Paget's camp," Breland said. "The fire could not have been too big, else it would have burned there, as well."

Hesitantly Turcotte said: "I think maybe I agree with Joseph, Noel. He came north from Paget's camp only a day or so east of here. A big fire would have burned that far. But I think also that we should remain here tonight and let the stock eat their fill. Maybe by morning Big John will have returned, and we will know more about what lies ahead."

"There is daylight left now," Breland argued. "And I smell snow."

Turcotte nodded carefully. "I also smell snow, Joseph, but I do not want to let such a thing goad us into an unwise decision. I do not want for us to be stranded without grass for the stock. It is a gamble to tarry, true, for there is no water here, but, if it snows, there will be water enough, and, if it doesn't, then tomorrow we will cross the burn and find a lake or river on the other side."

No one spoke for a moment. Then Breland looked at Turcotte, his expression restrained. "You speak wisely, René. I agree. We should remain here overnight to allow the oxen and horses time to graze. Tomorrow will be soon enough."

They ran their carts into a circle and lashed the wheels together. Then, while the older boys grazed the horses and oxen away from the caravan, the women set about making camp. Night seemed to fall swiftly that evening, as if the darkness were a shade drawn over the land. Only a pale band of soft pearl remained in the west when Charles Hallet and Jim Patterson, the last of the flankers, came in. As they threaded their mounts through an opening made in the carts, a number of half-breeds began to gravitate toward them. Pike had been resting beside Isabella's fire, but, when he saw the looks on the faces of the men as they dismounted, he pulled himself up with the aid of his rifle and hobbled over. He arrived just in time to hear Hallet say: "Very many. More than a hundred, easily."

"Tae hundred, 'n' nae a feather less," Patterson insisted. His eyes looked big in the imperfect light, his face drawn.

"Maybe two hundred," Hallet conceded.

Pike glanced slowly around the circle of half-breeds, noting their grim acceptance, the lack of surprise. They had been waiting for this news for two days.

"Where exactly?" a *métis* asked.

"East of here about three hours."

"And you are sure they crossed the burn?" Turcotte asked.

"They entered the burn, heading south," Hallet replied. "I don't know how far they went. We didn't follow."

A voice made edgy with fright said: "They will catch us on the burn and stop us there."

Eva McKay—a widow less than three days—cried: "This is madness! The Sioux will kill us all if we do not treaty with them!"

There was a muttering of agreement. Breland hushed it with an upraised hand. "*Non,* we cannot! To show weakness now would only invite disaster. We must remain strong."

Others—a clear majority, Pike thought—sided with Breland. A little round-faced half-breed with gaping front teeth said: "The Sioux are like dogs when they spot a crippled fawn, Eva. They would fall on us as a pack, and tear out our throats."

But another shouted: "If they stop us on the burn, our cattle and horses will starve within days."

Then someone else said: "Overnight, the oxen will crop the grass within a camp into the dirt. If they starve, it would be no more than twelve hours sooner than they would have on grass."

"That is true," said Pierre Campbell, the *métis* who'd offered Pike breakfast after the first day's fighting. "I came to hunt buffalo, not run from the Sioux."

"Oui!" shouted Baptiste LaBarge. "We are hunters, *non?* We must follow the buffalo."

Others took up the call, most of them agreeing with Campbell and LaBarge that they should go on. Only a few argued that there would be buffalo farther west, as well, and that it would be smarter go in that direction.

Pike took it all in absently. It didn't matter to him where they hunted. From here on, he waited only for his wounds to heal.

There was no fire in the lodge, and the darkness was complete save for a single star visible through a gap in the closed flaps covering the smoke hole. Celine lay on her back, staring at that twinkling bit of light. It reminded her of the ice crystals that used to form on the stone walls of her room at the Convent of Our Lady of Troy. Especially the outer wall, where the hoarfrost during the coldest weeks of winter sometimes grew more than an inch thick.

She focused her attention on the star because it took her mind away from the half-breeds' recent engagement with the savages. During the battle, while other women had stood behind their men and helped reload, or took part in the actual fighting with their own long guns, Celine had cowered among the hides piled behind Big John's carts, feigning deafness to Isabella's commands. She had been too terrified to help, but, of course, the stupid bitches—every one of them smelling of grease and blood and sweat—were too ignorant to understand that. Even though they'd yelled at her as if she were a dog, she hadn't cared. She was immune to their anger.

After the battle she'd attempted to prove her worth by helping with the wounded, but the jealous whores who had pleaded so selfishly for her assistance earlier now refused her every offer. So she'd retired to Big John's carts, where she busied herself handing out balls of pemmican to whomever passed. It was that evening that she'd gone to Gabriel to mend the rift the American had created between them.

Celine knew the American wanted her badly. Once she had considered the possibility of becoming his woman, but it had become obvious he wasn't the man for her. He didn't understand a woman, or those things that made a woman special. He had become too accustomed to the red-skinned harlots of the unholy *pays sauvage,* and seemed content to wallow in that life the way a hog wallowed in mud. It hadn't escaped her notice that Gabriel was much the same in many ways, but she also knew that Gabriel was still young and could be shown the errors of his thinking.

Besides, she was certain Gabriel was as dissatisfied with his life in the valley as she was. He just hadn't yet figured out how to correct his situation. Celine could help him. If Pike was too stupid to want to see Boston or New York or Montreal, Gabriel wouldn't be. He would take her to those places, and they would live in a splendor of warm homes and fine clothes, with succulent meals butchered and gardened by others. That was the life she craved.

There was a shout from one of the guards, an answering hail from somewhere outside the cordon. Celine sat up with a little, shivery cry, convinced the Sioux had returned for her. She stared at the dark wall of the lodge until the blackness there seemed to swim.

Isabella stirred, muttering something in Cree. Alec pushed his robes back and said he would go see. Voices outside rumbled low and cautiously, without meaning. The antelope hide door made a stiff, scraping sound as Alec exited the teepee, allowing a rush of cool air inside. Pike's voice came to her through the thin hide walls, explaining to Alec that someone was approaching the camp, and Alec replied that it might be Big John and Gabriel. At mention of his name, Celine quickly fumbled into her coat and moccasins.

She paused outside for bearings. It was brighter than she'd expected. Although the moon had long since gone down, the stars seemed bigger and more numerous than ever before. She joined the flow of half-breeds hurrying toward the far side of the caravan. Perhaps thirty or forty *métis* were already gathered at Nicolas Quesnelle's carts, with more appearing every minute. Someone asked who it was, and Quesnelle replied: "Big John and Gabriel."

Breland forced his way through the throng to climb onto the hub of an upturned cart. "Big John!" he called. "Is that you?"

"Aye, Joseph, me and Gabriel. We're alone, and no sign of hostiles the day long."

Celine's heart leaped for joy. For two long days she had feared Gabriel would run off and leave her to Pike. Instead, he had returned. What further proof did she need of his love?

Chapter Twenty-Two

The buffalo had drifted south and a little west from where Big John and Gabriel had last seen them, but they were easy enough to find. The *bois brûles* came at them from the east, with the wind in their faces, the musky tinge of the herd working on the high-strung runners like a stimulant. After laying over at the slough for a day to rest their livestock and scout for the Sioux, who had once again disappeared, the *métis* were eager to renew the hunt.

Big John's roan was as fractious as the worst of them, tossing his head and baring his huge teeth at any horse that came near. Although Big John had left the caravan riding old Solomon and leading the roan on a short lead to keep the runner as fresh as possible, he had been forced to switch mounts long before they reached the herd. Even from this more dominant position, it was a handful to keep the fiery stallion in check.

The sun was still hidden behind the distant curve of the prairie when the hunters came in sight of the herd, but its light was already gilding the higher crags of Dogden Butte, sliding the morning shadows slowly down its long flanks the same way a seductive woman lowered a skirt off her hips.

With no low ridge to take advantage of this time, Turcotte kept the hunters close until they were within eight hundred yards of the nearest bull, then ordered a line formed between himself and Charlo. With everyone in place, he wasted no time raising his hand above his head, then dropping it forward with a lusty: "Ho!"

As one, the *métis* began their advance. At six hundred yards, they went into a trot. It was here the line began to break apart, the roan and a few others pulling eagerly ahead.

The buffalo were scattered over the broad plain as far as the eye could see. From horseback, the country looked like a solid mass of curly brown and black and buff, although Big John knew that, while grazing, the shaggy animals would actually be spread fairly far apart.

It was a mixed herd of bulls and cows they were approaching, somewhat of an oddity this late in the season. Normally by now the larger herds would be split into smaller bunches of the same sex, excluding the youngest bulls, which would remain with the cows until they were two-year-olds. Big John couldn't help but wonder if having been run at least twice so far this season hadn't delayed the herd's natural winter division. Certainly it had made the bison more agitated. The *métis* were still five hundred yards away when a huge bull at the edge of the herd spotted them, shook its massive head as if in annoyance, then trotted off.

The effect on the buffalo around it was instantaneous. Within seconds, the animals at the periphery of the herd were loping away from the hunters, spreading outward from the point where the bull had entered the main herd like a ripple launched from a muddy bank. In less than half a minute, the entire plain was on the run, stampeding into the wind. With a ragged yell the hunters dashed after them. So quick were they to react that Turcotte's final—*"Ho! Ho!"*—was all but lost in the rush.

Big John's roan quickly pulled ahead of the main bunch. Only a handful—Charlo, Breland, Hallet, LaBarge, and three or four others on better horses—were able to keep up. Big John's eyes immediately began to tear in the freezing wind, and the pounding of the roan's hoofs beat a dull cadence he could feel inside the scabbed-over wound from One Who Limps's knife. The odor of the running herd seemed to sharpen as he closed with it, as pungent as fresh-made cider. Buffalo gnats, shaken loose and left hovering in the air, began to pepper his face, and cowbirds, startled from the backs of their hosts, squawked raucously overhead.

Fortunately for the hunters, the herd was too cumbersome to manage much speed. Within half a mile, Big John felt the first bruising slap of a heart-shaped clod of dirt, kicked up by a fleeing bison. Minutes later, he began the perilous endeavor of threading a path through the rear wall of slower beasts. He was mildly surprised that the buffalo seemed more aggressive than usual. Many of them grunted angrily as the big stallion ranged alongside. A few even attempted to hook the roan with their short, curving horns, as if they'd finally grown weary of the *métis'* harassment and intended to retaliate.

The roan was an old hand at this type of work, though, and it didn't take him long to worm through the older bulls and get in among the younger animals. With a slight pressure of his knee, Big John guided the straining runner alongside a three-year-old cow—a Small-Built One, in the vernacular of the plains tribes. Palming one of his brace of pistols from his sash, he thumbed the cock back to full, then leaned almost casually from the saddle and pulled the trigger. The Small-Built One seemed to shudder in mid-stride, then veered sharply away before tumbling to the ground. Quickly Big John plucked a length of green wool from his sash and tossed it after the cow. Then he reloaded while the roan picked out another animal.

They approached the next cow from the left, but just as Big John pulled the trigger, the buffalo dodged to the side. The pistol bucked in his hand but the ball missed its mark. The cow bellowed in pain and rage, lurching away with her foreleg swinging uselessly, the shoulder broken.

Big John cursed as he guided the roan after her with his knees. He didn't try to reload. Instead he returned the empty pistol to his sash and slid its companion free. The second pistol was already primed. As the roan came against the cow, he cocked it, thrust it down, and pulled the trigger in one motion.

The cow fell as if pole-axed, flipping head over heels into the roan. The stallion squealed and stumbled sideways. Big John grabbed the reins desperately, struggling to bring the runner's head up, to keep the horse on its feet. They might have made it if not for an older cow coming up from behind and bumping hard against the horse's hip, flinging him in the opposite direction. The roan squealed again as its legs tangled, and went down like a stone.

Big John spilled over the horse's head with a strangled cry. He landed on his shoulder, from there rolling smoothly to his feet. He heard the roan's harsh, deep-throated roar as it lunged upright, but the horse was lost from sight, hidden behind a surging brown wall of stampeding bison. Big John turned toward a bull hurtling toward him. He could see the small, raging eyes below the burr-matted mop of the animal's forelock, the sharp black horns lowering. The bull wasn't running blindly. It had swerved deliberately toward him.

For a moment Big John stood as if frozen, the bull lumbering at him in what seemed an almost tortoise-like speed. His mind told him he could dodge this animal easily if he wanted to, that all he had to do was step aside at the last instant and the buffalo would simply race on past. But his muscles refused to respond at the same speed as his brain. He felt as sluggish as a bear coming out of hibernation.

It was Joseph Breland who stopped what, for a moment, seemed inevitable. He appeared as if from nowhere, charging his black runner straight at the bull. As he came near, his pony gun belched a rosy lance of flame and smoke that mushroomed against the bull's shoulder. The buffalo grunted and seemed to draw in around the point of the ball's impact. Then its front legs buckled and its nose dug into the prairie sod like a blunted plowshare.

The great weight of the animal propelled it forward, but by then Big John's paralysis had broken and he was able to skip nimbly out of its path. As the bull slid past, Big John jumped onto its back, balanced precariously there for a scant second, then tipped forward across the back of Breland's saddle—a move so gracefully perfect, so completely improbable, that it would have been impossible to duplicate. Then Breland's hand grabbed his sash, holding him firm until he could swing a leg over the black's croup.

Breland's grin was strained as he glanced over his shoulder, although neither man spoke. Big John's roan was clinging to the side of another cow about forty yards ahead, and Breland guided his black horse after it. The roan's ears were laid back, his neck stretched parallel to the ground, as if determined to continue the chase alone.

With its double load, it took the black a while to catch up. When they came alongside, Big John drew himself up on one knee, then slid his other leg across the roan's back. He launched himself toward the runner with a twinge of the same gut-wrenching anxiety he'd felt when he first spied the bull bearing down on him, but landed squarely in the saddle and found his stirrups without difficulty. With a wave and a yell, Breland swerved away and was soon lost from sight. Calmly Big John reloaded his remaining pistol, then shot the cow at his side.

He killed four more buffalo before the roan became too winded to keep up. The herd had scattered considerably by then, and, when he looked around, he discovered that he was alone on a vast, hill-rimmed plain. Straightening in the saddle, he pulled the roan down to a canter. The stallion's neck and shoulders were dark with sweat, and a grimy lather had collected along the saddle's single, buffalo-hair cinch.

The herd continued to stream around him, rolling on west like a billowing brown carpet. There was no place to go for him to escape the running mass of bison, and there were still too many animals behind him to stop completely. He had no choice but to continue on at a lope until the bulk of the herd had passed.

Once the herd began to thin out, Big John slowed to a trot, although he kept a wary eye over his shoulder. Most of the buffalo avoided him by swinging wide to one side or the other, but occasionally he would have to bend the roan out of the path of a larger, more densely packed bunch. It was another ten minutes before he felt comfortable enough to turn back. Coming to his last kill, he pulled up to study the country around him for any sign of hostiles. When he was satisfied he was alone, he dismounted and drew his butcher knife.

The cow's hide was a good one. Not quite a silk, but with a definite bluish tint that was rare, and that would increase its value. He took extra care with the skinning, then folded it carefully afterward and tied it behind his saddle.

The second cow he came to was as thickly wooled as the first, but its hair was coarser and of a more common hue, and there was a thick, ugly scar across the ribs from some past goring. He spent less time on this one, and dumped the hide beside the carcass when he was finished. As rough as it was, he doubted if Isabella would bother tanning it for a robe, although she might want it for whatever leather she could cut from around the lengthy, poorly-healed wound.

He was cleaning his knife with a handful of grass when he spotted a rider hauling up atop a distant hill. It was Pouliot, and in broad sign he was asking for Big John to come, explaining that the lost hunter had been found. For a moment, Big John didn't know what he meant. Then he realized what Pouliot was trying to say and his head snapped back as if he'd been slapped. Swinging his leg awkwardly over the bulky blue hide behind his saddle, he reined toward the hill.

Pouliot waited for him, but, as Big John made his way up the steep incline, he could tell from the expression on the mixed-blood's face that the news would not be good. Drawing up, he said: "Ye're tellin' me ye found a missin' hunter?"

Pouliot nodded glumly. "We think so. Etienne Cyr, maybe. You come, eh?"

"Etienne Cyr was lost days from here," Big John said. "He couldn't have walked this far."

Pouliot shrugged. "You come," he said, reining his horse around. Almost reluctantly, Big John followed.

Pouliot led him into an area of rolling hills, keeping his mount to an easy jog. It was a twenty-minute ride to the shallow basin where a dozen other *métis* surrounded a crumpled buffalo. Big John spotted Gabriel's Baldy and Breland's black runner among them.

There were a few terse greetings as he approached. Several of the men pulled their horses out of the way to allow him to ride through. Breland was already dismounted, stooped next to the dead bison. Hallet and Turcotte were also on foot, standing just behind him. Breland looked up as Big John halted his runner, his expression stricken, confidence gone. Glancing at the cow, Big John noticed for the first time the swatch of fabric attached to her head.

"I saw this, but didn't know what it was until I came back," Hallet explained shakily. "I . . . I thought it was a coat, maybe. A piece of clothing."

Big John looked again, and his heart seemed to slam against the back of his throat. "By the Lord," he croaked. His breath was ragged as he stepped down, then moved closer. "Are ye sure, man?" he demanded huskily of Hallet. "Are ye positive sure?"

"It is the shirt Cyr wore the day of the hunt," Breland said. He was watching Big John intently, as if unable to look any longer at what lay at his feet.

Big John bent unwillingly over the cow's neck to study what was left of the corpse. There wasn't much. A deflated torso and a misshapened lump that had once been the head. The arms and legs were trampled stumps, the blood-stained remnants of a green wool shirt all that remained of his dress. The buffalo's short, curved black horn was impaled deeply into the pelvic bone.

"Look here," Breland said, brushing back the cow's long neck hair. Pushing his fingers into the thick inner wool, Big John discovered the narrow stub of a broken knife blade, the hair around it matted with old blood. Breland nodded soberly. "He was alive for a while. He tried to kill the cow with his knife, but the cow killed him, instead."

Big John walked back to his horse, using the time to compose himself. Casting an accusatory eye on Turcotte, he said: "Why haven't ye pulled him free, man? Do ye not have the stomach for it?"

"We tried, Big John." Hallet's voice quavered. "But he's . . . stuck. We were afraid he'd come apart if we pulled much harder."

Big John swallowed with difficulty. "Then he'll have to be buried with the horn in him." He mounted the roan, settling himself before looking up. The eyes of every man there were upon him. Big John took a deep breath, then let it out slowly. "He was me friend," he whispered. "I can't. . . ." The words trailed off as his gaze returned to the empty sack of flesh. No one moved. No one spoke. Finally, with a terrible groan, he started to dismount.

"No!" Gabriel said loudly, startling everyone. He slipped

from Baldy's back and strode over to the buffalo. Glancing at Turcotte, he said: "Give me your belt axe."

Turcotte handed it over. Gabriel pulled the hair back from the base of the horn and, with his fingers dangerously close, drove the bit into the hard, scaly protrusion. He worked swiftly and, as far as Big John could tell, never once looked at the corpse. The horn cracked before it broke, tipping Cyr's body toward the ground. With the next blow, Gabriel severed the horn completely. What was left of Cyr's body plopped into the grass, rolled once, then came to a stop.

Breathing slightly harder than the effort would have seemed to require, Gabriel returned the axe to Turcotte, then went to his horse. Silently Turcotte began to skin the cow. He would use the hide to wrap the body in. Big John glanced at Breland, but Breland was still staring at the corpse in morbid fascination.

"Wrap him tight, René," Big John said heavily. "We'll take him back to the caravan and see that he's buried proper-like."

"We can't," Breland said, tearing his gaze away from the body. "Marie must not see this, Big John. We will bury him here, and no one must speak of it to her."

"No, Joseph, we'll not be hidin' this from Marie. She has a right to know what happened to her husband, no matter how difficult the tellin' might be."

"We don't even know for sure that this is him," Hallet said.

"We know," Gabriel said flatly. He stared at Hallet until the hunter looked away, then turned to Breland. "We will do as Big John says."

This time, there was no debate.

Chapter Twenty-Three

Gripped by restlessness, Pike wandered away from the McTavish camp. Overhead, the stars were nearly obscured by a mantle of clouds that had blown in late that afternoon, and the moon had not yet risen. Only a few small buffalo-chip fires continued to dance and sputter in the stiffening breeze. Most of the half-breeds had turned in early, daunted by the reappearance of Etienne Cyr, nearly one hundred miles from where he had vanished.

Cyr's return had affected the *métis* deeply, more so than even McKay's death at the hands of the Sioux. They had gone through the motions of a funeral as if in a trance, then voted immediately afterward to move camp several miles closer to the herds. Even Cyr's wife Marie had watched with more dismay than grief as the broken remnants of her husband were lowered into its grave.

Pike shared their feelings of unease. Etienne Cyr's reappearance was unnerving; it dredged up too many childhood nightmares. Turning his back to the wind, he dug the fixings from the overlap of his capote. He packed his short clay pipe tightly, then lit it with flint and steel and a spark struck into a piece of char cloth. With the pipe drawing smoothly, he eased down against a dished cart wheel and carefully stretched his legs. Despite the stiffness, he was satisfied with the pull of muscle across his ribs, the dulling ache in his hip. The swelling in his knee had gone down, too, and, although he hadn't taken part in the day's chase, he was determined to go out tomorrow. Duprée had been bragging earlier that he planned to drop twice as many buffalo on his next run, but Pike had decided to make him a liar. Henri Duprée's time of reckoning had come at last, and the middle of a run seemed like the perfect place for it to happen.

The woman caught him by surprise, and Pike swore under his breath and stood, annoyed at having let her get so close without detecting her. The woman said: "You are *Monsieur* Pike, *non?*"

"Yeah, I'm Pike."

"*Oui,* I thought as much, but the night is so dark. I am Susanne Leveille, daughter of Jacques Leveille, of Saint Joseph."

"You skin for Charlo," Pike said, picturing her in his mind—an attractive girl, finely featured. A good worker, too, he recalled.

"I make Charlo's pemmican and cure the hides he takes, *oui.*"

"What do you want?"

"You will go soon, *non?* To the *montagnes,* I mean."

Pike's brows furrowed suspiciously. "Maybe."

"After the hunt, *non?*"

But maybe was all he was willing to give.

"You must say!" Susanne exclaimed with a quick stomp of her foot.

Shrugging then, deciding it didn't really matter, Pike said: "I don't intend to go back to the valley. When the caravan turns around, I'll keep moving west."

"You will take Celine when you go?"

He stiffened at that. "No."

"But you must!"

"No," he said again, bluntly.

"*Monsieur,* you must know that Celine has poisoned Gabriel's heart. He must be left alone if he is to ever find his way again. Surely you can see that?"

Pike doubted if he saw it quite the way Susanne Leveille did. Or Gabriel, for that matter. It was ironic, though, and more than a little humorous. He wondered if Gabriel knew how Susanne felt about him, that she was willing to humble herself in front of a stranger this way. Although Pike didn't know her well, he thought Gabriel would be a fool to cast someone like her aside for Celine McTavish. Yet there was no accounting for what a man might do if he thought he was in love. It was a strange medicine, more potent than the strongest Pass Brandy sold in Taos.

"It is true, *non?*" Susanne persisted.

Maybe, Pike thought, but that didn't mean he was going to saddle himself with a crazy woman.

"*Monsieur!* You must answer me," Susanne demanded.

"No," Pike said gruffly. "I want nothing to do with her."

"But she came to you. When you returned from the Chippewas. You, *monsieur.*"

"I don't want her, girl. It's her that wants, although I'm damned if I think she knows what it is she's looking for."

"Gabriel," Susanne replied simply. "It is Gabriel she wants."

But Pike wasn't convinced of that, either. Not in the way Susanne Leveille meant it.

"Then you will not help me?"

He shook his head, not caring whether she saw his silent response or not.

"Very well," she said stiffly, then turned away.

Pike watched the spot where she disappeared, thinking that maybe it would be a good thing if he did leave after tomorrow's hunt. He was getting the prickly feeling that he'd already stayed too long.

★ ★ ★ ★ ★

By morning the clouds had thickened into a dense gray canopy, stretching from horizon to horizon. Now and again they would spit a few small, grainy flakes of snow that took their time melting against the rapidly freezing soil. The wind had strengthened overnight, too, numbing where it struck exposed flesh.

Pike saddled the seal brown runner Michel Quesnelle had given him, his fingers stiff and clumsy on the latigo. From time to time he would glance across the camp to where Henri Duprée was saddling his own horse, boasting loudly to those around him of the buffalo he would take that day, the quantity of meat and hides he would harvest. Duprée had grown bolder of late, Pike thought, more arrogant. Familiarity had given him a confidence he'd lacked when he first arrived.

Big John walked up just as Pike finished. "I didn't think ye'd be goin' out again so soon."

"A man can't make meat idling about camp," Pike said.

"Well, and sure, but I'd say the women have enough to handle with what Gabriel and I shot yesterday. Isabella and I will be takin' a cart out later today to bring in what the wolves have left us. There's no reason ye have to hunt if ye don't feel up to it just yet."

"Figured I'd give it a try," Pike said. He pulled the heavy wooden stirrup down off the seat, then glanced at the sky. "Feels kinda like winter," he remarked absently.

"Aye, and here to stay this time. I can feel it in me bones." He lifted his face to the spiraling dry flakes. "I'm hopin' we can push on to Turtle Lake soon. 'Twill feel good to sit before a real fire again. We've used up most of the firewood we brought from Chain of Lakes in dryin' the meat after the last hunt."

"What's the matter?" Pike asked, grinning. "Buffalo shit don't suit you any more?"

Big John smiled good-naturedly. " 'Tis a fact dried dung

won't warm a man the way a good wood fire will, though 'twas shelter from the storm I was hopin' for."

Pike thrust a heavily moccasined foot into his stirrup and pulled himself up into the bulky cradle of his saddle. At the southern rim of the camp about twenty hunters had already gathered for the day's run, but only a few others were still readying their mounts. The majority of the men would remain behind today, most of those going out, as Big John and Isabella planned, to bring in the meat and hides they hadn't been able to retrieve yesterday.

Stepping away from the brown, Big John said: "Luck to ye then, Mister Pike, and watch yeself. We've lost too many good men already this season."

Pike made a chore of gathering the brown's reins, sliding them through his fingers until they hung evenly along the gelding's neck. A feeling of warmth came over him for this old man, and a sense of shame after that. He had done McTavish wrong by horning his daughter—had bit the hand that fed him, his ma would've said—but it was too late now. There was no way to undo his wrong without destroying what little trust McTavish still had in him, and, as selfish as it was, Pike didn't want to risk that. Not now.

To the south, Turcotte was already leading his hunters through a gap in the carts, and Pike touched the brown's sides with his spurs. He rode away without acknowledgment of McTavish's good bye, and, when he was free of the carts, he kicked the brown into a gallop to catch up with the rest of the party.

They angled more south than west, and by late morning came upon a small herd of several hundred buffalo, speckling the baseline of a range of snow-dusted hills. Turcotte called a halt, and the hunters crowded around him.

"Where 'ave they gone, René?" Patterson queried.

"Where do buffalo ever go?" Turcotte replied sourly, then answered his own question. "Wherever they please, but who ever knows where that is? Myself, I think we should hunt these. There will be enough, no?"

"Maybe too many, even at half that," another replied. His words caused a general uplifting of chins. The snow was coming down harder now, the flakes bigger and wetter, and it was finally starting to stick, turning the grass slick and white.

"I'm nae anxious tae run me pony o'er such mountains as these," Patterson said, inclining his head toward the low, jumbled hills behind the buffalo. "Such a land be made for sleds 'n' such, this time o' year, and nae a pony's hoofs."

Turcotte nodded glumly. He looked like he would gladly call off the hunt if anyone suggested it.

Pike, who had been hanging back silently, said: "Be a long ride out here for nothing if we turned back now."

"No one said we were turning back," Hallet replied, giving Turcotte a hard glare.

"Unless the American wants to," Duprée added in a snickering tone. He was watching Pike closely, his lips pulled back to reveal the jagged, yellow tips of his teeth.

"Non," Turcotte said almost wearily. "We came to hunt, and hunt we will do." He made a quick circular motion with his hand. "We form our line here."

Pike reined after Duprée, forcing his horse between him and Pierre Campbell. Duprée eyed him curiously in the thickening fall of snow, his dark, bearded face twisting in a frown. "I do not know you," he said, "but I think you must know me, eh? You watch me always, like the wolf watches the lamb."

"I saw you the first time at Qu'Appelle Post," Pike said. "You were leaving just as I rode in. I didn't recognize you then, but I learned afterward that it was you."

"And then you come here, to the valley?"

"I've been following you a long time. You and Rubiette."

Duprée's eyes widened. "François . . . ," he breathed with cautious understanding. "It was you? I thought maybe an Indian, a Sioux, at least."

At the far end of the line, Turcotte called—*"Ho!"*—and the *métis* started forward at a brisk walk. Only Duprée and Pike held back.

"Who are you?" Duprée whispered.

"Just a trapper, Duprée. And a friend."

"A friend . . . but not of mine?"

Pike shook his head. Duprée's self-assurance was crumbling rapidly. Pike could see it in his face, in the quick darting of his eyes.

"There was a Pike who traded for American Fur, out of Fort Union," Duprée said hesitantly, his eyes narrowing. "But he was. . . ." He licked nervously at his lips. "*Non.* That man, that Pike, I did not know him." He stopped, staring.

Leaning forward until his face was within inches of Duprée's, Pike whispered sharply: *"Weendigo!"*

The half-breed stared back as if seeing a ghost. Then he groaned and quirted his horse after the line of hunters. Pike held the brown back, breathing heavily. He wondered if he'd pushed it too far, too soon, by letting his anger get the better of him. If Duprée sought help from the others, it could ruin his plans.

But Duprée didn't stop when he caught up with the others. He didn't even slow down. Ramming his horse through the ranks of *métis* horsemen, he continued his mad dash for the distant hills as if hell itself were snapping at his heels.

At least half a dozen horses already keyed up for the run seemed to explode as Henri crashed his mount through the line. A couple bolted after him, their riders scrambling to regain control, and, with that, the race was on. Turcotte tried to call them back, but his own runner was lunging so frantically against its jawline bridle that it was all he could do just to keep his seat. A few held back with Turcotte, but the rest were quirting their horses furiously after Duprée. The run had started; nothing could stop it now.

Cursing, Pike drove his spurs into the brown's flanks. He swung wide around Turcotte and the half dozen or so with him. They were following at a lope, their faces dark with anger. Turcotte hailed him as he passed, but Pike was too intent on catching up with Duprée to respond.

The snow was falling heavier by the minute, feathering down out of the west on a dying breeze. In the gray light the flakes looked as big as silver dollars. The drumming of the brown's hoofs was muffled by the snow already on the ground, and the buffalo that had been clearly visible only moments before were now nearly imperceptible through the thickening veil of snow. Although Pike could see several riders ahead of him, he couldn't see Duprée. With growing panic, he knew he would have to catch up before they reached the hills. Once there, it would be anyone's guess as to which direction the half-breed took.

Although Turcotte had halted them nearly half a mile from the herd, the leggy brown gelding seemed to cover that distance in no time. The buffalo had already taken flight and were scattering into the hills to the west. Even though these mounds hardly warranted the notice of a man who had trapped in the shadows of the Tetons, they were still fair-size—steep, rolling nubs covered with brown grass rapidly disappearing under a blanket of fresh-fallen snow.

Most of the half-breeds continued straight into the hills after the main herd, but when Pike spotted several buffalo veering into the next valley to the south, being dogged by a man on a gray horse shaded similarly to Duprée's, he figured he had little choice but to follow.

He slowed to a trot as he entered the mouth of the valley. The trail of the buffalo was a broad, grayish swath churned through the wet snow, the tracks of a single horse conspicuous among the smaller prints of the bison. Riding alone, Pike's gaze shifted from hilltop to hilltop, lingered on the ravines, scrutinized every rocky outcropping. He knew Duprée would have the advantage here, if he had the courage to use it.

The hills seemed to lay in a convoluted tangle, without any discernible pattern. Coulées fingered down on either side—some almost as wide as valleys in their own right—but the man he trailed stayed with the buffalo, his tracks easy to follow.

Winding deeper into the hills, wrapped in a crepuscular world that was both sky and earth, Pike was able to keep his sense of direction only by the gentle slant of the snow. In time another buffalo trail came down a sharp incline on his right to merge with the one he was following, obliterating Duprée's tracks completely. Grimly Pike pushed on after the buffalo.

Pike saw bison in every direction, and knew they'd underestimated the size of the herd. Smaller bunches were strung out across the hills, agitated and on the move as the animals the half-breeds had run on the flats joined them. With the falling snow, Pike almost missed a flash of color moving over the shoulder of a distant ridge. He kicked the seal brown into a short lope. Although he hadn't been completely confident he was on the right trail when he'd veered off to the south, he was now. He figured he'd recognize that brilliant, emerald tuque of Duprée's in the middle of spring-green pasture. In a snowstorm, it stood out like a beacon.

At the next coulée leading in the same general direction as the far-off rider, Pike abandoned the buffalo trace altogether. Although the coulée snaked back and forth, it rose quickly. When it finally shallowed out about two-thirds of the way up the hill, he jumped the brown out of the ravine and dismounted, hobbling the horse and climbing the rest of the way on foot.

The wet snow was like ice under his greased, slick-soled moccasins. It took all of his concentration to make any progress without slipping and falling, and by the time he reached the crest, his toes were numb from digging for purchase.

The view from the top was spectacular, though limited. The land lay empty before him, without blemish. Not even the brown smudge of a buffalo marred the whitened countryside, although he could hear the ponderous approach of another herd coming up from the rear, the pop and click of joints, the clatter of horns, the hog-like grunts of the leaders, all accompanying a faint vibration through the ground that told him this bunch was large, but coming on slowly.

Pike glanced over his shoulder in annoyance. The floor of the valley he'd followed up from the plain, little more than a coulée itself now, ran past about eighty yards below him. The seal brown gelding still stood at the edge of the ravine where he'd left it, but had turned to watch their back trail, head high, ears perked forward. The brown whickered as the scent of the herd reached his quivering nostrils, and its rear hoofs shuffled restively. Swearing under his breath, Pike started back down the incline. The brown was a runner, and his instincts would be to go with the herd. Although the hobbles might slow him down, Pike knew they wouldn't stop him if he took a notion to run with the buffalo.

He'd gone perhaps a dozen paces when a small, mushrooming cloud blossomed from the side of the hill across the valley. He jerked to a stop just as the distant boom of a fusil reached his ears. At almost the same instant, he was struck a sharp blow to his side. His moccasins scooted out from under him and his rifle seemed to leap from his hands. He fell on his back, his head smacking solidly against the hard ground. White flashes strobed briefly in front of his eyes, then the sky overhead darkened.

Although unconsciousness never claimed him completely, his struggles against it occupied the next several minutes. Only slowly did the dull, cloudy light of the buffalo plains return. Groaning, he brought a hand to his face, then slid it around to the back of his head. His fingers came away clean, even though he expected blood.

Sitting up, he twisted around to examine his side. Duprée's shot had missed his body but shattered his powder horn, scattering black grains of DuPont over the snow like ground pepper. As that knowledge sank in, a feeling of panic gripped him, and he pulled his rifle into his lap. A dab of fine-grained powder remained in his priming horn, but not enough for a second charge. That left only the round still in the barrel, and no way to reload until he got back to camp and found a spare horn.

Despite the cold, there was a sheen of sweat across his brow as he struggled to his feet. On the hill across the valley, Duprée stood behind his pony, his fusil resting across his saddle, the muzzle pointed directly at Pike.

Chapter Twenty-Four

It was snowing heavily by the time Big John reached the last buffalo he'd shot in yesterday's run. The plain surrounding the marbled carcass was white and featureless, the air jittery with falling flakes. Dismounting, he looped his reins around one of the cow's horns, then stood a moment to survey what he could of the country.

With no real horizon to lay his eyes on, there wasn't much of an impression of place. Only the tracks of his horse and the snow-covered lump of the dead bison provided even a modicum of perspective. Little enough, he supposed, leaning his double-barreled rifle against the cow's woolly skull, although it seemed more than adequate when he recalled his first few winters in the *pays sauvage*. During those callow days of his youth, such scenes as this had often tyrannized his soul, breathing morbid life into visions of freezing to death alone and unloved, or succumbing to the wretched agony of starvation.

Nowadays, of course, and as long as the temperature remained above zero or so, he was more apt to welcome the solitude of a winter's storm.

Stooping above the carcass, Big John muscled his knife into the half-frozen flesh. Deftly he pared down the side of the spine, taking the *dépouilles* first. There had been some damage from wolves and coyotes to the first three buffalo he'd shot yesterday, one of the animals ravaged so completely its entire yield had been ruined, but none of the later carcasses had been molested, and the meat had remained fresh in the cold air.

Guiding his heavy-bladed butcher knife skillfully through the lean meat, Big John removed only the choicest pieces and laid them out in the snow. He had just finished the first side and was rolling the carcass over with the aid of the roan and a length of rope when he heard the muffled squeal of Isabella's cart. A few minutes later he spied her trudging through the curtain of snow, following the roan's tracks. She was wearing her heaviest shawl, and had thrust her hands into the sleeves of her capote for warmth. Visible beneath the blanket coat's hem were heavy wool leggings that extended down over the tops of her thick *souliers de boeuf,* the calf-high buffalo-hide moccasins she wore in winter, constructed with the hair turned inward.

The cart pony followed without lead, halting obediently when she flashed a hand in front of its face. Eyeing the partially butchered carcass, she nodded her approval. "It was a good run," she pronounced. "There is much meat for pemmican, and the robes are as good as last season's."

"Aye. Nary a silky in the lot, but naught that's truly bad, either, save for the one with the scar across her ribs."

"It has been a good hunt, McTavish. We will fill a cart with what we have taken today, and maybe fill a *taureau* to put in the second cart."

Drawing her knife, she bent over the carcass while Big John carried the meat he'd already removed to the cart. Working together, it didn't take long to finish up. Afterward, they cleaned their blades with handfuls of snow, dried them on their coat sleeves, then touched up the edges with a whetstone. When they were done, Isabella climbed into the cart and Big John mounted the roan and took the pony's lead rope.

They traveled without speaking through a white world no more than a few hundred yards from one end to the other. With the snow falling as thick as it was and the light fading, Big John began to fret a little about finding his way back. There weren't any landmarks to latch onto, just his own intuition and the vanishing back trail of the horses and cart. But if Isabella was worried, she didn't show it. Perched atop the pile of meat with a spare robe pulled over her shoulders for warmth, she quietly smoked a long-stemmed clay pipe. Now and again Big John would glance back at her and she would return his gaze expectantly, but she never breached the silence. Nor did he, for all that his thoughts kept leading him in that direction.

For some obscure reason, Father Denning's admonition that they marry, and in that way cease the impropriety of their relationship together, had come to him again that morning, as it had intermittently throughout their long journey to the buffalo ranges. Something had changed of late, subtle yet large. He had become aware of it only recently, but he knew Gabriel had sensed it much earlier, and maybe Charlo, too. Surely others had as well.

Marriage? He mulled the possibilities, wondering why he'd avoided it for so long. Although a Church union would always remain out of the question for him, there were alternatives. Hudson's Bay still offered a contract of marriage—insisted on it for its employees, in fact, although it was a difficult policy to enforce in the far-flung expanses of Rupert's Land—and there were the American settlements of St. Peter and Green Bay to the south. He wondered if a civil ceremony would be sufficient for Isabella, if it would lighten her guilt. Imagining that it would brought him a certain amount of pleasure. She asked for so little for herself outside of her religion, the one thing Big John was forever unable to give her.

Although he toyed with the idea of bringing up the subject now, an unfamiliar shyness came over him and he kept the roan pointed toward camp, his feelings to himself. He would think about it some more, he decided, and, if it still seemed like a good idea in a few days, maybe he'd ask her then. But not right now. There was something else nagging at him, and, looking back, he saw that Isabella felt it, too. Giving the cart pony's lead rope a sharp tug, he picked up the pace.

Half an hour later an ox dodged past them in the storm, wall-eyed with fright, bleeding from the nose, then vanished into the storm. Big John halted the roan long enough to put fresh caps on both nipples of his rifle, while Isabella slid to the ground and unhitched the cart pony. She was carrying her own shortened fusil now, and had slipped her bag and powder horn over her shoulder where they would be easy to reach. Pulling the cart pony alongside the vehicle's shafts, she jumped from them onto the animal's bare back. Big John signed—"Ready?"—and she replied that she was, and, side-by-side, they moved out.

It was a woman's keening they heard first, faint and low-keyed, as if she had been at it a while and was nearly cried out. They reined their horses toward the sound and gradually the caravan took shape out of the swirling maw. From beneath one of the carts came a flash, followed by a muted boom. Hearing the whuffing passage of the ball as it sailed overhead, Big John drew up.

"Hold ye fire!" he bellowed. " 'Tis Big John McTavish and Isabella Gilray."

A distant voice told them to advance slowly and keep their hands away from their weapons.

As they neared the caravan, Big John spotted an arrow jutting from an oaken hub. After that, his gaze was drawn to other arrows, embedded in cart beds or pricking the stacks of meat and untanned hides that had been dumped hastily between the vehicles. The woman's wailing grew sharper as they approached, accompanied by the softer cries of others.

Big John's muscles were taut as bowstrings when Joseph Breland stepped out to meet them. Joseph's face was riven from the corner of his eyebrow to his chin by a long, ugly gash, the clotted blood already starting to freeze in his beard. He was hatless, and his long black hair, wet with snow, was plastered to his skull.

"It was the Sioux, Big John," he explained. "They caught us by surprise."

A cart was rolled back, and Big John and Isabella guided their horses inside. Breland came along beside them, his hand on the roan's hip. Jacques Leveille waited for them by a small fire, his fusil cradled across his chest.

"We were breaking camp to move closer to the herds," he said, his voice strained with emotion. "They appeared out of the storm before we even knew they were there."

"Were there no guards?" Big John asked.

Breland nodded morosely. "Saint Germain and Rocheblave. Both were killed."

Isabella pulled her horse around and kicked it into a trot. She was heading for her own lodge, and the medical supplies she kept stored there in a parfleche box.

"The news is worse," Breland added reluctantly. "They broke through the carts. Nicolas Quesnelle's son Michel was also killed, as was Gavin McGillis, and . . . Big John, three women were taken. Lizette Hallet, Emmaline Pouliot, and. . . ."

Big John groaned softly.

". . . Celine. I am sorry, my friend."

Pike raised his rifle, sighting on the distant figure just visible at the far end of his wavering field of vision. He judged the distance at a little under one hundred yards, but knew the snow could be misleading.

Below him, the brown gelding whinnied as the first of the buffalo appeared around a bend to the east. Pike noted the herd briefly, then dismissed it from his thoughts. He focused on his aim, on holding his sights high on Duprée's chest. Then he gently stroked the trigger. The rifle bucked in his hands. Swearing at the powder smoke that hung like a billowing sheet in front of him, he half skidded down the steep slope until he had a view clear of the choking cloud. What he saw was Duprée's horse rearing against the gray sky, its front hoofs flashing. But the footing was too treacherous, and the animal's rear legs abruptly slid out from under it. Horse and man fell in an explosion of white.

Duprée's horse came up in an instant and fled over the brow of the hill, bucking as it went, but Duprée was slower to regain his feet. He stood and shook his head, then looked around empty-handed. Moving carefully down the slope, he plucked his fusil from the snow, shook it to dislodge any slush from around the lock, then lifted it to his shoulder. Pike's heart sank like a stone in water. He stood motionlessly, his breathing shallow, rifle hanging useless in his hands.

At first he didn't know what to think when Duprée lowered his weapon, then raised it again. When he lowered it a second time, a weak grin took possession of his features. Something had happened to Duprée's fusil. Perhaps it had been damaged in the fall, maybe kicked by his horse. Or snow had wormed through the touch hole to saturate the powder charge inside. Whatever the cause, Duprée couldn't get his smoothbore to fire, and Pike felt a momentary reprieve.

Lifting his voice above the rumble of the herd just then coming between them, Pike shouted: "Duprée!"

The man's head jerked up. Pike extended his arm away from his body, his rifle dangling from his fist. Then he let it drop, making sure it tipped outward into the snow so that Duprée didn't think it was a ruse. Drawing his knife, he held it above his head where the half-breed could see it. It was a hollow challenge, and it made him feel hollow inside to issue it, but perhaps if Duprée didn't know he was unable to reload, if his own fusil was inoperable. . . .

Leaving his rifle behind, Pike started down the slope. He kept his hands spread wide not just for balance, but to reassure Duprée that he was unarmed save for the knife. Duprée held back suspiciously until Pike was well clear of his rifle, then he angrily flung his own long gun aside and started forward.

The herd leaders were just disappearing over the top of the rise to the west when Pike reached the bottom of the hill. Behind them trailed a sinuous thread of buffalo, flowing between the two hunters like a cinnamon-hued river. Here, near the top where the valley had narrowed down almost to the size of a ravine, the bison were funneled in tightly, about a dozen abreast and packed shoulder to shoulder between the steep banks. A few of the beasts shook their heads threateningly as Pike approached, but the majority of them were so crammed in they didn't even notice him.

Pike halted at the very lip of the ravine, his toes about even with the surging brown humps of the bison. Duprée stopped opposite him, maybe thirty feet away. He lifted his knife provokingly. It was a Hudson's Bay dagger with a hole drilled through the bone handle that enclosed a slim, braided leather thong looped around the half-breed's wrist.

"You and me, eh, American?" Duprée shouted. "We see now who is the better man."

Pike's anger soared when he saw the pitted, whetstone-worn blade of the dag. Was this the knife the cocky little bastard had used on Arch? His voice taut with rage, he called: "How did man meat taste, Duprée? Was it tender, or tough?"

But Duprée was already denying it. "It is not me that is *weendigo.* It was François."

"You're a liar!" Pike shouted. "A god damned man-eating liar!"

At Pike's feet, a cow brushed the steep bank, loosening a small avalanche of dirt and tiny stones. Pike felt the scuff of her shoulder through the sod, the jolt of her massive frame beneath his moccasins. It seemed the most natural thing in the world to step out onto her wet back. No different than exiting his family's cabin door back home after the evening meal.

Duprée's eyes widened in astonishment. Then he laughed and hurried down the slope, leaping astride a buffalo that bucked once and shook its head, then settled back into the shuffling trot that marked the pace of the rest of the herd. Pushing to his feet, Duprée cackled gleefully as he crouched easily with one hand hanging onto the buffalo's long shoulder hair. "You and me, American! *Sacre,* I look forward to slitting your throat."

But Pike's zeal had waned. Balanced awkwardly atop the cow's sloping hips, he felt suddenly sick with dread. Duprée's quick response didn't surprise him. He'd seen Indians and half-breeds perform similar feats of recklessness in the past. But his own daring had left a brassy taste of fear in his throat. He'd never attempted anything so audacious in his life, and, even though he knew it could be done, he was almost certain it couldn't be done by him.

He swayed dangerously above the jogging cow, unable to find her rhythm. His toes and arches ached where they dug at the buffalo's sides. He might have whimpered if his throat hadn't been so constricted. Yet the bison seemed oblivious to her new burden, jogging on as if he were nothing more than an oversize cowbird.

Duprée's ridiculing laughter was nearly Pike's undoing. Looking up, he immediately lost his balance, and with a strangled yell he fell forward across the winter-furred hump of the next cow in.

Draped over the cow's back like a pair of saddlebags, Pike

clawed at the woolly hide. Beneath the surface of the densely packed herd there moved the current of a world all its own—pumping shoulders, oscillating hoofs, the splash of snow pounded into slush. And through it all, a thick, dank odor that nearly suffocated him.

Pike pushed and punched until he was able to wiggle back far enough to swing a leg over the cow. Lifting his face clear of the wet hide, he sucked in a lungful of frigid air.

Hooting scornfully, Duprée stepped onto the next buffalo in, straddling its back in a crouch until he was sure of his equilibrium, then pushing on to the third.

Pike watched in awe. Duprée's movements looked as graceful as a house cat's walking a back-yard fence. It reminded Pike of the Pembina hunters who had ridden out to meet him and Big John on the day they'd gone into Pembina Post to trade, the half-breeds standing nimbly upright atop their charging runners, as free as the wind itself. Above the reverberation of the herd, Pike heard Duprée's taunting words.

"You are clumsy, American. Like the bear, *non?*" Rising to his feet, Duprée eased onto the back of the next buffalo. "See? See how simple a thing this is for a *bois brûle?* I will cut your heart out while you sit there helpless as a newborn babe." He raised his hand, the dagger flashing in the pale light. Then his lips peeled back in a snarl. "Now we settle this thing between us for good, eh?"

Pike knew he'd never be a match for the agile half-breed. Not this way. He'd already lost his own knife when he fell across the second cow, although he doubted if he would have been able to do much with it, even if he'd managed to hang onto it. It was taking all his concentration just to keep his seat aboard the rough-gaited, oddly shaped bison. Meanwhile, Duprée was moving steadily closer, barely pausing as he eased from one animal to the next.

"Maybe I eat you, too, eh, American? What do you think of that?" The *métis* chortled. "Carve a piece off your ass, maybe? Arch, he was not so good as some. Not like a fat squaw whose flesh sizzles above the flame, but, *sacre,* if a man is hungry, he must eat, *non?*" He stepped onto the next animal and dropped to his familiar three-point stance of knee, the ball of his other foot, and one hand above the buffalo's spine. Although he made it look easy, as he drew closer, Pike could see the strain in the half-breed's face, the difficulty of matching the rocking cadence of the animal under him.

Still, his progress amazed Pike. On the flat plain below, Duprée had fled like a frightened child. Here, he seemed immune to fear. He was also no more than four or five more buffalo from Pike's side, although he would have to move forward now, as well as laterally.

His breath dragging raw across his throat, Pike rose to his good knee, careful to keep a tight grip on the thick wool of the cow's hump. Even then, he wasn't sure what he was going to do. He knew only that he couldn't just sit there like a lump of clay while Duprée skipped over and slit his throat.

"Do not be in such a hurry, *mon ami,*" Duprée chided from behind him. "Death should never be rushed. It must be savored, like the squaw, or whiskey."

The herd seemed to be moving faster, and, when Pike looked up, he saw that the narrow valley was widening as it neared the top, those animals in the lead picking up speed as they fanned out. Without the density of the packed herd within the narrow confines of the ravine, Pike knew he wouldn't stand a chance.

Swallowing back his fear, he straightened slowly, allowing his hips to rock instinctively to the gait of the cow. He could hear Duprée calling to him, but paid no mind to what he was saying. He took a long, awkward step toward the outside buffalo, planting his foot solidly against her hip. Then he pushed away from the cow he had been riding to leap clumsily for the lowering bank.

He landed in a heap on the side of the hill, crying out as his injured knee and bruised hip came into contact with the hard ground. The cow behind the one he'd jumped from lunged belligerently at him. It managed to hook the hem of his capote with one of her curved horns, and yanked him back toward the engulfing herd. But the heavy wool fabric ripped before she could pull him under, and Pike rolled free.

On his hands and one knee, he scrambled higher up the bank, but, when he finally stopped and turned around, Duprée was gone. The *métis* had disappeared without a trace, without even a sound of protest, while the flow of buffalo continued on without pause or swerve, spilling over the top of the rise like water over a falls.

It was another thirty minutes before the last of the buffalo passed on by. When the valley was clear, Pike went back. Duprée's remains weren't hard to find. They lay near the center of the ravine-like vale, mangled beyond recognition save for the dagger, still looped around his shattered wrist. Pike stared for a long time before he finally turned away, limping back down the ravine. He recovered his own knife along the way, and soon afterward met the seal brown gelding in its hobbles, following hesitantly after the bison. He rode back to retrieve his rifle, then climbed the opposite hill to claim the powder horn Duprée had tossed aside with his fusil.

He reloaded methodically, his movements slow but sure. He felt oddly disconcerted, as if his whole world had been jolted slightly off kilter. He'd felt this same way the day he'd abandoned François Rubiette, he recalled, wrung-out and dissatisfied, as if all he'd done still wasn't enough.

Tipping his head back, he stared into the swirling snow. The flakes were significantly smaller than earlier, feathering lightly on shifting breezes, though still accumulating. For a moment, listening to the gentle hiss of the snow as it struck his hat, he debated what he wanted to do, which way he wanted to go. Fort Clark lay to the southwest, an American Fur Company post where he would be known by name, if not by sight. He had credit built up with American Fur, enough to outfit himself back to the Rockies if that was where he wanted to go. And there was nothing to hold him here any longer. He knew the buffalo he'd harvested so far wouldn't be enough to compensate McTavish for the bay, but he doubted if Big John would care. There were a few odds and ends of supplies that would have to be left behind, but nothing vital. Certainly nothing worth the long ride back. It would be a waste of time to return, he told himself. Pure foolishness. Yet he didn't try to second guess his motives when he reined the brown in that direction. Some questions, he'd learned, were best left unasked.

Chapter Twenty-Five

There was no discernible sunset that night. The light just faded and darkness closed in. With the exception of Quesnelle's brother-in-law, Henri Duprée, the last of the hunters had returned at dusk, their expressions exhibiting the same incredulous shock Gabriel had witnessed on Big John's face when he'd learned of Celine's abduction.

After slipping through the gap in the circled carts, most of the *métis* had hurried off to their own lodges, needing to be with their own families for a while. Later, Gabriel knew, they would congregate at someone's fire, their emotions oscillating between remorse and anger.

The wounded, eight men and nearly twice that many women and children, were sheltered in teepees around the cordon. Three of the women and one of the men were injured seriously, but only Old Dan Keller's youngest son William wasn't expected to survive. William had taken an arrow in his lungs, and was slowly bleeding to death on the inside.

The Sioux had exacted their toll for the stolen buffalo. For the *bois brûles,* the price had been tremendous.

It had been Breland's idea to move camp a few miles closer to the herds, and, although several of the party had objected on the grounds that not everyone was in, the vote had gone to Joseph. The Sioux had struck while they were packing their carts and harnessing the stock, appearing soundlessly out of the swirling storm.

"Alec and I were in your lodge," Gabriel had related to Big John that afternoon, after his return. "We did not think it wise to leave, but we knew we couldn't stay if the others went."

"We did not even know the Sioux were nearby until we heard several shots," Alec had added.

At first Gabriel had thought it was a hunter's shot that cracked flatly across the camp, maybe taken at a wolf that had gotten too close to an ox. But when he heard Gavin McGillis's panicky warning shout, he knew there was trouble. He grabbed his musket and ducked outside just as the Sioux breached the northern wall of carts.

In the confusion of the next several minutes, it was difficult to tell just what was going on. Fusils roared in every direction, and the sharp ring of metal on metal—tomahawk against lance, sword against gun barrel—filled the air. Gabriel saw LaBarge's woman, Elaine, empty a pistol at a Sioux. When the Sioux kicked his horse after her, Gabriel shouldered the Bess, tumbling the Indian from his pony's back with a lucky shot. The Sioux immediately jumped up and leaped behind another warrior, and the two of them raced off.

A quirt lashed the top of Gabriel's shoulder—a coup struck—and he spun with the musket raised like a club, but the Sioux had already flown past.

That was when Gabriel saw Celine, stumbling from between a pair of lodges like a lost child. He shouted for her to go back, but she didn't hear him. He started toward her, reloading on the run.

He saw the three Sioux at the same instant they spotted Celine, and in his heart he knew there wasn't any way in the world he could stop all of them.

Sprinting across the churned snow, he rammed the big .75-caliber musket ball home without taking his eyes off the trio of warriors racing their ponies toward Celine. He cried out in frustration, his legs pumping furiously, but he was too far away. The Sioux swept past the girl without even slowing down, and, when they passed, she was gone.

Skidding to a halt, Gabriel threw the musket to his shoulder, but the big flint snapped down on an empty pan—a single, sterile click, just before the three Indians and their captive vanished into the falling snow. . . .

"When I reloaded, there was another Indian firing his bow at Antoine Toussaint, so I shot him, too," Alec was telling Big John proudly. "This was not Black Fish's war party," he'd added authoritatively, voicing what he'd already heard others claim. "There were not as many warriors, nor did they try to overwhelm the camp. They wanted only ponies and prisoners. One pass through, then they were gone." He snapped his fingers. "Poof."

Gabriel had been staring at the southern section of carts where he'd last seen Celine. When Alec finished, he'd said: "We will go after them. We will get her back."

Big John had nodded stonily. "Aye, lad, we'll go after 'em. By the Lord, we'll follow 'em to hell and back if that's what it takes."

Now, with the snow stopped and full darkness upon them, Gabriel and Big John mounted their horses and rode to the center of camp. Although most of the men were already there, only a few were mounted. Charlo sat his white runner at the far edge of the crowd, but, when Big John rode up, he guided it around without comment to rein in beside his old friend. Pike also waited just outside the main body of *bois brûles,* holding the reins to the seal brown runner Michel Quesnelle had given him.

Gabriel had viewed Michel's body only briefly that afternoon, just before his parents wrapped him in a robe for burial. Michel had been shot in the chest, then crudely scalped. Seeing him like that, his face waxen, cheeks already sunken in, it had been as if a giant hand had reached inside Gabriel and squeezed out all of the air. Fogged in emotion, he'd mumbled his condolences to a numbed Nicolas and Rosanna, then stumbled away.

It was at Joseph Breland's fire that the hunters gathered. Stepping close to the flames, Breland tentatively opened the debate. "I think this thing must be said first, that the blame for what happened here today has to be placed at my feet, and mine alone. I took it upon myself to call for a vote to move camp. It was my. . . ."

"There's no time for that," Big John interrupted. "We've the women to think of now."

"Big John echoes my own thoughts," Turcotte said. "Blame must wait for another time. Tonight we must finish burying our dead, then we should fortify the camp against further attacks. But I do not think a rescue party should go out until first light."

"First light be damned," Big John growled. "We'll be leavin' within the hour, and trackin' the bloody bastards through the night. We've lost enough time as it is."

Turcotte hesitated. "We cannot follow them after dark, Big John. In the morning, when the sun is full. . . ."

"No." Charles Hallet pushed his way to the front of the crowd. "It's true that there are clouds yet, but they are breaking up even as we speak. There will be a hunter's moon tonight. When it rises, there will be enough light that we can track them. I intend to ride with Big John. Others may follow as they wish."

Noel Pouliot stepped forward, looking more haggard than even the Quesnelles. His voice quavered when he spoke. "We have to get my little girl back. Her. . . ." He held up his arm, the same side as the one Emmaline had broken when she'd slipped on the ice. "It is not yet healed. She cannot. . . ." His voice broke. "A slave works so hard."

"We will go after her," Gabriel promised. "We will find her

and bring her back. We will bring them all back."

"She cannot work until her arm is healed," Pouliot insisted. "It will cripple her for life if she does." He stopped, and Monique laid her hand gently upon her husband's shoulder.

"Then I will lead the party that goes after them," Breland said.

"No, ye won't, Joseph," Big John replied. "Nor will I sit here listenin' to any more of ye talk." His voice turned harsh, lifting toward the handful of stars just beginning to appear through the broken clouds. "I do not care to hear what Joseph Breland has to say on the matter, nor what any of the rest of ye think, for 'tis not ye families that's been taken. I'll be goin' after 'em tonight, me and Gabriel and Charlo here, and Charles and Noel, if they wish. And any of the rest of ye that be of a mind to help. But no more talkin'." His voice dropped almost to a whisper. "Do ye hear me, now? We'll not be puttin' this one to a vote."

Big John pulled his roan away from the crowd. Gabriel and Charlo followed, and Pike fell in behind them. A deathly silence dropped over those still standing at the fire. Then Hallet found his voice. Pushing through the crowd, he shouted: "Hold up, Big John, Gabriel! I have to saddle my horse."

There were eighteen hunters assembled at the southern rim of the camp when the moon finally pulled free of the horizon and began its slow journey over the clouds. Big John felt a grudging satisfaction in the numbers. He had feared that most of them would be too chary of the Sioux returning to want to leave their families. He was embarrassed by his doubt, and by his earlier outburst at Breland's fire. He should have known the *métis* would not let down one of their own, no matter his blood.

It was as Hallet had promised, a hunter's moon glowing through the clouds, filling the eastern sky with a strange, filtered light. But it didn't penetrate the clouds the way Big John had hoped it would. Instead, the prairie stretched away to the south, dim and indistinct, a grim, frozen landscape that seemed suddenly inhospitable.

Big John would glance occasionally to the west, but the sky there had grown darker as the night progressed and more clouds rolled in. There was no hint of a break anywhere, nor even the faint light of a star any more, and the worry was that it would start snowing again before daybreak.

" 'Tis time we moved out," Big John announced. He hadn't bothered to dismount, and his impatience—with the light, the weather, the mixed-bloods, even with the roan—had been eating steadily at him ever since he'd ridden away from the council.

"It will not be difficult to follow their trail," Charlo promised him. "But we must not hurry, either. It would be even more disastrous to follow a hunter's tracks to the buffalo than it would be to wait until morning to find the right trail."

Big John didn't argue. Haste was important, but so was keeping their wits about them. Their task would be formidable enough as it was.

"Ye'll be doin' the trackin' for us, won't ye?" Big John asked Charlo. Although he knew just about any of them could have followed the Indians' trail, Big John wanted someone up front who could pick out the little nuances that might give them an edge when they caught up with the Sioux.

"I will do my best," Charlo replied. He looked at Gabriel. "You will ride with me, and hold my runner's reins if the need arises for me to dismount." When Gabriel nodded, the old Indian turned to the others. "You must all stay well behind Gabriel and myself, in case I have to backtrack. Is that understood?"

"It's understood," Hallet said curtly. "Get on with it, man. We've talked too much already."

Charlo's response was to silently guide his white runner through the carts. Free of the caravan, he kicked the horse into a lope. The others fell in about fifty yards behind.

Charlo set a swift pace, paying little attention to the trail until they were several miles out. Coming to the top of a low rise, he called a halt, then leaned from the saddle to lift a bison's severed head from the snow. Big John already knew that Charlo had followed the fleeing Sioux as far as he'd dared that afternoon, then marked the spot where he'd turned back with a cow's head. He didn't question how Charlo had led them here in the dark so unerringly. It was just part of the mystique that surrounded the old Indian.

Although they were forced to slow down after that, they still made good time. A few miles farther on, Charlo again signaled a halt. Dismounting, he handed his reins to Gabriel, then ventured forward on foot. No one spoke as he knelt at various spots to examine the trail, occasionally stroking the snow's surface or poking at it with his fingers. After several minutes, he returned to the white and motioned the others up. As they gathered around him, he said: "At this place another party has joined with the one we are following, and the trail grows much larger. Maybe seventy-five horses altogether, although not that many are ridden."

"The stolen horses, do ye think?" Big John asked.

In addition to the captives, the Sioux had managed to get away with nearly fifty head of *métis* horses, mostly cart ponies.

"Yes. My old mare is with them, but it is too dark to find her prints," Charlo said.

They rode on across the frozen landscape. The moon shrank as it climbed higher into the sky, its light weakening through the clouds. When Charlo finally dismounted to forge ahead on foot, Big John knew they wouldn't be able to continue much farther. Still, they had come a good ways, and by the time Charlo called a halt a couple of hours before dawn, Big John estimated they'd covered at least twenty miles. It had been a taxing night, but worth the effort, he decided.

They waited out the remaining hours of darkness in a shallow depression where there was at least the illusion of protection from the wind, should it rise before morning. They hobbled and picketed their horses nearby, then huddled in tightly packed groups for warmth. Several sat side-by-side with old friends in order to double up their robes but, despite their weariness, few slept. Most of them passed the night in muted conversations or long, catatonic-like silences.

They breakfasted on the trail, cheeks bulging like squirrels around frozen chunks of pemmican. As the sun came up, the tracks of the Sioux became easier to follow. With better light, Charlo set a pace that rarely dropped below a jog. Toward midmorning the sky finally began to clear off, and although the breeze picked up again, it was gentle and didn't drift the snow. By noon it appeared as if they might actually be catching up. Hindered by so many stolen horses, the Sioux were making poor time.

With the trail so clear, there was no need for the others to hang back, and Pouliot gradually let his horse ease ahead until he was riding at Charlo's side. It was he who first spotted the fork in the trail, nearly half a mile ahead. By the time they reached it, their spirits had plummeted.

Once again, Charlo scouted the site on foot. It took nearly thirty minutes.

"The captives are with the trail that goes to the right," he reported when he returned. "I think."

"You are not sure?" a *métis* asked in surprise.

Charlo shook his head. "No, I am not sure."

"Then we must also split up," Pierre Campbell said. He glanced around as if for support, but most of the *bois brûles* refused to meet his eyes.

"I'll be goin' to the right," Big John said softly, fixing Campbell with a steady look. " 'Tis not the stolen stock I'm worried about, ye see?"

"You think that is why I say we should split up?" Campbell replied defensively.

"The trail's plain to read," Hallet said. "The stolen stock was driven straight south, but this smaller party"—he indicated the broken path with his chin—"goes to the southwest. If that's the direction Lizette has been taken in, that's where I'll go."

"As it should be, Charles," LaBarge said tentatively. "But maybe Pierre is not so wrong, either." He nodded toward the left-hand branch. "What if Lizette or one of the others were taken in that direction? Just one. What of that?"

Hallet stubbornly shook his head. "I've known Charlo a long time, Baptiste. I've never known him to make a mistake about something like this. Not even when he says he isn't sure."

"But what about this one time?" LaBarge persisted. "This is what I ask."

"Go!" Big John thundered. He jerked the roan around to face LaBarge. "Go get ye stock if that's what ye want, and take the others with ye."

LaBarge reared back in his saddle. Then his gaze hardened. "That is not what I meant, Big John. You know that."

Coolly Big John said: "Don't be tellin' me what ye meant, Baptiste, and don't try to explain ye reasonin' for followin' the left-hand fork. And by the Lord, man, don't ye follow me, because I'll kill ye sure if ye do. Do ye hear me? If ye follow now, I'll break ye neck."

With his pulse roaring in his ears, Big John whipped the roan around and took off at a fast gallop. He heard others coming after him, but only a few. When he finally allowed himself a backward glance, he saw Gabriel and Charlo riding side-by-side, then Hallet, Pouliot, and Pike bringing up the rear. There was no one else.

It was late in the day when they reached the breaks of the Missouri River. The snow was melting rapidly in the unexpected warmth of the afternoon sun, the trail disintegrating almost before their eyes. Big John rode in a near stupor, his every muscle screaming for a rest, a chance to stretch and relax. His eyes felt dry and gritty, seared by the harsh glare of sunlight reflected off the glistening snow, and the top of his spine hammered at the back of his skull with the roan's every jolting step.

He knew the others felt as bone-weary as he did. He could see it in the drawn cast of their faces, the sluggish way they handled their reins. The cold and the long hours were sapping the strength of every man there.

It was still a little more than an hour before sunset when they came to a gap in the hills and spotted the wide, flat valley of the Missouri a couple of miles ahead. Charlo, riding in the lead, halted his white runner in the middle of the buffalo trace the Sioux had followed through the breaks. He waited for the others to come up beside him. Although it was too far away to tell for sure if the tracks of the Sioux horses continued across the valley, there was no mistaking the narrow ribbon of smoke that curled above the line of trees along the river.

Scowling, Big John said: "Why would they stop here?"

Charlo shook his head in puzzlement. "It does not make sense unless they thought we would not follow them through the night. If that is their thinking, then they must also believe that we are still very far behind."

"If that's it, they'll probably think we're a full day behind," Hallet said, his red-rimmed eyes brightening with hope.

"We should get out of this gap," Gabriel said. "If they are watching, they would spot us easily, even up here."

Charlo nodded and drummed his heels against the white's ribs. He led them into a narrow depression, then drew up once more. Sliding from his saddle, he silently handed his reins to Gabriel, then made his way over the shoulder of a nearby hill.

As exhausted as they were, no one else dismounted. Not even to stretch their legs. Big John had been carrying his double rifle slung across his back in a quilled leather case. He unsheathed it now and placed it across the saddle in front of him, prying the old caps off with a cracked thumbnail and replacing them with fresh ones. Everyone else reprimed or checked their flints. In the silence of the little hollow, Big John could hear the slow trickle of melting snow, the soft whisper of its settling. Already the gnarled fingers of tawny buffalo grass were visible on the south-facing slopes, and the ridge tops had been swept almost clear.

Big John kept glancing at the broken trace of the Sioux' passage where it cut through the hollow on its way to the valley. Charlo thought they were following at least fifteen riders. If all three *métis* women were with them, that meant no fewer than twelve warriors waiting in the valley below. Two to one odds, at best. His gaze shifted to Hallet, then Pouliot, Gabriel, and Pike, and he wondered what he'd gotten them into. He had lost control back where the trail forked, had once again allowed his temper to override reason. And in the process, he had gambled not only with their lives, but with the lives of the captives, as well.

By the Lord, what have I done? he thought miserably. *What terrible calamity have I set into motion with my stubbornness and pride?*

Charlo's return saved him from forcing an answer. Sliding down the slope of the hollow, the old Indian said: "The trail leads straight across the valley, into the trees near the fire." He looked at Pouliot and nodded. "It is them, my friend."

"Did you see Emmaline?" Pouliot asked almost fearfully.

Charlo shook his head. "The valley cannot be crossed within three leagues in either direction. I could not identify individuals from where I was, but I did see horses and men and some women. The women were making a bullboat to cross the river." He glanced at Big John. "I could go downriver and find a place to cross. Maybe that way I could get close enough to be sure."

Big John shook his head. " 'Tis the Sioux' trail we've followed this far," he reasoned. "I don't see how it could be anyone else."

"Besides, it would be dark before you returned," Gabriel said. "If they finished the boat before then, we wouldn't be able to stop them, and I haven't seen a buffalo all afternoon that we could use to make a boat of our own."

"Where'd they get a hide for a boat?" Pike asked.

"Maybe they stole it from us," Charlo said. "A fresh hide makes the best boat, but a flint would also work."

"Not without soaking it first, and it'd still have to dry," Pike replied.

"That is why they have the fire," Pouliot hazarded. "To shrink the hide."

" 'Tis of no matter where they got it," Big John said. "Green or soaked, 'twill still have to be fitted, and that takes dryin'."

A bullboat was a generally flat-bottomed, kettle-shaped craft of hide, with the hair left on and to the inside, then shrunken over a willow framework. It was awkward to paddle and easy to tip, prone to leaks and ruptures from hidden snags and, if not greased or treated properly, it would soon become water-logged and sink to the bottom. But on the open plains where buffalo and elk were plentiful and wood was as scarce as bathtubs, it made a quick, serviceable vessel. A bullboat could be constructed in a few hours. Saddle, rifle, gear, and clothing would then be tossed inside. A horseman could swim his mount across a river while towing the boat behind him.

Of all the people of the plains, only the *métis*—who removed the wheels from their carts and lashed them beneath the beds for added buoyancy—shunned the fragile rawhide crafts.

"What do we do now?" Hallet asked, his gaze shifting from Charlo to Big John.

"We'll have to go downstream until we can cross the valley without bein' seen, then come up on 'em slow-like," Big John said.

"What if they cross the river before we get there?" Pouliot asked.

"Then, old friend," Big John answered gently, "I fear we'll have lost 'em for good."

Chapter Twenty-Six

There was a hunter's moon again that night, dominating the eastern sky like a huge, sickly face. It was cloudless, as well, and in the frosty, star-studded clearness, the riverside woods seemed almost as bright as day.

Less than ideal conditions to be going up against an enemy as formidable as the Sioux, Gabriel mused.

They were waiting for Charlo's return from upriver, standing chilled and miserable within the sparse timber bordering the river. On his left, Gabriel could hear the gentle lapping of the Missouri's waters. An icy breeze flowing down the broad, shallow cañon of trees lining the river would now and again rattle the branches above them like the sabers of some distant army. Other than that, all was quiet and bitterly cold.

The snow that remained had frozen over when the sun went down. Now it crunched loudly underfoot every time a horse shifted its weight or position. Such conditions would make slipping up on the Sioux all the more difficult, Gabriel knew, yet of them all, he questioned only Pike's ability to move soundlessly over the crusted snow.

Studying the American from the corner of his eye, Gabriel decided Pike was as much of an enigma now as he had been on the day Gabriel and Big John had rescued him from the Chippewas. That he was hurting badly from the wounds he'd received from the Sioux was obvious. His left knee—the one that had been clubbed hard by a Yankton's rifle—was especially tender yet. But Pike hadn't complained once on the long, grueling ride, and Gabriel admired him for that.

Still, the core of his distrust for the American remained as strong as ever, and it had been growing steadily since the night of the attack by Black Fish's warriors, when Celine came to him expressing her fear that Pike wanted to kidnap her to the mountains. If abduction was indeed Pike's intent, then the time for him to put his plan into motion would be soon, Gabriel reasoned.

A low, sharp whistle pierced the night, and Gabriel, his nerves already twangy as a fiddle string, jerked his musket part way up. Close to the riverbank, Charlo stepped clear of a tree, waited until he was certain he'd been identified, then approached without a sound.

"It is them," the old Indian announced in a whisper. Glancing at Pouliot, he added: "I saw Emmaline. The little one is unharmed, although they make her work at the fire."

"And Lizette?" Hallet asked tonelessly.

"She is also unharmed." He paused a moment, then looked at Big John. "Maybe Celine has given them trouble. She is barefoot, and without her coat."

"Then they be punishin' her for her resistance?" Big John asked.

"Maybe," Charlo replied. "Lizette tries to show her how to help with the boat, but she . . . does not seem to listen."

"What of the bullboat?" Gabriel asked.

"They dry it over coals even as we speak. Lizette and Celine work on the boat while Emmaline cares for the meat. They must have shot a buffalo, after all, and cached its meat and hide before the attack."

"How many are there?" Pike asked.

"Twelve, but only three who watch. They have their robes and saddles in a pile next to the river. I think they intend to cross tonight."

"Well, I'm not surprised," Big John said. " 'Tis fools they'd be to slow down so soon after stealin' our women, whether they thought we followed 'em through last night or not."

"The bloody, black-hearted devils," Hallet muttered fiercely. "Another hour of snow and we'd not have been able to follow them at all."

"Aye," Big John agreed. "Our luck has held so far, but we don't have 'em back yet. Charlo, ye've been close to the buggers and have seen what needs seein'. What say ye, man?"

Charlo was quiet a moment, thinking. Finally he said: "There is no way we can approach them quietly on foot without endangering the women. What I think we must somehow do is go in very fast and each of us kill a man before they know we are among them. Then we must each of us kill another, before they can harm the women."

"That ain't possible," Pike said flatly. "The Sioux won't be that slow to react. Some of us are going to taste steel or lead tonight."

"Does that worry you?" Gabriel asked tersely.

"Not so much, sonny, but there's no point in ignoring it, either. Main thing is the women, and especially Noel's little girl. We have to get them out of there fast, before the Sioux have a chance to get at them. They'll kill them out of spite if we don't, sure as hell."

"There is truth in Pike's words," Charlo said thoughtfully. "But I think also there is a way to surprise them, even though they have men watching." He cocked a brow toward Big John. "The unguarded side, eh?"

"The river?"

"*Oui,* the river. Two men. We carry our guns such, tied." He lifted his fowler across both shoulders. "Our powder horns, too. We go into the water and pull ourselves upstream by roots. It can be done, and if the others wait until we attack, then the surprise will be complete."

" 'Tis a wee mite dangerous, old friend," Big John replied weakly, then, after a moment's reflection, added: "But, aye, it might work, at that. Sure, I'm game to try it."

"No, not you, Big John," Hallet said. "I'll go."

"And me," Pike interjected.

"No. 'Twill be me and Charlo doin' this."

"You're gonna be in freezing water up to your necks for nearly half a mile," Pike reminded him. "That's a young man's game."

But Big John was adamant. "No, Mister Pike, 'tis an old man's game, not to be played by those with a life ahead of 'em yet."

"Big John is right," Gabriel said, his voice suddenly choked and unsure. He looked at Hallet and Pouliot, then Charlo and Pike. Lastly he looked at Big John, and his fists clenched until his fingers ached. "Big John and Charlo should go. The rest of us must remain behind and be ready when the time comes."

"I don't like this," Hallet said. "It isn't right."

But Big John reply was quick and succinct. "Aye, friend, 'tis naught but right."

Charlo stepped forward to shake Hallet's hand, then Pouliot's and Pike's and Gabriel's. Big John did the same, though pausing before Gabriel, smiling warmly. "Ye watch yeself, laddie," he said. " 'Tis a hornet's nest we'll soon be walkin' into, and no way for it except to take us a sting or two."

Tears welled in Gabriel's eyes. He let them come, unashamed. "I will watch myself, Big John. You will do the same, no?"

Big John's smiled widened briefly, then disappeared. He went to the roan and began to strip, tying his clothes in a bundle atop his saddle. When he was naked, he dug a tin of bear grease from his saddlebags and coated his body with the heavy, pallid yellow lard until his flesh shone and the scars from his encounter with One Who Limps gleamed a bright, angry red. When he had greased himself as best he could against the icy waters of the Missouri, he drew on the lighter, deer-hide moccasins he wore beneath his heavy *souliers de bouef,* and his knee-length woolen drawers. He belted his knife and hatchet around his waist, then thrust a single pistol into the fringed scabbard with his rifle. He turned then and, without a backward glance, vanished into the trees. Charlo was only a few paces behind, skeleton lean, pale as a wraith.

Gabriel stared after them only a moment, then wiped the tears from his cheeks and went to where Baldy was tethered. He slipped out of his factory coat and tied it across the front of the saddle, then took off his bulky winter moccasins and secured them to his bedroll. He wrapped his bandanna over his mouth and nose to mask the frosty cloud of his breath, then readied the Brown Bess by feel. When he'd checked the belt axe and the two knives he carried at his waist, he was ready. He entered the trees as Big John and Charlo had done, quietly and without fanfare, and made his way alone toward the tiny, flickering glow that was the Sioux' fire, nearly half a mile away.

There was no fear in him, not even the familiar twinge of anxiety, just an incredible awareness. He felt every twig beneath the thin leather soles of his moccasins, could sense its tension and pull his foot back before it snapped. His toes glided into the crusted snow as if it were water, and his foot slid smoothly after them, with only minimal noise. He spotted an owl watching him from a high limb and changed direction before it whooed or flapped loudly away.

A time or two he thought he heard one of the others behind him, but the sound was always small and never carried far. He didn't even bother looking back. Gradually the light of the Sioux' fire strengthened. Drawing closer, he spotted the overturned bullboat propped on a low brace between the

Indians' camp and the river, its pale hull glowing dull red from the reflection of the coals beneath it. A woman stood nearby but Gabriel couldn't tell whether it was Lizette or Celine. Several men sat around the fire, talking animatedly.

Stopping, Gabriel finally looked back. Hallet was following in his tracks, but the others were still hidden from view. He nodded as Hallet came up, and the two men sank to a crouch.

"We will wait here a few minutes, before moving closer," Gabriel whispered.

Hallet cast a brief glance over his shoulder. "Noel and Pike are still coming."

Gabriel shook his head. "We will wait only a few minutes. We must not lag when Big John and Charlo begin their attack. That is the most important thing."

Hallet didn't reply. He'd spotted the woman standing beside the bullboat and was studying her intently. After a couple of minutes, he shook his head in frustration. "It could be Lizette, but I'm not sure." The bandanna over his mouth puffed in and out as he spoke, like the irregular beating of a heart, the oval patch of condensation right at his mouth whiskered with frost.

"Look," Gabriel whispered, nodding toward the Sioux camp.

A couple of warriors had stood and were making their way to the boat. Lifting one side free of the props, they examined the drying hide, commenting on its condition to one another. Lizette Hallet—in the increased reflection from the drying fire Gabriel could see her clearly now—stood silently to one side.

Hallet drew his breath in sharply, and, in a choked voice, said: "If I lose my Lizette. . . ."

"We will get them back," Gabriel said grimly. He moved his hand back to cover the musket's big lock. "Come, it is time to move closer."

With Hallet dogging his heels, Gabriel made his way carefully through the trees to a waist-thick limb, only recently fallen.

Smaller branches arched upward from it, tapering into a lattice of twigs pointing crookedly toward the river. Crouched within the limb's camouflage of twigs and branches, Gabriel surveyed the camp. He counted only eight or nine warriors, but remembered Charlo had said at least three of them were standing watch. Celine and Emmaline were sitting in the snow behind the bullboat, close to Lizette and within the light of the larger fire, although outside its circle of warmth. None of them had blankets or robes with which to combat the intense cold, although Lizette and Emmaline still had their capotes.

Only Celine had been stripped of her outerwear. She wore the same dark, heavy dress that she'd come to the valley in, and sat, hunched and shivering, beside Emmaline, rocking steadily back and forth. Gabriel thought Big John must have been right. Celine was being punished for something, and would have to earn her clothing back with obedience.

Hallet touched his arm, then nodded toward the flat meadow separating the trees from the distant line of hills they had come through that afternoon. It took Gabriel a couple of minutes to spot the warrior standing motionlessly beside a cottonwood, but, once he had, he soon picked out a second Indian, keeping watch about forty yards below where the first one stood. He tried to recount the braves lounging around the fire, but still couldn't tell whether there were eight or nine. That left at least one, and possibly two, unaccounted for.

Leaning close, Hallet whispered: "I saw someone moving near the river."

Big John and Charlo? Gabriel thought it probably had to be, although he knew it could also be one of the unaccounted for warriors.

Then he heard a faint thud from the river's edge, followed by a muffled cry, then a loud splash. The Sioux sitting around the fire sprang to their feet, and, at Gabriel's side, Hallet's fusil roared. One of the Indians at the fire was knocked spinning. A second later, Big John's rifle flashed from the darkness of the riverbank. Gabriel snapped a shot at the scattering warriors. His ball struck one of the braves in the back and slammed him to the ground, face first.

Lunging to his feet, Gabriel raced toward the Sioux camp, pulling his powder horn around to reload as he did. He kept his eyes on the warrior he'd shot, scrambling awkwardly into the brush, his shoulder glistening with blood.

Hallet was sprinting through the trees for his wife and Gabriel ran after him. Lizette was trying to pull Celine toward the river, but she was resisting, fighting back with slaps and kicks. Emmaline had already vanished. Most of the Sioux had also disappeared into the trees, but at least three of them were dashing toward the captives.

Gabriel cried an impotent warning as he spilled a haphazard powder charge down the barrel. He watched helplessly as the warriors closed in on the women, tomahawks raised. Then he heard the crack of Big John's second barrel, and saw in that same instant the flowering muzzle flash of Charlo's fowler.

Two of the braves rushing the captives were blasted off their feet. The third skidded as he spun toward the trees; he was darting into the timber when Hallet threw his reloaded fusil to his shoulder and fired on the run. The third warrior jerked and staggered, then dropped to his knees, from there toppling slowly to his face.

Thumbing an unpatched ball down the musket's bore, Gabriel rapped the butt sharply against the ground, then jerked it up to the cradle of his left arm and quickly primed the pan. He stopped then, the musket held ready, but there were no targets in sight.

The Sioux were gone.

The clearing around the fire was empty save for the saddles

and gear of the Indians. Taking his time now, Gabriel started to work his way around the camp in a large circle toward the river, being careful not to blind himself by looking directly into the brighter light of the clearing. Movement to his left preceded the cold whisk of an arrow paring the air close to his ear. He spun, shouldering the Bess, but the shattering crack of a rifle—Pike's rifle, he thought—interrupted his aim. He heard the startled cry of the Indian, then the loud splash of a body tumbling into the river.

A horse nickered from beyond the fire. There was a shout, a reply in Sioux, then the drumming of hoofs that quickly faded to the west.

There was another cry then, of pain and surprise, followed by a Sioux's triumphant shout. The cry was Pouliot's, or at least it had sounded like Pouliot. A short silence followed, then the night erupted once more with shouts and cries, the sharp cracks of rifles and the more hollow booms of the smoothbores.

Gabriel plunged recklessly forward. A Sioux sprang up before him, tomahawk flashing. Gabriel smashed him in the face with the musket's butt, slashed downward with the barrel. There was a grunt that nearly drowned out the dull, wet plunk of steel against flesh and bone. A warm, bloody mist showered the back of Gabriel's hand. As the Indian crumbled, he leaped over the body and ran on.

He saw Charlo come into the clearing, then dodge quickly to one side. He saw Big John approach the bullboat just as one of the Sioux who had been shot earlier sat up. The muzzle flash of the Indian's fusil lit Big John's face with an orange glow, staggering him backward.

Pouliot seemed to appear out of nowhere, the left side of his shirt bloody around the shaft of an arrow protruding from his shoulder. His fusil was gone, but he stepped up behind the warrior who'd shot Big John and cleaved his skull with a belt axe.

Leaving the hatchet embedded in the Indian's head, he strode rapidly to the bullboat and flipped it over with his good arm. Emmaline was crouched beneath it like a rabbit under a bush. She cried out in terror when the boat was lifted away, then cried again with joy and jumped into her father's arms. Holding her tightly, Pouliot darted into the shadows.

Gabriel had come to a halt when Charlo ran into the clearing, then had watched in stunned disbelief as Big John fell. Pouliot's rescue of his daughter took mere seconds. When he and the girl were gone, Gabriel's gaze was drawn numbly back to Big John's writhing form, the big Scotsman's hands clutching and clawing at his face from which came hollow, breathless shrieks that made Gabriel's scalp crawl.

Gabriel started forward, but hadn't gone more than a few paces when yet another scream yanked him to a stop. Pivoting, he saw Celine running toward the clearing from the direction of the open valley. A mounted Sioux was racing his pony after her. Gabriel shouted and lifted his musket, but the Sioux was already leaning from the back of his mount, his arm curling toward Celine's waist, her body partially shielding his.

Helplessly Gabriel watched the warrior grab Celine and pull her roughly across the horse's withers. Then a rifle cracked from the edge of the trees and the Sioux pitched limply from the pony's back.

Celine fell with him, sprawling in the snow. Gabriel ran to her side. Goose-flesh pimpled his arms as her unearthly screams raked the night. Her body jerked convulsively, and she was beating at the air and kicking at the snow as if still fighting off dead warriors.

Gabriel dropped to his knees at her side, leaning the Brown Bess against a tree. Celine's face snapped toward him, twisted with rage.

"You don't love me!" she yelled wildly. "You don't love me!"

He froze, transfixed by the stark intensity of her features, the lifeless depths of her eyes. He was only peripherally aware of her arm fumbling behind her. Then the look of hatred on her face faded. A smile twitched at the corners of her mouth. She came up fast, her hand flashing forward in a blur of polished steel.

A hand grabbed Gabriel's shoulder and yanked him back at the last instant. He fell in the snow and Pike stepped between him and the girl, holding out his hand to stop her rush. Celine screamed her frustration and lunged toward him, her arm darting like the strike of a snake. Pike grunted and spun away, wrapping an arm around the trunk of a tree to hold himself up. With his free hand he plucked clumsily at the hilt of the knife protruding from his chest, but he was too weak to pull it out. Then his knees buckled and he crumbled to the ground, dead before Gabriel could reach his side.

Epilogue

Placing the snow goggles in his hand, Isabella gently guided his fingers over the stone-polished cottonwood. The goggles were slim and one-piece, rather than the traditional two-piece units that were easier to make but harder to wear comfortably.

Big John smiled his approval as he fitted them gingerly over the bridge of his nose. Pulling the two leather thongs behind his head, Isabella tied them snugly in place. The fit was perfect, the result of previous sizings. The twin wooden orbs protruded outward like the eyes of a lizard, but were hollowed within, the inner surfaces blackened with a mixture of grease and soot to reduce glare. The overall result was bug-eyed but effective. The slits through which he peered were about a sixteenth of an inch wide and extended nearly an inch horizontally. On the prairies when the winter sun was at its brightest, the Crees often used goggles similar to these to prevent snow blindness, although it was June now, and snow blindness hadn't been a threat for months.

Opening his eyes slowly, Big John couldn't help a small wince at the sting of the midmorning sun, but his vision soon adjusted to the change in light and he found that the goggles actually helped more than he'd anticipated. By squinting, he was able to make out the bulky silhouette of the windmill, the darkness that vas the shadows within the open-faced shed. Beyond the shed, fringe of trees that lined the Tongue River was a solid, mist- wall, but to the east he could make out the splotchy brown of buffalo-skin lodges where the *métis* were gathering for the spring hunt.

It wasn't much, he supposed, this blurred and watery world, but it was more than he'd once expected. Isabella had finished the goggles in January, but it wasn't until the last few days that he'd felt up to wearing them over the tender, pink flesh of his face for more than an hour or two at a time.

Big John was sitting in the cane-bottomed rocker Isabella had moved outside for him, listening to the summer sounds—birds trilling along the river, the distant hum of locusts, the lowing of oxen from the big herd to the south. From the village there came the shouts and laughter of children, the calls of women from their lodges, and, farther off, the squeal of a Red River cart coming down the road from Pembina Post.

There would be a wedding that night if the priest arrived in time. Gabriel Gilray and Susanne Leveille, and about time, most of them agreed.

"Sacre," Turcotte had joked only that morning. "Maybe next year, Big John, if Gabriel can *capitaine* Susanne, then maybe we let him *capitaine* a hunt, eh?"

Turcotte's remark had made Big John's chest swell nearly to bursting with pride.

Isabella placed a hand on his shoulder and he covered it with his own. The Sioux's ball had missed his head, but the funneling blast of the ignited powder had charred his face horribly, searing the flesh clear to the bone along his cheek, ruining his sight forever. Yet sometimes he thought his partial blindness might be a blessing. His fingers had long ago told him his face was something he didn't want to see.

He'd been a long time recovering, and near enough to death at one point that Isabella had finally sent for a priest. Father Denning had arrived just after the Twelfth of Christmas in a dog sled driven by Joseph Breland, but by then Big John had passed his most critical stage. From that point on, his recovery had been steady, though agonizingly slow.

Emotionally there had never, amazingly, been much trouble. Neither bitterness nor anger. He had, instead, experienced an unprecedented contentment, a feeling new to him, and strangely comforting. His place in the valley was secure now. He had a woman, a wife actually, married in a traditional Cree ceremony—Denning had been adamant in refusing a Catholic service, and Big John still stubbornly spurned conversion—and through her, two fine sons.

Once, he had had a daughter as well, but she had hung herself in the same woods where her mother had committed suicide a dozen years before. Big John thought there had been a sort of collective relief among the *métis* in that, a sense of something no one really understood coming full circle. A completion rather than an end.

Big John had come to peace with himself in that, too. He supposed he was to blame in some ways, but it was a blame grounded mostly in ignorance. He rued only sending her away that first time. Perhaps none of this would have happened if he hadn't, although he was realistic enough to think that it probably would have. He had accepted Celine's death as he had his own blindness and loss of rank within the valley—with sadness and resignation, but no regret.

À la façon du pays, he had once told Pike.

The way of the land.

ABOUT THE AUTHOR

Michael Zimmer grew up on a small Colorado horse ranch, and began to break and train horses for spending money while still in high school. An American history enthusiast from a very early age, he has done extensive research on the Old West. His personal library contains over 2,000 volumes covering that area west of the Mississippi from the late 1700s to the early decades of the 20th Century. In addition to perusing first-hand accounts from the period, Zimmer is also a firm believer in field interpretation. He's made it a point to master many of the skills used by our forefathers, and can start a campfire with flint and steel, gather, prepare, and survive on natural foods found in the wilderness, and has built and slept in shelters as diverse as bark lodges and snow caves, and has done horseback treks using 19th Century tack, gear, and guidelines. Zimmer is the author of ten Western novels, and his work has been praised by *Library Journal, Booklist,* and *Publisher's Weekly* as well as other Western writers. Jory Sherman, author of *Grass Kingdom,* writes: "He [Zimmer] takes you back in time to an exciting era in U.S. history so vividly that the reader will feel as if he has been over the old trails, trapped the shining streams, and gazed in wonder at the awesome grandeur of the Rocky Mountains. Here is a writer to welcome into the ranks of the very best novelists of today or anytime in the history of literature." And Richard Wheeler, author of *Goldfield,* has said of Zimmer's fourth novel, *Fandango* (1996): "One of the best mountain man novels ever written."

Zimmer lives in Utah with his wife Vanessa and two dogs. His website is www.michael-zimmer.com. His next Five Star Western will be *Río Tinto.*